THE BINARY LEGACY PART 1

ISBN:
ISBN-13:

"To my incredible wife, Stacey, whose unwavering support and love have been the bedrock of this journey. Your presence made every word possible. I cherish you deeply.

To my beloved mother, Susan, whose memory remains a guiding star. Though we have lost you to cancer, your spirit continues to inspire and surround us with love. You are profoundly missed and forever cherished.

And finally, to our delightful pug, Willow, whose charming antics often made writing a delightful challenge. Your joyful presence has been both a distraction and a comfort, adding a unique rhythm to the creation of this book."

1

United Kingdom, December 2024

A few rays of light found their way through the stained glass windows of the old church hall, casting a glow over the small group of people who had gathered, ready to open up and share their struggles with addiction and pain during the weekly Alcoholics Anonymous meeting. James, an older man who seemed to have weathered many storms, stood to address the room.

'I would like to say a big thank you to everybody for sharing today. Before we wrap things up, Jackson has something he would like to say.'

Ellie, a nervous young woman much younger than the rest of the group, felt her throat lock with fear as she saw Jackson stand up. He was a large man with weathered skin, long, straggly hair, and a shy, unkempt beard. Tugging her tatty jumper sleeves around her slender arms, Ellie anxiously nibbled on her nails, silently fearing what would follow. Jackson scanned the room and surveyed the familiar and unfamiliar faces.

'Hello, many of you know me, but I'd like to introduce

myself for those who don't.' Jackson's voice quivered with apprehension despite having spoken countless times before. He cleared his throat as if he had to force out the words. 'My name is Jackson, and I've been sober for over five years now.' He took a deep breath before continuing. 'Today, I am not here to talk about myself,' He glanced at Ellie, whose cheeks flushed pink as she tried to disappear into her chair. 'I'd like to take this opportunity to address Ellie.' He gave her a small, sympathetic smile and nodded slightly in her direction. His voice was soft and reassuring as he spoke, hoping his words would bring her comfort and strength.

'Ellie, I am so proud of you. I've been privileged to see your transformation over the last year and witness the highs and lows you've bravely endured. As your sponsor, I am honored to present you with this one-year sobriety chip to celebrate this momentous milestone.'

Jackson approached Ellie and placed the chip in her trembling hand as everybody in the room focused on her, making her uncomfortable. Ellie's palms started to sweat, and a wave of nausea engulfed her as she stood before the group. She was no stranger to social anxiety, and speaking in public filled her with dread. Sweat trickled down her neck, and vertigo took over. Despite her uneasiness, Ellie stood firmly in the invisible spotlight.

'Thank you, Jackson,' Ellie stammered, feeling her heart beating in her chest. 'I don't deserve anybody's praise. I've done so many wrongs and hurt the people closest to me.' Her heart pounded, and she felt anxiety pulsing through her veins like electricity. She opened her mouth to speak, but no words came out - her mind had gone completely blank. 'Fuck,' Ellie muttered as she let out a startled gasp, remembering she was in a sacred house of worship. 'I'm so sorry,' Ellie whispered as she sunk back into her seat.

The group of people were stunned into silence at Ellie's outburst as James rose from his chair with a smile.

'Ellie, thank you for sharing, and congratulations on your accomplishment. If there are no other volunteers, then we will bring this meeting to an end.'

A cacophony of scraping chairs disrupted the silence, followed quickly by conversations that echoed throughout the hall. The tantalizing aroma of freshly brewed coffee and home-baked pastries drifted from the long table in the corner. Ellie stepped across the church hall, her shoes clacking against the polished wooden floor. She reached for a polystyrene cup from the table, hands trembling from the cold as she filled it with steaming coffee. Ellie brought the warm cup to her lips and curled her hands around it, eager to take in its comforting heat. Before she could take a sip, a man bumped into her from behind, causing her to stumble forward and spill some of the beverage onto her clothes. He steadied her with his hand on her arm, and in one swift motion, he fixed a tiny silver device onto the hem of her jumper. Ellie's head swiveled, and her piercing gaze locked onto Stephen. He had been watching her with an intense curiosity throughout the entire gathering, but she had played it cool until this moment. He was a good-looking young man in his late twenties with an air of charisma about him.

'I'm so sorry,' Stephen mumbled with a thick southern drawl. 'I need to watch where I'm going.'

Ellie's lips twitched into a faint smile as she blotted the last coffee stains off her jumper with the napkin.

'It's fine,' Ellie sighed, her lips quivering with suppressed anger. 'No harm done.'

A gentle smile formed on his lips as he poured a fresh cup

of coffee. He handed it to Ellie, her fingertips lightly brushing against his.

'I'm Stephen,' he said with a whisper. She smiled back, nodding in acknowledgment. 'You must be Ellie. Congratulations on your accomplishment. This place has clearly been good for you.'

She nodded, her cheeks tinging pink at the compliment.

'Well, I certainly wouldn't have been able to do it alone,' Ellie paused and cocked her head, allowing her gaze to linger on him a moment longer. 'you're not from around here, are you?'

'Is it that obvious?' Stephen asked with a self-deprecating laugh, running a hand through his hair before shrugging his broad shoulders. 'I'm here for work, but I'm originally from Texas.'

'Did you find the meeting helpful?' Ellie inquired, her eyes lingering on Stephen's face.

'Yeah,' Stephen replied with a nod, a sparkle in his deep brown eyes as he rested his hand lightly on Ellie's shoulder. 'I think I've found what I was looking for. Look, I have to get going. Are you sure you're alright?'

'I'm fine,' Ellie murmured, tugging at a strand of her hair nervously as she averted her gaze. 'See you at the next meeting?'

'Oh, you'll be seeing me again,' Stephen said with a wink as he grabbed his coat and quickly exited the building.

Ellie lifted the steaming cup of coffee to her lips, feeling its warmth spread down her throat. Her gaze drifted up to the large clock on the wall, its hands slowly ticking towards noon. Ellie knew Holly would arrive soon to pick her up, so she took one last sip of her drink and set it down. She quickly pulled on her red winter jacket and tucked her hair inside the hood before rummaging through her colorful bag for her gloves. Ellie paused in the doorway, her gaze lingering on the faces of those she had shared her journey with. She silently wished them peace and strength to carry them through the holiday season.

A chill that seemed to steal her breath away greeted Ellie when she pushed open the wooden door of the old church hall. Delicate snowflakes whirled around her body, creating an ethereal flurry of motion as they spun about in the air while gradually resting on the ground below. She pulled her coat tightly around her body and fastened each button carefully to block out the cold. Ellie's face lit up when she noticed her best friend's vintage red Volkswagen parked in the far corner of the parking area. Holly lounged against its door, wearing a sleek black coat and classic denim trousers. Not for the first time, Ellie marveled at how effortless her friend seemed to look; so graceful but strong. She was almost too perfect. It drove Ellie mad sometimes, yet she adored her. Across the street, she noticed a tall man shrouded in a long black coat with his chin tucked deep into his chest and dark sunglasses shielding his face. Her breath hitched, and she resisted the urge to look again as a chill ran up her spine, filling her with an ominous sense of foreboding. But it wasn't the first time her imagination took hold of reality. The door creaked open behind her, and Jackson emerged in a dirty brown trench coat that billowed around him as he struggled to pull it on.

'Ellie, Hold on a second!' Jackson shouted as he pulled out a crumpled pack of cigarettes and shook one from the box. He grabbed an old, dented cigarette lighter from his pocket and sparked it to life, the flame flickering in the wind. He cupped his hands around the cigarette and breathed deeply through the filter, feeling it fill his lungs with warmth and calm. The smoke billowed outside into the chilled night air in a soft, gray stream.

'I needed that,' Jackson whispered, securing the wool collar of his coat around his neck and running his fingers through his unkempt beard. 'I'm sorry for embarrassing you in there.'

'It's fine,' Ellie said. 'Is everything alright?'

'You forgot your chip,' Jackson whispered, reaching deep into his pocket and closing his fingers around the sobriety chip. He pulled it out and placed it in Ellie's open palm. She stared at it momentarily, her thumb tracing its worn ridges and noticing its faded coloring before meeting his gaze with a deep sadness in her eyes.

'I didn't forget it,' Ellie whispered, her mouth twisted into a frown. 'It's not something to be proud of. It's an awful reminder of how I failed.'

She lowered her head and tightly wrapped her arms around herself, a shield from the overwhelming memories trying to take over. With a slight trepidation, she handed the chip back to Jackson. His gaze dropped, and he took a few steps back, propping himself against the wall.

'It's a tough pill to swallow, admitting you've screwed up,' Jackson sighed. 'But you are selling yourself short. You have come a long way, sticking around here for a year.' Jackson paused to take another drag of his cigarette. 'Maybe my opinion doesn't hold much weight. After all, I'm just an old, broken-down, recovering alcoholic. Just remember, one day at a time.'

Ellie looked into Jackson's eyes, taking in the lifetime of knowledge and wisdom he had acquired. Though his face bore signs of sorrow, Jackson gave Ellie the chip with a determined stare. With a single nod, she accepted it without a word, carefully placing it in her pocket.

'Thank you.' Ellie whispered.

Jackson felt the weight of their conversation, their mutual understanding that he genuinely understood her struggles. He took her hands in his and gently squeezed them, letting Ellie know he was there for her.

'Listen, do me a favor and go home. Give yourself a break and spend time with your family over the holidays,' Jackson said, standing still momentarily to admire the snowflakes cascading from the sky. 'Just remember, I'm here for you. Promise me that you will call me if you ever feel tempted.'

He watched as the snow flurries swirled around them, settling atop their shoulders like a blanket of stars. Reaching into his pocket, he withdrew a red gift bag and handed it to Ellie.

'Merry Christmas.'

'You got me a gift?' Ellie gasped. 'You shouldn't have.'

'Open it.'

Ellie opened the bag and pulled out a fancy black jewelry box, and her face lit up with surprise and delight. Ellie's breath caught in her throat when she lifted the box lid. Nestled within the velvet lining was a finely crafted silver bracelet. Etched into its surface were the words, 'The journey of a thousand miles begins with a single step.'

A smile found its way onto Ellie's lips as she carefully lifted the bracelet and secured it around her wrist, looking up at Jackson with overwhelming gratitude.

'Thank you, Merry Christmas.'

Ellie beamed as she stood on her tiptoes and kissed his cheek. Jackson's cheeks glowed a subtle shade of pink as he chuckled.

'Merry Christmas, Kid.'

Ellie peered over her shoulder and noticed the man in

black had disappeared, convinced she had imagined him.

Jackson looked over at Holly, waiting patiently by her car as he lifted the cigarette to his lips for one last drag.

'You had better get going before you freeze to death.'

With a flick of his wrist, he sent the butt soaring through the air, resting on the ground and creating a layer of ash in its wake. The sky's darkness seemed to press down upon them; the grey clouds had thickened, and snowflakes spiraled slowly from the sky. Jackson watched as Ellie trudged through the veil of snow. Wrapping her arms close to her chest, she approached Holly. Without lifting her gaze, Ellie encircled her waist and pulled her close, pressing her face into the crook of Holly's neck. She rested there for a moment, absorbing her warmth.

'Shall we?'

Holly opened the passenger side door and offered her arm to help Ellie climb inside. She then turned, walked to the driver's side, grabbed the rusty handle with both hands and pulled it heartily. The door hinges creaked in response before giving way to a loud thud. Holly slipped inside, closed the door behind her, and cranked the key in the ignition. The car responded, shooting forward with a thick cloud of sooty black smoke trailing behind it. Holly caught sight of Ellie with her elbow propped up on the armrest and chin cupped in one hand, gazing out the window. Holly felt her face light up with a mischievous grin as she studied the far-off look in Ellie's eye.

'Who was the hot guy you were talking to?'

Ellie crossed her arms and sank into the aged leather seat, feeling its well-worn texture against her body.

'Holly! We're talking about anonymity here.'

'I mean, it's not like I'm ever gonna meet any of them,'

Holly sighed in resignation.

'He is just my sponsor,' Ellie explained. 'He's a genuinely nice man who has been through a lot.'

Holly glanced at Ellie and saw her pensive expression, her eyebrows drawn together and her lips pressed into a thin line as she gazed out the window. With a loving gesture, she reached out, placing her hand on Ellie's knee.

'I'm glad you have somebody who understands what you are going through.'

Ellie gazed out the window as the world went by, observing the trees peeking through the snow that swirled in the chilly winter breeze.

'You still with me?' Holly asked, noting Ellie seemed lost in her thoughts. She looked over at her friend and gave her a gentle nudge on her shoulder. Startled, Ellie gave out a yelp of surprise as she jumped and turned her gaze to Holly.

'Sorry, I was half asleep,' Ellie mumbled.

Holly's mouth twitched as she fought to suppress a smile and breathed an audible sigh.

'Well, can the awake half please pay me some attention? I am driving you home.'

As Ellie looked down at her lap, her eyes filled with tears. She ran her fingers through her thick, dark brown hair before tucking it behind her ear.

'I'm sorry, Holly,' Ellie said, her voice quivering as she shifted her feet nervously. It had been so long since she was home, and the guilt of disappointing her family weighed heavily on her heart. Holly glanced over at Ellie, her expression both sad and hopeful. She wished she could take away Ellie's pain, yet all she could do was offer her friendship and empathy.

'We all make mistakes, and you have paid for yours. You

are fighting your demons, and your family will be proud of you.'

'I don't think they will be proud,' Ellie whispered, biting her lip. 'I'm nervous about seeing Ashley again. I never wanted to hurt her.'

Holly noticed the distress on Ellie's face and offered her an understanding smile.

'Ashley knows it was an accident.'

'My family has given me so much love and countless opportunities. I want to show them I'm dedicated to becoming the best version of myself,' Ellie mumbled.

Holly looked at Ellie with a gentle smile.

'You need to stop being so hard on yourself,' Holly said in a determined tone as she reached over and grabbed Ellie's hand, squeezing it tightly. 'You worry so much about upsetting everybody else, and now you must focus on yourself. Listen to me, Ellie Jones, you are an amazing woman and my best friend in the universe.'

Holly carefully drove down the twisting forest road, her gaze flicking to the rear-view mirror with apprehension.

'What's up?' Ellie asked, looking over her shoulder.'

'A black car has been behind us for a while.'

'Are you sure?' Ellie asked hesitantly.

'It's probably just a coincidence,' Holly replied dismissively.

The tree trunks rose like silent giants on either side, their branches intertwined overhead to block out even the faintest winter light. The sky cleared as their car left the dark forest road, and the sun glowed through the grey clouds. Holly drove cautiously down the winding road of stately mansions, glancing anxiously in the rear-view mirror, watching the black Sedan disappear down a side road and out of sight.

'It's gone,' Holly sighed with relief.

Ellie nervously looked over her shoulder, wondering if someone had followed her. She had felt eyes upon her for weeks but wrote it off as just her paranoia.

Holly couldn't believe her eyes when she saw the floral displays lining the snow-covered yards. Each garden was a work of art, precision-cut and sculpted to perfection.

The many mansions stood in all their grandeur, reflecting the morning sunlight off their windows. The magnificent homes had balconies that overlooked lush lawns with trimmed paths featuring sculpted shrubs. Holly was amazed by the beauty of what lay before her. Magnificent iron gates towered above, each one unique in its intricate craftsmanship. She beheld the beautiful sights before her, feeling like she had entered a fairytale. Feeling nervous, Ellie averted her gaze from the luxury surrounding her and looked at her friend.

'I'm sorry for going on about my problems. It feels like all we've talked about this year.'

'Don't worry. I haven't been paying attention,' Holly chuckled. 'Just try and relax and enjoy Christmas.'

The tires crunched on the snow-covered gravel as they approached a large gate. Stretching her arm from the window, Holly tapped in a code on the keypad connected to the security box, and the gate opened. Holly proceeded down the driveway, breathing the fresh air from the open window. The large pond was alive with activity, hundreds of fish swarming in frenzied patterns, creating ripples that glistened in the light. A tranquil waterfall cascaded down the mossy rocks, its soothing sound crashing into the water below. The car made a tremendous noise as it approached the grand house, spluttering until it came to a halt with a loud bang. Ellie stepped out of the vehicle, and Holly trailed behind her, brushing her hand along the side of the car. Rust had covered the car's exterior, and dents had marred its once glossy paint job. Ellie reached into the trunk and pulled out an old, sizable brown suitcase and a shoulder bag decorated with colorful sequins. Holly's eyes widened as she observed the immense size of the house before them, and even though she had been there many times before, the magnificence still amazed her.

'Thank you for driving me home,' Ellie said, her voice laced with gratitude and a hint of sadness. Her eyes widened as she gazed up at the house. It was much bigger than she remembered.

'I was afraid I'd have to spend Christmas in our apartment alone,' Ellie sighed with relief. 'I'm so glad you get your first holiday away from home with Steve. Aspen for Christmas, that's amazing!'

'I think your parents would have helped you with your transport,' Holly giggled, motioning toward the grand house and the expensive cars in the open garage.

'I know they would help me, but I like making it alone.'

'Well, I'm not so proud, so if they ever want to send some money my way, I wouldn't complain. The old bug here could use a new stereo.'

'She still has a lot of life left in her,' Ellie chuckled, patting the roof as her gaze lingered on the rusted frame of the car and its dilapidated interior.

Ellie's eyes sparkled with joy as she carefully undid the brass clasps of her suitcase and removed a small box wrapped in festive red and green paper. She handed it to Holly, her hands trembling with excitement.

'You got me a gift?' Holly cried out, trying to contain her joy. 'Oh no, now I feel terrible. I completely forgot to bring yours with me.'

Ellie sighed, pretending to take the gift back.

'Don't you dare!' Holly screamed, clasping her hands together and jumping up and down. 'Please, can I open it now?'

A smile spread across Ellie's face as she saw her best friend struggle, knowing that she had no patience for such things.

'Promise me you will open your gift Christmas morning! Swear it on Santa's sleigh.'

Holly's expression dropped, and she rattled the present close to her ear, her eyes narrowing with focus as she attempted to figure out what was inside. After a few moments, she groaned in frustration.

'Come on. You know I don't have that kind of willpower.'

Ellie glanced up at the stone steps covered in snow leading to her parent's home.

'I should go inside and check if anybody's home.'

With a deep sigh, Ellie made her way to the grand entrance.

'Not so fast! Where is my hug?' Holly said as Ellie let go of her bags and tightly wrapped her arms around her.

'You have fun, okay? I can't wait to hear everything when you get back!'

'I will spare you some details,' Holly exclaimed with a cheeky wink.

'Gross!' Ellie chuckled.

Holly watched her approach the door as she returned to the car.

'Hey, good luck. I will see you in a few weeks.'

'Thank you. Enjoy your trip.'

Ellie felt a lump in her throat as she waved goodbye to Holly. Her long black hair blew in the breeze, and her eyes sparkled with excitement as the car engine roared to life. An arm emerged from the window, and a hand waved, sending Ellie one last smile before Holly drove away.

'Love ya, bitch!' Holly yelled as the car disappeared, leaving a plume of smoke in its wake. Ellie paused momentarily, a deep wave of nerves washing over her. Taking a deep breath, she grasped the coarse leather handle of her suitcase and hauled it up the steps. Ellie rummaged through her pocket, finding her old house key. She placed it in the door and smiled as she heard the lock click open, signaling she had returned home.

2

United Kingdom, December 2024

Ellie walked into the inviting hallway, greeted by the scent of gingerbread baking in the oven. The comforting sound of classical music and faint chatter from the kitchen filled the air as she hung her coat on the hook beside the door and carefully removed her black boots, laying them side-by-side on the shoe rack. She walked across the glossy hardwood floor, her bare feet leaving only a whisper in their wake. Ellie ran her fingers along the frames of the pictures hanging on the wall. There were family vacations to the beach, aunts and uncles huddled around a winter fireplace, and various photos of her and Ashley growing up. A wave of nostalgia washed over her as she paused to admire each memory. As she reached the kitchen door, the scent of her mother's signature fresh baked sugar cookies, with hints of cinnamon and nutmeg, floated in the air. She drew a deep breath, and her lips curved into a gentle smile. A warm, calming sensation flooded her body, filling her with contentment. A loud crash filled the room as her hand grasped the door handle. Her foot knocked a nearby potted plant to the ground.

'Ashley?' Alice shouted from the kitchen as Ellie gingerly stepped out behind the door, smiling.

'Hi, Mum,' Ellie whispered. 'Hi, Dad.'

Alice and Mike's eyes widened with surprise at the sight of their daughter, her presence an unexpected but welcome shock. Alice glided elegantly across the room, her black dress clinging to her figure and highlighting her shapely silhouette. Her dark hair was twisted into an intricate knot with a diamond and sapphire pin, and her earrings glimmered like stars in the night sky. Mike stood with an air of confidence, his muscular frame towering over Alice. His tailored suit fit him snugly, highlighting his broad shoulders and long arms. Alice rushed to Ellie, embracing her tightly and pressing kisses against her forehead. She was so overwhelmed that she could feel her hands shaking as tears flowed down her cheeks. Mike stepped forward, enveloping Ellie in his powerful arms, pressing her close to his chest. She felt the warmth and familiarity of his embrace, a comfort that made her feel safe. He stepped back, wiping away a tear before turning to Alice, who was smiling with delight. She stared at Ellie, taking in every detail she had missed during their time apart.

'It's so good to have you home. Come and sit down,' Mike offered.

Ellie entered the kitchen as Mike pulled a chair from the large table. Alice set a mug of coffee in front of Ellie, who eagerly wrapped her hands around it, enjoying the warmth that radiated from within.

'I tried calling you yesterday. We were getting worried,' Alice whispered.

Ellie's hands trembled as she traced the edges of the steaming mug, avoiding eye contact as Alice searched her daughter's face with concern.

'I lost my phone a few days ago,' Ellie mumbled. 'I had no way of letting you know I was coming home. I wanted to be with family.'

Alice stared at Ellie, her deep blue eyes radiating with a sense of compassion and worry. She reached out across the mahogany table and grasped Ellie's tiny hands.

'How have the meetings been going?' Alice asked.

Ellie gazed into her mother's eyes as they brimmed with emotion, hope radiating from their depths.

'They have been going well. I needed to be in a better state of mind before coming home.'

A tear slid slowly down Ellie's cheek, and she quickly wiped it away. She closed her eyes and inhaled deeply, trying to quell the swell of emotion.

'I never intended for all the pain and suffering I have caused. I'm so sorry.'

Alice held onto Ellie's hands tightly, providing comfort and reassurance.

'We just want you to be happy,' Mike said. 'We love you so much, Ellie.'

With a solemn expression, Ellie reached into her pocket and pulled out the small sobriety chip, placing it on the table between them. Mike's eyes lit up with admiration as he looked at the chip, taking Ellie's hand and giving it a comforting squeeze, a silent understanding that said more than any words could. Ellie's gaze softened as it fell upon a framed photograph of horses. They stood tall, their manes billowing in the breeze with a sun-streaked field behind them.

'How's Willow doing?' Ellie asked.

Alice couldn't help but smile, looking in Mike's direction.

She had been around horses her whole life, and they always brought her happiness.

'She's doing great. I hope you get to see her while you are home.'

Everywhere she looked, there was a tangible glimmer of holiday magic. Richly adorned trimmings hung from every corner of the room, and aromatic candles filled the air with a hint of Yuletide enchantment.

'This is just what I wanted, a traditional Christmas like we used to have,' Ellie sighed.

'Do you have any plans for the rest of the day?' Mike asked.

'I was planning to go to the coffee shop to ask for some shifts.'

The shrill ringing of the kitchen timer reverberated through the room, and Ellie's body jerked in surprise. Alice rose from her chair, walked across the linoleum floor towards the oven, and opened the door to reveal a fresh batch of chocolate chip cookies.

'They'll be delighted to have you back. I am sure Jasper will be overjoyed to see you,' Alice smiled.

'Mum!' Ellie snapped, shaking her head.

'Listen now, I always thought you two made the cutest couple. I can't help but remember how inseparable you have been since you were kids. You grew up side by side, and I will never understand why you broke up with him.'

'I had to end things with him. I dragged everybody down with me, and he didn't deserve how I treated him.'

'Maybe he wanted to help you; we all did. You took that choice away from us,' Mike whispered.

'Can we talk about something else, please,' Ellie insisted, reaching for a biscuit on the festively themed plate before her and taking a bite.

Anxiety washed over her as she tucked a strand of hair nervously behind her ear. She felt the urge to bite her nails, so she pulled her jumper down so the sleeves hung over her hands to protect them.

'Mum, Dad, would it be alright to ask you something?'

Alice approached the table and stood alongside Mike, wrapping her arm around his waist.

'Well,' Ellie whispered, her gaze fixed on the table.

'You are scaring us, Honey. You can ask us anything,' Mike said as he exchanged a worried glance with Alice.

Before Ellie could say anything, the kitchen door burst open, and her older sister, Ashley, strode in, focusing solely on her phone and the music pulsing through her headphones. She dropped her bag onto the floor and glanced up at Ellie.

'Oh my god, Ellie!' Ashley screamed as she dashed over to her, wrapping her arms around Ellie tightly. 'I can't believe it. I haven't seen you for so long.'

A smile crept onto Ellie's face as she held onto Ashley's hands. She was in disbelief when she saw the transformation Ashley had gone through since they had last seen each other. Her once-long blond locks were now short, framing her luminous face and radiating a newfound confidence. She wore a yellow sports bra that accentuated her toned stomach and glowed with an energy Ellie had never witnessed before. Her gaze fell to Ashley's prosthetic leg, and suddenly, the memories of the accident came flooding back, filling her with regret.

'I'm sorry I haven't called lately.'

'I was worried about you!' Ashley whispered.

Ellie's stomach churned as the image of Ashley lying motionless on the stretcher filled her mind.

'I'm so sorry, Ash.'

'I've told you a million times, I never blamed you for what happened to me,' Ashley assured Ellie as she pulled her close and wrapped her arms around her. 'You messed up, but we don't know it was your fault Bailey was spooked. It might have happened anyway.'

The warmth and compassion in her voice was unmistakable. Ellie bowed her head, trembling as tears trickled down her face. Her body shook with emotion as she placed her hands on Ashley's shoulders and gazed into her eyes.

'I understand I haven't been the best sister,' Ellie sighed. 'But I swear I'm making every effort to do better.'

Ellie held Ashley tight, the pressure of her embrace conveying what words could never express. When they finally pulled away, Ellie's eyes were glassy with tears that she quickly brushed away with a trembling hand.

'I don't know how you do it. How do you stay so strong?' Ellie asked.

'I'm not always strong, Ellie. There are moments when I want to give up, but I remind myself of the people who love me, which motivates me to keep fighting. I'm still here, healthy and happier than I have ever been. What hurt more than anything was my little sister leaving. Ashley hesitated, her eyes welling up with emotion as she stared at Ellie's sobriety chip on the table. She beamed with delight as she looked into her sister's eyes, her face illuminated with a warm smile.

'That tiny chip tells me you are changing your life, and I couldn't be more proud of you. I'm so happy you are home.'

Mike and Alice clasped hands as they watched their daughter's embrace. Tears glistened in their eyes and smiles stretched across their faces. The long-awaited reunion was finally here, filling the air with joy.

'I'm sorry for the sweaty hug. I just came from the gym,' Ashley chuckled as she stepped back, drawing attention to the gleaming metal of her prosthetic leg attached just above the knee. 'What do you think? I got this upgrade a few weeks back.'

Ellie beamed at Ashley with adoration, amazed by her poise and grace. She felt immense pride in her sister's beauty.

'You look amazing!'

'What are you up to today?' Ashley asked.

'Not much. I planned to head to the coffee shop to inquire about some shifts.'

Ashley flashed a broad, toothy grin, and her eyes sparkled with mischief.

'Let's get this show on the road,' Ashley beamed. 'I'll take a quick shower and put on something more ladylike. We're going to the coffee shop to catch up, and I will call Shreya so you can finally meet her.'

Before Ellie could say anything, Ashley had already disappeared up the stairs. Ellie glanced over her shoulder at her parents, smiling warmly.

'You were going to ask us something before hurricane Ashley blew in?' Alice asked.

'It's not important, honestly. I was going to ask what you guys wanted for Christmas?' Ellie asked, trying to sound convincing.

'Oh, alright, honey. You had us worried,' Alice said, knowing something else was weighing on her daughter's mind.

Ellie made her way to the kitchen door, turning around to face her parents before she reached it.

'It's so nice to be home; I missed you. I better go and get ready before Ashley whisks me away. Is my room still there?'

'Of course.' Mike said with a smile.

'See you tonight?' Ellie asked.

'Oh no! I forgot that we have an overnight business trip. I'm so sorry. We could cancel.'

'Please don't cancel because of me. You'll be home tomorrow night, and we can all have a quiet evening together,' Ellie said as she walked toward her parents and hugged them, savoring the moment before leaving the room.

Mike kissed Alice on the forehead and held her close, her head leaning on his broad shoulder.

'Our family is back together,' Alice smiled.

3

Ashley grabbed Ellie's wrist and guided her toward the car, her feet barely keeping up. Ashley had changed into a light cotton dress that was sunny yellow and patterned with vivid flowers. The fabric fluttered around her legs like a summer breeze as they raced toward the car. A wide smile formed on Ashley's face as she fastened the buttons of her denim jacket and admired the sun's reflection in the shiny yellow paint job and chrome accessories of her brand-new sports car. Ellie grabbed the door handle and pulled open the passenger side door. She slipped into the seat and felt a comforting embrace from the leather. Ashley climbed in, pushing the Start button with her thumb as the engine rumbled to life, reverberating through Ellie's body.

'I love your car!' Ellie remarked, taking in the new car smell.

'Thanks,' Ashley replied with a proud grin. 'Let's go for a spin!'

Ashley drove down the long driveway and headed south toward the local town. The asphalt glittered in the sunlight, reflecting off patches of slush and puddles from the earlier snowfall. Ellie looked at Ashley in awe; she still couldn't believe the changes in her sister. Suddenly, the speakers emitted an electronic jingle, signaling an incoming call. Ashely gave Ellie a knowing glance; it was her girlfriend, Shreya. Ellie smiled but also felt sad, realizing how much she had missed.

'Hi,' Ashley said. 'We're in the car on the way to the coffee emporium. I can't wait for you to meet Ellie.'

Ashley's face filled with joy when Shreya's voice came through the car speaker.

'I will be there soon. I had to pick up some papers from the office. I'm looking forward to meeting your sister.'

'See you soon. I love you.'

'I love you too,' Shreya said before disconnecting the call.

Ashley turned onto a road leading to the old town center, known for having the best shopping district in the area. She took her eyes off the road for a second to check on Ellie, who was tapping her fingers against the dash nervously. She knew Ellie's restlessness was never more apparent than when she was forced to sit still.

'I was so surprised when I saw you sitting in the kitchen,' Ashley said. 'Please promise me that you won't just disappear again.'

'I promise.'

'Pinky swear?' Ashley chuckled as she held out her little finger.

'Really?' Ellie smiled as she wrapped her finger around Ashley's.

As Ashley parked the car, Ellie's eyes widened when she saw the familiar sight of the coffee shop on the corner. Ellie's eyes twinkled as she gazed upon the large windows framed with enchanting Christmas lights and delightful decorations. Her heart filled with nostalgia, remembering all the memories of laughter and joy that she had shared with Jasper here. They stepped out of the car and onto the sidewalk, cautiously crossing the street before arriving at the coffee shop. Ashley gave her sister a quizzical look, her eyebrows cocked and her head tilted sideways.

'So, are you excited to see Jasper again?'

'Nervous more like it. What if he wants nothing to do with me?' Ellie whispered.

'Ellie, all he has done for the past year is ask after you.'

The smell of freshly brewed coffee and baked pastries greeted them when they entered the shop. Ellie looked at the young man standing behind the counter. The sun shone through the window, illuminating his caramel-colored skin and giving it a radiant glow. His green turtleneck jumper, the same color as his eyes, clung snugly to him, and a beige apron hung from his waist.

'Hi, Jasper,' Ashley gushed.

Jasper looked up from the register and saw Ellie standing behind her sister.

'Ellie, Your home?'

'How have you been?' Ellie asked as she approached the counter.

'Oh, nothing changes around here,' Jasper said nonchalantly.

'Is Fiona working today? I was gonna ask if I could get a few shifts while I'm back for the holidays.'

'Yeah, she's in the office if you want to go and check with her.'

Ellie paused momentarily and flashed Jasper a knowing smile before walking across the room towards the office door behind the counter. Jasper's eyes followed her every move as she walked, captivated by her presence.

'What?' Jasper whispered.

'You are just so adorable.' Ashley giggled, her hands cupping her chin while she leaned against the counter. Ellie's hand shook with trepidation as she knocked on the door, her knuckles lightly grazing the cold metal doorknob. Ellie opened the door, cautiously peeking into the room to see if anybody was there. A large wooden desk took up most of the space before a single window, letting in a small beam of light. A disorganized assortment of papers and newspaper clippings cluttered the walls. Fiona was sitting at the desk, focused entirely on her work, and didn't notice Ellie entering the room behind her. Her hair was held up in a tight bun with tiny round spectacles just above her eyes. She tapped away at the keyboard, her caramel skin glowing in the light and her black patent leather heels making a rhythmic sound against the wooden floor.

'Sorry to interrupt. Jasper said it would be alright for me to come and say hi.'

Fiona spun in her chair, quickly leaping to her feet and enveloping Ellie tightly.

'Ellie, It's so good to see you! How are you?' Fiona asked, taking a step back to look at her.

Ellie wrung her hands together, taking a deep breath, anxiously surveying the room.

'I'm alright. I came home this morning to spend Christmas with my family, and I was wondering if you had any hours you could throw my way. I know I let you down before, and I understand if you say no.'

Fiona smiled as she leaned back in her chair, picking up a cup of coffee from her desk.

'You probably won't believe me, but I was in a similar situation when I was younger. I know how hard it is to change your life, and it can be even harder when people don't even give you a chance to try,' Fiona said, shaking her head wearily. 'But it seems you are in luck. We have a few people off sick, leaving us short-staffed. Jaspers alone out there chasing his tail while I'm stuck back here.'

'When would you like me to start?' Ellie asked, her face lighting up with excitement.

'I know it's short notice, but how about now? I have to visit my husband in the hospital, and Jasper needs to pick up his brother. We were going to close early,' Fiona sighed.

'Sure, I can start as soon as I have had a drink with Ashley if that's alright?' Ellie said, her voice wavering with anticipation as she nervously tugged the cuffs of her jumper.

She was determined to make the most of this chance, but her stomach twisted into knots, thinking about slipping back into old habits.

'That's amazing; thank you. Would you be alright closing the shop later?'

'Of course,' Ellie said.

Fiona shuffled through a cabinet full of beige aprons and pulled one out, handing it to Ellie with a soft squeeze on her shoulder.

'You are a lifesaver. This one should do,' Fiona said, her eyes sparkling with appreciation.

Ellie shifted her weight from side to side and looked down at the tiled floor, biting her bottom lip anxiously. She then lifted her eyes to meet Fiona's warm gaze.

'About what happened between Jasper and me.'

'What happened between the two of you is your business,' Fiona smiled, shaking her head. 'He was devastated when you left but understood your reasons; we all did.'

Ellie nodded, her cheeks already beginning to flush as she moved to pick up the apron from the chair, readying herself to leave.

'He has always loved you, Ellie. That much I can tell you,' Fiona said as Ellie walked out of the office, her lips curved into a smile.

Jasper caught a glimpse of Ellie with an apron draped over her shoulder and broke off his conversation with Ashley.

'How did it go?' Jasper asked.

'Your mum was very understanding; she said I can start after my drink. You don't have to close the shop, and you can go and pick up Zack.'

'That's great; she was worried about losing business,' Jasper said, raising his eyebrows quizzically and looking at them both.

'So what can I get you to drink?'

Ashley stifled a laugh, looking sideways at Ellie. Her eyes crinkled with the recognition that such absentmindedness was typical of him.

'I didn't think you would ever ask! I will have a black coffee and get a chai tea for Shreya. What would you like, Ellie?'

Ellie slowly read through the menu, her stomach tightening as she looked at the options. She felt overwhelmed by the number of choices before her, unsure which one to pick.

'Just a breakfast tea, I think,' Ellie replied with a smile as Jasper tapped away at the old cash register.

'That'll be nine pounds and ninety-seven pence, please.'

Ashley rummaged through her purse, brushing aside lipsticks and tissues until her fingers grazed the smooth plastic of her credit card. She pulled it out and ran it through the machine, waiting for the familiar beep that told her the payment had gone through.

'I'll bring the drinks over,' Jasper said as he quickly placed the mugs under the steaming machine, filling them with the sound of bubbling liquid.

Ashley approached a table in the corner of the shop, draping her jacket over the back of the chair as Ellie followed suit, taking off her coat and tucking her hands inside the sleeves of her jumper. With a quick, nervous glance, she noticed Ashley's prosthetic leg glinting in the light under her short dress. Ellie tugged at the loose threads of her jumper, trying to keep her hands busy and stop herself from biting her nails. Across from her, Ashley let out a deep, contented sigh as she absentmindedly rubbed the top of her prosthetic leg.

'Does it hurt?' Ellie whispered.

'Not really. It just gets a little sore when I have been on it a long time.'

The door opened, and a young woman stepped through with a confidence that seemed to fill the room. The sun's rays seemed to caress her light brown skin as it glimmered in the afternoon light, and her dark eyes sparkled with joy. Her long black hair ran down her back like a wave of glossy silk as she removed her hat. As soon as Ashley saw the woman, she jumped up excitedly, grinning, when she realized it was her girlfriend. Shreya's heart leaped with joy as she sprinted towards Ashley. Throwing her arms around her, Shreya felt the warmth of Ashley's body against hers and smelled her sweet perfume. Taking Ashley's face in her hands, she kissed her lips softly.

'I have missed you. Shreya, I'd like you to meet my sister,

Ellie,' Ashley said.

Ellie rose from her chair, extending her hand for a polite greeting. Before she could respond, Shreya had already pulled her into a tight, comforting hug, leaving Ellie both surprised and touched.

'Sorry, I'm a hugger,' Shreya chuckled as she sat beside Ashley.

'It's really nice to meet you,' Ellie said with a smile. 'Where did you meet again?'

Shreya's heart raced as her fingers tingled with anticipation before finally intertwining with Ashley's warm, soft hand. She couldn't help but smile as she recalled the first time they saw each other.

'We met at the gym, in an aerobics class. As I watched her from across the room, I felt a spark I knew couldn't be ignored. After class, we went for coffee and talked for hours. It felt like I had known her my whole life; I think that's when I realized she was the one.'

Ashley felt her heart skip a beat as she glanced up at Shreya, her cheeks warming and her lips curving into a shy smile.

'I love you.'

'I love you too,' Shreya beamed.

Jasper walked up behind Ashley, the mugs on his tray rattling with every step. As he placed the drinks on the table, he felt his palms become sweaty as he glanced nervously at Ellie.

'Enjoy,' Jasper said before returning to the counter.

Ellie smiled as she watched him leave, filling her cup with the freshly brewed tea and adding a cold milk splash.

'Do you live around here?' Ellie asked.

'I did live with my parents, but unfortunately, they

disapproved of my relationship with Ashley. I grabbed whatever I could and moved in with a friend not too far from here,' Shreya sighed, her eyes filling with tears as she remembered the moment she opened up about her sexuality to her parents.

'Mum and Dad have been amazing. They said Shreya could stay for Christmas and move in until we find our own place,' Ashley said as she tenderly grasped Shreya's hand with a reassuring squeeze. 'She's just packing up all her things. It's our first Christmas together, so we want to make it memorable.'

Shreya savored the warmth of the chai tea, briefly closing her eyes in contentment. When she opened them again, her gaze fell on Ellie, who had just placed her mug carefully on the table.

'So, what do you do for work?' Shreya asked casually.

Ellie's lips curled into a gentle smile, Highlighting her warm, dimpled cheeks. She lifted the cotton apron from her lap and cradled it so Shreya could get a better look.

'Well, I start here soon,' Ellie sighed as she finished the last dregs of her tea before placing it back on the table.

A sudden, rambunctious cackle from a table on the other side of the shop reached their ears, and Shreya saw a group of children staring at Ashley's leg. Her face twisted in a scowl of anger as she stood, But Ashley's grip on her arm kept her firmly in her seat.

'What's going on?' Ellie asked, her voice tinged with confusion she sat with her back to the children.

'They are being disrespectful little shits, that's what,' Shreya spat. 'Laughing at Ashley's leg like that. They need to learn how to show respect!'

Ashley held both of their hands, her touch soft and

comforting, as a sense of calm filled her face.

'I appreciate you wanting to teach them a lesson for me, but this isn't the first time. It's just a need for more knowledge and respect. I'm proud of my body, and I'm not ashamed of my leg, so I refuse to hide it away. I love both of you for wanting to stand up for me, but let this one go.'

Shreya smiled at Ashley as Ellie stood up, the apron draped over her shoulder. She placed the mug on the tray and shook her head with a sigh.

'I love you, Ash,' Ellie said as she embraced Ashley tightly before stepping back and holding her arms open to Shreya.

'It was really nice meeting you,' Shreya said as she hugged Ellie.

'I had better prepare for my shift so they can get going. See you back at the house later?'

We were going to see a movie tonight; we can pick you up after your shift if you want?'

'Sounds great, thank you. I should finish about nine,' Ellie said. 'I have missed you so much, Ash.'

Ellie smiled and walked toward the door behind the counter to prepare as Ashley snuggled in next to Shreya, the softness of her hair brushing Ashley's arm as she rested on her shoulder.

'Your sister looks like a nice person. I hope she sticks around so we can get to know each other better,' Shreya whispered as Ashley kissed the top of her head and smiled as she watched Ellie leave.

'It's great to have her back; It looks like she's doing so much better.'

4

Ellie scoured the tables for any used cutlery and discarded items, gathering them and returning them to the counter. She carefully placed the mugs and cups near the sink and then disposed of the trash in the swing bin close to the door. Fiona walked out of the office, tightly winding her thick winter coat around her body. She pulled the scarf across her neck and secured her purse over her shoulder. She made her way toward the counter, where Ellie and Jasper stood in a fit of laughter.

'It looks like you two have certainly picked up right where you left off,' Fiona chuckled. 'I'm leaving now to visit your father. Don't forget to pick up Zack; He finishes school in half an hour.'

'Yeah, Mum, I just need to finish here before I go,' Jasper said with a nod.

Fiona smiled before walking to the door, feeling around in her pocket for her keys. The icy wind blew violently against her face, sending strands of hair flying in every direction. Ellie and Jasper watched Fiona open the car door, slide into the driver's seat, and give one final wave before starting the engine and driving away. Jasper smiled before counting the money in the register, preparing for the shift change.

'So what have you been up to this year?' Ellie asked.

Jasper's gaze fell upon Ellie, and his face flashed with surprise before the corners of his mouth pulled downwards into a frown. His eyes moved away quickly, but not before she could see the sadness lingering in them.

'It's been a challenging year, trying to balance looking after my brother, visiting my Dad in the hospital, and fulfilling my responsibilities here,' Jasper said. 'It's probably a good thing; It was unbearable when you left. I needed the distractions. I have missed you, Ellie.'

Ellie bit her lip, her gaze darting around the room, too scared to look him in the eyes.

'I am so sorry for hurting you and leaving suddenly,' Ellie murmured, her voice choked with emotion. 'Please don't think it's because I stopped loving you.'

Jasper stopped what he was doing momentarily and looked into Ellie's eyes.

I know why you did it, and I do understand. You needed some time away from everything to heal.'

Ellie grasped his hand, squeezing it softly.

'Yes, that was part of it, but I also had to protect you. I was being self-destructive, and it wasn't fair to expect you to carry all my bullshit,' Ellie whispered, gently raising her finger to his chin, redirecting his gaze toward her. 'But even so, I didn't want to leave you either.'

Ellie stood before Jasper. Her hands clenched nervously at her sides as she cleared her throat.

'I wanted to see you, Jasper. That's why I came back here and asked for work.'

Jasper counted the money in the register; his brows furrowed with concentration.

'So, do you have anybody special in your life?' Ellie asked nervously as she wiped down the counter. She paused and looked over at Jasper, watching as he seemed mesmerized by his task.

'No, not at all. As I said, I don't have time for anything like that,' Jasper said with a slight smile.

Ellie's heart skipped a beat at the thought that Jasper wasn't seeing anybody, and she couldn't contain the rush of joy that flooded her body.

'I can't believe it. Any girl would be lucky to be with you,' Ellie said.

Jasper tensed up and avoided eye contact while shuffling his feet nervously. His breath hitched as he finally looked up into Ellie's eyes.

'I've never been interested in anybody else; it's always been you,' Jasper whispered. 'A Christmas fair is coming this week; would you like to go with me?'

Jasper's sudden question caused Ellie's bright blue eyes to widen in surprise.

'Are you asking me out on a date?' Ellie asked, Her voice trembling.

Jasper nodded and stepped toward the coat rack to put on his winter Jacket as Ellie nervously tucked her hair behind her ears and followed him. Just as Jasper was about to leave the shop, he stopped and turned around.

'I'm sorry, I shouldn't have asked,' Jasper said, avoiding her gaze.

Ellie felt her face grow warm, and she tried to find an appropriate response.

'I would love to go out with you, but I don't want to hurt

you,' Ellie whispered, gently squeezing his arm.

Jasper smiled as he handed Ellie several keys.

'Then don't hurt me,' Jasper chuckled. 'I missed you, Ellie. Have a good night, and call if you need anything.'

Jasper's gaze lingered on Ellie momentarily. A chill ran through her as another customer stepped up to the counter. She watched Jasper walk away into the frigid winter air, his form soon hidden by the falling snowflakes. Her nerves tingled with anticipation, but was it due to fear or excitement? She had no doubt she'd see Jasper again tomorrow, but what would that hold in store?

Ellie's eyes flicked to her wristwatch. She felt the sharp edges of her apron as she straightened it and glanced around the room. The remaining customers were few - a middle-aged man in a business suit, crisp black with a navy tie, sitting alone in one corner. A young couple sat near the door, their faces close together, hands entwined, and whispering sweet nothings to each other.

'Only ten more minutes until closing time,' Ellie sighed.

The sound of bells on the door, chiming in the stillness of the shop, announced the day's last customer. He shuffled forward, his body thin and frail beneath layers of clothes that looked two sizes too big for him, giving him a worn and haggard look. His pallor was ghostly, and faint purple circles pooled beneath his eyes, making his face appear exhausted. As soon as he entered, Ellie wrinkled her nose as an all too familiar odor reached her nostrils. As soon as she caught the smell of the whiskey on his breath and the strong smell of beer emanating from his skin, it felt like a wave of nostalgia was pulling her back to a part of her past that she had put in a lot of effort to escape. Ellie could almost taste the sweet bitterness on her tongue. As she watched him approach her, she felt her heart beating with a blend of fear and dread that left her trembling. When he finally reached the counter. In frustration, he slammed his hand down, making Ellie jump with a muffled yelp. She tried her hardest to maintain professional composure, but the fear in her eyes and the tremor in her voice gave her away. Ellie took a deep breath and mustered all her courage before forcing a weak smile.

'Hello sir, how are you today?'

Ellie felt the man's eyes slowly run down her body, and she shuddered in response. Her heart began to pound, and a chill ran through her as she nervously crossed her arms over her chest. She could feel his gaze fixed on her as she heard chairs sliding across the floor and the rustling of coats as the young couple hastily retreated from the shop. The man sitting nearby observed the situation keenly, turning his head to listen to the exchange better. The drunk man leaned closer to Ellie, who was almost overwhelmed by the powerful aroma of alcohol.

'I want you to leave now! I don't appreciate how you are looking at me,' Ellie snapped.

The man sitting in the corner of the room leaped to his feet, his eyes wild and intense. He grabbed the drunk man by the shoulder firmly.

'It's time to go.'

The drunk man desperately tried to break free from the customer's iron grip, but he was no match for his strength. The tables and chairs clattered and scraped along the floor, bouncing off walls as he desperately fought for freedom. Ellie felt her body trembling from shock as her fingers wiped away a tear that had trickled down her face.

'Are you alright?' The man said as he approached Ellie.

'Thank you, what a creep. I think I'll close five minutes early if you don't mind finishing up,' Ellie said as the man picked up his mug and placed it on the counter.

'Would you like a hand cleaning up?'

'No, I'm fine. You have done enough,' Ellie whispered.

'Make sure you lock up after me; you never know who's around.'

The man walked out the door, and Ellie followed, dutifully locking it behind him. Her movements were slow and labored as she picked up discarded cups and mugs from the tables. Suddenly, Ellie stopped and leaned heavily against the wall, her body shaking with sobs she tried vainly to suppress. After several moments, she dabbed her eyes, then blew her nose into a tissue before picking up the phone to call Ashley.

'Hi, Ash. It's Ellie.'

Hi, I'm sorry, we ran into some friends and got invited to a party. I didn't realize the time.'

'Don't worry; I will get a taxi home. You guys have fun,' Ellie replied.

'Are you alright? You sound upset.'

'I'm alright, honestly,' Ellie said. 'I'm just tired.'

'Alright, be careful, and we will see you in the morning.'

Ellie jumped as she heard tapping coming from the doors. After ending the call and grabbing her bag, she glanced through the window and spotted a man standing outside in the shadows. Ellie gasped in fear, her heart pounding as she assumed it was the intoxicated man from earlier returning with malicious intent. But when she peered through the window, she sighed in relief to see the kind face of the man who had saved her moments before. Quickly unlocking the door, she welcomed him inside.

'Sorry, you scared me. I thought it was that man,' Ellie said.

'I'm sorry. I didn't mean to scare you. I think I left my phone by the table.'

Ellie followed him cautiously to where the man was sitting as his eyes shifted to the door.

'I was worried you might have left already.'

Ellie opened her mouth to reply, but the man cut her off before she could speak. His gaze shifted, and his posture tightened as he rotated to face her, a cold sneer spreading across his lips. His fists clenched tightly at his sides as the man stepped menacingly closer. Confused and terrified, Ellie scrambled backward as he closed the distance between them in two swift strides, locking his rough hand around her arm.

'You're hurting me,' Ellie gasped as she tried to escape his grip.

The man threw back his head and let out a menacing chuckle that filled the room's silence.

'Oh, I'm sorry,' The man snarled contemptuously. 'Don't make this any worse than it has to be. I am being paid handsomely to have you delivered alive, no matter what shape you may be in,' The man spat. 'I have to say I'm disappointed. I was told you might be dangerous. I have watched you for hours, and all I have seen is a pathetic little girl.'

He curled his hand into a tight fist and instantly struck Ellie's cheekbone as she felt the blow reverberate through her head. His hands closed around her hair like a vice and yanked her head back, tears streaming down her cheeks. She found her courage and pushed away from him with all her strength, driving an elbow into his ribs so hard she could hear the air rush out of his lungs. He released her with a snarl of rage, then grabbed tightly at the collar of her jumper, gripping it so hard that Ellie felt the fabric constricting her throat like a vice. She cried out in fear as he applied more pressure, the sound of her jumper tearing under his iron grip. Ellie felt a surge of adrenaline and wrenched out of his grasp with unexpected force; she immediately turned around and fled, her feet pounding against the ground as if poised for flight. He lunged forward, grasping her arm and yanking her body backward with such force that the table behind collapsed under her body as Her head crashed against the unforgiving floor with a sickening crack. He stumbled back in shock, his eyes wide in disbelief and horror at what he had done. His heart thundered as he inched closer and closer to her motionless figure, anxiously searching for any hints of life as he strained to hear even the faintest sound of breathing. Ellie felt a scream die in her throat as the man's rough hands closed around her upper arms, lifting her off the ground with surprising strength and slinging her over his broad shoulder. A chill rippled through her entire body as she opened her mouth to call for help, but only a silent gasp emerged. The man's shoes clacked against the pavement, each step echoing dread through the otherwise quiet night. His footsteps were steady and menacing, closing in on an ominous black van parked in the shadows. Ellie remained unable to move and too scared to breathe as the man wrenched open the van's side door violently. As he threw her inside, she felt all the air being knocked out of her lungs as she landed hard on the splintery floorboards. The man grinned as he watched Ellie cower before him, paralyzed with fear. An electric thrill surged through him as he reveled in a feeling of absolute control. His face glowed with satisfaction, unable to contain his smugness at the sight of her vulnerability. Ellie desperately tried to find the strength to move but felt utterly helpless. Without warning, the man was viciously thrown to the ground, his body crashing hard against the cold, wet path beneath him. Towering ominously above him stood an enormous behemoth of a man, raining merciless blows down on him with brute force and no trace of mercy. Ellie felt her eyelids grow heavy as a wave of fatigue overcame her. She tried to fight it, but the darkness was too powerful, and soon the world faded from view.

5

As the morning sun emerged over Portland, Oregon, its radiant light illuminated the sky, enveloping the city in pleasant warmth. The morning sun glinted off the pavement as commuters made their way to work, accompanied by a cool, crisp breeze. In the distance, a structure that twisted, curved, and arched like a double helix towered above the other buildings. The sun glinted off a sleek white car as it approached the entrance. A distinguished man in a charcoal suit stepped out from the driver's side and opened the rear door. As Rebecca emerged from the car, she ran her hands through her soft hair and straightened the grey skirt that hugged her toned legs above her stylish black heels. She tastefully tucked in her crisp white blouse and adjusted the designer handbag on her arm, exuding grace and elegance with every step.

'Thank you,' Rebecca said.

'Have a lovely day, Mrs. Ellis,' The man said with a polite nod.

She approached the sizeable white lobby of the building

and showed her security pass to the guards. It bore her name: Rebecca Ellis-Carter - CEO.

'Good morning, ma'am. Just go right through,' one of the security guards said as she passed.

'Good morning,' Rebecca said. Her voice reverberated through the grand hallway, resonating off the walls as she spoke.

As she entered the grand room, all conversation stopped, and all eyes shifted to her. She strolled toward the center of the room, taking in every detail of the marvelous sculpture erected in memory of her late father, David Ellis, who once held this very seat of power. She paused before it, her eyes swimming with emotion. Rebecca strode towards the glass elevator, marveling at how it captured and reflected the light in a dazzling array of colors. The buttons glowed with a red DNA helix as if inviting her to navigate the secrets of life itself. She reached out a perfectly manicured finger and pressed the button. Rebecca stepped inside the elevator, feeling a wave of apprehension hit her. A woman wearing a black skirt suit came in behind her just as the doors closed. Rebecca glanced briefly at her and noticed her long blond hair pulled back in a tight ponytail. The elevator slowly ascended, floor by floor. Finally, it stopped on the 27th floor with a slight jolt. Rebecca walked into a brightly lit room, illuminated with flickering screens lining the walls and bright sunlight shining through the large window. The young woman behind the desk had her sleeves rolled up, her long, red hair pulled back, and a pen tucked behind her ear.

'Good morning, Stacey. Any messages for me?' Rebecca asked.

'I have put all your mail on your desk, and Mr. Reed is waiting for you in the Conference room. He said for you to meet him there when you arrive.'

'Martin is in there now!' Rebecca snapped, her face contorted with rage as she abruptly turned to confront Stacey.

'I'm sorry. Mr. Reed has been there since he arrived this morning.'

Stacey watched, rooted to the spot with fear, as Rebecca marched resolutely towards the first door on the left - her head held aloft, defiantly, and her jaw clenched tight. Rebecca stepped into the room, squinting against the luminous glare created by bright spotlights reflecting off the stark white walls and a beam of warm sunlight spilling in from the window. The long, glossy wooden table shone brightly in the center of the room, surrounded by comfortable chairs. A large screen illuminated the room at the end of the table, and a man in an oversized, high-backed chair was facing away from her. She placed her bag on the table with great care, and the contents made a gentle clink as it settled down. She spread her hands across the top of the wooden surface, feeling its polished finish beneath her fingertips.

'I'm going to gloss over the fact that you are sitting in my chair and just ask you to get to the point, Martin,' Rebecca said.

The man slowly turned his chair around and stood up to face her. His tall, slender figure was a striking silhouette against his dark grey suit and neat, slicked-back dark red hair.

'I apologize, Rebecca. I didn't realize I had to ask permission,' Martin replied sarcastically as he carefully took a crisp piece of paper from his pocket and laid it on the table.

'What is that?' Rebecca asked.

'Well, this report is coming out of England claiming that

one of our operatives found her,' Martin said, sliding it across the table toward Rebecca.

'I'm sorry; why was I not informed immediately?'

'Listen, you wanted to be alerted if anything came up, and I'm alerting you.'

She gingerly picked up the paper from the table, her breathing escalating as she read. Her eyes darted across each line, devouring the words and their implications. When she finished reading, she slowly lifted her gaze to meet Martin's, her brow furrowed with confusion. Rebecca slammed her fist on the desk, her knuckles turning white in frustration. She read through the report again, shaking her head in disbelief.

'This makes no sense,' Rebecca said. 'It says here that she was attacked and beaten?

Martin's face hardened, and his eyes avoided Rebecca's as he clenched his jaw. She continued reading aloud, her mouth tightening with each word.

'It appeared he wanted some sick pleasure before someone helped her escape,' Martin said.

Rebecca didn't dare lift her head again as her hands slowly ran through her hair. She read the report word by word in a murmur, feeling as if the world around her had sunken away. It felt like an eternity until she finished reading, but when she finally looked up, all that remained was a deep sorrow for what had befallen her.

'We must get a handle on this before he talks. What possessed you to use such a high-risk asset?'

Martin leaned in close and spoke in a low, authoritative voice.

'I can assure you that we have taken care of the situation. The operative is no longer an issue, and our agents are searching the city for the girl. We have also set up surveillance around her family's house, monitoring it at all times.'

Rebecca slowly turned towards him; her lips pursed into a menacing expression as she bore her eyes into his very being. She silently nodded before turning away.

'Please get out of my sight,' Rebecca said.

She watched as he nodded and turned towards the door, but before he could take a step, she leaned in, and her lips brushed his ear as she whispered.

'From now on, all information goes through me,' Rebecca said. 'I appreciate your work here, but don't you ever think of demanding an audience with me in my father's boardroom again, understood?'

'Loud and clear, Mrs. Ellis,' Martin replied as he departed the office. Rebecca glanced back down at the file and saw a grainy black-and-white photograph of Ellie taken from surveillance footage. She smiled softly, running her fingers along the picture's edges.

'could it be after all this time?'

At that moment, an urgent knocking sounded from the door, and Rebecca quickly tucked the photograph back into the folder.

'come in!'

A sharply dressed man with slicked-back hair and a crisp white shirt strode through the room, his eyes widening as he approached Rebecca.

'Is it her?'

Rebecca gave him a gentle smile as she met his gaze and nervously ran her fingers through her hair.

'It's all so hard to believe. She looks just like Scarlett and is the same age. I had almost given up hope, but somehow I knew this day would come,' Rebecca whispered as she took a moment to reflect on the swirl of thoughts and emotions inside her.

'If it is her, then we have to be cautious. She could be very dangerous. Is it time to put Scarlett back into the field?'

Rebecca felt her face flush as she crossed her arms, and her lips tightened into a thin line. She was struggling to contain her emotions—she wanted to yell and scream, but at the same time, she didn't want to appear out of control.

'Not yet. Scarlett is still far too reckless; we all saw the destruction in China after her last mission. She's volatile and inexperienced, and I'm afraid the treatment isn't helping as much as I'd hoped. She doesn't know the details of this situation yet and must not find out.'

The man stepped closer to Rebecca, his face a grimace of worry.

'This is a hazardous situation. She's getting help, but from who?' The man asked. 'This girl is far too important, and we must handle this before she finds out too much. Shall I contact another asset in London?'

'I will handle it. I know just the person,' Rebecca said.

Rebecca's face was a blank mask as she shook her head, and the man responded with a slight bow before turning on his heel and walking away.

Rebecca slowly shut the door, sighing relief at the faint click that signaled it had closed completely. Then, she carefully adjusted each slat of the blinds until no light or view of the outside world remained. She stepped softly over to the table, her heels sinking into the thick carpet, and reached into her bag to retrieve her phone. Gazing intently at the contact list on display, she eventually decided on a number as she picked up the photograph of Ellie from the desk. Rebecca looked at the photo with gentle affection, her lower lip softly caught between her teeth, before putting it back into the file for the last time. Her heart raced as she dialed the number, listening intently for a sound signaling a connection. After what felt like an eternity, she heard a faint ringing. A loud crackle echoed over the line, and then a voice responded.

'Yes,' Piper said with a sophisticated poise, her voice smooth and elegant. Her British accent was alluringly detectable as it lingered in the air like a whisper of fine silk.

'I have a job for you,' Rebecca said. 'I am sending over the details now. Be warned; the target is not to be taken lightly. She could be very dangerous, so I'm sending you, Piper.'

Rebecca pulled the phone away from her ear, took images of the files before her, and sent them to Piper.

'I'm getting the details through now. Ellie Jones, she's just a small girl. How is she supposed to be dangerous?' Piper asked.

Rebecca heaved a deep sigh, her palms cupping her temples.

'I don't pay you to ask questions. I need The girl delivered to me unharmed. Can you handle that or not?'

'Consider it done. I will contact you when it's complete for payment.'

Rebecca disconnected the call, clicked the pen in her hand a few times, and then placed it in her pocket. She collected all the paperwork from the table, checking everything was in order, and tucked it into her bag before standing up. She glanced over her shoulder, taking in the sound of the ticking clock in the empty room, before she reached for the light switch and walked out.

6

United States of America, December 2024

Rebecca hurried down the hallway, her steps echoing off the hard walls. She stopped abruptly before a vast steel door with wires snaking across its surface and a blinking red light hovering above. The air around her vibrated with electricity, and a low, consistent hum came from within. Rebecca pulled a rectangular plastic ID card with a magnetic strip on the back from her pocket. She slowly swiped it through the metal reader, and after a soft beep, the light shifted from red to green, and the heavy door opened with a low, grumbling sound. Rebecca stepped into the laboratory, her eyes wide as she took in the spotless surfaces and heard the faint hum of the computers. In the corner, she noticed a tall, slender man with unruly dirty blonde hair and glasses perched on his nose. His lab coat hung around him like a protective shield, the crisp white fabric rustling slightly as he nervously shifted his feet when he saw Rebecca approaching.

'Hello, Doctor Wilson. How is Scarlett today?'

A beautiful woman on the other side of the lab glanced up from her microscope, her blonde hair gathered in a neat bun and her glasses perched on her forehead.

'What?' Rebecca asked.

Doctor Wilson swallowed, his Adam's apple bobbing in his throat.

'The guard was about to go in and take her food. She's not eating again,' Doctor Wilson said. Rebecca watched with a knot in her stomach as a guard, clad head to toe in black armor, appeared, his heavy boots thudding on the floor and echoing through the room's stillness. The guard marched towards a large door sealed shut by bands of titanium locks. Two men stood outside the entrance, wearing black suits tailored to their muscular frames. The two figures stood watch like sentinels, their shadows looming ominously against the wall. They held their weapons firmly, their fingernails dug deep into the hard steel, and their jaws clenched with fierce determination. The man at the door glanced over at Doctor Wilson, although his expression was unreadable. He nodded, and the door clicked open with a soft thud. Rebecca felt the sweat trickle down her skin as she examined the images on the large monitor before her. The whirring fan grew louder and more oppressive with each passing second. Her hands trembled ever so slightly as they rested on the plastic casing while she stared intently at the figure of the young woman on the screen. Scarlett and Ellie shared many similarities, the only visible distinction being their hair. Scarlett had pale blond hair that flowed gracefully to her collarbone and bore a unique tattoo of a black widow spider behind her left earlobe, its legs trailing down her neck. She was lying on the cold floor, her body tightly curled to fight the chill. Her white bodysuit hugged every curve of her figure like a second skin, and a silver collar with a bright emerald light encircled her neck with an ethereal glow that illuminated her pale complexion.

'Deactivate the collar.' Rebecca snapped.

Doctor Wilson blinked as he shifted his gaze from his colleague to Rebecca. His chair creaked as he leaned back, the leather squeaking with each movement. He clasped his hands together, trying desperately to hide the telltale tremble of his fingers.

'With all due respect, Mrs. Ellis,' Doctor Wilson said. 'Her behavior is becoming more and more concerning. The chances of success are almost nonexistent if we deactivate the safety protocols. There would be dire consequences.'

Rebecca stepped closer, her warm breath making contact with Doctor Wilson's cheek as she narrowed her gaze. He squirmed uncomfortably, the room's chilly air in stark contrast to the hot beads of sweat on his forehead. He felt Rebecca's intensity as she looked deep into his eyes.

'We need to take risks to determine if she is falling in line,' Rebecca said. 'You tell me you have been medicating her and conditioning her daily. I have to believe that she will learn to trust us. Deactivate it.'

Doctor Anderson approached the control panel with trepidation, her hand hovering over the deactivation button before pressing it reluctantly.

The heavy metal door slid open slowly. Inside, the room was utterly monochromatic. The entire structure was made of mirrored walls, creating a dizzying kaleidoscope of reflections. In the center was a glass prison cubicle that stretched up to the high ceiling. The bright white light cascaded down from the top, illuminating the young woman lying on the floor. Rebecca and the two Doctors peered intently at the security feed, holding their breath as they watched the guard enter the room.

'Open the door,' The guard whispered into his communicator as he approached the glass cell.

The door opened with a metallic click. The guard leaned inside the cell, his ears picking up the sound of Scarlett's shallow breathing as he collected the tray of food, and his gaze lingered on her motionless form lying on the floor.

Rebecca glanced at Doctor Anderson and felt her heart beating faster as she tightened her grip on her arm.

'Now,' Rebecca said.

As the guard turned to exit the door, the tiny green light flashing on her collar blinked out, and the red light illuminated, making Scarlett's eyes suddenly snap open to reveal her deep, emerald eyes. All at once, the guard's body went rigid, his face contorted with panic, and his forehead dampened with sweat. The young woman silently rose to her feet, her bare feet gliding across the floor as she strode up behind him with a menacing glint in her eye, her fingers clasped together darkly. Scarlett's gaze flickered to the security camera, her eyes burning with a cold, calculating light.

'Mother, is that you? What brings you back here again? Will you ever learn?'

Rebecca acted quickly and stopped Doctor Wilson from reactivating her collar by firmly gripping his arm before he could press the button.

'Leave it.'

Rebecca pressed the intercom, and her voice echoed through the chamber as Scarlett stood confidently behind the man. Her shoulders were straight as the light beamed down on her and glinted off her alabaster skin.

'Scarlett, you have a choice. Make the right one, and we can talk,' Rebecca said.

Scarlett slowly stalked around the man, her gaze searing into him. She moved around him with slow and steady steps, her eyes roaming and lingering on his body. Her lips curled into a smile as she noticed the dark stain spreading on his trousers, the puddle on the ground becoming more and more visible.

Scarlett's gaze became intent, her eyes narrowing as she focused on his face. She leaned forward, her eyes closing slowly as their bodies softly connected. Her lips met his, tasting the coffee he'd had earlier that morning. He trembled beneath her touch, and a thin layer of sweat glistened on his forehead. He saw a feral hunger in her eyes that filled his body with fear.

'You need to understand something, Mother. I hurt people because I enjoy it,' Scarlett chuckled.

'No!' Rebecca Said.

The man let out a blood-curdling scream as his face contorted with pain. His skin was pale, his veins visibly throbbing under his flesh, and he shook violently against the sheer force of the pain that coursed through him. Blood trickled over his face and streamed down from his eyes and ears, pooling around him on the ground. The man screamed until his throat was raw, his voice a broken whisper. His body shuddered as the life left him, and he slumped over in a crumpled heap on the floor. Scarlett smiled and lowered herself down beside him. She dipped her finger into the pooling blood and slowly dragged it up her arm, smearing it over her chest before taking a lick off her finger. Finally, she rose to her feet, her humming filling the room with a haunting version of Incy Wincy Spider as she stepped over his lifeless body and returned to the center of her cell, her hands atop her head. Rebecca shoulder-checked the guards, their faces cloaked in shadow, guns outstretched and trained on Scarlett. The bright red light on her collar suddenly changed to a bright green glow, and Rebecca felt relief.

Scarlett was standing in the middle of the cell, her eyes as sharp and intimidating as daggers, illuminated by the bright lights from the ceiling, firmly fixed on Rebecca.

As Rebecca spoke, an oppressive feeling of heaviness permeated the atmosphere.

'Why do you do it, Scarlett? You will never see the sun again or feel fresh air on your skin,' Rebecca whispered.

Scarlett didn't break her gaze away, not even to blink.

'What do you want from me? You keep testing me, hoping I will change, but this is me.'

Scarlett's lips twitched in a smirk, and the corners of her mouth curved up slightly, forming a wry expression.

'You know I am trying to help you, right? I'm your mother, and I love you,' Rebecca said.

Scarlett stepped forward, her gaze unwavering as she looked at Rebecca through the glass wall.

'You love me?' Scarlett chuckled as she turned her back on Rebecca.

'That's why I'm a prisoner here. That's why I'm treated like an animal and punished.'

Rebecca closed her eyes as a tear escaped, tracing a mascara-streaked path down her cheek. She wished she could have held it in, but the sorrowful sight of Scarlett was too much for her.

'The worst part is that I don't hate the cruelest tortures inflicted upon me. No, instead, it's the only time I feel even a sliver of life, a single spark to keep the darkness from fully consuming me.'

Rebecca looked at Scarlett again.

'You're here for your protection. I gave you a chance, and you failed. You were supposed to fly under the radar. What you pulled in China could have destroyed the organization.

We covered it up, but if the world knew what you did, your punishment here would pale compared to how the world would treat you,' Rebecca said.

Scarlett's hand came down hard on the glass, reverberating with a dull thud that made Rebecca jump.

'I failed? Are you fucking kidding? Scarlett said as she widened her eyes in disbelief. Rebecca leaned into the glass, resting her forehead on the cold surface.

'We trusted you! All you had to do was be discreet! Yes, the target was eliminated, but at what cost?! You brought a lot of unwanted attention,' Rebecca said. 'You showed me that you lack respect for authority and can't be trusted to handle tasks that require any responsibility, so you are here until I see some reliable change in your behavior. Are we clear?'

The room was tense as she turned away from Scarlett and took a few steps toward the door. Before walking out, Rebecca heard Scarlett's low laughter.

'Is something funny?' Rebecca asked.

'You asked me to kill, so I did my job, but now you dare to come in here and think that I won't do what I was born to do - what I love to do? You are mistaken, Rebecca. And one day, hopefully soon, you will understand that.'

Rebecca turned to face Scarlett again.

'Listen, whatever you think of me, I am your mother and love you. I am trying to protect you. I don't want to lose you.'

Scarlett chuckled under her breath.

'My mother? I haven't seen you for months. You say I'm dangerous, so I ask you, here and now. Kill me, please, and release me from your love,' Scarlett said.

'I can't bear the thought of you dying. You have so much to offer this world; you are special and one of a kind. I know you'll find your place,' Rebecca said.

'One of a kind, are you so sure about that?' Scarlett asked.

Rebecca stepped away from the glass in shock, trying to recompose herself.

'What do you mean?' Rebecca said.

Scarlett's lips curled into a smirk as Rebecca slowly stepped backward. As she reluctantly spun on her heels and made for the exit, Rebecca heard Scarlett's sinister laughter echoing through the room. As Rebecca walked away, the door slowly closed behind her, and the lights gradually dimmed, leaving Scarlett in the dark. Rebecca marched across the room and slammed her hands on the table, rattling paperwork and beakers, causing Doctor Anderson to flinch. Doctor Wilson cautiously followed behind her, clearing his throat.

'Mrs. Ellis.'

Her head snapped to attention, and she spun around, eyes blazing.

'What?'

'I tried to tell you she is changing, exhibiting signs of strange behavior. The conditioning is no longer working; instead, it's making it worse by reinforcing her damaged psyche.'

Doctor Wilson closed his eyes briefly before pushing his glasses up the bridge of his nose. Rebecca studied him with wide eyes, her brows knitted together in concern.

'What are you saying?'

'She's becoming more and more fearless and intelligent every day, so I fear there is no way we can keep her contained indefinitely.'

With a sharp nod, Rebecca moved towards the door.

'Get somebody in here to take care of that mess and get her

cleaned up,' Rebecca ordered over her shoulder as she exited the laboratory.

7

United Kingdom, December 2024

Ellie jolted awake with a start, the sudden burst of sunlight from the window searing her eyes. She groggily lifted her arm to shield herself against the brightness, dreading the cold morning air that was sure to follow. A soft groan escaped her lips as she shifted on the old leather sofa. The tattered red blanket slipped from her shoulders, sending a chill down her spine. She swung her legs around and placed them on the white rug below. But before she could stand, an intense pain shot through her. It started in the back of her head and spread to her temples. Ellie's breath caught in her throat as she clutched at the armrest of the worn blue sofa. She surveyed the room with a sense of disorientation, finally settling on the enormous brick fireplace that loomed over her in the corner. The yellow and orange flames within cast flickering shadows onto the walls, sending out a warm glow that lit up every nook and cranny of the space. A loud, ticking sound emanated from the old clock above, counting down each second like it was precious. Ellie's icy fingers traced their way over a throbbing welt on her temple as she stood up, trying to steady herself. In front of her hung an antique mirror, its cracked surface reflecting a barely recognizable woman.

Bruises ran down her arms and around her neck, and a shirt that didn't belong to her hung loosely off her, like a child playing dress-up in their parent's clothes. Ellie gingerly ran her fingers over the back of her head, feeling the thick stitches that held together the wound she'd received the night before. She shivered as a sudden chill ran through her body, and she collapsed onto the sofa, letting out a weak groan of pain. The clanking of pots and pans coming from the kitchen and the faint strains of music made her heart pound. The horrific events of the previous night replayed in her mind like a broken record. She could almost feel the man's rough hands grasping at her, tearing her jumper away from her body as if it were paper. Ellie sat up slowly and got to her feet, but as she pushed off the sofa, a wave of vertigo made her stagger and grab onto the wall for support. She stood still for a moment, trying to regain her balance.

When she finally stepped away from the wall, she looked toward the kitchen and saw a faint figure pacing around, their silhouette cast in the dim light spilling through the doorway. Ellie's eyes fixed on the main door to the house, her only way out. She stepped forward, but the floor creaked like a whale in distress. Every movement seemed amplified, each step echoing off the walls of the narrow corridor. Her chest tightened, her pulse quickened, and her eyes darted to the kitchen entrance, searching for any signs of movement. She stopped and looked at the kitchen door, watching the shadow of a person chop vegetables with quick and precise movements. She eased toward the front door, her heart pounding in her chest. She stepped lightly and cautiously, but the old wooden floor moaned beneath her feet, and the sound of chopping vegetables suddenly ceased from the kitchen. Fear turned her blood to ice, but she tried to push past it and run for the exit. Her leg throbbed from the injuries sustained in the attack, making it difficult to put weight on it as she hobbled towards the old oak door. Ellie gasped as her frantic tugging of the door handle proved futile. She spun around and was met with a towering figure, his height casting a heavy shadow on her. His hands were like vices on her arms, immobilizing her in fear. Her heart pounded as she felt the tension in his grasp. Ellie felt her heart skip when she saw the tall, broad-shouldered figure ahead of her. Her hands instinctively flew up to cover her mouth as recognition registered on her face. The man's grip loosened on her arms, and he stepped back with a look of reluctance. She took the chance to move away slowly, cautiously measuring the distance between them. Panic raced through Ellie's veins, and before she could stop herself, she took a step back and found herself pressed flat against the door.

'Jackson! What the fuck are you doing?'

Jackson nervously ran his fingers through his hair and cleared his throat before he spoke.

'I know this is overwhelming,' but I will try to explain what's happening.'

'Well, you can start with why I am in your house, how you knew where I was, and who the fuck attacked me,' Ellie screamed.

Her muscles tightened, her knuckles whitening as her fingernails dug into her palms. Jackson stood on the living room's threshold, hand outstretched in a gesture of peace. She fought the urge to scream and instead balled her hands into fists, letting out a deep sigh. She slammed her fist against the wall, challenging him silently, but still refused to move.

'Come on,' Jackson said, stepping closer to her with concern.

He stretched out his arm, lightly touching her back. She flinched, and a frown tugged at the corners of her mouth.

'You need to lie down for a while. You hit your head pretty hard.'

She reluctantly nodded and leaned into him slightly as he guided her towards the sofa. Her feet shuffled slowly, and Jackson stayed close in case she swayed. He sat her down carefully and propped up a pillow behind her head before handing her a glass of cold water.

'I understand you're confused, but I'm here to help,' Jackson said.

Ellie nervously took the glass of water in her trembling hands and raised it to her lips. Taking a sip, she was aware of his eyes watching her every move before placing it carefully onto the side table. She reluctantly leaned back into the pillow and closed her eyes, trying to bury away the feelings of doubt and uncertainty that were scratching away at her mind.

'Alright, I will tell you what happened, but you have to let me finish, as it's a lot to take in,' Jackson said.

His voice wavered as he opened a box of cigarettes, flipped one out, and used a lighter to ignite the tip. A thick cloud of smoke rose between them as his eyes darted about the room nervously.

'Was anything true, or was it all a lie? Is your name even Jackson?'

'My name is Jackson Carter, and everything you heard me say in the meetings was true. Your biological father had rescued you from a life of danger in America and asked me to bring you here and monitor you from a distance,' Jackson said. 'I promised him I would keep you safe.'

Ellie's back straightened, and her eyes widened as she edged closer to Jackson, disbelief filling her voice.

'You knew my birth father?'

Jackson nodded, his face filling with regret.

'I knew him, yes. A long time ago.'

The weight of his words hung heavily between them as Ellie struggled to find the right questions to ask.

'Do my parents know any of this?'

Ellie took a sip from her glass of water as Jackson's gaze shifted away. His hand trembled as he brought the cigarette to his mouth and held it there for a few moments before finally taking a deep draw, his closed eyes obscured by a veil of smoke that rose around him like a protective shield.

'I brought you to this country so you could be safe, but I couldn't tell them everything,' Jackson whispered. 'I couldn't risk putting them in danger.'

'I don't understand what this has to do with last night?' Ellie asked.

Jackson stood and began pacing the room, smoke trailing off his lips as he spoke.

'Your father wanted to keep you away from dangerous people, Ellie. They've been trying to find you for a long time and sent that man. That's why I hid you here, but now they know exactly where you are, and they won't give up.'

Ellie swallowed hard, her throat suddenly dry. She looked up at Jackson pleadingly.

'This has got to be a mistake. Why am I so important? I'm a nobody.'

Jackson crushed his cigarette in the ashtray and moved closer, settling into the sofa cushions beside her.

'Ellie, when you were a baby, you had this extraordinary

presence, something special and unique about you. You could do things that seemed impossible. Some people wanted to take advantage of your gifts for their own gain. That's why I have done everything in my power to keep you safe.'

Ellie stared in disbelief. She did not know what to say. On the one hand, she was sure this was all a mistake; she didn't possess any remarkable abilities. Yet, on the other, something in her gut told her that there must be more to it. Jackson slowly lifted his hand towards Ellie tentatively, his eyes radiating a plea of understanding. When she shrunk away in fear, he hesitated before gently placing his hand on the back of her neck and continuing to speak softly.

'Right underneath your skin is a micro device called an inhibitor. Your father placed it in your body before we left. It suppresses your powers so that you can have a normal life. Your father wanted you to live a peaceful life as a regular kid.'

Ellie's eyes widened, her mouth open in disbelief. She squeezed the bridge of her nose with trembling fingers and took a slow breath.

'I'm sorry, I just can't make sense of this.'

Jackson cleared his throat and squared his shoulders, his dark eyes locking with hers. His voice was gentle but unwavering.

'I'm sorry it has come to this, but they know where you are, and you're in danger. You need to conserve your energy and rest as much as possible so we can take out the inhibitor when you're ready.'

Her mouth fell open, and she sat back in her chair as if trying to distance herself from his words.

'What! You must be fucking crazy!' Ellie said.

She leaned back; her fists clamped tight at her sides. Her

eyes narrowed in disbelief as she shook her head.

'Even if I believed you, which I don't, there is no way I would let you cut into me like that!'

Jackson slumped back in the chair, running his fingers through his long hair as he stared out the window into nothingness.

His words were steady, but his eyes darted around the room, betraying his anxiety.

'I've been preparing myself for this day since we arrived here. Now they have found you; they won't stop. If they manage to apprehend you, they will do unimaginable things. You must allow me to help if you are to have any chance of survival,' Jackson said. 'We need to disable the inhibitor and figure out how to control your power before it's too late.'

Ellie's face drained of color as her gaze darted around the room, her hands trembling in anticipation. She spun to face him, her eyes wide with fear.

'I don't know how much more I can take,' Ellie said. 'Everything going on in my life has exhausted me beyond words. You know what I've been through, so you must understand why this isn't something I can accept. My stress levels are already through the roof; I can't handle anything else added to it. Please just let me go.'

Jackson stepped closer to Ellie and hesitantly reached out his hand, unsure how she would react. He could see the fear in her eyes as he gently touched her shoulder.

'I understand how scary this must be for you,' Jackson said. 'You're free to go. You're not a prisoner here.'

Jackson looked into her deep blue eyes and paused momentarily, feeling an air of uncertainty between them.

'I saved you from one attack, but I can't protect you from whatever is coming. You have a choice - go out that door as

Ellie, the woman who's defined herself by her failures, or stay and find out who you are. He moved closer, and she could almost feel the tension between them.

'And who is that, exactly?'

Ellie considered his words, torn between the door symbolizing her past and the unfamiliar path Jackson offered her. She slowly turned to him.

'An extraordinary young woman with gifts to change the world,' Jackson said.

8

United Kingdom, December 2024

Slowly, a thick curtain of fog crept over the Jones's sprawling estate, shrouding it in eerie grey light that gave the once-proud mansion an atmosphere of desolation. Suddenly, an electric bike appeared through a cloud of dust, its powerful hum breaking the eerie stillness of the night. It skidded gracefully over the gravel path before coming to a halt beside an enormous metal gate. Piper removed her helmet, feeling the chill of the winter air rushing over her. She trudged across the gravel, her heavy boots crunching with each step. As she reached the entrance gate, she determinedly swept her long chestnut brown hair away from her face and quickly secured it in a tight ponytail with a black hair tie. Taking a deep breath, she pulled a small remote device from her pocket and cautiously aimed it at the electronic keypad. When her finger pressed the button, the device emitted a gentle vibration that grew stronger and faster as it worked its magic. The heavy iron gates groaned as they slowly opened, creating an echoing noise that reverberated through the air. Piper stepped forward and stared at the majestic mansion before her, feeling an undeniable strength inside her. She took a deep breath as she entered the grounds, ready to face whatever lay ahead. Piper produced a thin metal tool from her pocket and stared at the door handle fixedly. She inserted it into the keyhole and moved it with unshakable confidence. There was a soft click, and the door laid open before her, beckoning her inside. She braced herself and pushed the door firmly, shoving it open with a loud creak. The hallway flooded with a shrill siren reverberating off the walls in an eerie echo. Instinctively, she clamped her hands against her ears to block out the deafening noise that filled every inch of the room. Piper's fingers moved frenetically across the illuminated surface of her device until she silenced the terrifying alarm that had disturbed the eerie stillness in the house. The only sound left was the faint ticking of clocks coming from different rooms, as if time held its breath in tense anticipation. Piper closed her eyes and inhaled deeply. She mustered up the courage to step into the dark hallway. The plush red rug beneath her boots felt like a cushion as she gingerly moved forward, allowing her eyes to adjust to the darkness. The grandfather clock in the corner drew Piper's eyes as it marked each second with a deep rumble that echoed off the walls and floors. Its mahogany frame was immense, reaching the ceiling like an ancient tree.

As its steady thumping rhythm created a feeling of unease within her, Piper clicked on her torch, its light illuminating a series of family portraits on the wall. She pulled the photo of Ellie from her back pocket and carefully unfolded it. Gazing at the image, she compared it to the many photographs on the wall and ran her finger along the frame's edge. Her gaze then shifted to the ornate Christmas decorations draped around the staircase. Colorful bells, strings of twinkling lights, and dried pine garlands glinted in the flickering light.

She marveled at the house's grandeur as she trudged up the long staircase. She stepped onto the plush carpet of the second floor and crept towards the first bedroom, where an enormous bed lay in wait. The frame was crafted from the finest dark mahogany and carved with beautiful motifs, further enhanced with glistening gold accents. At the foot of the bed, a long dressing table glinted in the light. It seemed to glow, embellished with intricate carvings and inlaid with shimmering crystal. On the surface, glass perfume bottles sparkled like diamonds beside jewel-encrusted boxes that reflected a rainbow of colors. Piper studied her surroundings with a heavy heart, feeling intense emotions. She wanted so badly to have what this family had, the beautiful home, the sense of security and belonging, but she also felt a feeling of deep sorrow at how different her life was from theirs. Piper wished more than anything that her life could be as grand and luxurious, but it seemed an impossible dream.

'This must be Mummy and Daddy's room.'

Piper took a few careful steps toward the next open door, craning her neck to determine what was inside. She pushed the door open with her fingertips and stepped into a small room - its walls painted in pale pink, shelves decorated with framed photographs, beloved stuffed animals, and mementos from childhood. Ellie's suitcase was open, overflowing with clothing and other items. Piper's eyes scanned the room until they settled on the old pine dresser, which stood in the corner, partially blocked by the suitcase. A white cork board decorated with photos of Ellie and her older sister Ashley hung beside it, adorned with colorful push pins. She watched from the window as a glossy black BMW approached the house. It glided to a stop with a quiet purr that sounded almost reverential, and she felt her stomach twist in anticipation. Mike opened the car door and gracefully stepped out, his broad shoulders filling out the tailored black fabric of his suit. He straightened out his tie and shut the door. As he walked around to the other side of the car, he opened the door for Alice, who glided out with elegance and poise worthy of a queen. Her dress was a shimmery blue fabric that clung to her curves in all the right places, and the slit on the side revealed a hint of her thigh. Piper hastily retreated from the window, her gaze lingering on the figure of Mike holding Alice's arm as they ascended the steps. She heard the front door open and close, followed by a chorus of voices and laughter in the foyer. A sudden, brilliant glow illuminated the room as he flipped the switch. Alice followed him inside, shrugging off her long winter coat and hanging it on the hook.

'That's strange. I thought the alarm would be on,' Mike said.

Alice sighed in relief as she slumped into the armchair near the door. She propped her elbow on the armrest and rested her chin on her palm, uncrossing her stiff legs to give them a good stretch. She slipped off one high-heeled shoe, then the other, relieved, as she wriggled her toes free.

'It should be,' Alice said, her voice a mix of puzzlement and concern.

Mike examined the alarm panel while Alice looked on, her heart beating faster with each passing second.

'Maybe one of the girls came home,' Alice said to reassure herself and Mike.

Alice followed Mike into the kitchen, wincing at the sudden brightness when he flicked on the light switch. She stayed close to him as they stepped toward the fridge, her eyes scanning back and forth for any sign of movement from upstairs.

Mike opened the fridge, pulled out two water bottles, and handed one to Alice. Just as they were about to leave the kitchen, an earsplitting crash shook them both to their core. Alice clutched tightly onto Mike's arm, her fingers digging into his skin as Mike wrapped an arm around her waist, his other hand still gripping the water bottle.

'What was that?' Alice asked nervously.

He smiled reassuringly at her before releasing his grip on her waist and slowly stepping forward.

'It's alright, honey. I'm sure it's just Ellie or Ashley. I will check.'

Alice nodded, her eyes wide and brimming with fear.

'Be careful, please.'

Mike's hand shook as he picked up a walking stick by the front door. He silently inched one foot in front of the other and stopped at the top step, his heart pounding. He held his breath and squinted into the darkness, searching for any sign of life. With a deep exhale, he flipped on the light switch.

'Ellie, Ashley, are you home?' Mike whispered.

He glanced over his shoulder and saw Alice, her knuckles white as she tightly clutched the kitchen door frame, her gaze filled with worry as she watched him.

'Please, Mike, come back.'

The chill of unease ran down his spine as he tiptoed through the hallway, not a sound emanating from any of the rooms. He twisted the brass knob of their bedroom door and peered inside. His gaze darted around the room, scanning for signs that something was out of place. He crept towards Ellie's room, his heart racing with dread.

'Is everything alright?' Alice called from behind him.

Mike frantically surveyed the room, his gaze falling on the jagged shards of glass scattered across the wooden floor. His eyes then turned to Ellie's window, the curtains billowing in from the cool night air. He ran his hands through his hair, desperately attempting to organize his racing thoughts as he shouted to Alice.

'Yeah, I'm alright. Ellie just left her window open, and a gust of wind knocked a glass over that smashed.'

Mike sighed heavily and allowed his shoulders to slump in resignation before briefly squeezing the bridge of his nose with his thumb and forefinger. He slowly turned away from the broken glass on the floor and descended the creaking wooden stairs, each step growing heavier as he drew closer to the kitchen.

'I will clean it up so nobody gets hurt. Alice? Where are you?'

His gaze darted around the room as he tried to find her. The upturned stool, the shattered plates scattered across the floor, and the air's eerie stillness made him feel like he had entered a living nightmare. The faint tapping noise coming down the hallway seemed to echo in every corner of his mind, making him hold his breath in anticipation. He crept towards it cautiously, feeling like each step was weighing him down more and more.

'Alice, Alice?' Mike said.

Taking tentative steps forward, he entered the living room and felt a chill run down his spine. Mike scanned the room until he saw Alice seated on the sofa. His heart sank as he saw Piper standing behind her, gun in hand, its muzzle pressed against Alice's temple.

'Please, take a seat next to your wife,' Piper spat.

Mike cautiously stepped across the room, his feet dragging with each step. He could feel Alice's fear before he even reached her side. Her body was shaking, and tears were streaming down her face. Without a word, he sat on the couch beside her and pulled her tightly against him, shielding her from Piper's view. Mike felt his stomach drop as the cold barrel of Piper's gun pressed against his forehead. He could feel sweat trickling down his temple and chills radiating down his spine.

'Take whatever you want. Just don't hurt her,' Mike begged.

Piper's smirk widened as she crept closer to the couple, their faces drained of color. With a menacing glint in her eye, she waved the gun at them with malicious intent.

'I don't care about your snobby crap. What I want is something much more valuable,' Piper said as her laughter echoed eerily around the room.

'What do you want, money?' Mike asked.

Piper dropped heavily into the chair before them and placed the gun on her lap like another accessory. With an air of indifference, she threw her scuffed leather boots onto the expensive coffee table, causing a delicate ornament to crash to the ground in a flurry of broken glass.

'I'm making good money, thank you very much. What I want is simple,' Piper pulled out a photograph of Ellie from her pocket and placed it on the table between them. Mike's face paled as he gazed at the photo, his mouth agape.

'What do you want with Ellie?' Mike asked, his voice barely audible.

Piper carefully folded the photo and slowly slid it back into her pocket. Her throat tightened, her knuckles whitening as she desperately tried to contain her emotions.

She took a deep breath and carefully leaned back into the chair, trying to keep her temper in check.

'Where is Ellie Jones? I must warn you: patience has never

been my strength. I don't care for the girl, but my employer wants her unharmed and back promptly.'

The air seemed to thicken as Piper waited for an answer. Mike's gaze darted to Alice, and he saw her pupils grow wide with terror. Her breaths were shallow and quick, each more fearful than the last as she stared at the woman before them.

'Please, this has to be a mistake. You have the wrong person,' Alice screamed.

Piper clenched her fists and screamed, her face contorting with rage. She upended the coffee table with one swift motion, sending books, magazines, and glasses crashing to the floor. Piper leaned in, her face looming closer and closer to Alice's with every breath. Unspoken rage burned in her dark eyes as she fiercely met Alice's gaze, pressing the gun barrel against her forehead. Before Mike could intervene, Piper raised the gun and thrust it into Mike's face. A sharp crack echoed through the silent room as he stumbled backward, bright red blood streaming down his white cheek from a deep gash. Piper's icy stare sent shivers down Alice's spine as she slowly returned the gun to her head and cocked it.

'You will tell me what I need to know, or you will watch your wife die!'

Piper swung the gun violently, connecting with Alice's temple and sending her to the ground with a loud thud. Mike felt his blood run cold as he watched in horror; Alice lay still with blood spilling from her forehead while Piper stood above her unmoving body.

'please stop!'

Mike scrambled across the cold floor, desperate to reach Alice. He was helpless as he watched blood spill from her head onto the ground. He clawed at the ground with his fingernails as he approached her still body. His pleas were met with Piper's chilling laughter, echoing through the room like a haunting fog. She knelt beside Alice and savagely grabbed her by the hair, yanking her off the floor and into an upright position. Disoriented from the shock of the blow, Alice could not fight back as Piper threw her on the couch, her body limp and lifeless.

'sit next to your wife,' Piper said.

Mike slowly inched onto the couch and embraced Alice, laying his head on her shoulder.

Piper's booted steps echoed in the room's stillness as she advanced towards the couple, gun raised and pointed straight at Mike, who had his arms protectively around Alice.

'This has been a waste of my time. You two are of no use to me anymore. I will find Ellie, and when I do, I will be much less gentle than if you had cooperated,' Piper said.

Mike's breath hitched as he leaned in to kiss Alice's forehead tenderly. He closed his eyes and savored the feeling of her warm skin against his lips, knowing it would be the last time he showed her affection before death's cold embrace took them both away.

9

Ellie slowly walked out onto the porch of Jackson's farm, the wood creaking beneath her feet. She carefully lowered herself onto the weathered wooden rocking chair, hearing its joints groan as she shifted her weight. She curled up in a thick blanket, tucking it tightly around her slender frame as she fought to stay warm against the chill of dusk. Jackson pushed gently against the door with one foot, careful not to spill the two mugs of steaming tea in his hands. He inched closer to Ellie and offered it to her. She sat rigid, her eyes wide, as she snapped out of whatever distant thought had captured her mind.

'Thank you,' Ellie said as she took the hot mug of tea from Jackson, cupping her hands around it and warming her fingers.

Jackson settled into the chair beside her, producing a pack of cigarettes and striking a match. She watched with disdain as he lit up, her nostrils flaring as a cloud of smoke drifted before her face. Her lips curled into a tight purse, and her eyes darted away in a silent judgment.

'You know those things will kill you, don't you?'

Ellie felt a twinge of disappointment as Jackson gave a low chuckle, his mouth forming a slight smirk while exhaling a smoke stream.

'Thanks for the warning, kid,' Jackson said. The corners of his mouth curved slightly upward as he raised one shoulder in a half-hearted shrug. 'Plenty of things have tried to kill me before, and nothing has succeeded yet.'

Jackson leaned his bulky frame against the porch railing, admiring the stars twinkling in the night sky. He lifted a cigarette between two fingers and inhaled deeply, letting out a slow stream of smoke that rose, fading into the darkness like a whisper.

'So, were you in AA because you needed help or just because you were spying on me?' Ellie asked.

As his gaze drifted to meet her blue eyes, a flood of memories rushed over him. He thought back to when he had isolated himself from everyone as he struggled with his addiction, the days spent without laughter, hope, or purpose, all feeling too heavy for his weary heart.

'Oh, I needed help. When I brought you to this country, I had nothing. I had to learn how to survive quickly. That's why I needed to find you a nice family so you could disappear and live a normal life.'

He slowly exhaled a plume of smoke, watching the wheat fields ahead of him.

'I needed to stay close,' Jackson whispered. 'So I took a job at this old man's farm.'

The ember on the end of the cigarette glowed brighter as he inhaled deeply.

'Paid hardly anything, but I had a roof over my head and food on my plate.'

Jackson's fingers trembled as he crushed the filter between them.

'The incessant nightmares and the fact that I couldn't sleep, no matter how hard I tried, drove me to seek solace in the bottle.'

Ellie hung her head low as a wave of understanding washed over her. She felt the gravity of his words tugging at her spirit, the realization that he was talking about something she had been trying desperately to forget.

'It didn't take long before I was drinking round the clock. Then, old man Bill passed away, and nobody came to claim his farm. The years passed quickly, and your parents didn't want me around you while I was drinking. I tried to contact them, but they didn't want to know. I couldn't blame them. That's when I went to AA. It took a long time for sobriety to take hold, but eventually, it did. Imagine my surprise when you walked into the group. I asked if I could be your sponsor because I genuinely wanted to be there for you.'

Ellie cupped the mug of steaming chai between her palms and inhaled the sweet aroma before bringing it to her lips. The tea scalded her tongue, but she savored each comforting swallow and let its warmth seep through her body. Her eyes drifted downward as his words echoed in her mind.

'I'm so sorry, Jackson,' Ellie said. 'You never really spoke about your life in America. Did you have a family back home?'

He hesitated for a moment before finally replying.

'I had a wife, but we separated before I left.'

Ellie slowly trailed her fingertips across the back of her neck. She felt a deep curiosity about what powers lay dormant within her.

'What is this thing inside me?'

Biting her lip, she waited for a response.

'Your parents were scared when you were born because they could see strange abilities within you. They worked in a multi-billion dollar industry, with a division that supplies military forces with special operations weapons,' Jackson said.

Ellie's heart dropped like a stone in the pit of her stomach as Jackson spoke. His voice echoed in the heavy silence, and he paused to take a long drag on his cigarette, the tip glowing orange in the darkness.

'When they uncovered your gifts, the company sought to weaponize you. Your parents were scientists who developed a microchip that was inserted into your central nervous system to keep your powers contained.'

She felt the weight of their words in her chest.

'How did they find me?' Ellie asked.

'They've been trying to track you down for years. I thought they had lost interest, but it seems they have eyes everywhere,' Jackson sighed.

Ellie sprang to her feet, anguish in her expression.

'If they found me, they know where I live.'

She stopped, horrified at the thought of her family in danger. She ran her fingers through her hair with trembling hands as tears filled her eyes.

'Jackson! I must warn Holly and my parents.'

Ellie's breath quickened as desperation rose in her voice.

Jackson reached into his pocket, pulled out his phone, and offered it to Ellie. With shaking hands, she dialed the number. After a few agonizingly long rings, the call connected to Holly's voicemail.

'Fuck!' Ellie yelled desperately, knowing she couldn't explain the situation over a voicemail message. 'Holly, it's

Ellie. Please don't return to the house for any reason before your flight. I will explain everything later. Just trust me on this one.'

Ellie hung up the phone, and her hand shook as she entered her parent's number. She held her breath, willing the other line to pick up, and each passing second felt like an eternity.

'Come on, answer.'

She anxiously tapped her foot on the floor, waiting for the call to connect. The dial tone suddenly changed, showing a successful connection, and she could hear faint breathing on the other end.

'Hello?'

Piper's silky British accent drifted through the phone, causing Ellie's heart to beat faster.

'Hello Ellie, it's so good to hear your voice. I would very much like to meet in person if you could come and join us,' Piper said.

Ellie could hear the fear in her voice as she tried to steady herself against a wall.

'Who are you? Please don't hurt them!'

'I would hurry. Your parents don't have long,' Piper said.

Suddenly, two sharp, echoing gunshots cut off the line.

Ellie's mouth dropped open as her gaze shifted towards Jackson, her pupils dilating with fear. The phone slipped through her trembling fingers and crashed to the floor.

'Your parents?' Jackson asked.

Ellie's face drained of color as she quickly turned and dashed towards the black truck parked by the barn. Jackson trailed just behind her, the sound of their breathing the only thing breaking the tense silence.

'Ellie, wait! It's too dangerous!'

Jackson stepped forward, arms outstretched to prevent Ellie from leaving, but she quickly brushed him aside and continued.

'They are my family. You said I'm not a prisoner, so I am going. Either help me or get out of my way,' Ellie screamed.

She jumped into the driver's seat and started the engine. Jackson rolled his eyes, rushed to the car's passenger side, and leaped inside. The vehicle roared, its tires squealing, as it sped away, leaving a cloud of dust in its wake.

'Ellie, for God's sake, slow down! Are you trying to get us killed?'

Jackson shouted as the car careened towards the Jones's estate. The speedometer needle quivered at its highest point, and Ellie refused to let off the accelerator. With a screech of tires, the car stopped mere inches from the iron gates.

Ellie leaped from the car and sprinted towards the house as Jackson followed.

'Stop, it's too dangerous!'

Ellie's legs were burning as she sprinted towards the house, but before she could reach it, Jackson lunged forward and clasped his hand firmly around her wrist. She whipped around to face him, her chest heaving as her breath came in short, ragged gasps.

'Ellie, please stop.'

Before either of them could move, Jackson spotted somebody behind a tree in the distance.

'It's a trap!'

Jackson reacted quickly, spinning around and shielding Ellie with his body. The deafening sound of a gunshot reverberated through the air, and he crumpled to the ground before her. Through blurry eyes, she saw Piper's hands move methodically, reloading her gun. Tears of rage blurred her vision as she stepped forward, opened her mouth, and let out a feral roar that made her throat feel like it was ripping apart.

'What did you do to my parents?'

Ellie felt a powerful surge of energy course through her body towards Piper, lifting her off the ground and throwing her like a rag doll. Her tiny frame crashed through tree branches on the way down, leaves raining around her as she crumpled onto the ground. Ellie stumbled back in shock, glancing at Jackson, who lay motionless on the floor. He stirred, blinking slowly.

'I'm alright. It was just a sedative. Check on your parents.'

With one more look of uncertainty toward Piper's body, Ellie ran into the house. Ellie's mouth hung open, and her stomach seized as her eyes glanced from one corner of the room to another, trying to piece together what had just happened. Her father, Mike, lay motionless on the floor in a pool of blood. Ellie gasped as she backed away from the carnage before her. Splashes of red decorated every wall, and shards of glass covered the ground. Alice was motionless on the sofa, her pale blue dress stained with crimson. Ellie sprinted to Mike, her mind racing with dread. She hovered over him, fingers trembling as she felt along his throat. Tears of relief filled her eyes when a faint pulse thumped against her fingertips. Fearful yet determined, Ellie raced to Alice's side and repeated the process, letting out a deep sigh when she found the same steady beat. With shaky hands, Ellie grabbed the phone from the side table and dialed emergency services, her voice full of desperation as she begged for an ambulance immediately.

'Stay with me; help is on the way,' Ellie said, holding Alice close.

Jackson slunk into the room, leaning against the wall.

'Are they alright?'

'My parents are dying!' Ellie sobbed.

Jackson's heart raced as he reached for Ellie, her hand trembling in his. The room was illuminated all around them by dazzling blue flashes piercing the darkness, and the sirens' howl was deafening. Paramedics rushed past Jackson and Ellie toward her parents.

'We need to get out of here, Ellie.'

'I can't leave them.'

'We need to get answers from the woman that did this. Your parents will be in safe hands.'

Ellie looked at Mike and Alice as Jackson led her out of the house, passing where Piper's body was moments before.

'She's gone!' Ellie whispered as Jackson looked at the broken branches covered in blood.

'We need to get you back to the farm where you are safe,' Jackson said as Ellie threw her arms around him, crying into his thick coat.

'come on, Kid, let's get out of here.'

10

With a slow and steady pace, Piper made her way up the old, creaky stairs of her hotel building, her left arm hanging as she used the handrail for extra support. Her feet felt like lead with each step, the pain growing more unbearable. Finally, she reached the top and, with a heavy sigh, leaned against the wall to catch her breath. Suddenly, out of the corner of her eye, she saw a woman in a long dress stride toward her with determination. Her eyes widened with concern when she noticed the large blood stain on Piper's shirt and the noticeable pain on her face.

'Are you okay? Do you need any help?'

Piper kept walking, trying to maintain dignity despite being in obvious distress.

'I'm fine,' Piper said curtly, not looking back as she reached her room.

She pushed open the door to her tiny room and stumbled over to her bed in front of a window that overlooked the city below. She fell onto the edge and winced as pain shot through her body. Her hands shook as she slowly unzipped her heavy leather jacket. She paused momentarily before pushing it off her shoulders, allowing it to slump onto the floor. With a deep breath, she reached down to untie the laces of her thick-soled, steel-toed boots and kicked them off with a resounding thud. Piper's stifled yell echoed off the walls as she gingerly pulled her blood-soaked grey shirt over her head, which fell softly. She took a deep, shuddering breath and, with a groan, pushed herself up and shuffled over to where the mirror hung by her bed. Even though her legs felt like lead, she was determined to face her reflection in the mirror. She gazed at her ravaged body, horrified by the sight of deep cuts and lacerations crisscrossing her chest, stomach, and back. Blood pooled around the wounds, dripping down her pale skin. Piper entered the bathroom and winced as she peeled off her tight leather trousers, careful not to move too quickly or put pressure on her tender ribs beneath. She kicked aside her underwear and stepped into the porcelain bathroom tub, scalding hot water already flowing from the shower head. She looked up as the warmth of the water cascaded over her tired body. The water was like a balm, soothing the ache in her muscles and washing away the dirt and dried blood from her body. Her mind reeled with shock at what Ellie had done to her. She'd never endured something so traumatic before. After turning off the shower, Piper grabbed a soft towel from the chair beside her and wrapped it around her shivering frame. Gingerly, she limped back to the bed and placed a hand on the wall for support. She held her breath as she lowered herself onto the edge of the mattress, trying to minimize the sharp pain in her ribcage. She gritted her teeth as a low, guttural moan escaped her lips. Her face and neck muscles were tense, and her eyes squeezed shut as she endured the pain. Piper sat on the edge of the bed, phone pressed against her forehead as she willed it to grant her the courage to make this call. Taking a deep breath, she dialed, waiting for an answer.

'Hello?'

'Mum, I won't be home tonight,' Piper said. 'I'm sorry to ask, but can you have Emily another night?'

There was a brief pause before her mother replied with concern.

'What's going on? You sound troubled?'

'I'm fine,' Piper said. 'I had to stay later than I thought at work. I'll be home tomorrow.'

'Of course, I'll look after her. She's here if you want to say goodnight?'

Piper held her breath, willing herself not to break down, but tears spilled over her cheeks despite her best efforts.

'Please.'

After a few moments, a tiny voice came through the phone.

'Hi, mummy.'

'Hi baby, are you having fun with Nanny?'

'Yeah, but I miss you, though,' Emily said.

Swallowing hard against the lump forming in her throat, Piper recomposed herself.

'I'm sorry I can't make it home tonight. I will see you tomorrow; I promise.'

'See you tomorrow, mummy; I love you.'

As Piper's tears streamed down, she whispered back with a deep pain that felt like her heart was breaking.

' I love you too, baby.'

Piper hung up the phone, opened the wardrobe, and rummaged through, searching for something light that would not aggravate her injuries. Suddenly, the door knocked, making her jump, dropping a soft, white cotton shirt she had picked out. Piper's slender fingers searched beneath the side table until they felt the cold metal of the pocketknife. She had kept it hidden there for emergencies. She grabbed it in her sweaty palm and shuffled to the door.

'Who is it?' Piper asked.

'Room service.'

A sense of unease swept over her as she looked through the peephole and saw an unfamiliar man pushing a silver-domed trolley. He stood proud in his navy blue uniform, crisp and professional, with golden epaulets on the shoulders that glinted in the light. Holding her breath in anticipation, she opened the door only a fraction of an inch, enough that if he looked up, he would catch sight of her face but not her body.

'I didn't order any room service,' Piper said.

'This was ordered for this room, Miss.'

Piper vigilantly monitored him until he was out of sight, then bolted the door and slumped against it for support. Painfully dragging herself back to the bed, she placed the knife on the side table. Releasing a sigh of relief, Piper untied the towel around her head and massaged out the moisture from her tangled locks. She heard a faint whisper behind her and sensed an overpowering presence. She slowly turned around to see a man shrouded in darkness, his face hidden by the shadows of night. The only feature she could make out was his cold, dead eyes. Before she could react, his strong hands were already around her neck. She felt an ice-cold piano wire cutting into her skin as it tightened with each passing second, sapping away the life within her. Every part of her body screamed in agony as she looked into the mirror, watching helplessly as the reflection of the tall, thin man pulled the wire tighter. Piper felt her heart pounding like a jackhammer as she thrashed and writhed, striving to escape his menacing embrace. She summoned her strength as she pushed against the wall with her feet, desperately trying to escape his clutches. With one last surge of power, Piper felt herself lurch backward on top of him, finally freeing herself from his paralyzing grip around her neck. Her fingertips scratched against the cold floor, leaving behind blood trails as she stretched her arm as far as it could go, barely grazing the handle. With her last bit of strength, Piper flung herself forward and snagged the knife. She felt a sudden sharp tug of pain on her ankle and glanced back to see the man's fingers wrapped around it. His grip grew tighter, and Piper cried in agony as he dragged her towards him. With all her strength, she twisted around and drove the blade into his arm, finally freeing herself from his grasp. With a manic gleam in his eye, he grasped the blade sticking out from his arm and yanked it free. He dragged his tongue across the knife edge, tasting the salty iron of his blood. The man raised his leg in the air, bringing his heavy boot crashing down on Piper's ribs with a sickening crunch. She screamed in agony as she felt her breath knocked from her lungs. The man's fingers tangled in her hair, yanking her up with a violent tug. He tossed her onto the bed like a rag doll, sending blankets and pillows flying around the room like a tornado. Piper lay still on the bed, gasping for air, feeling the weight of his malicious intent. He sneered with delight as she writhed in pain, a predatory grin stretching across his face. He crawled onto the bed beside her, a wave of frigid air emanating from his body as he silently pressed into the mattress. His breath caressed her neck like a ghostly chill, sending shivers down her spine and haunting her with its icy presence. His fingers curled through her locks with desperate need, breathing in the sweet scent with a primal hunger that chilled his blood.

Before he could react, she lunged forward, her forehead smashing into the bridge of his nose with a sickening crunch. He stumbled back, blood dripping from his nostrils and chin as he swiped away the crimson liquid with an eerie chuckle. He savagely seized her by the arm, yanking her up and propelling her with unmitigated force toward the mirror until it exploded into a million tiny shards. The impact threw Piper violently backward, her body slamming into the hard ground with a terrifying thud. She lay there, still and silent, her skin drained of all color and smeared with crimson blood. He stalked to the bathroom with calculated strides, jerking on the faucet until the bathtub was brimming with water. The man returned to Piper, seething with rage, his breath coming in menacing snorts. He gripped her fragile body with brute force and effortlessly lifted her into the air. She felt as light as a feather in his arms as he carried her with determination back to the bed. She could barely keep her eyes open or utter a sound as she faded in and out of consciousness. He threw her onto the bed, disregarding her well-being, like she didn't matter. He sat next to her and traced his fingers along her body, unhooking the towel with an impatient tug, throwing it to the ground, and revealing her naked body. His eyes burned into hers with a fierce intensity as he took in every inch of her. As he surveyed her battered body, a smile of perverse pleasure crept across his face. His ecstasy grew with every new bruise and cut until it felt like an electric current running through his veins. His primal urges were awoken as he feasted on her disfigured form, delighting in the destruction of her perfect beauty. His lips curled into a sickening smile as he ran his fingertips against her smooth skin. Her body stiffened at his touch, and she felt a chill as his fingers ran up her thigh. His breathing grew heavier, and he moved closer to her, digging his hands into the curves of her body like a wild animal searching for its next meal. His fingers burned with a cold hunger as they trailed circles of dread across her skin. He lingered on her neck, brushing his thumb lightly against it as if relishing the thought of snuffing out her life source. His fingers graciously traced the shape of her collarbone like a vulture awaiting its feast. His gaze followed his finger as it snaked its way up her arm to the silver ring she wore on her finger. With a vicious twist, he plucked it off and pocketed it without a second thought, claiming her in more ways than one. He scooped her light body into his arms and carried her away, following the soft light of the bathroom where unspeakable horrors awaited her. With a trembling grip, he lowered her unresponsive body into the tub, the water sloshing against her skin. As the hot bathwater lapped around her neck and chin, he hastily tucked a few strands of her hair behind her ears, letting his seething breath linger on her face. His hands were steady as he pulled out a sharpened blade from his pocket and pressed its icy edge against the curves of her skin, barely restraining himself from breaking through the fragile surface. He seized her wrist in an iron grip, the blade's pressure threatening to pierce and break her delicate skin. Her breath hitched in her throat as he carved a path across her wrist with the knife, slicing through her flesh until vivid crimson blood filled her palm and dripped into the bathwater, creating a swirling red sea around her body.

The man's iron grip wrapped around Piper's other wrist, and he dragged the razor-sharp blade along her delicate veins. Her eyelids lazily flickered open as she watched in horror at the pool of crimson liquid that was oozing out from her body. With every drop, she felt what life she had left slowly slip away. When the man realized she was gone, he pulled out his phone and dialed a number he knew by heart.

He waited impatiently for what felt like an eternity until the line connected.

'Target eliminated.'

The man's thick Cockney accent filled the room, and then there was a long pause before a man's voice broke the silence.

'Thank you for this, Alastor. I'm not too fond of loose ends. Mrs. Ellis likes to deal with people as spineless as she is. You have all that you need. Find the girl and kill her. I want her gone.'

As the line went dead, a sudden chill descended over the room. Alastor slowly approached Piper's body, his heavy boots pounding a somber rhythm on the aged wood. He dragged his hands through the tangled mess of his long, unkempt blond hair as he slowly scanned the room. The cloying aroma of death lingered heavily in the air, and he inhaled deeply, savoring the scent. He knelt beside her body, his fingertips lightly tracing the strands of her brown hair that were still damp, taking in every feature of her face. His cold blue eyes glinted with malicious glee as he stared down into her unseeing eyes. He stood up, his every movement sending waves of creaking through the floorboards as he clicked off the lights and plunged her into a permanent night. With a final smirk, he shut the door behind him, leaving her in the darkness.

11

Jackson's bleary eyes slowly opened, and he saw the worn, faded fabric of the sofa cushions beneath him. His head throbbed as he attempted to rise, causing his vision to swim and a wave of dizziness to wash over him. He quickly scanned the room, his eyes resting on the familiar shape of his brown coat in a crumpled heap near the door. His heart pounding in his chest, he was hit with a wave of silence and stillness, with no sign of Ellie.

'Ellie, where are you?'

Jackson slowly rose to his feet, pressing one hand against the wall to steady himself. He took slow, deliberate steps across the room, his bare feet connecting with the chilly hardwood beneath him. He glanced at the clock, realizing it was afternoon, and he had been asleep for quite a while. His heart began to race as he walked toward the kitchen. The morning sun shone through the window, warming the room after days of snow and grey skies. Its rays danced on the walls, creating a cascade of golden light that brought a feeling of hope. Jackson slowly opened the door and spotted Ellie, her figure silhouetted against the fence at the edge of his property. A rooster and about a dozen chickens were pecking at the ground for food near her long black boots. He noticed Ellie talking on his phone as he approached her and rested beside her on the fence.

'How are they doing?' Ellie asked, a note of hope laced throughout her question despite the trace of fear in her voice.

'There's little change. They are stable but still unconscious,' Ashley's voice was so faint that Ellie could hardly discern what she was saying. She held the phone with a trembling hand, and tears of grief streamed down her face as she wept silently.

'The doctor said they are lucky. They would have died if the bullets had hit a few inches on either side. What happened, Ellie?'

Ellie's stomach sank as she heard the quiver in her sister's voice and felt a wave of guilt crash over her. She fumbled with the edge of her shirt, desperately trying to mask the panic rising within her. The image of her parents lying in hospital beds, hooked up to machines, replayed in her head. She knew that all of this was because of her.

'I can't tell you everything yet, but I know people are after me, and I'm scared. Please stay with Mum and Dad and keep them safe. Could you and Shreya stay with friends for a while? I need a few days to figure out what's happening.'

Ellie's eyes filled with desperation as she waited for Ashley's response.

'I think we can, but I don't understand. Did you do something, Ellie? Are you drinking again?'

With a single tear filling her eye, Ellie shook her head, realizing that her past mistakes would forever define her.

'I'm so sorry, Ash. I promise I am not drinking, and I have done nothing. This is all just a huge mistake.'

Jackson stood beside her, his eyes full of fear and worry as he heard the conversation unfold. Ellie took a deep breath and felt her heart sink.

'I will call again later to see how they are doing, but please let me know if there are any changes.'

'Please be careful. I nearly lost you once, and that cannot happen again,' Ashley sobbed as she disconnected the call.

'I love you,' Ellie whispered.

She gently handed the phone to Jackson before wiping away a tear.

'I thought you had disappeared.'

Jackson's voice was low and heavy as he swiftly reached into his pocket, pulled out a cigarette, and lit it with a flick of his wrist.

Ellie's thoughts drifted as her eyes locked onto the distant horizon, her expression void of emotion.

'I'm sorry I used your phone,' Ellie said.

Jackson pulled a crumpled cigarette from his pocket, put it between his lips, and lit it. He sucked in the smoke with a long draw and then lazily exhaled it into a murky gray cloud.

'How are your parents?' Jackson asked.

'They're in intensive care, but they are stable. Ashley wants answers, and I don't blame her for that. Why should they have to suffer because of me?'

Ellie's voice tightened with frustration as tears filled her eyes. She wanted to remain strong, yet she could feel the anger at the injustice slowly bubbling inside her. Jackson took another long drag, letting the smoke linger before exhaling it slowly.

'This world sucks sometimes, kid. Good people always seem to get the short end of the stick. But it isn't your fault.

You've done nothing wrong and need to stop blaming yourself.'

Jackson flicked his cigarette onto the ground and stomped down, extinguishing it before returning his gaze to Ellie.

'You look different,' Jackson chuckled. Ellie had traded his baggy t-shirt for denim trousers and a gray vest top. She had tightly secured her long, dark hair into a high ponytail that curved down her neck.

A crooked smile tugged at the corners of his lips as Ellie nervously laughed and ran a hand through her hair.

'Yeah, I thought I would wear something more my size. Sorry, no offense!'

'None was taken, kid. But you better not have thrown away my shirt - that was one of my favorites!'

Jackson's face lit up as he spoke, amused by the thought.

Turning away from him, Ellie stared at the fields again, and her face dropped.

'What did I do to that woman last night?'

Jackson didn't meet her gaze; instead, he looked off into the distance, his mouth opening and closing, searching for words.

'I was going to tell you.'

Jackson's voice broke as he reluctantly finished his sentence.

'Tell me what?'

Ellie stepped away from Jackson in anger, anticipating his response.

'When you were unconscious after the attack, I removed the inhibitor.'

Jackson's gaze fell to the ground as Ellie's eyes widened, and her mouth opened in shock.

'What the fuck, Jackson! You cut me open without me

knowing! You had no right!' Ellie screamed.

Jackson studied the ground, his broad shoulders slumped and eyes cast down. He shifted his weight from one foot to the other, refusing to meet Ellie's gaze. The air seemed to thicken with remorse as he shifted uncomfortably.

'I knew it was the only way. It would have been painful, and you felt nothing that way. I should have waited and given you a choice. I'm sorry.'

Ellie's hand gently swept across the back of her neck as she stepped closer to Jackson and looked into his eyes.

'I want to see it,' Ellie snapped.

Jackson lowered his gaze to the floor and offered a slight nod. He gestured for her to follow him, and they returned to the house. Jackson pulled open the kitchen drawer and carefully pulled out a folded cloth bundle. He laid it on the old wooden table and opened it to reveal a tiny pill-shaped device no bigger than a few millimeters.

Ellie stepped closer, her gaze sharpening as she examined the mysterious object.

'That thing has been suppressing my so-called powers?'

Ellie looked in awe as Jackson gave a firm nod.

'I helped design it with your father,' Jackson said.

Ellie pulled a chair from the table and sat down heavily, her thoughts racing with confusion and apprehension. She looked at the tiny object, feeling the question's weight in her chest.

'So what happened?' Ellie asked.

Jackson hesitated as if weighing his words carefully.

'The simplest term would be telekinesis. As a baby, you could move objects with your mind.'

Ellie felt a chill run down her spine, and her heart began pounding in her chest with the possibilities she never knew existed. Was she ready to embrace this new identity?

'Like magic?'

Ellie stared at him in confusion, hoping for reassurance as Jackson smiled slightly and nodded.

'In a way. Yes. In scientific terms, it's the ability to interact with or manipulate matter or another aspect of a physical system through non-physical means.'

'So, like magic?' Ellie whispered.

'Yes, like magic. We need to find out if you have any other abilities, and we need to learn to control them. What happened last night was driven by passion and rage. It's unstable and dangerous.'

Ellie looked up at Jackson nervously, her eyes wide with worry.

'I shouldn't have left if I'm dangerous. What if they were trying to keep me there to ensure people were safe?'

Jackson shook his head firmly.

'Trust me. They're not interested in protecting anyone but themselves. I have a loyal friend who still works at the company. He contacts me with any information that would compromise you. That's how I knew you were in danger that night. I just wish I had arrived faster. Ellie, there is another woman with powers who is far more dangerous than you could possibly imagine. She is contained right now, but if they ever let her out of there, I'm not sure how we would ever be able to stop her.'

Ellie's eyes widened as she listened to Jackson, absorbing all the information. Her mouth was slightly open in surprise, and her hands were clenched tightly in her lap as she struggled to process it all.

'Another woman? How did we get to be like this?' Ellie asked.

Jackson sighed and ran a hand through his long, wiry beard.

'There have been a lot of things done there that I'm not proud of. So many mistakes.'

'Am I one of those mistakes?' Ellie asked.

'Listen to me, Ellie Jones. You are not a mistake. You could be the most important person on the planet.'

Ellie's tired eyes scanned the device in Jackson's hands, confusion and fear written all over her face.

'How will I know how to control anything if I don't know what I can do exactly?'

Ellie bit her lip anxiously as Jackson sighed and ran a hand through his hair.

'This isn't an exact science. There has never been anybody like you, so we're making this up as we go along.'

Jackson tried to offer a comforting smile, but Ellie could still see the uncertainty in his eyes.

He held the inhibitor in the palm of his hand and smiled sadly, a hint of nostalgia shining in his gaze as Ellie looked over at him with tired confusion.

'My parents told me I was adopted when I was five but never gave me any other details. I didn't want to bother them and seem ungrateful, so I accepted it and assumed my parents didn't want me. I was going to ask them when I returned home but couldn't.'

Jackson looked at Ellie as he lit up another cigarette and exhaled slowly.

'I can honestly tell you that your parents never wanted to give you up. You were a gift to them, and they wanted what was best for you.'

Ellie's gaze lingered on Jackson as she studied him intently.

'What can you tell me about my parents? How well did

you know them?'

'I knew them very well. They both worked together in a science division of one of the biggest companies in America. Your father was one of the most innovative men I knew, and your mother was beautiful, determined, and brilliant. Her father was the head of the company, so naturally, she felt like she needed to prove herself.'

Jackson's voice softened as he spoke, as if he was allowing himself to think about the past for the first time in a long time.

'Do you know if they're still alive?'

Ellie's voice quivered with fear as Jackson sighed heavily, his shoulders slumped in despair.

'As far as I know, they both passed away. Not a day goes by that I don't wonder if I could have done more to help them.'

Ellie reached out and squeezed Jackson's hand in sympathy.

'I'm sorry for everything you have been through. I never thanked you for helping me back at the coffee shop. I don't know where I'd be if you hadn't shown up.'

'Don't mention it, kid,' Jackson said as he turned to switch on the kettle behind him. He turned back to Ellie and gestured to the mug on the table before her with a nod.

'Well, from what we can deduce, your brain can access parts that every other human on the planet can't. Now your inhibitor has been removed, you should be able to do it again.'

Jackson stepped back and motioned for her to try it.

Ellie took a deep breath and stared down at the mug on the table before her.

'What am I supposed to do?'

Ellie stared at Jackson, giving her an encouraging smile.

'Just start small. Move the cup,' Jackson said.

Ellie's hands were shaking as she clenched her fists on the table. Desperately trying to focus, she closed her eyes and took a deep breath. Jackson moved around the table and placed his hands on her shoulders, steadying her as his calming words echoed in her head.

'Empty your mind,' Jackson whispered. 'Focus entirely on the mug and feel the energy between you and it. Remove every other thought from your mind and concentrate.'

Ellie squeezed her eyes shut and clenched her fists in concentration as Jackson watched the mug intently, but there was no movement. After a moment, Ellie looked away in frustration while Jackson continued to focus, desperation apparent in his expression.

'Don't give up. Just imagine that it's only you and the mug, nothing else. Relax and feel the energy.'

Ignoring the doubts in her head, Ellie took a deep breath and repeated Jackson's words in her mind. She opened her eyes, intent on the pale blue mug in the middle of the table. She concentrated, silently willing it to move with all her mental strength. Suddenly, ever so slightly, it began to wobble. Ellie gasped and pushed back her chair, standing up.

'I did that!'

Ellie looked at Jackson's face and saw a triumphant smile spread across his face.

'Yes, you did,' Jackson said. 'We have a lot of work to do.'

'I felt it. I felt something in my body,' Ellie gasped.

Jackson walked towards the coat rack and started pulling on his long brown coat.

'You just took your first step in a much larger world,' Jackson said as Ellie looked on in confusion.

'Where are you going?' Ellie asked.

'We need something to eat. I'm just going to the store. Why don't you have a shower and we will eat when I get back? You must be starving.'

Ellie hadn't allowed herself to think about food all day, but as soon as Jackson mentioned a late dinner, her mouth began to water, and her stomach rumbled with anticipation.

'Please don't be long.'

'Just be careful and don't answer the door or go outside,' Jackson said. 'Make yourself at home.'

Jackson pulled on his heavy, scuffed brown work boots, took a deep breath, and opened the door. A frigid gust of wind swept past him and into the house. He slammed the door shut, and Ellie jumped at its loud bang. She shivered in the now silent room, feeling suddenly alone.

Ellie trudged up the creaking stairs of the old house. She opened her suitcase, which she had collected from her parents' house, and carefully laid the clothes on the thin blanket. Ellie trekked to the bathroom and turned on the bath taps. She wiped away the steam that had already formed on the mirror and looked at her reflection, her face illuminated by a single light bulb dangling from the ceiling.

Outside, Jackson's black pickup roared to life and pulled away down the driveway. The gravel crunched as headlights lit up from the darkness and crawled towards the house. Alastor stepped out of his car, its paint dull and its bumper rusting. He tugged on his worn gloves before looking up to see Ellie in the second-floor window, illuminated like a beacon beneath her warm lamplight. She pulled her vest top off, and her hair cascaded down her back in long waves. His breath caught as he watched her move gracefully across the room toward the bathroom. Determined, he marched up the path and climbed the stairs to the porch, his long blond hair tossed about by the night's chilly breeze.

12

<u>United Kingdom, December 2024</u>

Alastor trudged towards the farm, his boots struggling to gain purchase in the thick mud while the cold winter air had no visible effect on him. He paused outside the door and tilted his head to the side as he heard the faint sound of a radio coming from Ellie's bedroom. He bent down and picked up a rock from beside the entrance, studying it intently, then suddenly thrust it against his forehead with enough force that blood trickled down his face. His expression remained unchanged, and he made no sound. He approached the door and pounded on the sturdy oak with a loud rap. Ellie emerged from the steaming bath, skin red and wrinkled, and wrapped herself in a fluffy white towel. As she dried off, the radio played her favorite song in the background. Suddenly, a loud banging on the door jolted her back to reality. She turned off the radio and slipped into snug leggings and a clean, comfortable vest top. Heart pounding, she crept to the top of the stairs and peered down at the space below, wondering if her mind was playing tricks on her. Jackson's advice before he departed still echoed in her mind. She was about to return to her room when a voice called from outside.

'Is there anybody home? I need help. I have been in an accident on the road just outside your farm and need to borrow your phone,' Alastor said.

Ellie stood nervously at the top of the stairs, her heart pounding in her ears as the persistent knocking echoed throughout the house.

'Please, I know somebody is home. I don't mean any trouble. I'm hurt.'

Ellie nervously bit her nails and twisted her hair as she descended a few steps, her eyes drawn to the window at the bottom of the stairs. She peered outside as the man hobbled away, one hand cupped around his forehead as the wind blew his long, unkempt blonde hair around his face. Ellie's fingers trembled as she cracked open the door and peered through the narrow opening. Standing silhouetted in the waning light, Alastor slumped over, coughing and wheezing, muttering something inaudible.

'Hello!' Ellie said.

The man turned towards her and hobbled closer.

'Miss, please. May I use your phone? I need to call for my car to be picked up.'

Ellie's heart sank. She glanced back at the safety of the farmhouse, then returned her gaze to the man and shook her head in silent resignation. She stepped aside With heavy feet and opened the door wider to let him in, closing it behind him.

Gently brushing off his coat, he looked into Ellie's eyes with a silent expression of gratitude.

'Thank you,' Alastor said. 'So, would it be alright to use your phone?'

Ellie scanned the room for Jackson's cell phone and noticed

it lying on the side table, its screen glowing in the darkness.

'Please come in and make your call.'

Ellie motioned towards the armchair just inside the door as the man slowly shuffled over, wincing with every step, and collapsed into the chair with a soft sigh of relief.

'Let me get you some water and a cloth for your head,' Ellie said, passing him the phone.

Without hesitation, she marched across the room and into the kitchen while Alastor fished a small device from his pocket. He opened Jackson's phone and inserted it into the back panel, then held it to his ear without dialing a number.

'Hello, I have been in an accident and need my car picked up,' Alastor said. 'Just off Loganberry Road and outside an old farmhouse.'

Ellie walked back into the hallway and handed him a glass of water. He cupped his hands around the glass and took a few grateful sips.

'Thank you, Miss,' Alastor said. 'They're on their way.'

Ellie leaned close to examine the cut on his head, her long, wavy hair cascading around his face like a curtain. He inhaled deeply, taking in the sweet coconut scent of her shampoo, and closed his eyes in a blissful trance.

Unaware of his reaction, she gingerly dabbed the wound with a damp flannel, but he didn't flinch.

'Does it not hurt?' Ellie asked.

Alastor suddenly snapped back to reality and groaned in pain.

'Sorry,' Ellie said as she gently dried the wound with a clean cloth.

'What's your name, miss?' Alastor asked.

'Ellie.'

She offered Alastor her hand as she smiled warmly. He

hesitated but accepted her handshake, his eyes widening as he noticed the silver ring on her right hand sparkling brightly.

'My name is Scott,' Alastor said. 'Thank you for your kindness. I had better be going and wait by my car.'

Alastor stood and turned towards the door, offering a weak smile.

'You are welcome,' Ellie said.

She turned to take the bloody flannel and throw it away but suddenly stiffened as she felt his warm breath on the back of her neck. Before she could turn around, a sharp prick in her neck sent a neuromuscular blocking agent streaming through her veins. Her eyelids fluttered as he watched, her breathing slowing until suddenly, she began to collapse. He leaned forward and caught her in his arms, cradling her body against him as her eyes shut completely.

'That was almost too easy.'

Alastor carried her up the winding stairs and into her bedroom. He barged through the door, not slowing his pace as he brought her close to his chest. He thrust open the door with a swift kick and confidently strode into the room. In one smooth motion, he tossed her onto the bed like a ragdoll, her hair spilling across the blanket. Ellie's eyes were slightly open and surveying her surroundings, yet her body felt heavy, and no sound escaped her lips. Alastor grinned and strolled away to the bathroom, and she heard the tap turn on as he settled in to watch it fill. Each second felt like hours as she waited for his return, tears streaming down her cheeks until her eyes fell heavy in despair. The sound of the water stopped, and he walked back towards Ellie with heavy footsteps.

'Don't worry. I'll be here with you until the end.'

Alastor knelt beside the bed, his face level with Ellie's. He ran a hand gently through her wet hair and held her fingers in his own. He took a deep breath before slowly sliding the silver ring off her finger and tucking it into his pocket.

'Please,' Ellie whispered.

She felt her waning strength, and her eyes fluttered shut, but she forced them to remain open. The tears gathering in her eyes suddenly spilled down her cheeks as the sound of Jackson's warning echoed through her mind. Ellie followed Jackson's instructions and cleared her mind of any distractions. She felt the power within her grow stronger as she concentrated, her breathing slowing to a steady rhythm. Ellie opened her eyes and focused on the man before her. The air around her seemed to vibrate with his presence. A feeling of energy, almost like electricity, surged through her body. Rage ran through Ellie's veins as vivid memories of the past few days flooded her mind.

Alastor's fingers slowly trailed up Ellie's thigh and across her ribcage as he cautiously grabbed the hem of her shirt. Ellie closed her eyes tight, feeling the heat of rage rising in her chest. She took a sharp intake of breath before exhaling through gritted teeth.

Alastor lifted Ellie's shirt over her head, his eyes raking across her body hungrily. Then suddenly, a sharp shock of pain shot through him like an electric current. He gasped and curled up in agony, writhing as the fire-hot torment seared his skull, and he clamped his hands over his temples, screaming in pain.

'What the fuck are you doing, you bitch!' Alastor screamed. Tears of frustration and pain rose in Ellie's eyes as her anger swelled. She remembered coming home to her parents covered in blood and felt a fire of hatred burn inside her chest. She mustered all her strength with newfound determination and unleashed an ear-splitting scream. Alastor stumbled backward, covering his ears with his hands while screaming in pain. His face twisted in agony as he stumbled across the room, never having felt such intense pain. Alastor heard the rumbling of Jackson's truck approach outside, and his heart turned to lead. Without hesitation, he dashed to the stairs, taking them two at a time. When Jackson opened the front door with a jingle of keys, Alastor shoved him aside so hard that several bags careened from his grasp. Fear and bewilderment were written across Jackson's face as he fell back against the door frame. He ran up the stairs and paused in the bedroom's doorway, his breath catching in his throat as he saw Ellie lying on her bed, unable to move. When her eyes landed on Jackson, a stirring of hope twinkled in the depths of her soul. A faint glow illuminated her face as her lips curled up slightly.

'Stop him!' Ellie whispered.

Jackson scrambled down the stairs and leaped into his truck. The engine came to life with a roar as he sped up the dirt path leading to the main road. In frustration, Jackson slammed his hands against the steering wheel as he heard the hum of Alastor's engine in the distance. With unwavering conviction, Jackson jammed his foot on the pedal, determined to make up for the precious time that he had lost. Even though he was driving through a treacherous terrain marked by deep crags and sharp stones, he trusted in his skills behind the wheel. Every bump, every jolt, only served to fuel his fire. Alastor felt his heart pounding as he glanced into the rear-view mirror and saw Jackson's car right on his tail. The road ahead seemed alive with danger, with sharp turns almost impossible to navigate and fallen trees blocking their way. Jackson drove beside him, his eyes blazing with malice. With desperation coursing through his veins, Alastor extended his arm, pointing a gun at Jackson with a firm grip. With no thought of the consequences, Jackson crashed into the driver's side of Alastor's car, pushing it towards an enormous tree at an alarming speed. Alastor shut his eyes and gripped the steering wheel with white knuckles, feeling the tires slip on the slick pavement. His eyes widened in terror as he heard the thunderous sound of breaking glass and felt the impact of his car against the massive trunk of a redwood tree. Jackson slammed on the brakes and leaped from the truck, his feet pounding as he ran towards the wreckage. Alastor's car was a twisted pile of metal, the hood raised to reveal its destroyed engine. Thick black smoke rose from within, filling the air with an acrid smell. Alastor lay slumped over the wheel, his face bathed in crimson blood. Jackson ripped the door open and yanked him out by his shirt collar, sending him sprawling onto the hard pavement. Alastor was barely conscious, gasping for breath between bouts of laughter as clots of red liquid flew from his mouth.

'Who are you? Who sent you?' Jackson screamed.

With one last sputtering laughter, Alastor vanished into the darkness, slipping away while gargling on a pool of his blood.

'Fuck!'

Jackson's hands shook as he frantically searched Alastor's pockets, pulling out the items one by one: a jingling set of keys, several packs of gum, his cell phone, and seven rings in assorted sizes and shapes. He held them up to the light, examining each one with mounting anxiety. Jackson tucked the rings into his pocket before taking the phone with trembling hands and nervously fumbling at the buttons until he found the list of most recent calls. His heart raced as he saw the name displayed, prompting him to quickly press down on the last one. A stern and demanding voice answered the call almost instantaneously.

'Is it done?' Martin asked.

"Who is this?' Jackson demanded before the line disconnected abruptly. With a sigh, Jackson tucked the phone away and returned to his truck; home was calling him now more than ever.

Jackson slowly opened the door to the kitchen, and a heavy silence hung in the air. Ellie was seated at the table, her face illuminated by flickering candlelight, her eyes distant and unfocused. She had wrapped herself in a thick wool blanket, and he could see the exhaustion evident in her slumped shoulders. She raised her gaze to meet his, and he felt the force of her sorrow. Tears glistened on her long lashes, and the question in her eyes begged for an answer he couldn't give.

'What happened?'

'He's dead,' Jackson said as he pulled out a chair and sat opposite Ellie. 'Things are far more dangerous than I realized.'

Jackson's gaze softened as he took in Ellie's state.

'What did he do to you?'

Ellie shifted uncomfortably in her chair.

'He drugged me, and I couldn't move. I think he was going to kill me, Jackson! Ellie sobbed. 'He took the ring that Ashley gave me.'

Jackson's fingers trembled as he reached into his pocket and pulled out the rings he had retrieved from Alastor. He placed them carefully on the table, and Ellie gasped when she recognized her ring glinting in the light. She picked it up quickly, the weight of it heavy in her palm, and slid it back onto her finger.

'Thank you,' Ellie said.

Jackson's hand was warm as he slowly reached across the table to touch hers. She looked up, her eyes still wet with tears, and met his gaze. His gentle grip wrapped around her cold fingers, and for a moment, all was still.

13

Rebecca burst into the science division, her heels clicking like a ticking clock. She gritted her teeth and balled her hands into tight fists as she marched determinedly towards Doctor Robinson. The air around her seemed charged with electricity, and her eyes blazed with rage. The doctor's pulse quickened as she backed away from Rebecca's fierce presence.

'Scarlett requested to see me, did she?' Rebecca growled as she slowly walked across the room to the security monitor with a stern expression.

Her eyes had an intensity that permeated the air, and she leaned forward to take in the image on the screen. Scarlett stood tall in the center of the cold, pitch-black room, her gaze locked on the only entrance as if she anticipated an impending arrival. Doctor Robinson's heavy footsteps echoed through the room as she moved slowly to Rebecca's side.

'She has not moved all morning,' Doctor Robinson said.

Rebecca glanced at the empty plastic tray near the door.

'Did she eat this morning?' Rebecca asked.

'Yes, the first time in a week,' Doctor Robinson whispered.

Rebecca stood tall, inhaling deeply before exhaling a soft sigh of relief. Doctor Robinson's face softened as she glanced up at Rebecca and nodded toward the control panel.

'Shall I open the door for you?'

Rebecca inhaled a deep, shuddering breath. Her rigid spine straightened as her gaze focused on the metal door ahead. Doctor Robinson glanced at Rebecca, who gave a barely perceptible nod, and she pressed the button to unlock the door. A faint hissing sound accompanied its mechanical opening. A shiver ran through Rebecca's spine as she entered the room, passing the security guards. The fluorescent bulbs flickered, illuminating the somber chamber in a ghastly light. Scarlett stood in the middle of the glass cell, her figure as still as a statue - almost ethereal in the harsh lighting. Her pallid complexion seemed to glow like porcelain, and on her face rested a self-assured smirk directed right at her mother. Rebecca stepped hesitantly toward the cell as her gaze met her daughter's piercing stare through the thick glass wall. An awkward silence hung heavy in the air as Scarlett continued to study her mother, yet Rebecca could not muster any words.

'Hello, Mother, I am honored. Two days in a row!?' Scarlett chuckled.

A faint, bittersweet smile curved Rebecca's lips as her eyes flashed with intent.

'Hello Scarlett, how are you today?' Rebecca whispered. 'You asked to see me. I have to say I'm curious?'

Her hands trembled as Scarlett motioned for her to come closer. Rebecca inhaled deeply and braced herself before approaching her daughter. Scarlett glided around the perimeter of the prison cell, her fingertips lightly tracing the cold, transparent walls.

'I just asked you here for some girl talk,' Scarlett said.

Rebecca, already occupied with other thoughts, brushed the idea off with a disinterested sigh.

'I don't have time for games. I have a lot to do.'

Scarlett stopped and slowly pivoted towards Rebecca, her voice dripping with malice.

'Oh, do you mean my replacement?'

The color drained from Rebecca's face as shock kept her mouth agape, unable to comprehend what she was hearing.

'Who? What are you talking about?'

Scarlett's gaze was cold and unwavering as she looked down at Rebecca, her features betraying no emotion. The room seemed still as they locked eyes, a silent battle of wills between them.

'My sister,' Scarlett whispered.

Rebecca felt as if icy tendrils were wriggling through her veins. Her heart raced inside her chest like a hummingbird attempting to escape its cage. Scarlett's face twisted in rage as her piercing gaze bore into her mother. Rebecca shifted uncomfortably under the scrutiny, unable to meet her daughter's eyes.

'Why didn't you ever tell me I had a sister?' Scarlett asked, her words dripping with venom. 'What could have made her want to leave our perfect family?'

Rebecca blinked back a tear before straightening her posture.

'Who has been telling you these lies?' Rebecca uttered in a strained voice.

Scarlett slammed her fists against the glass wall, feeling her bones vibrate.

'Would you stop with all the bullshit, lies, and deceit already?' Scarlett screamed.

'You've been fed lies, and I will not be a part of it,' Rebecca spat as she spun away from Scarlett, stalking towards the door with her head held high.

She was about to take a step forward, but Martin stepped sharply in front of her before she could move, his arm stretched out and blocking her path. His eyes were wide and intense, almost as if daring her to try and pass him.

'Martin! What the fuck is going on?' Rebecca demanded incredulously, taking an involuntary step back as he slowly advanced into the room. Martin's strides were solid and purposeful; his gaze held a powerful force, even from across the room. Rebecca could feel herself flush as she met his smoldering eyes.

'Rebecca, or should I say Mrs. Ellis? The lies you have been telling this young woman end here and now. I know what has happened in this department, and it ends today.'

Rebecca stepped closer to him, her cheeks flushing crimson and her eyes blazing with intensity.

'You don't have any authority here!' Rebecca shouted, her fists shaking at her sides. 'You don't know what you're talking about!'

Desperate to escape the looming danger, she made a mad dash for the door. However, it seemed as if Fate had other plans as it slammed shut with an echoing thud before she could reach it. Her chest tightened at the sound, and her whole body quivered in fear at her current predicament. Her eyes then wandered up to the security camera perched in the corner of the room. Taking a deep breath, she balled her fists together and began endlessly pounding the cold metal door.

'Let me out!' Rebecca yelled through clenched teeth, her

desperation growing with each passing second, to no avail.

Martin stepped forward, and his face contorted into smug satisfaction.

'You thought you could get away with anything just because of your last name, right?' Martin said. 'Your dad was a genius that built this company from nothing. He would be so ashamed of you right now.'

His tone turned even more acidic and venomous as he continued.

'The board has decided, and unfortunately, you're no longer the CEO of this company.'

'This is an outrage!' Rebecca spat.

Suddenly, the sound of the door to the cell clicked open, and Rebecca froze in fear, her heart pounding in her chest and her palms sweating. She could feel a cold chill run down her spine as Scarlett slowly walked out of her cell, her bare feet silent on the cold, concrete floor as she stalked behind Rebecca. Scarlett's voice trembled as she spoke, her hands clenched into tight fists.

'What's the matter, Mother?' Scarlett screamed, her eyes flashing. 'You don't think I'm capable of hurting you, do you? Martin revealed your twisted lie, how you've kept me confined like a caged animal since my birth and denied me the same fucking freedom as my sister. Now you plan to bring her here and dispose of me just like everyone else who doesn't meet your standards?'

Rebecca's eyes swam with tears, and she looked pleadingly into Scarlet's emerald gaze.

'No, I just wanted us to be together,' Rebecca pleaded, wiping her cheeks with the back of her hand. 'I thought she could help you, understand you.'

Scarlett shook her head and ran her thumb tenderly down

Rebecca's cheek, wiping away the tears.

'Work with me? That's funny. You said it yourself. I don't work well with others,' Scarlett said.

'What would you have me do, Scarlett?' Rebecca murmured.

Scarlett grinned as she circled Rebecca, her movements predatory and menacing. Her emerald eyes glinted with sinister pleasure.

'I don't want you to do anything. Martin here has cut my strings, and now I am nobody's puppet.'

As if by an unseen force, Rebecca could feel her body go rigid and her gaze locked with Scarlett's. Moving closer, Scarlett reached up to the silver collar around her neck that had suppressed her powers. With a click, the collar fell free and into Scarlett's palm. Rebecca trembled as Scarlett triumphantly held it in plain sight, relinquishing the last vestige of control. Rebecca's eyes followed Scarlett's every move. The collar fell at Rebecca's feet with a loud crash that echoed in the room.

'Please, Scarlett, let me go?' Rebecca begged.

Scarlett sneered, her lips curling with delight.

'Oh, I plan on letting you go,' Scarlett whispered, 'And then I'm going to meet my long-lost sister and take everything from her before I finally end her life.'

Scarlett's glacial stare bore deep into Rebecca, the heat of her gaze igniting a fire in Rebecca's soul.

'Please don't!' Rebecca pleaded.

'I think you forgot something,' Scarlett whispered as she leaned into Rebecca's ear.

Rebecca shuddered as the heat of Scarlett's breath seared her flesh. She was paralyzed with fear as Scarlett continued in a chilling tone.

'You just forgot how to breathe.'

Struggling for air, Rebecca felt herself gasping for oxygen, panic overwhelming her senses until Martin stepped up behind Scarlett and firmly gripped her shoulder.

'That's enough, Scarlett. If I may, perhaps death is not the right punishment for her,' Martin said.

Scarlett slowly turned, her emerald eyes burning with unrelenting rage. Martin hesitated, uncertain how to proceed. He knew that no words could ease the pain that gnawed away at Scarlett's soul.

'What do you propose?' Scarlett asked, her voice thick with bitter loathing.

Martin looked at her steadily.

'Make her feel as much anguish and despair as you have felt. Take away what she holds most dear. Make her witness all that is yet to come.'

Scarlett's gaze sharpened into a cutting glare.

'Make her suffer?'

Without hesitation, Martin nodded.

'Yes. While Rebecca has enjoyed a privileged life, you have been in a cage like an animal. Take away her possessions and status, strip her naked, and let people see the real her with no facade or mask to hide behind,' Martin said as he looked into her eyes and continued, his voice unwavering and robust. 'Place her in the same cage you have spent your life in; let her know what it's like to be powerless and without choice.'

Suddenly, Rebecca collapsed onto the ground, her breath coming in shallow rasps. Scarlett stared down at her mother before turning to Martin, her expression one of resignation.

'Maybe you're right. She has to be held accountable.'

'Open the door,' Martin commanded.

The large door slowly opened with a heavy creak, and a

commanding figure emerged. She had the stature of an Amazonian warrior, with long blond hair pulled tightly into a ponytail, revealing her striking face adorned with a tattoo of three stars under her right eye, a sign of her rank as captain of the security division. Her black and grey armor clung to her powerful physique, while two other officers clad in similar uniforms flanked her menacingly on either side.

'Scarlett, I will deal with your mother. I have arranged the private jet for your travels, and some clothes for your comfort are in the laboratory,' Martin said.

'Thank you,' Scarlett said in a low voice, her eyes lingering on Rebecca's still body on the cold floor. 'I'll see you when I return.'

Turning away, Scarlett released a deep breath as she passed Doctor Anderson. The doctor shrank back from her, averting her gaze, a look of terror on her face. Scarlett approached the desk and ran her fingertips along the smooth surface. On top of the pile laid a tastefully arranged outfit: a red leather jacket with zip accents, snug red leather trousers, and dark boots. She caressed the fabric appreciatively, admiring its quality.

Martin stepped back and lunged forward with a wide grin on his face.

'Get her on her feet!'

Rebecca felt the men's firm grip on her arms as they pulled her to her feet.

'I knew this day would come,' Martin chuckled. 'I wish I could stay and enjoy the show, but I have a company to save. She's all yours, Jade,' Martin said as he walked away.

'Right, we have our orders. You can do this the easy way or the hard way,' Jade said coldly while her eyes scanned Rebecca's body.

'Take off your clothes, Mrs. Ellis.'

Rebecca felt her heart sink at the request and abruptly stepped back, shaking her head in disbelief.

'You can't be serious!' Rebecca said defiantly, her voice quivering as tears streamed down her cheeks.

'Either take your clothes off, or I will take them off for you,' Jade spat.

Rebecca trembled as she freed her arms from the guard's grips and stood motionless before Jade.

'You have worked for my father and me for over fifteen years; you don't have to do this,' Rebecca pleaded.

'Last chance,' Jade said.

Rebecca's chest heaved with sobs as she struggled to unfasten the tiny buttons of her light blue shirt. Her fingers trembled, and tears blurred her vision, but with one last tug, the fabric slipped from her shoulders and pooled at her feet.

'Don't take all day,' Jade said.

Rebecca's hands shook as she reached behind her back and pulled down on the tiny zipper of her black skirt, feeling it release and loosen around her waist before slipping down her legs. Her hands quickly fumbled to remove her heels, dropping them to the floor. She could feel the room's cold air biting through her skin as she shut her eyes tightly. She dragged down her tights with trembling fingers and stood shivering under the captain's gaze. Her toes curled against the cold floor as a chill ran up her bare calves. She closed her eyes, attempting to calm herself but only intensifying her racing heart. Her fingers trembled as they fumbled with the clasp of her white bra, and in a single swift move, she yanked it off, sending chills over her skin that made the hairs stand on end. With arms shaking, she released her underwear and kicked it away. She had never felt so exposed; covering herself with one arm over her breasts and the other hand shielding her modesty, she wished desperately for anything to hide behind. Jade grabbed a white jumpsuit from the table and threw it on the floor next to Rebecca's feet, similar to the one Scarlett was wearing.

'put this on.'

Rebecca crouched to grab the jumpsuit and hastily put it on, tugging it up her legs and over her figure, trying to conceal herself as quickly as possible.

'Now get in the cell.'

Jade's eyes bored into Rebecca's with a menacing intensity, and without warning, she felt a vice-like grip on her arm as she dragged her across the room. She was thrown violently into the cold cell and crashed hard onto the concrete floor, feeling every scrape and bruise from the impact as she lay there in shock. The glass door shut loudly as the guards picked up her discarded clothes and left the room. Jade stood at the glass, her expression stern.

'For what it's worth, I'm sorry. I'm just following orders.'

Jade spun on her heel and marched out of the room as the door shut behind her. Rebecca was left alone, paralyzed with terror as darkness engulfed her like a hungry predator. Her scream pierced the silence like a knife through flesh, echoing off the walls in a cacophonous symphony of horror.

14

Ellie dragged her feet across the kitchen floor, exhausted from another sleepless night. She lowered herself into a creaky wooden chair at the kitchen table, her attention immediately drawn to Jackson's phone. A heavy silence descended on the room, only broken by an occasional creak from the wobbly chair and Ellie's quickening heartbeat. As she nervously chewed her thumbnail, her gaze flickered between the time and Ashley's number before pressing the call button.

'Hi Ash, I'm sorry I didn't call last night,' Ellie said. 'Is everything alright? How are Mum and Dad doing?'

The line went silent for a few moments until, finally, Ashley spoke. Her voice was heavy with fear and worry.

'They are doing better. Mum woke up last night, and they are running more tests on Dad. It's been a long day, and we still don't have all the answers, but they seem confident. That's all I know right now. What's going on, Ellie?'

'It's something about my biological parents. I'm unsure whether Mum and Dad knew anything about who they were,' Ellie paused and exhaled a sigh of despair. 'How are you and Shreya coping?'

'We're going back to our parent's house tonight,' Ashley replied, determined despite her exhaustion. 'I want it to be perfect for when they come home.'

'I really don't think that is the best idea,' Ellie said, her voice shaking with worry. She could hear Jackson's heavy footsteps as he made his way from the upper level of the house to the stairs.

'The cops are still outside monitoring the house,' Ashley replied softly. 'Everything will be alright.'

'Please be careful, Ash. I love you so much. I will visit Mum and Dad as soon as possible.'

'Okay,' Ashley replied, her voice tense with worry. Ellie could almost picture her shuffling nervously back and forth while they talked. 'I love you too.'

The line crackled before disconnecting, leaving an ominous silence in its wake. Ellie took a deep breath to steady her nerves, placed the phone back on the table, and sat motionless, her sorrow radiating from her slumped frame. She tucked her head between her arms as her shallow breaths matched the encircling metronome of the clock's ticking. Jackson stepped into the room, and a wave of smoky air followed. His cigarette hung from one corner of his lips, smoke winding around his face as he walked. Glistening droplets of water clung to his combed black hair as he sat down, his large frame sinking into the chair's cushion. The wooden legs squeaked as he pulled them towards the table, and the scent of his aftershave hung heavily in the air. He glanced at Ellie and smiled warmly before taking a seat.

'Good morning,' Jackson said as Ellie groaned in response. She slowly lifted her head from the pillow, revealing a wild mane of hair strewn wildly around her shoulders and face, cascading down over her neck.

'How are you doing, kid?'

Her temples pulsed with a dull ache, and her fingers trembled as she massaged the sides of her head. Fatigue blanketed her shoulders, making it difficult to focus. Her throat tightened around her words as she spoke.

'My head feels like it's going to burst open from being drugged and attacked - again! I swear I'm going insane.'

Ellie took a deep breath, closing her eyes and resting her forehead in her hands.

'I just spoke to Ashley, and Mum's awake. The doctors are confident they will both make a full recovery.'

Jackson pushed his long hair away from his face, exposing eyes filled with worry. He attempted a gentle smile, his voice barely above a whisper.

'That's good news.'

Jackson's knuckles were white with tension as he clutched the arm of the chair, feeling a determination settle upon him.

'We have to be ready for what's coming. That man last night won't be the last, and we need to prepare ourselves,' Jackson said, his voice filled with conviction.

He pushed himself up from his seat and went to the window, running a hand across the sill as he stared at the golden sunrise illuminating the barn in the distance. When he turned back around, Ellie stood there watching him with an expression full of questions.

'You ready?' Jackson asked with a twinkle in his eye and the hint of a smile curling his lips.

'Ready for what?' Ellie replied, her eyebrows raised in curiosity.

'We must figure out how to teach you to control your

powers,' Jackson said.

Ellie gracefully stood from her seat, her graceful curves highlighted by the slender grey leggings that clung to her figure. Her black crop top displayed a sliver of her toned midriff, ending just above her waistline.

'Well, you look ready for a tough workout,' Jackson said as he opened the door, and a gust of icy wind blew inside. The warmth that had just filled the house, with its cozy scent of burning wood from the fireplace, was replaced with a chill that settled in Jackson's bones. Silence descended upon the fields, and soft white snow blanketed the landscape. Ellie felt a chill travel up her spine as they drew closer to the barn, making her shoulders tense and her breaths quiver into tiny puffs of mist. Goosebumps ran up her arms, and she hugged herself tightly, trying to stop the tremors that had started convulsing her body. Jackson reached out his hand, wrapping his fingers around the weathered handle of the barn door. He yanked hard and felt it give away with a deafening groan. The breeze that blew out was warm and humid, carrying the scent of hay and animals. As Ellie stepped inside, she could feel the warmth of the barn on her skin. Awe seemed to pour over her as she looked around the enormous room. The high, vaulted ceiling was reminiscent of a grand cathedral, with arched beams of wood and metal that soared above her in splendor. Dilapidated trailers lined the walls, packed with straw and warped wooden pallets in a disorderly fashion. Splendid light from the second-floor windows danced down to the Dusty grounds below, painting strips of shadows across the floor. Ellie shielded her gaze from the sun, its brilliance blazing and glimmering off the hulking green John Deere tractor.

'She's something, isn't she?' Jackson asked as he let out a delighted whistle.

'It's - large,' Ellie responded playfully, though her brow furrowed in confusion. She glanced up at Jackson with curiosity glittering in her eyes. 'So, what are we doing here?'

Jackson strode confidently towards the tractor, then crouched down to pick up an old oil can from the ground.

A mischievous glint sparkled in his eyes as he gestured to the tractor.

'We're going to see what you can do, Ellie. I want you to move that.'

Ellie's gaze shifted toward the large tractor, and her eyes widened in shock. She let out a low whistle as she pondered his request.

'Are you fucking kidding me!' Ellie said. 'There is no way I can move that!'

A booming laughter left Jackson's lips.

'There is no difference between that coffee mug and this tractor,' Jackson said calmly. 'You just need to think outside the box. Your mind is much stronger than the power of muscle strength. You can do this if you focus.'

With a clear sign of her frustration, Ellie rolled her eyes and crossed her arms. She clenched her eyes shut tightly, gritting her teeth as she concentrated all her energy on the tractor. She outstretched her arm before her, imagining an invisible force between their energies. Her veins pulsed with power as sweat began to slick across her forehead. She stood there in utter stillness, feeling a slight breeze over her skin as if almost willing the tractor to cooperate with her. Jackson stepped closer and placed a gentle hand on her shoulder.

'Come on, Ellie,' Jackson murmured, 'you can do this.'

'I'm trying!' Ellie shouted through gritted teeth.

Every muscle in her body was tense, like coiled springs ready to snap at any moment. Ellie whirled around in a swift motion to confront Jackson.

'No, it's impossible,' Ellie muttered as she shook her head.

Jackson stepped forward, his hands slicing through the air with frustration.

'You didn't even try! You gave up before you started!' Jackson shouted.

The fire within Ellie's eyes ignited as she turned toward him, her eyebrows knitting together in fury. The surrounding atmosphere seemed to sizzle with tension as she glared at him with growing animosity. Ellie closed her fists so tightly that her knuckles whitened as she looked up at Jackson with fierce defiance in her eyes.

'What do you want from me? Don't you know? I'm a complete fuck-up,' Ellie screamed, her voice full of spite as she turned her back on him. 'My entire life has been one big mistake, so why should it come as a surprise that I disappoint you too?'

Jackson roared and lunged towards the end table, snatching an empty can. With impressive speed, he hurled the can towards Ellie, and it connected with the back of her head with an ear-splitting thud, causing her to clutch her scalp in shock and spin around to look at him, her eyes wide with bewilderment.

'What the actual fuck, Jackson!' Ellie shouted in disbelief.

'If you don't want to get hit, don't,' Jackson replied as he threw another can her way, which she batted away with her arm. 'Not with your body, with your mind,' Jackson screamed before throwing a third can.

Ellie roared in frustration, her voice echoing off the barn walls.

'Would you fucking quit it,' Ellie shouted at the top of her lungs.

'No, because I'm not a quitter like you!'

Ellie's sparkling blue eyes had turned to glinting steel. A cold chill ran down her spine as she stared Jackson down with an icy determination. Before Jackson could utter another word, he suddenly grasped his head in agony, collapsing to the floor. Ellie was awash with a wave of electric energy as her senses heightened. Before she could comprehend what was happening, the massive tractor was hovering ten feet in the air and suddenly flew through the side of the old barn. The impact of metal against wood reverberated throughout the barn as debris flew everywhere like a firework display. Ellie's heart plummeted as a surge of fear coursed through her veins. Jackson lay motionless on the ground, surrounded by splintered wooden planks and shingles from the roof. Without a second thought, Ellie sprinted over to him and knelt beside him, her hands flying to her mouth in shock and panic.

'Jackson! Oh my god! Are you alright!? What have I done?'

Jackson shifted his weight, sending a few bits of hay flying as he sat up. He looked over at the broken wood planks that had once made the wall of his barn, and a gust of cold air whistled through the jagged, gaping hole.

'I'm sorry I pushed you so hard, kid. You never do anything by halves, do you?' Jackson said, a hint of admiration in his voice.

'Are you alright? I don't know what happened.'

Jackson rubbed the back of his neck, wincing.

'I'll be fine; you pack quite a punch,' Jackson whispered.

'That's what happened with that stranger last night,' Ellie murmured.

Her fists clenched tightly, and her stare was transfixed into the distance as if she were reliving it all again.

'I felt angry, and suddenly he started screaming in pain.'

Jackson's piercing gaze seemed to see right into her soul, causing Ellie to feel exposed and vulnerable beneath his stare.

'You're an empath,' Jackson said.

Ellie's eyes widened in disbelief as she shook her head frantically, trying to make sense of the incomprehensible words that had just escaped Jackson's lips.

'A what?' she whispered as confusion clouded her mind. 'I thought you said it was telekinesis.'

Jackson's hand trembled as he slowly extended it to Ellie. She took it warmly and leaned into him, lending her strength to keep him from collapsing back to the dirt floor. With her help, he was able to take a few tentative steps before coming to a stop.

'Well, there's more than meets the eye with you, isn't there?'

Ellie's eyes widened, then darkened again with frustration.

'What the hell is an empath?' Ellie asked, her voice heavy with emotion.

Jackson pushed a hand through his hair and took a deep breath.

'Well, empathy is an emotional state of being that allows one person to connect emotionally and cognitively with another person.'

The gears in Ellie's mind turned at lightning speed as she tried to process what Jackson had said.

'In English, please?' Ellie asked meekly, her voice far softer than before.

'Basically, it means that when you experience emotions such as anger, pain, hate, or love, you can transfer those feelings to another person.'

Ellie lowered herself to the floor slowly, drawing her knees into her chest and wrapping her arms protectively around them.

'So my amazing power is that I can hurt people and throw things around,' Ellie asked sarcastically, her lips curling into a sneer.

'That's putting it very simplistically, but yes, that's the basics,' Jackson replied, his voice low and steady as he nodded slightly.

'You said there is another woman; can she do the same things?' Ellie asked, her voice quivering with fear.

Jackson's face was a pale mask of terror; his hands tightened into fists as his blood turned to ice.

'Well, I have been told that she, too, had developed telekineses. But she also has grown powerful with psychokinesis,' Jackson swallowed hard and continued in a calm voice. 'It's similar to what you just demonstrated but where you can influence the mind and make people feel things. She can fully take over people's minds and make them do as she wishes. Very dangerous indeed, if used irresponsibly.'

The room felt suddenly still as the gravity of the situation sunk in.

Ellie climbed to her feet, brushing the dust off her leggings.

'Let's get out of here. I saw your cigarettes on the side in the kitchen,' Ellie said as she inclined her head towards the house, then walked over to the gaping hole in the barn wall.

'I'm so sorry about your tractor,' Ellie whispered.

Jackson nodded, his face heavy with disappointment.

'Me too,' Jackson said with a sigh. 'I loved that thing.'

Jackson padded across the wooden floor, scooping his cigarettes off the kitchen counter as Ellie filled the kettle with water from a nearby tap and set it on the blue-flame burner of the stove. She looked out the window, the sun casting its amber hues behind the old barn as wispy clouds slowly crossed the horizon. Then, just as Jackson was about to open his cigarette packet, his phone's shrill ring caused him to jump. He quickly answered, and his body nearly froze when he heard Andrew Duncan's voice roll through the receiver.

'Jackson?' Andrew asked, his voice sounding strained on the other end of the phone.

Jackson felt a tightness in his stomach as he had a feeling he knew why Andrew was calling. His voice was heavy with concern as he looked over at Ellie.

'What is it?'

Andrew hesitated, and Jackson's gut twisted even further.

'I'm sorry to call; I have some terrible news,' Andrew whispered.

Jackson could feel his pulse quicken, and dread filled his chest as he waited for Andrew to continue. He could feel the seconds tick by as Andrew struggled to find the words.

'Martin and the board of directors have taken over the company,' Andrew said.

Jackson stared wide-eyed in bewilderment, attempting to rationalize the situation.

'Rebecca?' Jackson asked.

'She's alive,' Andrew said, his voice strained with emotion. 'But there's more. Scarlett is free and on her way to London as we speak. She has imprisoned Rebecca. Martin is pulling the strings now, Jackson.'

'Fuck!' Jackson muttered under his breath. 'We have work to do.'

'I've contacted Doctor Clark. He's made an inhibitor collar - if it comes to it, we can use it to stop Scarlett from hurting anyone,' Andrew said.

'Where is Doctor Clark?' Jackson asked, realizing they needed to act fast if they had any hope of saving Ellie.

'Wales.'

'Fucking Wales!' Jackson shouted, frustration coursing through him now that he had a plan but no way to execute it in time without hours of travel involved.

'I have to go, Jackson,' Andrew said, disconnecting the call.

'Who was that?' Ellie whispered from behind him, alerting Jackson to her presence in the room and reminding him that he wasn't alone in this fight.

Jackson's body shuddered as the meaning of the words sunk in. His mind raced, desperately trying to deny what he had just heard. But he remained rooted in place, unable to escape the harsh reality. Jackson slowly shifted his gaze towards Ellie, and they locked eyes in a moment of shared distress. He held her stare, trying hard to keep his emotions contained.

'An old friend. What I feared most has happened: the young woman I told you about is coming here. We have to go on a trip.'

'Where?' Ellie asked, her voice trembling.

Jackson paused, dreading the answer that seemed inevitable.

'Wales,' Jackson said.

United States of America, December 2024

Andrew Duncan sat rigidly in his chair at the immense Portland facility, his fingers blazing across the keyboard with relentless energy. With every passing second, the pile of documents on his desk seemed to grow more intimidating as he raced against the ticking clock. He was jarred out of his concentration by a sudden loud bang as the door to his office crashed open, sending a jolt through his body and causing his desk papers to flutter. A security guard entered first, followed closely by Martin and a tall woman with a stern expression. It was Jade, head of security for the facility. As Martin marched towards Andrew, his imposing form cast a long shadow across the office floor. His shoes were heavy and beat a loud rhythm that echoed through the room. Approaching Andrew, Martin's steely grip closed around his shoulders like a vice, sending shockwaves of pain through him with every squeeze.

'Andrew,' Martin spat, his blue eyes full of malice. 'Do you consider me a fool?'

Martin stepped forward and loomed over Andrew, the tension rising every second. His body posture and demeanor exuded menacing energy that seemed more potent than any physical harm could ever bring. Andrew trembled and nervously pushed his glasses up onto the bridge of his nose, squinting to try and steady his gaze. His heart pounded in his chest as beads of sweat formed on his forehead, yet he still managed to keep his voice level and firm.

'No,' Andrew declared firmly.

Despite the danger of the situation, Andrew refused to back down. Martin strolled around the office and gracefully settled himself on the edge of Andrew's desk. Jade, who towered above them both, glared as Martin smirked in Andrew's direction, like a predator toying with its prey.

'So, how's your old pal Jackson Carter doing?' Martin drawled with an air of nonchalance.

Andrew trembled as fear surged through his veins. His heart raced as Martin's gaze darkened, bearing down on him with contempt. Sweat drenched Andrew's clothing, and he fought against the urge to flee - still, he remained composed.

'I don't know what you mean?' Andrew said in a voice that sounded weak even to himself.

Martin rose to his feet, his face twisted in pure rage.

'So, you do believe I'm a fool,' Martin said as he approached Andrew, his hands balled into fists at his sides.

Jade reacted swiftly, her fingers like steel as they clamped around Andrew's arm and yanked him up. His body trembled in terror, not expecting the vice-like grip of her hand. She pulled him closer until he could feel her breath on his neck.

'No! Don't do this! Jackson isn't the enemy!'

Martin glared at Andrew with blazing intensity as the atmosphere thickened into an oppressive silence.

'You have made a big mistake, Mr. Duncan.'

'I won't tell you anything,' Andrew said.

'You don't need to,' Martin said with a smile.

Jade marched Andrew towards the door, her grip on his arm digging into his skin as she dragged him away. Martin scanned the room intensely, his gaze lingering on every detail. He carefully sat behind Andrew's desk, letting out a satisfied breath as he felt the expensive leather chair envelop him. His fingers flew across the phone's keypad as he dialed a number and spoke into the receiver.

'This is Martin. I need the computer forensic team ready to go now!' Martin's voice was firm and commanding, feet propped casually on Andrew's desk.

15

Scarlett's hands firmly clenched her seat armrests as the plane descended, its powerful engines rumbling in the backdrop. The aircraft gradually diminished speed, gracefully gliding towards the ground like a majestic bird ready to land. Scarlett pressed her nose against the cold glass, gazing at the endless sea of clouds stretching beyond the tiny oval window. She watched curiously as the aircraft curved around the large runway below her. Her veins pulsed with anticipation at the thought of her mission ahead. The sleek jet descended from the heavens. Its roaring engines shook the earth, leaving a cloud of dust in its wake. The airplane glided onto the runway effortlessly and soon came to a screeching halt, leaving behind a billowing cloud of smoke. A tall figure stood next to an imposing black limousine, a man clad in a sharp suit who seemed to have been expecting their arrival. The hinges of the plane creaked in protest as the door opened. Two men, dressed impeccably in tailored suits and crisp hats, stepped out into the open air. Scarlett followed them, a compelling vision of beauty, filling the atmosphere with a magnetic sense of power. Her black and red leather jacket curled around her body like a protective shield - tailored to fit her curves perfectly. Scarlett made her way toward the vehicle, her heart thudding in anticipation. The driver stepped forward and opened the car's rear door. His lips curved into a polite yet professional smile as he took Scarlett's suitcase, handling it gently as he placed it inside the trunk.

'Here you go, Miss Ellis,' the man said in a posh British accent. 'I hope your flight was satisfactory.'

'My name is not Miss Ellis. That's my mother's name,' Scarlett spat.

Scarlett drew in a sharp breath as she opened the door to the car. The moment she stepped in, an intoxicating aroma of luxury and opulence filled her senses. Every detail was flawless, from the gleaming silver champagne bucket next to the flat-screen TV to the pristine white leather seats that beckoned her forward. Scarlett couldn't help but stare in awe as her gaze stumbled upon a mesmerizing woman sitting across from her.

She pulled her thick, fiery red hair back into a tight ponytail and propped her glasses on top of her head. The pristine white shirt tucked into her sleek black pencil skirt accentuated her toned thighs. Majestic heeled shoes elongated her slender legs, completing the look. Scarlett felt a chill run through her when she slowly tilted her head. The woman's bright blue eyes were like two shining gems that seemed to have a strange power over her. Scarlett felt like time had stopped, and she was captivated by the woman's gaze.

'Who are you?' Scarlett asked.

'Sabrina Scott,' the woman replied in a posh British accent, accompanied by a warm smile. 'Martin requested me to escort you and assist with your needs.'

With a scoff, Scarlett reached for the phone Martin had given her, rapidly pressing the speed dial button before holding it up to her ear.

'Scarlett, it's good to hear from you,' Martin said as his voice on the other end was steady yet stern.

'Why the fuck do I have a chaperone?' Scarlett asked.

'Sabrina is just there to help you navigate the city and get you anything you might need,' Martin said. 'You are on your way to one of the most luxurious hotels in London. Ellie Jones will still be there tomorrow, so go out and enjoy yourself for the first time in your life. You're only a teenager for a few more months.'

Scarlett looked out of the tinted window, feeling awe and excitement as she saw the bright city lights for the first time. Everything seemed so big, so alive, and for a fleeting moment, she forgot why she was here. She cleared her throat, bringing herself back to reality.

'Have you found out any new information?' Scarlett asked.

'We found out who had been leaking information,' Martin replied.

'He was talking to my father, wasn't he?'

'Yes. What would you like me to do with him?'

Scarlett contemplated her options before responding in an even tone.

'I will handle him when I return. Please keep me updated.'

Martin heaved a heavy sigh before his voice fell away into nothingness. The line went dead, leaving Scarlett in the presence of Sabrina. The stillness was almost suffocating until Sabrina broke it with a wicked grin, and her eyes slowly moved across Scarlett's body. The car rolled forward with the sound of a whisper, its progress followed closely by the growing light of London. The city beckoned them closer, and its luminescence steadily spilled onto their faces as they advanced into the city's embrace. Sabrina's lips curved into a smile as she reached up, her fingertips lightly brushing against her glasses before settling them onto the bridge of her nose.

'I am looking forward to working with you. I have heard all about you.'

Scarlett's face hardened, and she crossed her arms over her chest. Her voice was cold and firm.

'If you had, you wouldn't look forward to being anywhere near me.'

Sabrina slyly shuffled over to the seat beside Scarlett. Her arm brushed against Scarlett's with a feather-light touch, causing her to recoil with surprise. Sabrina laughed softly, her eyes glinting with amusement as she moved into Scarlett's personal space.

'Do you mind me sitting here?' Sabrina said as she handed Scarlett an envelope. 'This is everything you will need, money and identification.'

Scarlett reached out and took the envelope from Sabrina's hands, relishing in her perfume's light yet powerful scent. A complex mixture of berries, jasmine, and musk teased her senses, awakening them with each sweet breath. She shivered almost imperceptibly at the sight of the outside world as she nervously glanced at the busy streets.

The car came to a gentle halt as Sabrina peered out the window, her blue eyes wide in anticipation.

'We're here,' Sabrina murmured, barely able to contain her excitement.

The smartly suited driver stepped out of the car and opened the passenger door, offering his hand to Sabrina, who gracefully emerged. She shot him a quick smile before glancing down to ensure her skirt was straight, adjusting it ever so slightly with her slender fingers, her high heels clicking against the pavement as she stepped onto the sidewalk. He returned his hand to Scarlett, who accepted it without hesitation, her gaze never wavering from the grand building before them. Scarlett pulled her jacket closer to her body as a shiver wracked her frame, and she took a deep breath of the crisp night air. She watched Sabrina climb the steep stone steps, her movements graceful and unhurried. They arrived at the reception desk, where Sabrina quietly spoke to the attendant before receiving a single key card. She gestured for Scarlett to follow her, but the young woman was rooted to the spot, her gaze fixed upon the hotel's grand entrance. Paintings hung from the marble wall, and diamond chandeliers sparkled like stars in the night sky. Sabrina glanced over her shoulder and smiled.

'Scarlett, are you coming?'

Scarlett felt excited as she and Sabrina stepped into the regal glass elevator, slowly ascending to the twenty-third floor. The vast cityscape at their feet melted away until all that was left was the grandeur of the skyline in the distance. Scarlett felt like she was on a magic carpet ride as they strode down the marble-clad hallway, their footsteps ringing through the air with each step until they reached their destination. Her emerald eyes sparkled with amazement at the sight before her as Sabrina unlocked the door and swung it open. Scarlett gasped as the light from many twinkling crystal chandeliers filled the luxurious room. Plush leather couches encircled a large flat-screen television, creating an inviting seating area that beckoned her in. Scarlett took small steps into the grand space, her eyes widening with wonderment as she explored. Sabrina stood close behind her, smiling as she watched Scarlett's reactions.

'Is there anything I can do for you before you settle in?' Sabrina asked.

Scarlett's eyes lit up as she saw Sabrina, and her lips curled into a gentle smile. Slowly rotating on the spot, Scarlett broke their eye contact and returned to staring out the window. The twinkling lights of London's nightlife glittered on the pane like a million tiny stars, and Scarlett sighed deeply with contentment.

'I shall be just fine,' Scarlett said with a nod.

'I will just go and freshen up. Shout if you need anything,' Sabrina said as she shared a smile.

Scarlett grunted as she heaved the suitcase off the ground and onto the couch. She unzipped it and carefully lifted the lid, revealing a neatly-packed interior. A variety of clothing in an array of colors and textures welcomed her. Reaching inside, she pulled out each item individually, layering them onto the cushion beside her. Her eye caught a glimpse of a vivid green blouse that was so small it seemed almost unwearable and a short black skirt. Scarlett tenderly ran her fingers along each garment, admiring the exquisite fabrics. Her gaze eventually fell on the grand mirror. It had been a while since she'd seen her reflection, but now she was inexorably transfixed. She gingerly traced the delicate silk lines of her black widow spider tattoo with her fingertips. It was an intricate reminder of the ill-fated mission to Tokyo. Scarlett held up the shimmering green top and held it against her chest. She tilted her head in appreciation as she envisioned how she would look in it. Her heavy eyes carried with them an air of anticipation. Suddenly, she caught a glimpse of Sabrina in the reflection behind her entering the kitchen, the mist from her shower trailing behind her like a ghost. Her long red hair was slick against her back, and the thick white towel wrapped around her body was the only thing between her skin and the crisp air of the kitchen.

'I didn't mean to startle you,' Sabrina chuckled as she gazed at Scarlett before approaching her from behind.

'Wow, that would look great on you if you don't mind me saying.'

Scarlett's heart raced as she suddenly came to a halt, her fingers gripping the shirt tightly. A flush of embarrassment and anger washed over her, and without hesitation, she angrily flung the garment onto the ground. How could she have allowed herself to be so foolishly captivated by such an item?

'I was just seeing what was in here,' Scarlett said.

Sabrina carefully knelt, her fingertips lightly grazing the silky fabric of the blouse before scooping it up and presenting it to Scarlett.

'You would look amazing in this. Try it on?'

Scarlett stared at Sabrina, her green eyes sparkling with rage.

'Do you know what I'm capable of?' Scarlett hissed through gritted teeth.

'Should I be scared of you?' Sabrina said as her lips curled into an amused smirk.

Scarlett took a deep breath as she looked at her reflection in the mirror.

'You should be.'

Sabrina stepped forward, her fingers lightly brushing against the back of Scarlett's shoulder. She held up the emerald green top, its fabric catching the light and shimmering as she draped it gently around her slender frame.

'Come on, try it on. Enjoy your freedom this evening,'

Sabrina encouraged her with a warm smile and absolutely no fear.

'Why? It's ridiculous,' Scarlett said as her doubts lingered.

'Martin said you needed to have fun tonight. Get dressed, and I'll take you to a local nightclub,' Sabrina said with a wink.

Scarlett looked at her reflection in the mirror, illuminated by the lamp's glow on the dresser next to them. Her short blond hair was in disarray, and she had a deep crease between her brows as she weighed Sabrina's invitation. After a few moments of introspection, she took a deep breath and exhaled resignedly.

'Fuck it,' Scarlet said. 'I'm in.'

'Change your clothes,' Sabrina said with a mischievous glint as she strode to the bedroom, spinning around and giving Scarlett a joyous wink before closing the door.

Scarlett slipped out her vest top and leather trousers, revealing a black lace bra and matching panties. She stared at herself momentarily before reaching for the black skirt and pulling it up her legs. She removed her bra, grabbed the emerald green blouse from the back of the chair, and slid the straps over her shoulders. She brushed her strands of hair back and studied herself in the reflection. Moments later, Sabrina emerged from the bedroom. The living room's light danced off her exquisite dress, a garment that shimmered like a diamond in the night. The stylish black heels sparkled as they graced her long legs, and a gorgeous open backless design revealed the toned perfection of her arms and shoulders.

'Scarlett, I think you need help with that?' Sabrina asked as Scarlett fumbled desperately with the clasps of her top.

Sabrina's lips curled into a smile as she stepped closer to

Scarlett, tenderly securing the fastenings on her top.

'You look beautiful.'

Sabrina glanced down at Scarlett's back and gasped in shock, noticing the deep-rooted scars crisscrossing her skin. Sabrina's lips turned into a delighted smile as her eyes landed on Scarlett's neck. She couldn't help but reach out and let her fingertips trail against Scarlett's intricate spider tattoo.

'Why a spider tattoo?' Sabrina asked.

Scarlett took a deep breath, trying to steady herself as memories of an old lullaby entered her mind. The sounds of something so long ago yet close to her heart sent a shiver down her spine.

'When I was a child, my mother sang me a song about a spider every night. It was one of the last happy moments in my life.'

Scarlett tightly closed her eyes to shut out the overwhelming flood of memories. The lullaby that soothed her to sleep countless nights now echoed in her mind like a tormenting monologue, stirring up a mix of bitter emotions - pain, regret, betrayal.

'Why are you doing this?' Scarlett asked hesitantly.

Sabrina moved closer and looked into Scarlett's wounded eyes, her voice low and pleading.

'Look, I know you have had it rough,' Sabrina said as she gently reached out to take Scarlett's hand. 'I just want to be your friend. I'm guessing I would be your first one?'

Sabrina turned Scarlett around to face her and guided her to the couch. Sitting down gingerly on the edge of the cushion, Scarlett felt Sabrina leave for her bedroom before reappearing moments later with an armful of makeup bags.

Sabrina knelt before Scarlett and looked up at her with

shining eyes.

'Please let me do your makeup.'

'Not big on personal space, are you?' Scarlett said as Sabrina opened the bag and pulled out an eye pencil.

Sabrina's precise and gentle strokes illuminated Scarlett's features as she carefully applied the dark black eyeliner. Sabrina's agile fingers moved quickly and skillfully, blending her eyeshadow to make it stand out. Scarlett's face was inches from Sabrina's, and the heat of her breath flushed her cheeks. She shifted uncomfortably as she watched Sabrina unsheathe a blood-red lipstick from its case and press it to her lips, lining them meticulously with a steady hand.

'Hold still,' Sabrina whispered.

Scarlett took a deep breath and exhaled slowly, calming herself down.

'We are all done,' Sabrina said after what felt like an eternity of silence, grabbing Scarlett's hand and leading her back towards the mirror. The two stood before their reflections, and Sabrina smirked at Scarlett's wide-eyed expression.

'What do you think?' Sabrina asked with a hint of admiration in her voice. Scarlett stared in disbelief, taking in every detail of her reflection.

'Thank you,' Scarlett whispered.

'Let's go,' Sabrina said with a smile, tossing Scarlett a thick winter coat before approaching the door.

16

A frigid blast of winter air pushed past Sabrina, making her shiver and wish she had worn a heavier coat to protect against the night chill. As goosebumps raced across her skin, Sabrina rushed into the waiting limousine, eager for its warmth and safety from the cold, followed by Scarlett. The car glided effortlessly through the city streets, weaving in and out of traffic like an ethereal creature. She glanced over at her companion, Scarlett, looking out the window in wonderment. Although she did not understand all Scarlett had been through, Sabrina couldn't help but feel a surge of joy as she watched her face light up with excitement for what these new experiences had to offer. The limousine purred to a stop outside the lavish Fuse Nightclub, its walls lit up by garish neon signs. The pounding of bass thundered into the night, echoing off the building and shaking the street beneath their feet. Scarlett felt her heart racing as Sabrina tightened her grip on her hand and led her up to the imposing figure standing guard at the entrance; he was dressed head-to-toe in black, and his mirrored sunglasses reflected the light of the signs in an almost threatening way.

'Hey Steve, is it cool to go in?' Sabrina asked.

'Go right in, honey,' Steve replied.

Scarlett's eyes nervously flitted around the grand lobby, taking in all the well-dressed people.

'Do they know you?' Scarlett asked apprehensively.

'I come here regularly,' Sabrina said. 'Stick with me.'

Scarlett felt overwhelmed as they stepped into the lobby. Sabrina gracefully slipped off her coat and handed it to the woman at the cloakroom desk.

Scarlett tugged on Sabrina's hand, guiding her toward the doors that led to the dance floor.

'I shouldn't be here.'

'Don't be silly. This is exactly where you need to be,' Sabrina said confidently.

'It's too dangerous. You don't understand.'

'I don't believe that, Scarlett.'

'You said you know all about me, what I have done,' Scarlet said, her voice low and threatening. 'I could kill everybody here, including you.'

'If you were going to kill me, I would be dead already,' Sabrina said, looking calmly into Scarlett's eyes.

Sabrina slid off Scarlett's coat and handed it to the cloakroom desk before retaking her hand and leading her toward the dance floor. Sabrina cut through the frenzied mass of people, her Red locks bouncing in time with her steps. Scarlett trailed behind, careful not to lose sight of her friend in the chaotic sea of strangers. Sabrina's destination became apparent when she stopped abruptly and turned to Scarlett with a playful glimmer in her eye.

'Let's have a drink,' Sabrina said.

Startled by the suggestion, Scarlett watched Sabrina gesturing towards the bar behind them with a mischievous smile.

'I only drink water,' Scarlett replied hesitantly, a soft blush spreading across her cheeks.

'Not tonight, love. Tonight, you are my honored guest in this foreign land, and since you are over eighteen, you shall have a few drinks with me.'

Sabrina's grin widened as she affectionately patted Scarlett on the shoulder.

'Two shots of vodka, please.'

The barman's calloused hands meticulously placed two crystal glasses filled to the brim with ice-cold vodka in front of Sabrina and Scarlett, who glared at each other.

'To your new-found freedom,' Sabrina said, lifting her glass.

Scarlett took a hesitant sip before her eyes widened, and she choked on the overpowering taste of alcohol.

'You alright?' Sabrina chuckled.

'What the fuck was that?' Scarlett asked between gasps.

'It tastes like shit, but I thought it might loosen you up,' Sabrina smiled as she motioned for another round, tracing circles with her glossy black nails in the air.

The barman obliged, placing two more shot glasses on the glistening oak counter. Scarlett and Sabrina clinked their glasses together, the crisp sound of glass ringing between them. Scarlett threw back her drink, feeling a burning sensation as it coursed through her veins. Sabrina smiled broadly and let out a little squeal as the beat of a song came through the speakers.

'I love this song!' Sabrina screamed as she grabbed Scarlett's hand with an iron grip and tugged her onto the dance floor despite her protests.

Scarlett's anxiety rose with each step as the mass of bodies pushed into her. Sabrina, however, moved confidently and effortlessly to the beat, her hips swaying in time with the music. Sabrina spun and swayed, her body a white-hot blur of motion that seemed tailor-made for the dance floor. Scarlett, on the other hand, remained still as marble, her arms crossed over her chest and eyes wide with unease. She watched Sabrina's elegant movements as if they were an art form. Sabrina clasped onto Scarlett's hands and gently moved her side to side, spinning her around in a calm, peaceful dance.

'Come on, dance with me?' Sabrina asked, her grin wide and inviting.

Scarlett looked around the dance floor, taking in the couples locked together in a tight embrace, swaying to the music in perfect harmony. Scarlett's heart raced faster as a strange urge began to fill her chest, a call for her to join the chaotic display of emotions that surrounded her. Scarlett stood at the edge of a precipice, engulfed in a struggle between the light and dark desire that had followed her since childhood. The darkness seemed to take form around her, stretching its fingers out in a whispered invitation to succumb to its will. Sabrina looked into Scarlett's eyes and noticed her gaze was beginning to wander. Scarlett felt her strength waning as Sabrina's delicate hands encircled her wrists, drawing Scarlett closer until her cheek rested against Sabrina's shoulder. The warmth of Sabrina's embrace filled Scarlett with an unfamiliar and uncomfortable emotion, yet it sent shivers down her spine. Scarlett closed her eyes, aware of the heavy breathing on her neck. The sweet aroma of Sabrina's perfume filled her nostrils, and Scarlett felt a wave of longing overwhelm her. Despite pushing away the temptation, Sabrina had already begun to work her magic; her slender arms wrapped securely around Scarlett's back while their bodies moved as if connected by an invisible cord. The music was like a succulent lullaby that they twirled and danced to, drowning out the chaos surrounding them.

'Martin told me to look after you and to show you around, no strings attached. I will be honest with you. I kinda like you,' Sabrina said, a shy grin appearing.

Scarlett stared back at her, her eyes seemingly heavy with sorrow.

'You don't know me,' Scarlett murmured. 'Nobody does.'

Sabrina stepped closer, her hands slowly cradling Scarlett's face.

'You don't scare me,' Sabrina whispered. 'In fact, if I'm being honest -- I think you're beautiful. So deal with it.'

A deep breath broke through Scarlett's quivering lips, bringing a glimmer of hope. A hint of a smile curved at the corners of her mouth as she spoke again.

'Then maybe you're more fucked up than I am.'

Sabrina's fingers moved lightly across Scarlett's lower back, tracing the map of scars etched into her skin as they swayed in the music-filled air. Scarlett tensed and swiftly drew away from Sabrina's touch as if involuntarily shocked by an electrical current. Her emerald green eyes widened as her face grew stiff.

'Please don't touch them,' Scarlett hissed menacingly, her voice strained with emotion as darkness descended upon her features.

'How did you get them?' Sabrina asked hesitantly, not wanting to anger Scarlett further.

Scarlett shook her head, her lips trembling anxiously as the fire ignited in her eyes again.

'I don't want to talk about it.'

Sabrina tucked Scarlett's hair behind her ear and smiled.

'Then we don't talk about it,' Sabrina said as she held Scarlett's hand and smiled.

Sabrina felt a sudden, unwelcome hand grip her lower back and trail down to her bottom. She pulled away, pushing the man backward with enough force for him to stumble.

'What the fuck do you think you're doing?' Sabrina spat.

Scarlett stepped forward, ready to defend her friend, but another man moved between them with an arrogant smirk.

'My friend here is just trying to have some fun.'

Scarlett's heart filled with rage when she watched the man slip his hand around Sabrina's ribs and grip her breast. In an instant, Sabrina lashed out, fist connecting squarely with the man's nose and breaking it; a spray of blood followed as he fell back onto the ground.

'what the fuck, you stupid bitch!' The man shouted as he knelt beside his friend and quickly assessed the situation before rising to his feet with clenched fists, ready to strike. His arm froze mid-air at her presence, and his expression changed from fury to confusion. Scarlett closed her eyes and concentrated, holding him in her mental grasp as she circled him. Tears of anger began to stream down her face.

'All I wanted was a night away from my pain,' Scarlett screamed. 'Thank you for reminding me who I really am.'

The man's eyes widened in fear as he screamed in agony, his lower jaw moving oddly beneath Scarlett's controlling gaze. The skin around his mouth stretched taut and popped as his jaw bones began to dislocate from his face, ripping through flesh.

Blood sprayed in a wide arc as he collapsed in a heap on the ground as the people around them scrambled away, screaming in terror. Scarlett knelt beside the fallen man, her face determined. She reached out with one trembling hand and let her fingertips drift through the blood pool surrounding him. She took a deep breath and used her index finger to paint a swath of bloody fingerprints across her chest as if it were some ancient ritual. Sabrina carefully positioned herself behind Scarlett, taking a small step forward.

'Scarlett,' Sabrina whispered. 'are you alright?'

Scarlett shook her head and turned to look at the carnage she had caused.

'I couldn't help myself.'

Sabrina glanced down and kicked the lifeless body, an expression of defiance on her face.

'They deserved it. They all do,' Sabrina said. 'Never try to be anything other than who you are.'

Sabrina clenched her fingers around Scarlett's chin, forcing her to gaze into her eyes.

'Do it! Embrace your power,' Sabrina commanded, her voice echoing ominously around the nightclub. Without hesitation, all the doors in the club flew shut like a single gunshot in the air, trapping everyone inside as they scrambled desperately for an exit. Panic spread through the crowd as Sabrina's power filled the room. The chaos spiraled as three security staff approached them.

'Don't move!'

Scarlett tilted her head to the side and unleashed her power over the man to the right, forcing him towards a glass table. Wielding his fist, he punched it with such force that it shattered into tiny, jagged pieces. His hand throbbed as he grasped a jagged glass fragment, and he felt it slice his flesh and fill his palm with blood. In a blink of an eye, he plunged the sharp shard into one guard's neck, slashing through flesh and muscle, causing a fountain of scarlet liquid to gush outwards and drench his companion. Turning to face the last guard standing, he lunged forward, stabbing him five times quickly before pushing him away and gripping the glass tightly. He plunged it deep into his heart, causing himself to collapse onto the cold ground.

Sabrina intertwined her fingers with Scarlett's and stepped over the security guards.

'Please!' The man who had dared to touch her screamed out from the ground, blood spilling from his broken nose.

Rage erupted inside Sabrina as she raised her high-heeled shoe above the man's face. She brought it down with an almighty force, driving it through his eye like an arrow piercing a cloth. Sabrina and Scarlett pushed through the chaotic crowds, frantically trying to escape as screams and cries of terror echoed around them.

'All the exits are blocked,' Sabrina said through clenched teeth, her gaze piercing the masses of people desperately struggling to force open the doors.

Cries and screams bounced off the walls as they pushed and clawed, their faces etched with despair.

Scarlett froze in place, her eyes blazing and her arms stretched to the heavens. In a deafening roar, the hundreds of bodies in the nightclub rocketed to the mirrored ceiling with immense velocity, crashing into it and causing it to shatter into an intricate mosaic of broken glass. Sabrina's eyes widened in amazement at the sight of writhing bodies above her, suspended in a frozen moment of horror. She glanced over at Scarlett, whose eyes were blazing with power as she clung to her waist.

'You are so sexy right now,' Sabrina said.

The club doors creaked open, and Sabrina gazed at

Scarlett, who was humming Incy Wincy Spider in a spine-chilling tone. Scarlett released her grip on the bodies as the melody faded away, watching them plummet thirty feet from the ceiling onto the unforgiving floor below. Sabrina's wide eyes followed the bloody chaos unfolding before her. Bones were breaking, screams were ringing throughout the club, and suddenly, all were silenced when the ceiling splintered like thunder. Thousands of tiny shards of mirrored glass rained down on the broken bodies like deadly hail, slicing flesh and cutting deep until there was nothing but an eerie silence. Sabrina stared at the carnage before her in awe.

'What an incredible sight,' she murmured. 'Let's get you out of here.'

Scarlett and Sabrina strode out of the nightclub, only to be met by a wall of blinding blue-and-red flashing lights. Six police cars screeched to a stop, blocking any escape from the scene. Officers spilled out, guns drawn and aimed directly at them.

'Freeze, don't move a muscle!'

Scarlett raised her arms in defiance, and with a powerful wave of her hand, all six police cars rose high above the petrified officers. With a vicious swipe of her arm, the vehicles crashed down, smothering the officers like a boulder. The sound of crushing metal shook the air as the metal coffin closed in on its prey, swallowing them whole with a gruesome finality. Sabrina softly clasped Scarlett's hand, then led her through the pandemonium.

Sabrina opened the hotel room door, the bright overhead light illuminating her shimmering dress. She stepped inside, and Scarlett silently followed, still with a blank expression in her eyes. Sabrina walked to the sofa and slipped off her shoes, letting them drop to the floor without a sound as she sank into the cushions. She turned to find Scarlett in front of the large mirror on one side of the room. Scarlett bent her neck to get a better look at her reflection, eyes tracing every jagged scar that ran across her back. Sabrina watched silently, biting her lower lip.

'I'm sorry for touching them,' Sabrina said. 'I didn't want to upset you.'

Scarlett shifted from one foot to the other, twisting her hair around her finger.

'It's not you,' Scarlett whispered, desperately trying to keep her voice from shaking. 'I'm just not used to that kind of physical contact.'

Memories of being reprimanded for being who she was came flooding back; all the times her mother had tried to mold her into something she was not, punishing any mistakes made along the way. Sabrina approached Scarlett and placed a gentle hand on her shoulder, her touch warm and comforting.

'I know,' Sabrina said. 'I understand if you don't want to talk about it.'

As Sabrina looked into Scarlett's emerald eyes, she slowly pulled back her long red hair, revealing the dozens of small circular burns across the back of her neck.

'My father wasn't the man everyone thought he was,' Sabrina said. 'He would come home drunk and belligerent, ready to take out his anger on anyone who crossed his path. Most nights, it was just me and my mom there for him to take it out on,' Sabrina continued as she looked away, fighting back tears of anger.

Scarlett's eyes widened as she saw the scars on Sabrina's

neck, still raw and pink against her fair skin. She reached out and gently ran her fingers over them, feeling Sabrina shiver beneath her touch.

'I'm so sorry,' Scarlett whispered.

'It was a night I will never forget. He was about to kill her, and I had no choice. I didn't think; I just acted. I picked up the kitchen knife and let my rage overtake me. I stabbed him repeatedly until nothing was left,' Sabrina said, covering her neck with her hair and brushing away a tear.

'It's okay,' Scarlett reassured her. 'You did what you had to do.'

Sabrina nodded slowly, wiping away her tears.

'I swore from that day on that no one would ever push me around again,' Scarlett said firmly. 'I accept who I am and make no apologies for it. Neither should you.'

'What I am is a monster.'

Scarlett's tears mixed with her mascara, creating tracks of black down her ashen cheeks. Sabrina's gentle touch brought Scarlett back to reality. Her long fingers felt cool against Scarlett's heated skin as she lifted her chin until their eyes met. Her soft lips glowed pink against her flawless white skin as she smiled warmly.

'Well, you're my kind of monster,' Sabrina said as she inched closer to Scarlett, barely grazing her neck with the softest kisses.

'What are you doing?' Scarlett muttered nervously, a flood of sensations rushing through her body.

Sabrina tenderly brushed Scarlett's hair away from her face and leaned forward until their noses were inches apart.

'Doing what I can to make you feel better,' Sabrina whispered, her breath smelling of mint and lavender. 'Would you like me to stop?'

Scarlett paused, gazing into the depths of Sabrina's azure eyes.

'No,' Scarlett uttered, her tone definitive.

Sabrina entwined her fingers with Scarlett's and steered her toward the bathroom. Marble walls and floors gleamed from the light cascading down from the high ceiling.

In one corner was an open shower with a luxurious rainhead, which Sabrina turned on with one swift wrist motion. The cascading water created a heavy mist that stole the light from the room. Scarlett felt her heartbeat quicken as Sabrina's delicate fingers traced the contours of her body, and goosebumps appeared along her skin. Her breathing hitched as Sabrina's hands moved ever lower, and her eyes drifted closed. The clasps of her top released with a soft click, and Scarlett felt her top fall away from her shoulders, like a blanket of silk gliding to the floor. Sabrina tenderly ran her hand down Scarlett's cheek and felt the warmth of her skin. She slowly moved her hands down to Scarlett's chest, tracing the edges of her breasts with her gentle fingertips. Scarlett felt a thrill of electricity course through her body as Sabrina unclasped the zipper of her skirt and drew it down over her legs. Sabrina ran her fingertips up Scarlett's thighs, sending waves of sensation through her body. As Sabrina removed her underwear, she was left feeling vulnerable and exposed. Sabrina stepped back, and her eyes glided over Scarlett's body. Sabrina reached behind her own back, her fingers tracing the length of the zipper as it slowly descended. Sabrina felt the dress loosen around her body, revealing her sun-kissed skin to the soft glow of the bathroom light. Scarlett felt warmth wash over her as Sabrina unclasped her bra and stepped out of her underwear.

Every movement displayed her graceful femininity, igniting an aching hunger deep within Scarlett. They stood silently in the middle of the bathroom, both anticipating their impending embrace. Scarlett stepped closer and tentatively surveyed Sabrina's body with her eyes. It was the first time she'd seen someone without any clothing, and she was mesmerized. Taking her hand, Sabrina guided it to her chest and let Scarlett explore her body freely before guiding her toward the shower. The warmth of the water cascading over them sent sparks throughout their bodies. Sabrina shifted her fingers softly across Scarlett's chest, washing away the dry blood and letting the water run clear. Scarlett's pulse pounded in her ears as Sabrina moved nearer until their lips were a breath apart. A flutter of anticipation filled Scarlett's stomach, and she sighed softly, leaning her forehead against Sabrina's. Her heart raced with the realization that this was happening. Scarlett trembled, her eyes wide and uncertain. Sabrina cupped her face in her hands and brushed their noses together, then pressed her lips against Scarlett's in a long, tender kiss. Scarlett felt like she was melting into the kiss as she grabbed Sabrina's waist with both hands, her fingers running through the silky strands of her red hair. The warm water cascading over them was like a tantalizing caress, intensifying their passion until Scarlett felt like she was becoming one with Sabrina in that divine moment.

17

United Kingdom, December 2024

Ellie approached the stairs of the farmhouse. The old floorboards groaned beneath her bare feet as she descended into the hallway, her pulse quickening with every step. Ellie gingerly opened the creaking kitchen door, where the smoky aroma of Jackson's cigarettes and morning coffee consumed her senses. A gust of cold wind brushed against her face as she slowly pushed open the door leading to the farm, and the scent of hay and freshly cut grass with a hint of woodsmoke filled the air. The clucking of the chickens drew Ellie's attention, and she spotted Jackson in the barn, tossing out a handful of grain from a red feedbag. The birds fluttered around his feet as they pecked at the scattered kernels on the dirt floor. Ellie gracefully lowered herself onto one of the rickety chairs surrounding the large kitchen table. She slipped her black boots on, taking time to lace them up. Ellie stepped out of the farmhouse and inhaled the fresh country air. She advanced slowly towards Jackson, her leather gloves squeaking as she flexed her fingers. He was perched on a stool, hands shielding his face from the wind while he struck a match and lit a cigarette.

'Are you ready?' Jackson said in a low and commanding voice.

The question hung heavy in the air, and Ellie shivered from anticipation and fear. Her heart beat faster as adrenalin coursed through her veins.

'Scarlett might be here already. You're powerful, but your abilities are unreliable. We need an edge if we're going to be able to stop her from hurting anybody. We need an inhibitor collar,' Jackson said firmly, yet the compassion in his eyes was evident.

'Why can't we use the device that was in me?' Ellie asked, her voice a frustrated whisper as she squinted against the sun.

'It was damaged when I removed it, and besides, I don't have the gun to inject it here.'

Ellie fixed her gaze across the farm, watching the chickens engage in their mindless scurry across the dirt. Content in their blissful ignorance of the outside world, they seemed to live each day shrouded in serenity, contrasting with Ellie's tumultuous life. A twinge of envy struck her as she watched them, wishing she could feel the same carefree attitude they appeared to possess. Jackson rose to his feet, gently setting the two buckets on the shelf. Jackson quickly snatched up his long, brown coat that had been slung onto the ground. The fabric was mottled with mud and dirt, yet Jackson remained unfazed as he draped it artfully over his shoulder.

'Shall we?' Jackson said, his arm extended towards the black truck parked nearby. Its rust-coated exterior glinted in the sunlight.

Ellie looked up from her feet, hesitant. An uneasy feeling stirred within her chest as she thought of the long journey ahead.

'I guess,' Ellie said, her voice heavy with apprehension. Jackson gave an assuring nod, which did nothing to alleviate Ellie's growing anxiety. She shuffled forward, her feet heavy with the weight of her exhaustion. She tightly clasped her long green coat around her body, hoping to ward off the icy chill. She cautiously opened the old door, its hinges screaming in protest after so many years of use. She gingerly lowered herself into the leather seat, feeling the cracking material groan beneath her weight.

Ellie's gaze shifted out the window to behold a breathtaking scene; golden rays of sunlight cascaded down from clouds in the sky, brushing against vast fields of wheat that seemed to stretch on for eternity. The strains of a classical composition radiated throughout the truck, and Ellie settled back into her seat with a deep exhale. Jackson glanced over his shoulder at Ellie, nestled against the windowpane. Her blue eyes seemed transfixed on the blur of passing landscapes, her hands folded serenely in her lap.

'Why so quiet over there, kid?' Jackson asked.

Ellie exhaled a shaky sigh, her voice tight with emotion.

'Sorry, I'm not good on long journeys. Everything that has happened keeps playing through my mind like a broken record,' Ellie whispered as tears welled in her eyes. 'I don't think I can do what is expected of me, Jackson. All my life, I wanted to know who my birth parents were and ask them why they gave me up. Now I just want to forget the last few days and be with my family that loves me for who I am.'

Jackson couldn't help but feel sorrow as he looked at her. His heart ached when he thought of how she had been through so much in such a short time, but he knew he had to stay strong for her sake. He pressed his lips together tightly and turned his gaze away from her.

'I'm sorry, kid. I wish it hadn't come to this. It was bad enough when all they wanted to do was take you and try to control you. But now Scarlett is free,' Jackson said as he peered at Ellie, unsure of finishing his words.

'What is it, Jackson?' Ellie asked.

She wants you dead. She is a very dangerous person, Ellie.'

'She wants to kill me? why?'

'Because of what she has been through. The company has raised her like a weapon in isolation. That has made her a bloodthirsty killer. In her mind, she's the apex predator and sees you as a direct threat,' Jackson said as he reached out, placing his hand on Ellie's shoulder. 'Try not to worry. We will find a way to keep you safe and end this.'

Ellie nodded, her eyes blurry with tears. She had experienced so much in such a short time, and her days had been a never-ending blur of activity, uncontrollable emotions, and shifting realities. The exhaustion of it all was starting to take its toll, and she couldn't shake the feeling that she was trapped in time, unable to make sense of it all. Jackson shifted in his seat and cast an anxious glance in Ellie's direction.

'How have you been since our last meeting?' Jackson asked, letting his words linger in the air as Ellie regarded him with an intense stare.

'No, I haven't had a drink,' Ellie snapped. 'It's not like your farm is stocked with booze anyway.'

Jackson's expression softened as he reached out and softly patted her arm.

'I'm still your sponsor, Ellie,' Jackson murmured reassuringly.

Ellie glanced at him from the corner of her eye, a mischievous grin tilting up the corners of her mouth. Her smile faded as she locked eyes with his profound gaze. Jackson closed his eyes, took a deep breath, and slowly exhaled. He opened his eyes and gave Ellie an encouraging smile, squeezing her arm gently with one hand.

'I am very proud of you,' Jackson said, his voice low and full of admiration. 'You are dealing with so much and have a heavy burden. But remember that I'm here for you. Anything you need, I'm here.'

As they drove closer to the bridge, it seemed to stretch forever. Cars were lined up bumper-to-bumper for as far as the eye could see, clogging the entrance and exit ramps of the vast structure. Jackson's frustration was palpable as he slowed the car to a crawl. The fog had transformed into an eerie mist, almost like a seething entity surrounding them. Visibility was next to nothing, and the further they drove, the thicker it seemed to get.

'Shit! Looks like an accident up ahead,' Jackson grumbled under his breath.

Ellie wound down her window and took a deep breath of air. She peered intently, desperately trying to determine what had caused such a traffic jam. But through the white veil, all she could make out were dark shapes of cars slowly merging in the fog.

'I'm gonna look,' Ellie said, opening the door. 'I can't see anything.'

Jackson watched Ellie's figure vanish into the thick fog, her silhouette becoming a hint of movement.

She carefully picked her way through the stalled cars, peeking inside each one as she passed. As she approached the bridge, she stopped to take in the eerie silence that hung over the scene. Her steps echoed off the metal framework as she crossed and bent to peer inside a sleek red convertible. A chill ran down her spine as she saw a man inside; his body was still and motionless. He clung to the wheel of his car, each knuckle crisp white from the strain. Panic had taken control, evidenced by the beads of sweat that ran down his face and dampened his collar. The only sound was his erratic breathing as he shook under the unrelenting fear.

'Excuse me, sir,' Ellie whispered, 'are you alright?'

There was no response as Ellie looked questioningly at the man, then shifted her gaze to the other car beside her. Inside sat a woman in the driver's seat and a child in the back seat. Both had similar expressions of fear and panic on their faces, but like the man, they remained motionless.

'Are you alright?' Ellie asked again, gently knocking on the window this time. Still, there was no reply. Ellie whirled around and sprinted back towards Jackson, her feet pounding on the pavement, echoing in her ears. She saw the terror painted on his face as he clutched the steering wheel of his truck so tightly that his knuckles had turned white. His brown eyes were wide with fear, and he silently begged for help. Fear ran up her spine as she stepped into the eerie silence. Thick air clung to her like a heavy blanket, muffling the sound of her breath and pounding heart. Suddenly, a distant sound of a woman humming drifted through the foggy stillness, stirring something deep within her. Her chest rose and fell as she drew in a deep breath, then yelled into the abyss of the bridge. The acoustics were extraordinary, her voice reverberating off the walls and echoing until it faded. She heard a faint humming that grew louder with each step closer to its source. Her boot heels clicked like a metronome on the pavement below while her racing pulse screamed for her to turn around and go back. She was met with the same terrifying scene as she passed car after car, drivers sitting still, paralyzed by fear. Ellie felt a wave of

164

dread wash over her as she approached the haunting sound. She crept closer until she could make out two figures through the misty fog. They were locked in an embrace, wrists entwined, swaying gently. From here, Ellie could make out the unmistakable outline of two women.

'Hello?' Ellie called out cautiously.

The soft, lullaby-like melody of Incy Wincy Spider suddenly ceased, replaced by a thick, oppressive silence. Ellie took measured steps forward, her heart pounding in her ears as fear threatened to take over. As she moved closer, a chill raced down her spine when an eerie laugh pierced the stillness like a dagger. When the haze parted, she saw two figures in front of her. A wave of shock rushed through her body at the sight of Scarlett, her mirror image dressed in a wickedly inviting red leather suit with a nefarious smirk on her face. Beside her, Sabrina stood tall, her tight leather outfit showcasing the curves of her athletic figure. Sabrina leaned against her motorcycle's glossy, chrome-lined frame and smiled. Scarlett had one hand on her hip while the other pointed accusingly at Ellie, her face twisted with arrogance. A chill ran down Ellie's spine as she looked between them. Sabrina was electric with excitement, while Scarlett seethed with contempt. Ellie knew she couldn't escape as an oppressive chill engulfed her. Sabrina cackled loudly and waved her over with an evil glint in her eye.

'You must be Ellie Jones. It is a pleasure to meet you. I would very much like to introduce you to your Sister Scarlett,' Sabrina chuckled.

The air suddenly felt thicker, and Ellie felt she couldn't breathe. Every muscle in her body tensed as her mind raced with questions and confusion. She glanced at Sabrina, who looked a little too pleased with herself.

'I can see you are ignorant to many truths,' Sabrina said.

Scarlett's intensity burned from her emerald eyes as she slowly swept her gaze across Ellie's face. She examined every detail: the subtle arch of her eyebrows, the shape of her nose, the softness of her cheeks and lips. Ellie shifted in place uncertainly, not understanding the scrutiny.

'Look, I don't understand what's happening. I don't have a sister,' Ellie said, her voice quivering with confusion. Scarlett's lips curled into a knowing smile, and she took a step closer, her boots echoing on the road.

'I know. It came as a shock to me too,' Scarlett whispered. 'I feel like we were both in the dark about our family.'

Ellie's cheeks flared red, and her tiny frame shook as she spoke, her voice wavering between anger and fear. Her jaw was tight, and her veins throbbed with rage.

'Jackson told me what happened to my parents. They died a long time ago. I don't know who or what you are,' Ellie spat.

Scarlett's laugh cut through the oppressive silence like a lightning strike in the night sky. Each step closer seemed to increase the tension between them. Scarlett squeezed Ellie's hands tightly, her knuckles stark white against Ellie's skin. Her eyes were narrowed, her gaze malicious and icy cold.

'He told you everything, did he? Well, I saw our mother just a few days ago. She was beaming with joy at the prospect of seeing you soon. But now she'll never get to meet you. It's so sad that the plans had to change. The news of your death will certainly devastate her,' Scarlett said.

Ellie's lips parted, and her skin blanched. Her chest rose and fell in short, fearful gasps. Scarlett's eyes gleamed with malice as a cruel smirk curled her lips.

'How are your fake family doing?' Scarlett asked.

Ellie's knees trembled, her heart racing as she stepped

back, her hands shaking.

'I don't know what you think I have done to you. I had no idea I was special until a few days ago,' Ellie murmured, barely able to get the words out before Sabrina stormed forward, her face red and contorted in a fury.

'You are not fucking special!' Sabrina screamed, her hands balled into fists.

Scarlett stepped between them, her body blocking Ellie from Sabrina's onslaught. She was calm and composed, her face tranquil as she studied Ellie. A heavy silence filled the air, and Ellie's heart pounded in her ears. She didn't dare to breathe as Scarlett's smile widened into something more cruel.

'are you going to kill me?' Ellie asked.

'I'm not going to kill you yet. That would be too easy, and that's not what I want.'

Scarlett's eyes ran over Ellie's body, taking in every detail. Sweat beaded on her forehead, and her hands trembled as Scarlett stepped closer.

'You're not going to kill her?' Sabrina screamed, her eyes widening as she took in the situation.

Scarlett reached out, her fingers weaving through Ellie's long brown hair and her face twisted into a malicious smirk. Her breath was hot against Ellie's ear as she leaned in.

'Oh, I will kill her,' Scarlett whispered. 'But I want her to feel pain. I want her to experience the agony of loss.'

As these words echoed in the air, Ellie felt a chill run down her spine, for she knew there would be no escape from Scarlett's evil clutches.

'I know everything about you, sister, including how pathetic you are.'

Ellie's throat felt like it was closing as Scarlett slowly

reached out and dragged her fingernail down her cheek, gathering a tear and pressing it between her lips. Scarlett's icy green eyes pierced into Ellie, sending a wave of discomfort that made her shrink back. Her gaze was intense and held disdain as Scarlett slowly examined her from head to toe. Scarlett slowly turned towards Sabrina, her grip on her friend's hand tightening as she met Ellie's gaze. The corner of her mouth twitched upward as a malicious smirk crossed her lips. Her voice echoed, saturated with malice and fury.

'I will take everything from you. I will destroy your world. I will kill you when it pleases me,' Scarlett said.

'Don't bother with your little road trip,' Sabrina said. 'There is nothing good waiting for you there.'

Ellie's heart pounded wildly in her chest as the repercussions of Sabrina's words seemed to shake the earth. Her feet felt rooted to the ground, unable to move. Sabrina climbed onto the glossy black motorcycle as Scarlett sat behind her and wrapped her arms tightly around her. She turned her head to the side, her green eyes meeting Ellie's.

'Let's find out, Ellie. Are you really a good person?' Scarlett said with a smile.

A loud rattle filled the air as the blue car beside them trembled violently, inching closer and closer to the edge of the bridge. Ellie's eyes widened with fear as she watched the vehicle teeter precariously on its back two wheels, moments away from plummeting into the dark abyss below. Her body froze in shock and terror as she saw a woman and baby inside, unaware of their impending doom. She gasped for breath, her chest tightening like an iron fist until a strangled cry, laced with anguish, finally broke free of her lips.

'What are you doing?!' Ellie shouted, the desperation

ringing in her voice. Scarlett's gaze flashed with malicious delight.

'I'll be seeing you soon, Ellie,' Scarlett said as she looked into the distance towards Jackson's truck and smiled. 'Tell Daddy I said hello.'

Sabrina revved the engine of her motorcycle with a menacing growl. The bike surged forward in a roar, leaving Ellie in the dust, paralyzed with terror and confusion as she watched them disappear into the horizon. Scarlett's control ruptured, unleashing a cacophony of increasingly intense car horns, slamming doors, and piercing screams. The chaos suffocated her senses, yet Ellie heard the faint whirring of tires spinning against the bridge's slick pavement. She felt her heart drop as she watched in horror as the car teetered at the edge of the bridge without hope of clinging on. People scrambled for safety as Ellie clenched her eyes shut and held up her hands as if they could conjure a magical force field to keep it from falling. Fear shook her veins, but she tried remembering what Jackson had told her about her power and envisioning a force field around it. The car jerked to a stop, shaking on its axis as if being pulled in both directions. Jackson's voice boomed out as he appeared behind Ellie, his eyes darting to the car where the woman was hysterically crying.

'Ellie!' Jackson roared, sprinting towards the teetering vehicle and yanking open the door at the back. He snatched the baby carrier from its seat and placed it on solid ground before turning back to Ellie, who seemed drained and defeated.

'I'll get you out of there,' Jackson yelled, his unwavering determination radiating from him like a furnace. Desperation shone in the woman's wide eyes as she fought against her bonds.

'Hurry!' Ellie begged, and Jackson gave her an encouraging nod before scrambling back into the car's rear seat. His skilled fingers flew over the seatbelt, clicking it open in less than a second. Nimbly scooping the woman into his arms, he slid her out of the car and gently placed her on the ground. The woman hugged her baby tight to her chest, gasping for air amidst sobs of relief. Jackson watched as Ellie opened her eyes, shock and fear emanating from every inch of her being before the car plummeted over the edge and exploded in a deafening blast below. Ellie crumpled to the ground in a heap as Jackson dropped to his knees beside her and took in the full horror of what had just happened to them both. He reached out hesitantly and shook her shoulder carefully.

'Are you alright?' Jackson asked.

Ellie shook her head and sobbed uncontrollably. Jackson looked around at the chaos, then quickly rose to his feet and offered her a hand.

'Come on; we have to get out of here.'

Ellie accepted his hand and slowly got to her feet.

'That was Scarlett, wasn't it?' Jackson asked nervously as they walked back to the truck. 'We need to get that inhibitor.'

Ellie stopped in her tracks and looked at him, still in shock.

'It's over,' Ellie said as her words hung heavy between them, like a fog of grief. She continued walking, not waiting to hear Jackson's reply.

As they approached the truck, they were left speechless by the sight of cars desperately trying to escape the bridge ahead.

'Fuck!' Jackson spat out through gritted teeth as he slammed his fists against the steering wheel. Then he turned to Ellie, his eyes pleading for answers.

'What did she say?'

Ellie gazed out the window as if looking into another world, still trying to process what had happened.

'She told me to say hello to our father,' Ellie whispered before finally turning back to Jackson, who looked utterly stunned, as if he had seen a ghost.

Jackson stared out the window, his eyes distant and unfocused. He knew this conversation would be difficult, and his heart raced in anticipation. Ellie glanced at him, her face a mixture of sadness and anger.

'Is it true?' Ellie asked. 'Is she my Sister? Are you my father?'

He slowly turned to face her, and she saw the guilt in his eyes.

'I'm so sorry, Ellie. I was going to tell you.'

She turned away and leaned her head on the window, tears streaming silently down her cheeks.

'Take me home,' Ellie whispered.

Jackson turned the key in the ignition, and the truck roared to life. He threw it into reverse, and they left the bridge in uneasy silence.

Ellie stared out of the window, silently watching the world pass.

'Are you going to listen to what I have to say? I will tell you everything, I promise.'

Ellie turned to face him, her face tired and void of emotion.

'You expect me to trust you after all the lies you've told me? My entire life has been uprooted. I'm expected to accept that I have gifts and that people are trying to kidnap me! And then I find out that the woman who wants to kill me is actually my Sister and that you, who I have trusted the most this past year, are my father!' Ellie said.

Jackson's gaze dropped as he tried to process what she'd

said. He tapped a cigarette on the steering wheel before lighting it and taking a long drag.

'Kid, I knew you couldn't handle hearing all that at once, so I was trying to give it to you in pieces.'

'I can't handle it, Jackson!' Ellie screamed.

Jackson placed the cigarette on his lips as Ellie wiped away a tear and gazed at him intently.

'No more fucking lies!' Ellie said. 'You need to tell me the truth now, whatever it is. Whatever you've been holding back, no matter how hard it is to say, I need to know,' Ellie paused, her voice softening. 'I'm listening.'

18

The first sign of dawn spilled through the tall windows of the lab, scattering warm, golden light across the cold, metallic surfaces. Every machine was awake and humming, the bright LEDs twinkling in the silent room. Gradually, the lab filled with researchers, their white coats rustling as they settled into their stations. Their enthusiastic chatter disturbed the quiet of the morning as they prepared for another day of discovery. As a woman with shoulder-length black hair approached her desk, she noticed that Jackson, with whom she shares the workspace, was asleep. His head rested on his arm, and a gentle snore escaped his lips. She approached him cautiously and gently tapped his shoulder to wake him. He was seated with his head down, breathing quietly.

'Jackson, are you alright?'

His eyes snapped open, and he hurriedly rolled up his sleeve to check his watch, his brow furrowed with confusion and concern. His eyes widened as he quickly glanced at the wall clock.

'Shit, is that the time?'

He frantically grabbed the pile of paperwork strewn across his desk. He crammed it haphazardly into his filing cabinet as the woman stepped away to her workstation, throwing him a concerned look over her shoulder. Jackson pulled out his phone and tapped the screen, his fingernails scratching against the surface. He inhaled deeply and held it against his ear. He waited for a response, absentmindedly running his thumb over the two-day-old stubble on his chin. Jackson anxiously waited as the phone rang, his heart racing. Finally, on the fifth ring, Rebecca answered with a clear and polished tone.

'I'm sorry,' Jackson mumbled, 'I fell asleep at work. Have I missed your appointment?' There was a pause on the other end before Rebecca replied.

'No, I just got here myself. Please hurry.'

Amidst the flurry of activity, Jackson quickly removed his lab coat and hung it on a coat hanger before leaving his desk. As he rushed for the door with his suitcase, he almost stumbled over a man murmuring to himself in the hallway.

'Sorry,' Jackson said over his shoulder as he continued for the exit. 'I'm just leaving now!' he said as everybody in the lab watched.

With apprehension, Jackson pushed open the heavy wooden door to the Doctor's office and stepped inside. The waiting room was silent except for the enormous clock ticking above the reception area. Jackson shuffled to the desk, noticing that Rebecca wasn't in the waiting area. An older woman was sitting behind a stack of paperwork, tapping away on her keyboard. Nervously, Jackson scratched the back of his neck and cleared his throat before looking up at her.

'Excuse me, could you tell me if my wife has gone in? I'm a bit late.'

'May I have her name, please?' the woman asked as she smiled kindly at him.

'Rebecca Ellis-Carter,' Jackson answered as she quickly typed the name in and glanced at her screen.

'Yes, she was called in a few moments ago, in room two.'

'Thank you very much.'

With his heart pounding, Jackson jogged quickly toward the room. His knuckles trembled as he rapped on the door.

'Come in.'

As Jackson pushed the door open, he found Rebecca seated, her eyes red and swollen from crying. The Doctor stood tall in the bright light, his long white coat billowing as he moved. His thick-rimmed glasses glinted in the sun streaming in the window, and his expression was grave and stern.

'Mr. Carter?' The Doctor asked.

Jackson sat next to Rebecca and gently held her hand, using his thumb to rub soothing circles on her back. He looked at the Doctor, his face full of concern.

'What's wrong?' Jackson asked.

The Doctor hesitated briefly before speaking in a gentle and understanding manner.

'I am very sorry to be the one to tell you this. The cancer has returned.'

Jackson's breath escaped him as he slumped in his chair, almost feeling the invisible blow to his abdomen. He gazed at Rebecca, who had widened her eyes in shock and had tears shining on her cheeks. After that, he turned to the Doctor in a state of disbelief.

'What?' Jackson exclaimed, his face growing pale. He

leaned forward on his chair, anxiously wringing his hands. 'I thought it was under control, and there was more time! What can we do? Is there another treatment option?'

The Doctor's facial expression became gentler as he sadly shook his head.

'I'm afraid not. The treatment just isn't responding anymore.'

As Jackson looked at Rebecca, his chin started to tremble.

'How much time do we have left?' Jackson stammered.

The Doctor sighed and avoided eye contact as he sat behind his desk.

'I'm sorry, Mr. Carter, it has spread to the pancreas. We don't have much time.'

'There has to be something!' Jackson said.

Rebecca gently touched his shoulder and looked into his eyes as tears streamed down her cheeks.

'Jackson, stop. We have to accept this.'

Jackson gently squeezed Rebecca's hand, and his gaze locked with hers. Tears shimmered in her eyes, like a reflection of the sadness inside.

'We will fix this, Becca. We have to.'

Jackson and Rebecca emerged from the Doctor's office to find his aging blue Firebird. Chunks of paint had flaked off, revealing patches of gray metal beneath. Jackson opened the passenger door for Rebecca with a loud creak, and she hesitated before finally entering the car. The interior was musty with the smell of old leather and cigarettes, and she settled into her seat, sinking slightly into the cushion. She looked out the window, her gaze distant and unfocused, and an uncomfortable silence filled the air. Jackson looked over at Rebecca, cleared his throat, and nervously shuffled in his seat.

'Can we talk about this?' Jackson asked, his voice soft and hesitant.

Rebecca composed herself and gazed into his eyes with intensity.

'Take me to work!'

Jackson took a deep breath and glanced back towards the road.

'I'm taking you home,' Jackson said.

'We've been preparing for this,' Rebecca said, her hands clenching into fists. 'The research is nearly ready. We knew this day would come.'

Jackson ran his hands through his hair, feeling frustrated and confused. He shook his head, unable to reconcile the internal struggle he was experiencing between wanting to give up and unwilling to surrender.

'I've been up all night trying to figure out why the formula works on paper but not the animal trials. It's like the results don't transfer,' Jackson said, looking over at Rebecca and tightening his lips. 'We are nowhere near human trials.'

'Well, we might need to be sooner than we thought,' Rebecca said, her voice barely audible in the loud car.

'Just because the Doctor said you don't have long doesn't make it true. They are wrong all the time,' Jackson said, softly stroking her hair with a shaky hand as they drove back to the facility, their unspoken thoughts filling the car with an unbearable heaviness.

The clock ticked slowly into the evening, and everyone else had left the lab for the day except Rebecca and Jackson, who stayed behind to finish their paperwork. The air was thick with the smell of coffee as they scrambled to fill out forms, crossing off items on their never-ending to-do lists until the last sliver of sunlight vanished from the sky.

Jackson sank into the chair and stretched his legs out with a weary groan. He glanced at Rebecca, her body slumping against the chair, her eyes heavy with exhaustion.

'Let's get you home so you can rest.'

Rebecca lifted her head to meet his gaze and attempted a smile.

'I'll have plenty of time for that soon enough,' Rebecca said as her words trailed off into a sarcastic murmur.

'Not funny!' Jackson's expression hardened, his eyebrows furrowed, and his lips pressed into a thin line.

He stood up, pulling off the long white coat and throwing it over the back of the chair before raising his arms above his head in an extended stretch.

'We should be getting the results back soon,' Jackson said.

Rebecca attempted to stand, but exhaustion quickly overwhelmed her, and she sank back into her chair. Jackson rushed to her side and gently took the coat from her shaking hands. She pushed a stray lock of sun-kissed hair behind her ear and smiled, her blue eyes suddenly alive with emotion.

'Do you remember when we first met?' Jackson asked, the corners of his mouth lifting into a rueful smile.

Rebecca laughed and shook her head, resting it in her hands.

'Of course, I remember. You were an intern here. You looked so helpless and scared. I felt sorry for you and asked if I could train you,' Rebecca said. 'You were eager to learn and impress me with your enthusiasm.'

Happiness filled her face as she remembered the sense of possibility she felt back then. Jackson leaned back in his chair and nodded. His eyes softened as he recalled the moment he first saw her.

'Yup, I nearly lost my job because of your distractions,'

Jackson said.

'My distractions!' Rebecca snapped back with a chuckle.

Jackson grinned, his eyes twinkling with nostalgia.

'You looked stunning that day,' Jackson said, his gaze lingering on her as if imagining the scene again. 'I can still recall it like it just happened. You looked so beautiful in the sunlight, so stunning it almost seemed unreal.'

'I looked stunning? You mean I don't anymore?' Rebecca said with a smile.

His gaze traveled up her face, and he could see fine lines of exhaustion around her eyes.

'You still are stunning. Every day, I thank god that you came into my life.'

Rebecca looked away from him and studied the files on her desk, occasions where they had worked together to make a positive change.

'We have done a lot of good here. We can be proud of that,' Rebecca said.

Jackson smiled and reached across to take her hand in his.

'Hey, don't go talking like it's over.'

The sudden beeping of his phone made them both jump, and Jackson snatched it up from the table. A frown creased his forehead as he read the message, and then he flung the device away with an agitated curse. Slumping back into his chair, he glared at the opposite wall while Rebecca stifled a laugh.

'Another failure?' Rebecca asked.

Heaving a deep sigh, Jackson sat up straight in his chair and nodded curtly.

'I will fix this, I swear,' Jackson said. 'I won't stop until I do. There must be something I'm missing.'

He checked his watch and let out a sigh. He then looked

over at Rebecca, who was falling asleep in her chair and was struggling to keep her eyes open.

'It's getting late,' Jackson whispered. 'Let's go home and start again in the morning.'

Rebecca's head lulled to the side, and her eyelids slowly fluttered open. She shuffled in her chair and reached out with a shaky hand, stretching for Jackson's reassuring grip.

'Can you get me some water before we go? I need to take my medication,' Rebecca asked.

'Of course. I will run down to the vending machines and be back in a few minutes. Can I get you anything else?'

Rebecca's lips stretched into a thin line as she slowly shook her head. She opened her mouth to speak, but no sound came out. She kicked off her high heels one by one, wiggling her toes and exhaling with relief. With a gentle touch, Jackson caressed her face and brushed his thumb across her lips. His gaze locked into hers so profoundly that she felt a shiver up her spine.

'I love you, Becca,' Jackson whispered. The air in the room felt charged as he kissed her softly and moved away, but before he could reach the door, Rebecca spoke. Her voice was low but filled with emotion.

'Hey Jackson, I kinda love you too.'

After a few moments, Jackson walked back into the lab, his heart pounding and a bottle of water clutched in his sweaty hand.

'Sorry honey, I bumped into Andy. I couldn't get away.'

Jackson stood by the doorway and watched Rebecca from a distance. She was slumped in her chair, her arms hanging lifelessly at her sides while her head rested against the back of the seat. Her deep breaths told him she was fast asleep, and he felt a wave of sadness wash over him as he approached. He crouched beside her and gently shook Rebecca's shoulder.

'Wake up, honey, you need your pills,' Jackson said in a soft but desperate voice.

When she didn't stir, Jackson increased the force of his grip on her shoulder but still received no response. He reached for Rebecca's limp arm with trembling hands and felt a sharp pang in his chest when an empty syringe fell to the floor. Tears welled in his eyes, and his breathing became ragged as he realized what had happened.

'No! Becca, what have you done!'

He pressed two fingers to her neck and then checked for a pulse at her wrist, his heartbeat pounding in his temples. His hands shook as he pulled out his phone, fumbling with the buttons before dialing for an ambulance. He saw a crumpled piece of paper near her other hand. Jackson carefully picked up the note and unfolded it, anxious to see what message she had left.

'Jackson. I hate that I have to write this letter to you. You would never let me try this, but I am almost out of time. I have to do this, even if it means the end. If it works, I can come back to you, and we will have made a medical breakthrough that could save many lives. But I can't even begin to think about that possibility if it doesn't. You've been by my side through so much, and I will never be able to thank you enough for that. You are the most incredible man, and I was blessed to be your wife.'

Jackson dropped to his knees, sobbing. His tears mixed with the ink of Rebecca's letter and bled into its creases.

He wrapped his arms around her and gripped her tightly.

'Please don't leave me, not now.'

He heard sirens in the distance and glanced at the letter

one final time before crumpling it in his hand.

Two weeks had passed, and Jackson had not left Rebecca's side. Sitting in her hospital room, basking in the sun's warm rays that flooded in through wide-open windows, he lay his head against her chest and clutched tightly to her hand, interlacing their fingers. As he listened to her labored breathing, a tear escaped his eye and ran down his cheek. Suddenly, the door swung open, and a nurse bustled into the room. She was a petite woman with a blond bun, and her crisp white uniform almost glowed from the orange hue of the sun. She held a clipboard in her arm, her eyes darting around the room as she checked Rebecca's vitals. Jackson stirred, barely conscious, and spotted the nurse standing at the foot of Rebecca's bed. He opened his mouth to say something, but she forestalled him with a gentle smile.

'Sorry to wake you, sir.'

'Is there any news?' Jackson asked.

The nurse carried on with her duties and smiled at Jackson.

'The doctor will be in shortly.'

After completing her task, she left the room and shut the door with a click. Jackson cast his gaze back to Rebecca's sleeping form, still motionless in the bed. He felt his heart stop when the Doctor walked into the room. He clung to the arms of his chair, eyes fixed on the physician's face, searching for any hint of good news.

'Have the test results come back yet?' Jackson asked.

The Doctor's expression softened, and he took a few steps forward and stopped by Rebecca's side.

'Your wife's cancer has gone, Mr Carter.'

His voice was calm, almost in disbelief. He shook his head

slowly and walked towards Jackson, placing a comforting hand on his shoulder.

'Her readings are strong and healthy,' The Doctor said.

Jackson's jaw dropped, and for a moment, he was speechless. He stared at the Doctor with shock and confusion, and his eyebrows raised in disbelief.

'She doesn't have cancer?' Jackson asked, almost not believing his own words.

'It makes no sense,' The Doctor replied, shaking his head. 'Whatever she did has worked. I have never seen anything like this in my life.'

'Why won't she wake up?' Jackson asked, his voice quivering.

The Doctor looked him in the eye and offered a comforting look.

'She will wake up in her own time,' The Doctor said, his hand firmly on the door handle. 'Trust that she will return to us when she's ready.'

'Is there something else?' Jackson asked nervously.

The Doctor nodded, his expression serious.

'We found something else in your wife's blood tests.'

Jackson gasped, his face ashen, and he ran a shaking hand through his thick hair. He blinked as if struggling to understand the Doctor's words.

'What?' Jackson asked. 'You said she is healthy.'

The Doctor cleared his throat and adjusted the thick-rimmed glasses on his nose. He took a slow breath before speaking in a gentle yet authoritative voice.

'Mr. Carter, your wife is one month pregnant.'

Jackson was stunned and felt as if the room was spinning around him.

'What! That's impossible.'

The Doctor's smile was warm and kind as he gently placed his hand on Jackson's shoulder. His touch was firm yet gentle, with a hint of reassurance. He lingered for a moment before stepping back and nodding farewell. Jackson sunk back into the chair, grasping Rebecca's hand tightly, tears of relief streaming down his face.

'We did it, honey. The cancer's gone. You're going to be alright,' Jackson said. 'We are gonna have a baby, can you believe it?'

19

United States of America, July 2007

The laboratory was a hive of activity. Scientists in crisp white lab coats filled the room, conversations echoed off the walls, and the clinking of beakers and test tubes created an almost constant hum. Jackson sat hunched over his microscope, wholly absorbed in his work, until he felt a presence by his side and looked up to see a tall blond woman. She smiled, her gaze warm and inviting.

'Hey Jackson, how's it going?'

'I'm nearly done,' Jackson replied.

A hush descended over the laboratory as Rebecca stepped into the room. Her heels clicked quickly on the tiled floor, and an ominous energy followed her. Employees averted their gaze everywhere she turned, and a palpable tension arose. When she stopped at Jackson's desk, his heart sank. He couldn't tell whether anger or something else had taken hold of her features.

'What's going on?' Jackson asked tentatively, his voice tight with anxiety.

The woman standing next to Jackson suddenly found

herself the target of Rebecca's intense gaze.

'Do you mind? I want to speak to Doctor Carter.'

The woman timidly nodded back at Rebecca's icy gaze and quickly scurried away. Jackson sat motionless, barely able to breathe under the weight of Rebecca's eye.

'I'd like to talk to you,' Rebecca said firmly, 'can you come to my office, please?'

Jackson's expression was solemn as he trailed Rebecca out of the lab. They traveled down the stark, white hallways that gave off a faint hum of electricity and echoed with each footstep. She paused before her Father's old office and pushed open the door. Inside, everything was pristine, and vibrant whites filled every corner - from the walls to the furniture that appeared almost too perfect to be touched. The only thing that broke up the monotony was a large oil painting of Rebecca's Father hanging on the wall. Rebecca adjusted the laptop on her desk before gracefully lowering herself into the plush executive chair. Her bright blue blouse with its deep V-neckline added a splash of color to her black, calf-length skirt and sheer tights ensemble. Her long, blond hair framed her face, and when she directed her gaze toward Jackson, it was almost as if she were trying to read his thoughts. He shifted in his seat, feeling too exposed by the intensity of her look.

'I have been trying to contact you for weeks,' Jackson said.

Rebecca's lips curved into a strained half-smile, and she wriggled her toes inside her shoes as she tried to make herself more comfortable in her chair.

'Yes, I have been busy,' Rebecca answered dismissively. Her gaze held Jackson's for an uncomfortable amount of time.

'Do you know why I have asked to see you?'

'You mean it's not because you missed me?' Jackson said as

he swallowed loudly and took in the room, scanning the walls and furniture. His eyes glanced back towards Rebecca, who waited expectantly for an answer.

'I want to see them, Becca. You can't keep them from me!' Jackson shouted.

Rebecca stood, her palms pressing onto the desktop as she adjusted her skirt and stepped around the office. She paused and took a deep breath, looking at Jackson.

'I understand you want to see them. I'm sorry, but it's just not possible.'

Jackson's eyes narrowed, his face turning crimson. His fists slammed into the desk, and a loud thud echoed. The force of the impact made the stationary quake and the papers scatter. He seethed, his voice low and trembling with controlled anger.

'The best place for them is in a home with their Father, not being kept in cages like animals. They are children, not weapons.'

Rebecca averted her gaze from him and focused on the large painting of her Father that hung on the wall. She searched for something to say, but the words didn't come quickly.

'You know it hasn't been easy for me to step into his shoes. Our girls are miracles, and I want them to be protected. Can you imagine what the world would do to them if they knew what they could do?'

Rebecca's hands trembled as she looked up at him, her mouth slightly open. She breathed, and he could see the desperation in her eyes as tears welled up.

'No different to how you treat them,' Jackson said as he closed his eyes, took a long, steady breath, and opened them again. 'Look, I am trying to understand. I created that cure so

I didn't lose you. But now, I have lost you and my daughters. I don't understand. I always loved you.'

Rebecca sat back in her chair and crossed her legs, her face expressionless, her hands resting calmly in her lap. The room was silent, apart from the clock ticking on the wall.

'Things are different now. I know you don't see it, but what we're doing here will change the world.'

'Why did you call me here?' Jackson asked, crossing his arms and averting his gaze.

'I understand why you destroyed the formula. You were scared and angry. But I need you to recreate the serum for me.' Rebecca said in a soft voice.

Jackson laughed as he shook his head in disbelief.

'That's what you want? I destroyed it because it fucked you up!' Jackson shouted. 'What happened to you?'

'Cancer,' Rebecca screamed, her voice heavy with sorrow. 'I was about to die. But look at me. I'm alive, Jackson! Have I changed? Yes, I am now running a multi-billion dollar company, and I have two children who can potentially destroy the planet If they wanted.'

Rebecca sat in her chair and placed her hands on the table.

'We'll replicate your work. It's inevitable. All you have done is slow us down, but you can't stop progress, Jackson,' Rebecca said.

'You can't create more of that poison!' Jackson yelled, his face reddening and his chest heaving.

Rebecca shook her head slowly and stood, her eyes hard and unyielding.

'I can do whatever I please. Think about it. You can be a part of the solution or remain the problem.'

I will promise you this. If you don't help, I will ensure you never see your girls again,' Rebecca said as she edged towards the door. Jackson remained seated for a few tense moments before finally standing, his jaw tight and veins bulging in anger. He slowly exited the office without looking away from her until the very last second.

Jackson's heart raced as he hurried down the corridor and stumbled a few times due to his haste. His mind was spinning with thoughts of escape, and he had devised a plan. When Jackson reached Andrew's office, the door was slightly ajar. He knocked lightly, and Andrew opened it with a cheerful smile, but seeing Jackson's serious expression, his face grew grave.

'What do you need?' Andrew asked as Jackson walked in and closed the door.

'I need your help. I need to get my daughters out of here tonight!'

Jackson's eyes widened in alarm, and a multitude of emotions flickered across his face - fear, despair, confusion. His breathing became shallow and raspy. Andrew stood motionless and silent. He maintained an unwavering gaze on Jackson as time seemed to stand still. Then, the slightest nod of his head broke the tension.

'I have a plan. I've got a security officer uniform so you can move about undetected and a key card that will get you into any area in the facility.'

He swiveled his chair towards his computer, a large flat-screen monitor set atop the desk. He rested his fingers on the keyboard, then tapped out a quick string of commands and watched as the screen responded to his touch.

'Rebecca is leaving for business at six this evening. That's your window of opportunity.'

Jackson loomed behind Andrew's chair, watching how he masterfully moved his hands across the keyboard. Andrew typed the commands like a professional pianist playing a well-known piece of music.

'There's more,' Andrew said. 'I think I have located the twin's location. It is well-protected and off the grid. Rebecca has it guarded, but I think I can get you in. I will get you clearance for a shift change with the guard on duty.'

Andrew glanced at Jackson with a smug smile. 'We won't have much time, but I think I can get you in and out without being detected.'

Jackson shook his head and let out a gentle laugh.

'I don't know how you do it.'

Andrew stood up and rested his hand on Jackson's shoulder. He smiled at him and nodded.

'I wish you luck, old friend. You have gone through a lot. Get your girls out of here and start a new life,' Andrew said.

Jackson nodded, held his hand to Andrew, and gave it a firm but friendly shake.

'I will. Thank you for everything,' Jackson said. 'You have been a good friend.'

'Do you have that inhibitor ready?' Andrew asked.

'Yes. I hope it works.'

Andrew passed Jackson a black two-way radio and patted him on the back reassuringly.

'I will be with you every step of the way, talking you through it. Remember that I have eyes everywhere. I've got your back.'

Jackson walked out of Andrew's office, unsure of his fate.

Jackson put on the uniform reluctantly. He pulled the fabric over his body, feeling the material's cold against his skin as he fastened each strap and button with an audible groan. He stepped away from the wardrobe and looked up and down in the mirror, taking in the navy jumpsuit, shiny black shoes, and white hat that made him look completely different.

'Jesus, I look like an asshole,' Jackson sighed.

The Kevlar armor hugged his torso tightly, and the glossy black gloves fit snugly around his wrists. He picked up the heavy helmet and placed it carefully on his head, feeling a wave of claustrophobia as his face disappeared into the darkness. Taking a deep breath, Jackson stepped out into the corridor and felt like a stranger in his skin. He crept along the hallway, his heart pounding as he hurriedly passed crowds of suited employees. His body tensed when two burly security guards emerged around the corner and began marching toward him. He lowered his gaze, sure they could sense his deceitful presence, but to his amazement, they gave him a subtle nod of recognition as they passed by, acknowledging him as an equal. Jackson cautiously scanned his surroundings, glancing back and forth to ensure he was alone. He pulled the two-way radio Andrew had given him out of his pocket and cautiously brought it to his lips.

'Andrew, can you hear me?' Jackson whispered.

'Yes, I can hear you,' Andrew replied. 'Are you ready? How does the uniform fit?'

'Yes, I'm ready. The uniform is a bit snug. I think that's more my fault than yours,' Jackson chuckled.

'The room you are looking for is on level thirty-three,' Andrew said. 'Take the elevator and let me know when you get there.'

Jackson stepped cautiously down the deserted hallway, his scuffed boots tapping a hollow rhythm. He stopped in front of the elevator, its walls made of thick glass panels and a polished steel frame that glinted when the overhead lights hit it. Jackson jabbed his finger at the call button, and when the elevator doors opened with a gentle whoosh, he felt his pulse quicken. Sweat beaded on his forehead as he stepped inside, breathing a sigh of relief as the doors closed behind him. The elevator shuddered to a stop at the thirty-third floor, and he stepped out onto the dark, silent hallway. He felt weighed down by the heavy black helmet he had to wear. His hand grasped for his radio, and he pressed the button, waiting for a response.

'Andy, I'm on the level. What now?' Jackson asked.

'I can see you on camera. Just carry on straight down the corridor. I will tell you when you are there,' Andrew instructed in a calm, steady voice.

Jackson shuffled his feet, his every movement betraying the fear that seemed to course through his veins. His leather boots squeaked and echoed off the walls of the lonely hallway, echoing in his ears with each step.

'It will be the next door on the right,' Andrew said.

Jackson stopped before the metal door, its luminescent red light pulsing rhythmically. His palms were slick with sweat, and his heart raced in his chest as he clenched the keycard tightly in his fist. He could feel the extra weight of the combat suit pulling him down but mustered every ounce of courage to swipe the card through the security pad. To his surprise, a soft green light illuminated from around the edges of the keypad, and with a metallic hum, the door slid open. Jackson stepped into the room and took a moment to take it all in. Everything he saw pointed to another science division, but this one appeared infinitely more advanced than the one he worked in. A security guard stood by a second door, his back against the wall, holding a sleek black weapon.

'Are you here to relieve me of my post?' The man asked in a

low, steady voice.

'Yes, I was given orders to replace you,' Jackson said.

The guard gave a curt nod and slowly approached the door, leaving Jackson alone. He removed his helmet with a relieved sigh, feeling suffocated by it only moments before. His gaze then shifted to the door the guard was in front of, another keypad next to it. He raised his radio to his mouth and pressed the button again.

'Andrew, I'm in. There's another door. They must be here!' Jackson said urgently.

'Good luck.'

Jackson swiped his key card, and the door slid open, revealing a large room. He stepped inside and took in the sight of a wall displaying vibrant children's drawings. His eyes misted over as he moved closer to examine the artwork. He ran his fingers lightly over each picture before choosing one to slip carefully into his pocket. On the floor lay scattered toys and equipment used for medical testing. Jackson swallowed hard and reached down to pick up a battered teddy bear. As he approached the far end of the dimly lit room, his heart racing, his eyes fixated on two small beds. One had a fragile figure lying beneath a thick patchwork quilt. He pulled back the cover and saw a petite brunette girl with a sweetly freckled face and rosy cheeks, lost in peaceful slumber. A silver collar encircled her neck, glinting in the light. As he stepped over to the other bed, beads of sweat formed on his forehead, and he fumbled for his radio.

'Andrew! We have a problem. Scarlett isn't here!'

'what? I haven't seen anything on the records about a move. Hold on, and let me check,' Andrew said.

Jackson walked back to the other girl and picked her up. Her eyes opened briefly, and they were still the beautiful blue he remembered. He let out a soft sigh and scooped her into his arms.

'Ellie, I've missed you,' Jackson murmured, kissing her forehead gently before laying her back on the bed and expertly removing the inhibitor collar from her neck. He opened his bag and gingerly pulled out an injection gun he had invented.

'I'm sorry about this kid.'

Jackson clicked the trigger, but no sound came out. A puff of air brushed against her skin as her slumber remained uninterrupted.

'Shit, Jackson! I'm so sorry. Rebecca must have made the call last minute,' Andrew said.

'Are you fucking kidding me!'

'We'll have to abort and try again,' Andrew replied.

Jackson suddenly heard the heavy door to the other room creak open, and he stiffened, his eyes wide with fear as he turned around to see the imposing silhouette of a woman. As she stepped closer into the light, Jackson recognized her as Jade, head of security. Her firm expression did not miss a beat as her gaze settled on Jackson, who stood frozen.

'No need for identification,' Jade said. 'I know you don't work for me.'

Jackson shifted his feet anxiously as she walked closer.

'What are we going to do with you?'

'Look, I know you don't know who I am,' Jackson said, 'But I have a right to be here.'

Jade smiled, her eyes wide. She slowly reached for her radio, her fingers gliding along its smooth black surface.

'Oh, I do know who you are, Mr. Carter. I'm sorry to inform you that you have no right to impersonate a security officer and enter restricted areas.'

Jade's hand slid to her shoulder holster and rested on her gun.

'Please,' Jackson begged, as his eyes darted across the room, looking for an escape.

'Send a team to level thirty-three, restricted room one,' Jade said as her gaze shifted back to Jackson.

'Hold your hands out in front of you.'

Jackson's jaw tightened, and he shook his head in defiance.

'Have it your way.'

Jackson inhaled, instantly overwhelmed by the firm, acrid smell of electricity that hung like an intangible fog. The sound of a thunderous hum followed and made his skin crawl. His eyes widened with terror as he watched Jade's body convulse uncontrollably before her legs crumpled, and she fell to the ground. Jackson quickly shot his eyes at Andrew, who stood still with a smoking stun gun in his hands, its electric current crackling through the air.

'What the fuck!' Jackson whispered.

Andrew stepped forward and pulled the electrical connector out of Jade's neck, his eyes never leaving Jackson's face. Andrew's voice was laced with urgency as he spoke.

'It was too late when I saw her heading for you. I had no choice. You need to get Ellie out of here now. It's over if they find you here. Security is on its way! They'll lock down this building so you can't exit the main entrance. You'll have to go through the parking level. Take my car,' Andrew said as he threw Jackson his keys.

'What about you?' Jackson asked as he looked at Andrew in horror.

Andrew bent down and picked up Jade's gun. Its weight seemed incongruous in his hands. He held it out to Jackson, and his voice wavered.

'You will have to shoot me, just in the arm, so they don't think I helped you. Hurry, we don't have long.'

Jackson held Ellie's tiny body against him with one arm, the other shaking as it clutched the gun tightly. His eyes were closed, and he mouthed a silent apology before pulling the trigger. The gunshot reverberated off the walls as Andrew stumbled backward, his expression shifting from shock to pain as he felt the bullet rip through his arm.

'Go!' Andrew shouted as Jackson carried Ellie from the room, 'look after your daughter. I will do what I can for Scarlett.'

Jackson's heart thundered as he saw the dozen armed guards bearing down on him. He darted into the elevator and frantically mashed the button for the parking garage, not daring to look behind him. As the elevator descended, Jackson could hear a cacophony of alarms blaring from the facility. Desperately clutching Ellie, Jackson sprinted to Andrew's car and placed her onto the seat before hopping in himself. He cranked the engine and pulled away from the parking garage, the tires squealing against the pavement. Jackson slowed his car at the entrance, memories of days gone by clouding his vision as he scanned the facility. He remembered the day he met his wife there, and a wave of nostalgia passed over him. His gaze softened as he looked at his daughter, who had fallen asleep in the seat next to him. Tears welled up in his eyes.

'I'm sorry, Scarlett,' Jackson whispered, tears burning his eyes. 'I'll find you.'

20

The truck was heavy with an unspoken burden, the air thick with tension. Ellie slumped in her seat, her shoulders shaking as she fought to keep her emotions from spilling. Jackson cleared his throat before he began, shifting his body slightly towards Ellie.

'I should have told you the truth about where you came from long ago,' Jackson sighed.

His eyes were heavy with exhaustion, his gaze weighted with sorrow that seemed to settle like a physical burden on her shoulders.

'I can't believe it,' Ellie said. A mix of shock and anger pulsed from her voice.

'You are my father? And my mother, she is alive?' Ellie asked.

Jackson pulled the car into the long gravel path that led to the farmhouse.

'I don't expect your forgiveness or to even understand why I didn't tell you sooner,' Jackson said as he shifted in his seat. 'I was scared.'

Ellie stared at him. Disappointment and hurt flooded her face, and she ran her hand through her hair, tucking it behind her ear.

'I just feel I can't trust you,' Ellie replied. 'I need some time to process everything.'

The truck slowly rumbled to rest, and Ellie emerged. Jackson stayed in the shadows, letting her lead the way. He knew there was no way to make this right; all he could do was let her go and pray that she would understand his choice one day. Jackson's heart tore apart as he watched Ellie walk away and enter the home without glancing back. He knew then that he'd never be the same again. Ellie watched the sun dip below the horizon from the window, a single tear slipping down her cheek. She was numb from shock, and all she could think about was what had happened on the bridge with her sister. With her head bowed in sorrow, she crawled onto her bed and curled up into a ball, sobbing until exhaustion finally put her to sleep.

She awoke to the sound of the door slowly creaking open. She quickly sat up and ran a hand through her tousled hair before wiping away any trace of tears from her face. Jackson stood in the doorway, his face grim and his eyes sad. He stepped forward slowly with his hands clasped behind his back as he anxiously sought Ellie's forgiveness for his actions.

'Can I get you anything, kid?'

Ellie let her feet slide to the floor and looked into Jackson's eyes. With a heavy heart, she shook her head and walked to the window that overlooked the farm.

'I know you were in an impossible situation,' Ellie said. 'I just need some time.'

With a deep breath, Jackson nodded in understanding. The shrill sound of a phone ringing filled the air, and Jackson tensed, shock registering on his face as he pulled out his phone from his pocket. His hands trembled as he looked down at the screen. He slowly pressed the answer button with his thumb, hesitation evident on his face as he lifted the phone to his ear.

'Hello?' Jackson whispered, fear laced in his voice.

The only sound that came through the receiver was a gentle inhalation and exhalation.

'Hello, Daddy,' Scarlett said.

Jackson stumbled as if he had been struck in the stomach, his eyes widening.

'Scarlett! How did you get this number?'

'Is that really the first thing you say to the daughter you abandoned?'

Jackson ran a hand over his face, pacing the room.

'I know an apology won't compensate for what has happened, but I am so sorry.'

'An apology won't fix this,' Scarlett said sternly. 'I need to speak with Ellie, please.'

Jackson stole a glance at Ellie, who was nervously nibbling on her bottom lip, and her whole body was trembling. He opened his mouth to speak, but the words died in his throat as Scarlett spoke up, her voice thick with emotion.

'There will be a time for catching up, but for now, I want to speak to my sister.'

Jackson's eyes closed as he took a deep breath.

'Please, Scarlett. I know what has happened to you, but I have to believe there is good in you,' Jackson said. 'Ellie has done nothing wrong.'

'The fact that you believe there is good in me shows how delusional you are. Put my sister on the phone, or more people she loves will die.' Scarlett said sharply over the phone.

Jackson looked at Ellie with a heavy heart and held the phone out to her.

'I'm sorry, kid, she wants to talk to you,' Jackson said as Ellie's shaking hand took the phone and held it to her ear.

'What do you want?' Ellie asked.

'Well, if it isn't my favorite sister. I enjoyed our chat this morning. I was so happy to meet you finally.'

Ellie closed her eyes and pressed her fingertips against her temples, willing the sound of Scarlett's voice to dissipate.

'What do you want from me?' Ellie pleaded, her body shaking in fear.

'Oh my dear, we are only just getting started. I wanted to invite you to a party!' Scarlett said, her cruel laughter reverberating in Ellie's ear.

'What are you talking about?'

'Well, I have arranged a little girl's night at your parent's house. Ashley can't wait to see you. Oh, and come alone. If I see Daddy or anybody else with you, I will kill your sister and her beautiful girlfriend,' Scarlett said as the phone died, leaving only fear and dread in her wake.

Ellie dropped the phone and stumbled over to her suitcase, her feet barely able to carry her weight. She yanked out a pair of black boots and desperately pushed them onto her feet. Throwing open the closet door with shaking hands, she grabbed her red winter coat and quickly zipped it up to her neck. Jackson stood in the corner of the room, unsure of what was happening but seeing the fear on Ellie's face.

'What is going on?' Jackson asked.

'I have to go,' Ellie replied, her body still shaking with fear.

'You can't go, Ellie. She is baiting you. I will come with you,' Jackson said as he stepped forward.

Ellie put a hand on his chest, halting his motion. She could feel the muscles tense under her fingertips as he fought against her. She knew it would be hard to stop him, but she couldn't risk Ashley's life.

'I'm sorry you can't come. Scarlett will kill Ashley,' Ellie said in a firm voice but held a hint of fear. 'I have to do this alone.'

Jackson knew she wasn't ready to face Scarlett alone, and he was terrified about her intentions with Ellie.

'I need your truck,' Ellie said, grabbing the keys in his hand.

Jackson reluctantly held them tight, knowing she wouldn't be stopped. He eventually released them with a sigh.

'Please be safe, Ellie,' Jackson pleaded, his brow creased with worry as she nodded and dashed out the door.

Jackson's black truck inched closer to Ellie's family home. She stared out the driver's window as a chill ran down her spine. The mansion stood shrouded in darkness, its shadows reaching out like long fingers warning her of an ominous presence. The windows of the once-warm home were now like eyes, gaping into the night, watching her approach. Ellie stepped out of the truck, bracing herself against the sting of the cold winter air on her face. As she pushed back a lock of hair, she noticed a figure standing by the door. Ellie took a deep breath and walked closer, her steps light and quick. As she grew closer, she saw a woman standing confidently with her shoulders pulled back and her chin held high. She wore a sleek red evening dress that hugged her curves, with two long thigh-high slits that showed her long legs and a plunging neckline that showcased her delicate collarbone. Her long, fiery red hair danced in the wind like burning flames. Ellie's heart sank as she recognized the woman from the bridge earlier that day. Sabrina stood before her, a wide grin stretched across her face.

'Welcome home, Ellie!' Sabrina said excitedly. 'We have been looking forward to your company. We can get the party started now.'

Ellie stepped closer to Sabrina and glared at her defiantly.

'If you've hurt my sister,' Ellie spat, but Sabrina cut her off.

'You will do what exactly?' Sabrina said, her smirk never slipping. She waved a shiny silver collar in front of Ellie's face as Ellie stepped back in defiance.

'This is your party favor. Turn around and let me put it on,' Sabrina said, her voice heavy with implication. 'It's unfortunate, but Scarlett insists that you wear it.'

Ellie stiffened and reluctantly turned away, her anger like fire in her veins. She felt Sabrina's warm breath on the back of her neck as she brushed Ellie's hair aside to secure the collar over her neck, closing it with an audible click. A shudder ran through Ellie at the sensation of Sabrina's fingertips trailing across her skin.

'All done,' Sabrina whispered, taking Ellie's hand and leading her into the house.

Ellie stepped into the foyer, and her eyes immediately darted to the family portraits on the wall. Each picture was a knife twisting deep in her gut, as she realized with a sickening horror that someone had meticulously excised every image of her from within their frames, leaving only gaping black voids where her face should have been. Ellie entered the dining room, her heart pounding as a shiver crawled up her spine. The eerily familiar whistling of the nursery rhyme she heard on the bridge filled the room, echoing and reverberating off the walls until it felt like it was all around her, suffocating and paralyzing her with fear. The sound grew louder as the light from the dozens of candles flickered across the room, casting shadows on the grand table in its center. Ellie noticed the windows overlooking the backyard pool, and her gaze came to rest on her sister, Ashley. She was frozen solid in her chair, and terror was etched across her face as she stared across the table at her girlfriend, Shreya. Ellie looked at Shreya, who sat rigidly in her chair, her eyes wide with fear. Scarlett perched atop the table like an ominous shadow, her white vest and black leather trousers stark against her pallid skin. Every moment felt like an eternity to Ellie as dread filled her veins like poison. Scarlett's eyes lit up as she spotted Ellie walking into the room, and the whistling stopped. She hurriedly waved her over, her mouth breaking into a wide smile. Sabrina grabbed Ellie's arm and guided her to the chair in front of Scarlett, pushing her down onto it with an unexpected force. Fear stiffened Ashley's already pale face, radiating a chill from her wide eyes.

'Why are you doing this?' Ellie asked, her voice trembling.

Scarlett's dark laughter echoed off the walls as Sabrina crept behind her. Scarlett's heart stuttered in her chest as Sabrina's fingertips grazed along the exposed skin of her arm, sending a shiver down her spine. Sabrina's arms wrapped around Scarlett from behind, clasping tightly like shackles around her waist. She felt Sabrina's breath on her neck before she rested her chin on Scarlett's shoulder, claiming her with a possessive intensity that made Scarlett's head spin.

'I told you, I want to see you suffer, to feel pain. But as I found out, physical pain is too easy. It's the emotional stuff that will haunt you - the suffering that will eat away at your soul until there's nothing left.'

Ellie's vision blurred as tears filled her eyes; she glanced at Ashley and blinked them away.

'I'm so sorry, Ash.'

Scarlett gestured towards Ashley and nodded in encouragement.

'Go ahead, Ellie, tell her why you are sorry.'

'I'm sorry I wasn't a better sister. I don't know why she is doing this,' Ellie said as her lip quivered.

Scarlett's brow furrowed as she studied Ellie with intense concentration.

'I'm struggling to decide,' Scarlett said, her voice tinged with sorrow. 'Are you a better version of me or just another one of life's letdowns, like I was? Mother had such grand dreams for you, but I simply cannot envision it.'

With a smile, Scarlett stopped and gazed at Sabrina.

'Where are my manners? Sabrina, could you get our guest a drink?'

Sabrina treaded lightly to the Jones's cupboard and ran her finger along their carefully preserved wines and spirits. She grabbed a bottle of white wine and a crystal glass, catching Ellie's eye. Sabrina walked beside Ellie, delicately placing the glass before her and pouring the golden liquid inside. She began to swirl it under Ellie's nose, sending a tantalizing aroma of citrus and oak into the air as she grinned slyly. Ellie felt her body grow heavy with temptation as she inhaled the sweet fragrance.

'Come on, drink up!' Scarlett said.

Ellie slowly opened her eyes, and with a snarl, she whipped the glass of wine out of Sabrina's hand, and it shattered onto the floor. Ellie's fury manifested into action as she slammed her fists onto the table and jumped to her feet, her face burning with rage.

'What do you want from me? Yes, I had it all, but that doesn't mean I had it easy. Yes, I have a loving family and certain privileges you could never dream of—but it's not like I asked for it, so don't you dare put this on me!'

Scarlett's eyes narrowed as she stalked around the table and stopped with her face mere inches from Ellie's. She could feel the heat coming off Ellie's body, but the rage that consumed her was even more intense.

'Yes, you had it all, and what did you do with it? You threw it away! How could all of this not be enough for you? You are just a drunk pathetic failure and a piece of shit!' Scarlett spat out the words before whirling around and striding back to her seat. She leaped onto the table and glared at Ellie with evil eyes.

'Where were we? Oh yes, I almost forgot about your surprise,' Scarlett said.

Sabrina placed her hands on Ellie's shoulders, pushing her back ever-so-slightly into the chair. Her face, stern and determined, was just inches away from Ellie's own. Sabrina's gaze locked in with Ellie's, and Scarlett's eyes glinted as her fingers entwined together, and she leaned in closer.

'I have a party game for you. It's a simple game of choice,' Scarlett said.

'What are you talking about?' Ellie asked.

'You get to be a hero and save a life. But you can only choose one, Ashley or Shreya,' Ellie's eyes widened as the gravity of the situation hit her. Scarlett's lips curved up in a smile as if she knew what weight this decision held.

Ashley and Shreya's faces drained of color, their eyes filled with terror. Tears streamed down their faces as they remained unable to move, their breaths coming out in short, ragged bursts.

'What? No!' Ellie said, desperation strangling her voice.

'Well, the rules are you have to choose one, or they both die, and you get to watch,' Scarlett said.

Sabrina walked over to Ashley and sat on her lap, gently tracing her finger along Ashley's cheek.

'This one is cute. It would be a shame to hurt her.'

Sabrina slowly got up from her seat, her heels clicking against the hardwood floor with each step as she walked around the table. She approached Shreya and sat down on her lap, a mischievous grin spreading across her face.

'This one looks feisty. I don't think I could make this choice.'

Ellie shot Scarlett a glare, her eyes full of contempt.

'What the fuck is wrong with you?' Ellie spat. 'No wonder you were locked up, you psycho. Just let them go, and we can end this. You can kill me if you want. Just leave them out of it.'

'As I told you, I will kill you when I choose to,' Scarlett said as she shook her head. 'Choose!'

Ellie jumped at the demand as Ashley sat motionless, sobbing as she stared at Shreya.

Ellie clasped her shaking hands together in one last desperate plea.

'Please.'

Scarlett's eyes narrowed, and her lips pursed as Sabrina moved closer to Ellie, pressing her bony chin into the soft hollow of her neck. She began counting slowly down.

'10...9...8...7...6...5...4.'

Ellie's eyes widened, willing this madness to stop, but Scarlett's voice didn't waver.

'3...2...1.'

'Ashley! I choose Ashley to live!' Ellie screamed.

Scarlett's mouth curved into a delighted smile as Sabrina stepped forward and kissed Ellie's flushed cheek softly.

'Well done,' Sabrina said as she approached Ashley, resting her hands on her shoulders.

'Did you hear that, sweetheart? Your sister chose you to live,' Scarlett said. 'Now, I'm not a monster. I'll let you say goodbye,' Scarlett said.

Suddenly, Ashley felt a release from Scarlett's invisible hold, and she leaned forward with determination, her breath coming in ragged gasps as the realization of what was occurring dawned on her.

'Please don't kill her. Take me instead. I can't lose her! Please!'

'I'm sorry, your sister has made her choice,' Scarlett said, her voice devoid of emotion.

Ellie looked at Ashley compassionately, her eyes brimming with sorrow.

'I'm so sorry,' Ellie whispered, feeling helpless against the cruelty of fate.

'Please!' Ashley pleaded, though her words went unheard.

Scarlett leaned in close to Shreya, her eyes glinting as she whispered something in her ear. Suddenly, Shreya's face contorted in fear as she struggled to breathe, gasping for air as if she had forgotten how. Ashley tried to stand but was pushed back into her chair by Sabrina's iron grip. Tears streamed down Ashley's face as she watched helplessly as Shreya's complexion began to turn red.

Ashley's eyes widened as she locked eyes with Ellie, silently pleading for help.

Ellie roared, launching herself from her chair and plowing straight into Sabrina. With a single vicious swing of Ellie's fist, Sabrina flew onto the ground like a discarded rag doll, a thin trickle of blood running down her chin.

'That was a mistake,' Scarlett said.

Ellie ripped frantically at the collar around her neck, but it wouldn't open. Shreya's eyes did not flutter this time. They were open wide in shock as the color drained from her skin like an ebb tide.

'I love you, Shreya!' Ashley said as Scarlett released Shreya, and her body slumped onto the cold wooden table.

Scarlett's eyes were ablaze with a wild fury, and she pressed her fingers into Ellie's cheeks, turning her head from side to side as if examining a work of art.

'You don't get it, do you? I am in control now. I will break you down until you are nothing. Don't squander your one moment of peace tonight. Comfort your sister. You will be hearing from me soon.'

Scarlett's gaze softened when she saw Sabrina lying dazed on the floor. She gently helped her up and wiped away the blood dripping from her lip.

'Are you alright?' Scarlett asked.

Sabrina nodded and touched Scarlett's cheek with her fingertips before kissing her lightly. Hand in hand, they made their way slowly toward the door. Ashley scrambled towards Shreya and held her limp body tightly in her arms, stroking her hair gently.

'I'm sorry, Ash,' Ellie whispered.

'Please go. I don't know what is happening, but Shreya had nothing to do with it.'

Ellie moved slowly towards Ashley, arms outstretched. Her eyes filled with tears as she reached for her sister.

'Go!'

Ellie felt a lump rise in her throat as she looked at Ashley, cradling her lover's lifeless body, Shreya. Tears welled up in

Ellie's eyes, and she had to turn away from the heartbreaking sight. She stumbled out of the room, her heart heavy with grief and regret. Ellie could hear Ashley's anguished cries echoing in the hallway as the door closed behind her.

21

Jackson trudged across the creaky wooden porch, his heavy boots battering against the timber with each step. He reached into his pocket with a shaking hand, retrieving a crumpled pack of cigarettes. The flame of his lighter illuminated the darkness as he lit the tip, taking in a deep breath before it flickered away. His eyes scanned between the driveway and horizon for any sign of his truck. A faint glimmer of headlights shone through the night sky, indicating its approach. Jackson leaped off the porch in anticipation, sprinting towards the gravel path. Ellie hesitantly stepped out of the truck, feet rooted to the ground by fear and apprehension. The tension between them was palpable as they met eyes. Jackson seemingly begged for answers while Ellie kept silent, her gaze distant and voice barely audible. With a desperate sigh, she trudged across the property, gravel crunching beneath her feet. She shuffled past him; her head hung low with unimaginable grief. Jackson hastened towards her with a dread that filled the air, his eyes wide with desperation. She stumbled onward, her gaze hollow and distant. Her mind was numb, and she didn't notice him behind her until he leaped forward and grasped her arm. With a punishing clutch, he tugged her to a stop and compelled her to look back. She clenched her fists tight and yanked away in revolt, her stance tense. He stepped backward in awe of her anger.

'She killed Shreya! I watched it happen right in front of me,' Ellie screamed.

Jackson's face softened as he looked upon her. Tears streamed down her cheeks as her aimless eyes wandered here and there. He wanted to stretch out and take her into his arms, but all he could do was stand still in anguish, desperately wishing he could somehow rid her of the pain and hurt she felt at that moment.

'I can't do this anymore. I want everything to be over,' Ellie mumbled, tears tumbling down her cheeks.

Jackson moved haltingly, bowing at the waist until their eyes were even.

'No, Ellie,' Jackson said, his voice soft and reassuring. 'You can't give up.'

Jackson's gaze drifted to the collar around her neck, and he reached out to touch it.

'What is this?'

Ellie stepped back, brushing off his hand.

'They made me wear it,' Ellie whispered. 'It stops my curse.'

Jackson moved closer, scrutinizing it with his eyes.

'Oh my God,' Jackson said in awe. 'They have built a new inhibitor. I have never seen anything like this!'

'Maybe we should leave it on,' Ellie said.

'Look, I know how you are feeling. But we need your abilities to stop Scarlett or more people will get hurt,' Jackson said. 'Come on, let's go inside and get this thing off.'

Ellie followed Jackson into the kitchen, her feet dragging as she slumped into one of the wooden chairs. She sank her head into her hands and tried to hold back tears while Jackson moved behind her. He traced his fingers along the collar until he found the clasp, then opened a drawer and pulled out a small, sleek device. Holding it up to the collar, he twisted it slightly until it began to hum, louder and more high-pitched with each click. The sound reverberated through the room like a living thing, filling Ellie's ears and making her shiver.

'What are you doing?' Ellie asked.

'This may be more advanced than what I worked on, but the principle is the same. This thing looks for a locking mechanism and should release it.'

Moments later, a click echoed in Ellie's ear, and the collar fell into Jackson's hands.

'Got it,' Jackson said with a smile.

'Great,' Ellie said as she stood and headed for the stairs.

'Where are you going?'

'I'm gonna go to bed,' Ellie replied as she walked up the stairs, her boots echoing off the wooden steps.

Jackson sat at the table, mesmerized by the intricate looping lines of silver engraved on the metal casing of the collar in his hands. His fingertips delicately traced the curves of the design, feeling the cold smoothness against his skin.

Ellie shuffled into her bedroom, each step feeling like the world's weight was on her shoulders. She released a deep and exhausted sigh as she collapsed onto the corner of the bed. She leaned down and undid the laces of her heavy boots, grunting as she eased them off her feet. The air was cool on her skin, and she sighed in relief. Ellie slipped out of her jeans and tossed them into a pile on the floor. She flopped back onto the mattress and pulled the blankets around her body like armor. Every ounce of fatigue evaporated as Ellie nestled in, shutting her eyes tightly and wishing for the outside world to dissolve.

Ellie was jolted awake by the cacophony of animal noises outside her window. Peeling open her eyes, she squinted against the bright yellow rays of sunlight that beamed through her bedroom curtains. In shock, she glanced at the alarm clock and realized it had passed noon. With a heavy sigh, Ellie slowly dragged herself out of bed, her bare legs instantly attacked by the cold air, which made her whole body shiver. She stepped cautiously across the creaking floorboards, feeling each footfall reverberating through her body. She opened her suitcase and feverishly rummaged until her fingers brushed the soft material of her black leggings. With a deep breath, she pulled them on and glanced in the mirror at her reflection. She felt a wave of anxiety wash over her as she descended the stairs to the kitchen. Jackson was outside, working hard to feed the animals. The sunlight streamed in from the windows and glinted off Jackson's phone on the counter. Ellie hesitated, her hand trembling as she reached for the device. Her gaze shifted to the rolling hills beyond, and a chill ran down her spine. Tears welled up in her eyes as she dialed Ashley's number, hoping she was okay. But after many unanswered rings, grief filled her heart as the call disconnected. She wanted to scream or cry but remained motionless. With trembling hands, she dialed another number.

Later that evening, Ellie sat on the porch, watching the sun slowly dip beneath the horizon. She wore a black floral dress, its hemline brushing against her knees, and black boots glinted in the twilight. Jackson walked up to her, a myriad of emotions on his face. He leaned against the railings and cleared his throat.

'You haven't moved all day,' Jackson said.

The air was silent until Ellie stirred. Barely lifting her chin from her chest, she peered up with glassy eyes devoid of emotion. Her skin was ashen, unmoving like a still lake in the early hours of winter.

'You gonna do any training today?' Jackson asked, his voice laced with trepidation.

'No,' Ellie snapped, her voice heavy with disdain.

Jackson flicked his gaze to the horizon as the roaring sound of an approaching vehicle echoed through the air. He held his breath as he waited for the car to approach, and finally, a green sedan appeared along the path.

'Get inside, Ellie!' Jackson said. Ellie watched as the car pulled up alongside her and came to a stop. The door creaked open, and Jasper stepped out. The light glinted off his black leather jacket, which fit snugly around his slim frame. His denim trousers were cut to perfection, showing off his physique. Jackson eyed Jasper suspiciously as he approached them. In a split-second, Jackson stood protectively between Ellie and Jasper.

'Who are you?' Jackson asked, his voice like thunder rumbling through the night air.

Jasper smiled warmly, stepping forward and extending his hand toward Jackson in greeting.

'I'm Jasper. I'm Ellie's friend. You must be her uncle?'

Jackson's expression turned to worry as he tried to take Ellie's hand and keep her with him, but she pulled away.

'Ellie, please! This is dangerous,' Jackson pleaded.

Ellie's glare melted away as she locked eyes with Jasper.

'Please wait for me in the car. I won't be long,' Ellie said.

Jasper nodded before turning and walking to his car.

Ellie straightened her posture immediately, and a new resolve flowed through her. Her mouth thinned into a line as she stepped closer to Jackson.

'I know you think you're shielding me from something, but your control over me ends now. You've been telling me what to do for days, and enough is enough.'

Jackson's face hardened, and his body tensed. Ellie's words felt like a sharp blade slicing through his heart, yet he tried to hide the pain. He clenched his fists until his knuckles turned white, then willed himself to unclench them. Taking a deep breath, he attempted one last plea in a strained voice.

'It's not safe out there; Scarlett could find you. I'm only trying to protect both of you.'

Rage boiled in Ellie's veins as she pushed Jackson back with a strength that surprised even him.

'Fuck you, Jackson! You can't keep me safe. I'm going out, and tonight, I'll try to be like any other normal girl.'

Jackson watched in shock as she spun around and marched toward the car, her head held high with purpose. He felt his frustration flare up at her defiance, but he didn't move to stop her.

'Fine, go out and have fun. Get your friend killed, and then maybe you can go out for a drink afterward. You can't be helped, Ellie,' Jackson screamed.

Ellie's chest heaved with each raspy breath, and her knuckles turned white from the force of her clenched fists. With a sudden flurry of motion, she spun around, her eyes blazing with an undying fury that made even Jackson take a step back. Her arm jutted out from her body, and an invisible force sent Jackson hurtling through the air and crashing through a wooden fence. Ellie stared at him fiercely for a moment, daring him to move again before turning on her heel and striding towards Jasper's car, leaving Jackson sprawled in the dirt behind her. Jasper's car roared away and disappeared into a plume of dust. Suddenly, Jackson's phone buzzed in his pocket, and he pulled it out, recognizing Andrew's number.

'Jackson, I'm sorry to call, but something has happened,' Andrew whispered. 'It's Scarlett. She's on her way back here to kill Rebecca. You need to do something.'

Jackson felt his stomach drop, and a chill ran down his spine. He just watched Ellie walk away, and now Rebecca's life was in danger. His jaw clenched with determination, and everything faded as he focused on saving Rebecca's life.

'I will get a flight out straight away,' Jackson said before abruptly hanging up the phone.

Andrew hung by his wrists from the ceiling, his body trembling from exhaustion. Painful welts covered his bare torso, his skin sliced and slicked by his blood.

Andrew felt like he were a marionette, controlled by the strings of Jade's will. She snatched the phone from his ear and pocketed it with a triumphant smirk. He wanted to scream but was mute; she had stripped him of all power. He hung his head in shame, unable to meet her gaze.

'Well done,' Jade said, her voice dripping with mock admiration. 'It looks like your children will survive another day.'

Andrew slowly raised his gaze to meet Jade's. His breaths were shallow and ragged, like a broken engine struggling for air. As their eyes locked, she lightly traced her finger along the ridge of his chin, lifting it slightly so they were fully connected.

'What are you going to do with him?'

'That is not your concern,' Jade said with a cruel smile before storming out of the room without another word.

22

Ellie stole a glance at Jasper, and as their eyes met, intense feelings of guilt swept over her. She could sense his confusion but could not bring herself to tell him what had happened since they last saw each other in the coffee shop. Her heart ached to reach out to him, yet something inside kept her from doing so.

'I'm so sorry about your Mum's shop,' Ellie whispered. 'Is everything okay?'

Jasper turned to her with a worried gaze.

'The shop will be fine; the insurance will cover it,' Jasper said. 'I was worried sick about you, Ellie! I had to hear from Ashley that you were staying with your uncle. Why didn't you call me sooner?'

As Jasper rounded the corner, Ellie held her breath, listening to the faint strains of laughter and music in the distance. His eyes widened as light spilled from the funfair, casting a riot of hues across the night sky that lit the entire street in kaleidoscopic patterns. Ellie laid her hand on his shoulder, feeling an icy ache of regret seep through her veins.

'I'm sorry, Jasper. I didn't tell you everything because I'm not sure I believe it myself.'

Jasper looked at Ellie skeptically.

'Are you sure you want to be here? We could go somewhere else if you'd rather,' Jasper said.

Ellie glanced around the carnival grounds as they pulled into the parking area. The air was thick with the aromas of popcorn and cotton candy, and the lights dazzled in their brilliance against the night sky. Music drifted in from far away rides, and a fresh wind blew past them through the window. Taking a deep breath, Ellie turned back to meet Jasper's gaze, her eyes twinkling in the soft light.

'No, I want to be here with you.'

Ellie's heart raced as she glanced at Jasper from beneath her long, thick eyelashes. She looked into his eyes and felt the familiar warmth of adrenaline wash over her. Her skin tingled with excitement, but a wave of guilt threatened to pull her away from the moment. Jasper put the car into park and turned towards Ellie with eyes full of anticipation.

'We're here! I'm so happy you wanted to come with me!' Jasper said.

Ellie gave his arm a gentle squeeze and looked into his eyes.

'Jasper,' Ellie whispered. 'You're an amazing guy. The way I feel about you never changed.'

A small smile tugged at the corner of her lips as she leaned against the worn leather seat. They both stepped out into the frigid winter night, and Ellie shivered as her hair blew around her in a wild frenzy. Tugging at the hem of her dress, she regretted her bold choice of such a short skirt on this bitter night.

'Oh, why did I not choose a longer dress!' Ellie muttered

between chattering teeth.

They marched steadily towards the park entrance, and screams of joy shook the ground beneath their feet. As they drew closer, a brilliant array of neon lights and a cacophony of noises erupted into life around them. The purple and yellow hues from the neon glinted on their faces as they stepped forward, entranced by the sheer energy of the place. Ellie and Jasper stepped through the carnival gates, captivated by a dazzling skyline. Multi-colored lights blinked in an erratic rhythm, accompanied by pulsing music from thrilling rides like rollercoasters, Ferris wheels, and merry-go-rounds. The cloyingly sweet smell of candy floss wafted invitingly over them as they stood awe-struck. Jasper's gaze flared with worry as he noticed Ellie's body trembling. He swiftly removed his coat and draped it around her shoulders. His strong hands enveloped hers, and he gave her fingers a tender yet resolute squeeze, conveying a comforting assurance. Ellie slowly tilted her gaze towards Jasper, her lips twitching before they split into a warm yet timid smile. She felt hope blossom inside her heart for the first time in weeks.

'Thank you. I should have brought a coat, but I just wanted to get out of there.'

Jasper grinned, tugging Ellie closer as he plunged into the crowd of merrymakers. Raucous laughter and a cacophony of joyous conversations penetrated the air. Excitement bubbled within Ellie as they meandered down the path, admiring each stall. Ellie's heart soared as she looked upon the sizeable wooden booth housing a barrel of water with an array of plastic ducks bobbing inside. The carnival lights illuminated the bright colors of pink, yellow, and orange ducks while the laughter of game-goers blended harmoniously with the atmosphere. A slight smile curved across her lips as she recalled all the countless times she had cherished this very game as a child, the joyous noise of carnival games and rides surrounding them.

'I have always loved this stupid game,' Ellie murmured.

Jasper looked on as Ellie's eyes lit up at the sight of the stall. Vivid memories of her parents bringing her and Ashley to these events when they were kids came flooding back, coaxing a broad smile across his face. Jasper reached into his pocket and pulled out his wallet, handing the money over to the large woman with bright pink cheeks who wore an apron that looked two sizes too small.

'Well, let's go,' Jasper said cheerily, gesturing towards the game.

'There you go, honey! Go hook a duck!' The lady said joyfully, her eyes crinkling in the corners and her rosy cheeks dimpling with merriment.

Jasper turned to Ellie and placed the bamboo stick in her hands.

'Ready?'

'Can you help?' Ellie asked playfully.

Jasper stepped behind her, their fingers entwining around the stick. His index finger grazed over the back of her hand, sending a warmth radiating through her body. The sound of his laugh, the warmth of his embrace, the way he looked at her during a shared moment of joy, all these sensations flooded back instantly. Her body ached for the love they had once shared, and she was overwhelmed with emotion. Suddenly, the plastic duck at the end of their line rose from the pool, and the woman unhooked it and smiled at the number underneath.

'That's number ten, anything from the bottom row!' The woman said, gesturing to a line of stuffed animals and cheap trinkets.

Ellie looked around, her eyes settling on a small pink bear.

'I want that one!' Ellie said eagerly, holding her hands and cradling it against her chest when the woman handed it to her.

'Thank you. I know it's stupid, and it doesn't matter what duck you get, but I love it,' Ellie said, looking up at Jasper.

His lips curled into a warm smile as he laced his fingers through hers, and they walked further into the fair. The wind ruffled Ellie's hair, and the light from the nearby Ferris wheel illuminated Jasper's face.

'So what was all that about with your uncle?'

The smile on Ellie's face dwindled as she glanced over at Jasper.

'He has just been overprotective since the attack.'

Ellie desperately wanted to tell him all she had been through, but the words caught in her throat when she looked into his eyes. She couldn't understand it herself, let alone try to explain it to someone else.

'How are your parents doing?' Jasper asked.

Ellie bit her lip and looked away, her gaze drifting to the bright stall beside them. She shrugged, her hands fidgeting with the hem of her skirt.

'I'm going to try and visit them soon. But really, I want to be in the moment with you tonight, if that's okay.'

'Of course.'

Jasper cautiously nodded. His eyes widened as he looked up at the giant Ferris wheel, and his face lit up excitedly.

'Shall we?'

As Ellie peered into the sky, she felt her stomach drop. But then she looked into Jasper's eyes, bright with joy and excitement, and something inside her stirred. Taking a deep breath, she forced herself to move forward.

'Well, I'm not great with heights, but what the hell.'

'I will protect you,' Jasper said.

They stepped inside the metal box of the Ferris wheel, and Ellie suppressed a shudder as she noticed its peeling red paint and the rust creeping through its joints. The wooden seat was hard and uninviting, and the metal bar over their legs seemed flimsy and inadequate for safety. Suddenly, the wheel began moving slowly at first, rocking back and forth as Ellie gripped Jasper's arm. Sensing her fear, he scooted closer and slid his arm around her shoulders.

'Is this okay?' Jasper asked.

'Of course it is.'

The Ferris wheel rose steadily, the gentle whir of machinery taking them higher and higher with each rotation. Ellie felt excited as they reached the top, and their carriage swayed gently in the cool night air. She gazed at the glittering array of stalls and rides below them, feeling as if she'd left all earthly worries behind. Beads of sweat formed on her forehead as the seat rocked beneath her, sending flutters through her stomach.

'What was that?' Ellie asked nervously.

'Relax,' Jasper said, his gaze flitting to the other passengers queuing up the stairs below. 'They're just letting more people onto the ride.'

Ellie felt her cheeks flush, embarrassed that she had assumed the worst.

'Oh. I'm sorry.'

Jasper looked around the breathtaking horizon, and then his gaze fell upon Ellie, snuggled up against him ever so tenderly. His heart swelled with joy as he wondered how lucky he was to have someone so special to share this moment with.

'I can't believe I'm here with you. I have missed you so much, Ellie. I wish you had just let me in before you left. You didn't need to deal with everything alone. You may not see it, but I know how strong you are, and I'm proud of you.'

Ellie pulled away slowly, her gaze meeting the ground as if it held some secret answer she sought.

'Jasper,' Ellie sighed softly, 'you shouldn't be proud of me. My life has been nothing but a train wreck since I succumbed to addiction. It cost me everything, the people I love and care for the most.'

Jasper delicately grazed his thumbs over her cheeks and gazed soulfully into her eyes, exuding a profound gentleness. He tenderly trailed his fingertips through her hair, pushing the locks away from her visage with an affectionate caress.

'Well, I think you are kinda perfect,' Jasper whispered.

Ellie tipped her head back and released a soft giggle, the corners of her lips tugging into a playful smirk.

'Then I think you are clinically insane!' Ellie said, still smiling. 'But thank you.'

Ellie closed her eyes, feeling the warmth of Jasper's breath on her lips as her heart pounded in her chest. Her hands trembled with anticipation as he slowly inched closer until their lips were just a whisper apart.

'Your eyes have never looked more beautiful,' Jasper said.

Ellie's lips parted slightly, and her eyes widened as Jasper leaned toward her. His thumb brushed her cheek softly as his lips met hers, sending a spark of electricity through her body. He pulled away slightly, caressing her face as he looked into her eyes. A shudder of excitement ran through Ellie as she pulled him back to her, her muscles tightening around his body as she kissed him passionately. She grabbed his shoulder with one hand and ran the other up his back, feeling the warmth of his skin beneath her fingertips. Jasper's fingers ran down Ellie's neck, creating a trail of fire that sent shivers up her spine before they wove through the strands of her hair. His every touch left her aching for more as he reawakened a forgotten passion between them that seemed to have been lost in time. The car on the Ferris wheel gave a gut-wrenching lurch, throwing Jasper and Ellie out of their momentary bliss. Their eyes met, locked together in an unyielding gaze. A gentle blush washed over Ellie's cheeks as her hand rose to tuck away strands of hair behind her ears nervously. The Ferris wheel came to a jerky stop at the bottom, and they stepped out, still clasping hands. As they looked into each other's eyes, their faces lit up with joy as they made their way through the crowd, blending in seamlessly.

Jasper stopped in his tracks, his eyes widening with astonishment. His gaze was captivated by the colossal red-and-white striped tent that soared above them, a golden sign dangling from its peak that glittered: House of Mirrors.

'Shall we?' Jasper asked as his face filled with excitement.

Without delay, they crossed the threshold into the world beyond the looking glass. A kaleidoscope of beauty greeted them, with each mirror shifting and changing its size and shape as they ventured further into the hall of wonders. Jasper strode up behind Ellie, his hands confidently encircling her slight frame. Their bodies were distorted by the curvature of the mirror, appearing almost comically small. He stood behind her, close enough that she could feel the heat of his body through her clothes. His fingertips glided over her bare skin as he trailed light kisses from her neck to her shoulder. Ellie and Jasper tentatively approached the full-length mirror, not knowing what to expect. When they saw their reflections, they were unable to contain their laughter. Their images had been distorted beyond belief, making them look like grotesque caricatures of themselves. They moved along the walls, passing numerous mirrors, each reflection more surreal than the last. Finally, they stopped in front of a door with an ominous sign that warned against entering.

'This looks scary!' Ellie said as she tightened her grip on Jasper's hand.

They pushed the door open cautiously and were consumed by the darkness. Everywhere they looked, a dance of light shifted across the walls, from one mirror to another. The maze seemed to lead somewhere – perhaps out of this confusion – but every corner felt like a dead end. Flickers of reflection spun around them until it felt as if they were ceaselessly looping in circles with no way out. Ellie's eyes darted across the room, taking in the eerie display of mirrors. Everywhere she looked, a reflection of herself stared back with hollow eyes. The feeling of being watched crawled up her spine like fingers caressing her skin. A dull panic began to spread as Ellie's mind raced for any sight of Jasper within the vast area. She launched into a desperate search among the glittering glass, hoping against hope that he might be waiting in one of its distorted reflections. Ellie recoiled in horror as she looked at her reflection in the mirror, but it wasn't her face gazing back at her. It was the visage of her sister Scarlett, distorted into a menacing scowl filled with rage and hatred. Her eyes locked with the reflection as if in an unspoken challenge until Ellie finally broke away, unable to bear the sight any longer. She shook her head, trying to free herself from this haunting image. The room felt too quiet, and Ellie wondered if she was losing her mind. She clamped her eyes shut, her heart pounding in her ears. As Ellie peered around the corner, all she could see was her sister Ashley embracing Shreya's lifeless body while silent tears streamed down her face. Her heart racing and breathing shallow, Ellie scanned the room as if looking for a way out. Everywhere she looked, Scarlett stared back at her. Then her gaze fell upon Jasper, lying there motionless with his eyes wide open and the floor beneath him soaked in crimson red. Ellie froze in agony as an anguished cry rippled from her lips. Her legs buckled beneath her weight, and she crumpled to the ground, squeezing her eyes shut with all her strength. Ellie could barely believe it when she felt Jasper's arms around her. She was flooded with relief and happiness; it was like coming home. But just as quickly, Ellie was overcome with terror. She remembered all too vividly the corner where she had seen him lifelessly sprawled out moments before. Although his embrace felt so comforting, she couldn't help but feel a chill as if he would be snatched away from her any second.

'You're alive?' Ellie whispered, struggling to believe it was true. Jasper looked into Ellie's eyes with confusion and distress.

'What happened? I was right behind you, and suddenly you were gone. I heard you screaming.'

Jasper reached out and grabbed her hands, pulling her into an embrace. As she hugged him close, her mind raced with Jackson's warning that Jasper would be in danger if he stayed with her. Ellie felt the tears pressing against her eyelids, threatening to fall at any second. She wanted desperately to keep her arms around Jasper's neck and stay a little longer, but she knew it was time for her to go. His forehead creased with worry as he noticed the tears spilling from her eyes. Even in the dark, he could see her expression had turned to sorrow. He tried to say something, anything, that might make the pain go away, but his words seemed stuck in his throat as Ellie slowly stood up and stepped back, shaking her head slightly.

'I shouldn't have come here. I'm sorry,' Ellie said, refusing to meet his gaze.

'What do you mean? Did I do something wrong?'

A chill ran down Jasper's spine as Ellie stepped closer, her gaze pleading silently. She reached up and cupped Jasper's face in both hands, a warm pressure against his skin.

'No, I can't explain right now, but you are not safe around me.'

As Ellie spoke, a dull ache throbbed in her chest. Jasper stared at her, his eyes wide with confusion and fear.

'Please, you're not making sense,' Jasper whispered.

Ellie's eyes brimmed with tears, and her bottom lip quivered as she turned away. The sound of her stifled sobs lingered in the air even after she fled the room. Jasper stood in shock for a few moments before surveying the area, noticing Ellie's pink teddy bear lying near his feet. He crouched down, brushing off its fur before picking it up. Taking one last look around, he clenched the small toy in his fist before pushing open the door and leaving.

23

Ellie slowly made her way down the sidewalk, her shoulders slumped and head down as cold rain mixed with tears on her face. She didn't look up to see the large man barreling towards her until it was too late. He plowed into her shoulder like a bull, sending her staggering sideways before she could regain her footing.

'Watch where you're going!' The man shouted.

She remained silent, and her head bowed in defeat. The aching grief in her chest weighed her steps, making every inch forward seem like trudging through molasses. She walked along the line of shops, her movements labored, only coming to a stop when she reached an off-license. In the window, she could see bottles of every shape and size. Glittering bottles of ruby red wine, crisp whites, and vibrant liqueurs lined the shelves like a rainbow made of glass. She stood motionless, her eyes glazed over. Her mind raced with a jumble of emotions, and she desperately tried to fight the irresistible urge that kept pulling her towards it. She felt overpowered by the force, but her body stayed rooted to the spot. She took a moment to reflect on everything she had been through to get where she was today, yet the same struggles that had plagued her for years still lingered. As she surveyed her dismal surroundings, the allure of a stiff drink became increasingly more appealing than it had just moments before. Ellie felt the familiar tug in her chest, knowing that having a drink was not the solution to her problems. Yet she still pushed open the shop door as though it were calling to her like a siren's song. The little bell jingling above her head made her jump back in surprise, and for a moment, she hesitated. But it wasn't enough to stop her as she entered the lion's den. Ellie looked around the store and saw a tall man wearing wire-rimmed glasses and sporting an impressively waxed handlebar mustache behind the counter. Their eyes met momentarily, and he gave her a warm, friendly smile. Ellie kept her gaze fixed on the tiled floor, desperately trying to avoid the intense longing for alcohol gnawing away at her. She could almost feel the chill of the ice cubes against her lips and taste the warmth of the alcohol as it went down her throat. Her longing was so intense that she felt helpless to deny it. She slowly floated across the floor, her movements haunted by the memories of what once was. She stretched out her trembling hand and cautiously took a bottle of whisky from the shelf as if it were a precious rosebud on the edge of wilting. As she stared longingly at the bottle in her hands, her heart raced with anticipation as she debated the consequences of taking that first sip. She had worked hard to stay sober for so many months, yet she longed for a drink to bring her temporary comfort. Her head screamed at her not to give in while her body ached for relief. Tears filled her eyes as guilt and temptation overwhelmed her, and she found herself unable to move away from the bottle's cold embrace. The man behind the counter looked at Ellie with immense sympathy and concern. He could tell by the deep lines creasing her forehead that she had been crying for hours, and the bags under her eyes were a dark purple compared to her pale skin. Her lips quivered as she tried to form words, and he could see tiny traces of tears still glistening on her cheeks. He reached out a steady hand, and his reassuringly gentle voice startled her but brought a slight sparkle of hope into her eyes.

'You know, my mother, God rest her soul, had a saying,' The man said. 'Even the darkest night will eventually end, and the sun will rise.'

She stared at the glossy golden bottle of whisky and hesitated, trying to summon the will to put it back on the shelf. The lights above her shone brightly, and the store seemed to close around her. She felt her determination slipping away. Finally, she held the bottle close to her body and walked up to the counter, her heart pounding as its weight pressed down on her trembling hands. The man, wearing a spotless white apron and thinning black hair, glanced up briefly before quickly turning his attention to the register. His nimble fingers flew across the keys as he tapped in the price for the bottle. He took it from her and placed it carefully into a paper bag. With a deep breath, Ellie stepped closer to the glass door and felt goosebumps rise on her skin at the chill of the night air streaming in from outside. Her hand shook as she reached for the doorknob, and with a quick twist of her wrist, she opened the door and stepped out into the night.

'Goodnight, Miss!' The man said as the door closed behind her.

Ellie pulled Jasper's coat tighter around her body and walked into the darkness stretching before her. Ellie shuffled further down the street, her fingers tightly gripping the paper bag with whisky inside. She closed her eyes and lifted her face to the sky, feeling the gentle tickle of snowflakes on her skin as they began to fall. Suddenly, a cold gust of wind blew flakes in all directions, and visibility dropped dramatically, engulfing her in a flurry of icy white. She pulled the coat closer over her body and quickened her pace, relieved to see a taxi pulled into the side of the road. She opened the rear door and was greeted by the acrid smell of smoke as she glanced at the driver, who flicked his cigarette out the window.

'Where to?'

Ellie was uncertain about what direction to give him, feeling like she had nowhere else to go. She felt unwelcome at her parents' house and scared to return to Jackson's farm, but it was the only place she could think of. Taking a deep breath, she reluctantly gave him the address and prayed that Jackson would be fast asleep when she returned so she could lose herself in a bottle of whiskey without anyone questioning her. Ellie's heart raced at the thought of being able to drink again, and she couldn't take her eyes off the bottle. Ellie stepped out of the Taxi, her breath crystallizing in the gust of wind and snow. Her eyes adjusted to the darkness, taking in the rolling fields of white, the fence posts dotting the perimeter like skeletal fingers. She slipped her hand into her pocket to retrieve a crumbled wad of notes, paying the driver before he drove off in a cloud of exhaust.

With the bottle of whisky clutched in her hand, Ellie carefully made her way up the gravel path towards the farmhouse door, feeling every pebble through the soles of her shoes. She fumbled with the latch, pushing open the creaking door and squinting into the darkness beyond. Ellie was immediately overwhelmed by the smoky aroma of burning wood. She glanced into the living room and saw the crackling fireplace radiating warmth. The wooden floor creaked under her feet as she strode towards the bottom of the stairs, straining for any sound that Jackson might be home. But the farmhouse was still, silent except for the occasional rustle of wind outside. Ellie slowly scanned the room, taking in the sound of the ticking clock and the faint crackling of the fire. She stepped closer to the hearth, feeling the warmth of the flames on her chilled skin. She sat down on the sofa, her gaze fixed on the brown paper bag she had placed on the coffee table. Her fingers ran through her dark hair before she pulled it back from her face, tucking it behind her ears. Taking off her shoes, Ellie placed her feet on the soft rug, curling her toes as she closed her eyes and sighed deeply. She leaned forward, drawn by an irresistible force. The brown paper bag was compelling, and she couldn't take her eyes off it. Her slender fingers snaked in and extracted the bottle of whisky that shone with a dark golden light cast by the flickering flames. She became entranced by it as if ensnared by some otherworldly enchantment. Ellie gently ran her fingertips over the smooth surface of the whisky bottle, relishing its cold touch. She stood and carried it to the kitchen, its golden liquid sloshing against the glass sides with each step. With one hand on the table, she pulled a tumbler glass from the cupboard and carefully set it down as she sat in the wooden chair. She grasped the bottle of whisky and slowly unscrewed the cap.

As she tipped it forward, a heady aroma of peat and toffee wafted up to her nose, and she let out a sigh of pleasure. Carefully pouring the amber liquid, she ran her fingertips over the ridges of the glass and took in the power of what she held in her hands. Ellie closed her eyes and took a deep breath, letting the sadness wash over her. When she opened them, she looked over at the side table and placed her glass down with a shaky hand. Stepping up to the table, she noticed a handwritten note with her name on it in messy loops. On top of the paper sat her AA sobriety chip, and the weight of it seemed to pull at her chest. She picked it up, letting its cold surface sink into her skin as guilt and disappointment coursed through her veins.

She carefully unfolded the paper, and her hands trembled as she read the words.

'My Dearest Ellie, It pains me to leave you like this with nothing more than a note as my goodbye. I wish I could find the courage to face you so I can apologize for all the wrong words I said and for dragging you into my mess of life. I heard Scarlett is returning to Portland, and Rebecca is in danger. And so, I will end this - not for my own sake but for yours. All I want is for you to be safe. I understand if you can't forgive me, but please try to forgive yourself for all that has happened. I can never have the right for you to call me your father, but you will always be my daughter, and all I want is to keep you safe.'

Ellie felt her throat tighten as she read the letter. The guilt in her chest swelled with each passing moment of inaction, forcing her to refold the letter and place it on the side table. Despite her best efforts, Ellie had failed him. She shuffled over to the glass filled with whisky and held it to the light. Its golden hue glimmered in the dark as if it were a reminder of past sins. She stood trembling, arm pulled back, gripping the glass tightly. She knew what would happen next but felt powerless as if something else controlled her actions. The liquid inside seemed to plead with her, begging her not to pour it out. The smells that emanated from it comforted and confused her all at once. She slowly tipped the glass, watching the liquid disappear into the sink. Her fingers quivered as they grazed the bottle, and an internal struggle raged inside her. She desperately wanted to open it and succumb to its seductive call, but at the same time, she knew what she needed to do. She gripped the bottle with both hands and reluctantly tipped it over the kitchen sink, eyes shut tight to block the sight of its contents pouring out. Tears started streaming down her face as she felt a sense of pride swell up in her chest. Finally, with one last deep breath, she lifted the recycling bin lid and let the bottle go. Ellie walked up the stairs to her bedroom and stood before the mirror. She rummaged through her purse and pulled out a cleansing wipe, which she used to dab at her eyes delicately. She gently wiped away the tear-streaked mascara and foundation, revealing fresh skin. Taking a deep breath and letting it out slowly, she applied a light moisturizer and gave herself a small smile in the mirror. She hastily ripped her dress from her body and scrambled to locate the denim trousers she had thrown around the room the night before. Her fingers fumbled with the buttons as she hopped on one foot, trying to pull on a pair of old sports shoes. She quickly changed into a soft black vest top, grabbed Jackson's keys from the kitchen table, and rushed out of the house. She could feel the crisp night air as she jogged to the truck parked in the driveway. After unlocking the door with a click, she hopped in and settled behind the wheel. The vehicle shuddered and groaned as she pulled away from the house, gravel crunching beneath its tires. Ellie took a deep breath and tightened her grip on the steering wheel as she drove the winding road, heading away from the farm's open fields. Her eyes were dry - she had turned away from the distractions of alcohol and towards her newfound purpose.

The looming silhouette of the hospital loomed ever closer as Ellie's heart raced in anticipation. She was eager to see her parents and to express the love that she had for them. As she entered the building, her feet echoed off the sterile, glimmering floors. She approached the registration desk, where a kindly woman typed away at a computer.

'Can I help you?' The receptionist asked.

Ellie stepped closer and offered a warm smile. 'Could you please tell me where Mr. and Mrs. Jones are? They were brought in a few days ago.'

The receptionist tapped away at the keyboard, and After a few moments of silence, she looked up at Ellie.

'They're in Room 4 on the recovery ward.'

Ellie smiled, her heart hammering in her chest as she approached the hospital map. The metal elevator was icy cold to the touch. Its hinges squeaked as she entered and pressed the button for the correct floor. With a low rumble, it slowly ascended. Her stomach filled with nerves as she hadn't seen her parents since that fateful night when Piper attacked them. Ellie stepped through the metal doors, and a sign caught her eye as she wandered down the hospital corridor. It hung next to a door - Recovery Ward. She crept slowly down the hallway, pausing at each doorway to take in the muted conversations that could be heard from within. She passed rooms where family members hugged and reassured one another, rooms filled with whispered encouragements of hope. After a few minutes, she stopped outside a room where two white beds lay side by side. Taking a deep breath, she pushed open the door to find her mom, Alice, and dad, Mike, propped up on pillows in their respective beds. Ellie's sister Ashley stood off to the side, her hands clenched tightly at her sides. Her eyes were round and glassy as she stared off into the distance. Ellie could feel a tug in her chest, a deep sadness that Ashley refused to even look at her. Alice and Mike's faces beamed with warmth, but

Ashley's gaze was distant, and Ellie felt that whatever bond they had once shared had crumbled away. Ellie tentatively stepped into the hospital room, and Alice waved her closer. The atmosphere was taut, and Ellie could feel Ashley's reluctance to have her there. Taking a deep breath to steady herself, she bent down and embraced Alice, then moved over to Mike's bedside and hugged him. The embrace was warm but brief, as though Ashley's disapproval was hanging in the air. Ashley stood, her hands trembling as she zipped her pink coat over her black vest. She swallowed hard before speaking, her voice a soft quiver.

'I'm gonna go.'

Ellie's face crumpled, and Alice saw the tension rising between her daughters.

'Please, girls, sit and talk this out. I can't bear to see you two like this,' Alice said, pushing herself up in her hospital bed. 'It's not Ellie's fault, sweetheart. We all loved Shreya, but it's not Ellie's doing.'

Ashley glanced at her mother with a pained expression-- her eyes glassy with tears.

'If she hadn't returned, none of this would have happened. You were attacked, and Shreya was killed - who is to blame here?'

Mike groaned, shifting himself in his bed to face them all better.

'Ellie didn't know anything about it. When we adopted her, we were told she was special, and we had to keep her safe.'

Ashley looked back and forth between them, her face scrunched up in confusion.

'What are you talking about?' Ashley asked.

Ellie's complexion drained of color, and she slowly turned

her head toward Mike. Her eyes widened with surprise as she saw the strained expression on his face. He exhaled sharply, his attention briefly shifting to Alice before allowing it to drop away from them as he hung his head.

'We only knew what we had to know,' Mike whispered. 'I had known Jackson for a while through work, and he asked us to look after you.'

Ellie's eyes grew wide, and she stumbled back, her arm automatically rising to cover her open mouth.

'Wait, you knew who my biological parents were all this time!'

'What the hell is going on? What am I missing?' Ashley asked as she looked on in confusion.

'The woman who killed Shreya,' Mike said as his voice trembled. 'she's Ellie's twin sister. Their father worked for a huge weapons and science facility in the States, and they were both born with special abilities. He tried to rescue them both, but he could only save Ellie. Now her sister is free, and she wants to hurt Ellie -- we got caught in the middle of all of it.'

Mike's words shook Ashley to her core, leaving her wide-eyed and speechless. She couldn't escape Ellie's gaze as she grappled with everything that had just been said. Hot tears pricked at her eyelids, and Ashley felt an intense void expand within her.

'How could you not tell me?'

'We thought after all this time it would have caused more pain than good. We were wrong.'

'I just miss her so much.'

Ashley's lip quivered, and her chin shook as the tears fell. Alice touched Ashley's arm. Her touch was soft and comforting. She spoke in a low voice, full of sorrow and understanding.

'What happened was a tragedy,' Alice whispered. 'We will miss Shreya deeply.'

Ellie stood close to Ashley but stayed silent. Her gaze was kind yet hesitant, desperate for some sign of forgiveness from Ashley. Ashley kept her expression neutral as the tears rolled down her face, but the corner of her mouth twitched ever so slightly, enough of an indication for Ellie to take a deep breath and exhale in relief. Ashley paused in the doorway, her eyes heavy with emotion as she looked at Ellie.

'Look, I do love you, Ellie,' Ashley said, her voice trembling as she closed the distance between them. Her arms wrapped around Ellie in a comforting embrace, and despite the chill in the air, the warmth of Ashley's body seemed to thaw Ellie's fears. 'It's just every time I look at you. I see her face staring back at me.'

Ashley stepped back, holding onto Ellie's hands momentarily before releasing them. She looked into Ellie's eyes with an intensity that made Ellie shiver; there was a darkness in Ashley's gaze that seemed to be searching for something inside Ellie.

'We'll be okay. Just promise me one thing if you ever see Scarlett again.'

Ellie nodded slowly, her throat suddenly dry from fear and anticipation.

'Anything,' Ellie said.

'Make her pay for what she did,' Ashley said as she walked towards the door, her steps echoing on the floor.

Ellie slowly spun around and sank into the wooden chair beside her mother. Tears began to stream down her face as she stared in disbelief.

'I can't believe you both knew,' Ellie said as Alice reached out and tenderly held her hand.

'We just wanted to protect you,' Alice said, her voice full of regret and sorrow.

Mike glanced at Ellie and ran a hand through his thick, sandy-brown hair.

'Where have you been?'

Ellie fidgeted, her fingers twirling around her dark, wavy hair strands.

'Jackson saved me when a man tried to take me. He's been letting me stay on his farm to help me control my abilities.'

'Your abilities?' Alice asked.

'Jackson removed a device from my neck that was suppressing what I could do,' Ellie said. 'I wish he had left it alone now.'

Alice and Mike shared an understanding glance before Mike pushed further.

'So, you've been with Jackson? Did he explain things to you?' Mike asked.

'Yeah, where I came from, and that he's my father,' Ellie whispered, biting her lip, looking away as she finished.

Alice and Mike exchanged an anxious glance as Ellie leaned forward and blinked back tears.

'I'm sorry I didn't come sooner. I was so scared I'd never see you again.'

Alice embraced her warmly, erasing all anxiety with the intensity of her hug. Ellie felt the tension release in her shoulders, and her eyes glimmered with gratitude. A soft smile slowly spread across her face as Alice finally let go.

'You know, I have been searching for answers all my life, unsure of my identity and background. But now I realize it doesn't matter. You two have always been my parents; your love is enough for me. For too long, I have blamed the world for my struggles when, in reality, I was the one who had to stand up and accept responsibility.'

Mike's eyes filled with emotion as he looked at Ellie.

'You will always be our little girl,' Mike said.

'You know, I was so close to having a drink tonight,' Ellie said proudly. 'It was right there, but I didn't do it.'

Alice smiled and looked at Mike, her eyes filled with admiration.

'That must have been tough,' Alice said. 'I'm so proud of you.'

Ellie nodded and glanced down at her feet.

'I just couldn't do it. I don't want to be that person anymore.'

'Where is Jackson now?' Mike asked.

Ellie pulled a crumpled note from her pocket and handed it to Mike. He read it quietly, his face darkening with worry when he finished.

'He's gone to Portland alone?' Mike asked, looking up at Ellie.

'Yes,' Ellie replied. 'Apparently, my sister's returned to Portland, so I'm safe for now.'

Alice's eyes were heavy with exhaustion, but her face lit up upon hearing the news.

'We should be able to come home tomorrow. Please come and stay with us. We're safer together,' Alice said.

'Are you sure?' Ellie asked, her voice full of emotion, shocked that they would want her back in their house.

'Of course,' Mike said without hesitation.

Ellie stood between the hospital beds, her gaze alternating between Alice and Mike. She took a deep breath before slowly kneeling in the middle of them. With her arms outstretched, she welcomed them both into an embrace that felt like it would never end.

'I love you guys!' Ellie said, and for a few minutes, they stayed like that, clinging to each other tightly.

24

Jackson pulled up to the imposing presence of the facility, a chill creeping down his spine. The imposing grey walls rose before him, and he could feel a thousand memories threatening to wash over him like a wave. He was overwhelmed with dread at this place that had once been integral to his life. His heart felt like it was beating out of his chest as he watched the guards patrol the grounds. A sense of dread crept up his back, and he could feel a lump forming in his throat. He focused on controlling his breaths, but as the guard got closer and closer to him, he felt all the air being vacuumed out of him, leaving him lightheaded with adrenaline. Jackson's hand shook as he fumbled for his phone in his pocket. Taking a deep breath, he finally pulled it out and squinted at the screen to dial Andrews' number, counting each ring with dread blowing up in his chest like a balloon. He tried to steady himself by watching the scuffling of his shoes against the pavement while he waited for an answer.

'Jackson, Are you here?' Andrew asked as the phone connected.

'I have just arrived. How do I get inside?' Jackson asked, desperation lacing his words.

'I have given you all-level clearance; just scan your thumb on the doorplate, and you'll have access to wherever you need to go. You need to come to the restricted science division. It's where you found Ellie,' Andrew said as the phone disconnected.

Jackson's hand shook as he pulled a crushed packet of cigarettes from his pocket and lit one. He took a deep drag, letting the smoke fill his lungs before exhaling and stepping towards the main entrance of the building. His gaze was fixed on the ground, avoiding eye contact with the guards on duty. His thumb hovered over the security scanner, sweat beading on his forehead. Jackson closed his eyes and took a deep breath before flicking away the cigarette butt and pressing the button. There was a momentary pause before a green light illuminated, and the doors slowly opened. Jackson stepped inside, his shoes squeaking against the floor. He stopped in his tracks and looked around the large foyer with awe, taking in the intricate details of its design. An eerie silence hung in the air, and a single beam of sunlight streamed through the large windows, creating ghostly silhouettes on the marble floors. Jackson tried to shrink away as he walked past the giant statue of Rebecca's father, which stood in the lobby's center. He couldn't shake off the feeling that its cold eyes were following him, slicing through him like razor blades. Jackson entered the elevator and pressed the button to take him to his destination. As the doors shut behind him, he felt a familiar lurch of the lift starting its ascent. A knot formed in his throat as he watched the ground level slowly fade from view outside the glass walls.

Jackson's mind raced with a million questions. Where was Scarlett? What secrets were hidden in this place? Anxiety slowly crept up on him as the silent elevator doors opened before him, unleashing a new wave of fear and dread. Jackson crept down the quiet corridor, his footfalls echoing off the walls. The light from his flickering torch barely reached far enough to determine what was ahead of him. He tightened his grip on the handle and inched forward, feeling a chill run down his spine as he ventured deeper into the unknown. As he approached the door to the science facility, his hands were slick with sweat, and his heart raced. He wiped them on his trousers before pressing his thumb against the cold plate. A moment later, a small light turned green, and the massive door slowly slid open. Jackson stepped into the dark and silent room, a sense of dread looming heavy in the air. He took a few tentative steps forward, and his eyes struggled to adjust to the dark. In the corner, he noticed a hunched figure suspended from the ceiling, ropes biting into the man's wrists and ankles. As Jackson recognized the familiar face, his stomach dropped— it was Andrew, contorted and lifeless like some grotesque puppet hung from a cruel puppeteer's strings. His shirt lay bunched on the floor, and Jackson could see a grim map of torture, welts, and bruises covering Andrew's chest like a macabre painting. Jackson's flesh crawled with dread as he hesitantly edged closer. Andrew's eyes locked with his, desperation and guilt etched into his face.

'What happened to you?' Jackson asked.

'I'm so sorry, old friend,' Andrew whispered. 'It was a trap. I had no choice.'

The hum of the automatic doors broke through the tense silence, and then they slid open. With a determined march, Jade stepped out, her tall frame clad in a sleek black suit of armor. A legion of security guards flowed behind her like an unstoppable tide, their matching suits of body armor making them look menacing and powerful. The sharp edges of their armor glinted menacingly in the light. Jade marched into the hall with a presence that commanded attention. When she reached Jackson's side, she tipped her chin up and arched an eyebrow. Her smirk was taunting and unreadable.

'Do you remember me, Mr. Carter?'

Jackson shuddered as vivid memories of the night he broke free of the facility flashed through his mind.

Jackson's body was paralyzed with fear. His eyes flitted between Jade and Andrew in sheer terror.

'I remember you. Please, let Andrew go!'

Jade slowly ran her index finger along Andrew's skin, tracing the faint raised lines left behind from his recent wounds.

'What we have planned for you is far worse.'

Martin stepped through the doorway, a menacing grin stretching across his face. A low, rumbling chuckle emanated from him as he rubbed his hands together in anticipation. His dark eyes glinted as they landed on Jackson.

'Oh yes, oh yes!' Martin murmured. 'Jackson Carter, it has been too long.'

Jackson's jaw clenched as Martin scanned him up and down, waiting for a response. The air between them seemed to thicken with tension, and Jackson felt every muscle in his body tense until all he wanted to do was flee.

'What have you done with Rebecca? Where is Scarlett?' Jackson asked.

Martin stepped forward, his cruel smirk widening with every inch. As he opened his mouth, his eyes glinted with malice, and Jackson felt a chill run down his spine.

'You still don't understand, do you? Scarlett isn't here. She's still with Ellie. She still needs to finish her mission.'

Jackson's blood ran cold, and his heart raced like a pack of wild horses as his mind conjured up the thought of Ellie, utterly oblivious to Scarlett's looming presence. Terror filled Jackson and drained every ounce of color from his face. Martin stepped menacingly closer until their faces were mere inches apart, and in a low, rumbling growl, he spoke each word deliberately with painful emphasis on the truth.

'Your wife was too naive to recognize how valuable Scarlett is,' Martin said before stepping back and daring Jade to meet his gaze as he glared at her with a fierce and intimidating air of authority.

'I have somewhere I must be. Being CEO of a multi-billion dollar company is not easy,' Martin said, gesturing to Jackson, surrounded by Jade's security detail. 'Mr. Carter needs somewhere to stay for the night. See to it that he gets to his accommodation and is made as comfortable as possible.'

Martin spun on his heel, eyes twinkling with delight. He threw his head back and laughed as he strode out the door, the broad smile still stretched across his face. Jade's fingers dug into Jackson's wrist as he led him through the door into a vast, empty room. As they stepped into the room, an array of fluorescent lights hummed to life, illuminating the glass cell hidden in the darkness.

Jackson's heart raced as they approached the cell where Rebecca was shaking in terror.

Jackson's heart stopped as she lifted her head. Her eyes were wide and terrified, tears streaming down her pale cheeks. She had curled herself into a ball with her arms wrapped protectively around her legs.

'Rebecca! What have they done to you?' Jackson shouted.

Jackson pulled away from Jade's tight grasp, his eyes

conveying a steely determination as he crossed his arms.

An impenetrable wall of security officers converged on him, their massive guns poised and ready. Rebecca watched in horror as a chill ran through her body.

Jade's gaze was cold as she looked into Rebecca's eyes, her former boss now sitting before her in fear. As Jade stepped closer, her boots thudded on the floor with each stride, and although part of her wanted to do her job and be professional, another part of her felt a deep sadness at seeing a once powerful woman so broken.

'What the fuck is wrong with you,' Jackson said.

Jade's eyes were cold and calculating as she stalked around Jackson. She ran a finger down his chest, making him flinch. Her lips twitched into a smirk when he failed to react further.

'Remove your clothes,' Jade whispered, her voice dripping with malice.

Jackson felt like his feet had been welded to the ground as his gaze shifted to Rebecca - What had they done to her? He forced himself to remain calm despite the fear and humiliation that threatened to overwhelm him, not wanting to give Jade more satisfaction.

'I don't have all day,' Jade said. 'Strip.'

Jackson's eyes darted around the room, taking in the menacing faces of the security officers poised to strike at any moment. He glanced over at Rebecca, trembling violently in fear; a wave of nausea twisted through his body as he realized his inevitable fate. His hands shook as he fumbled with each button on his shirt, desperately trying to undo them as quickly as possible. His eyes filled with a determined rage as he finally released the last one, sending the shirt flying off his body and onto the ground with one swift tug.

He squared his shoulders and raised his chin high, exposing his chest and displaying the intricate tattoo of two turtle doves in flight, a tangible sign of his twin daughters. Jade's gaze was stern as she pointed her index finger toward Jackson's trousers, her lips pressed together in frustration. Jackson took off his mud-encrusted boots with a single, swift motion, never once taking his eyes away from Jade. He clenched his jaw and reached for the button of his jeans. He pulled them open one by one, then slid them down his lean frame with purposeful determination - not out of embarrassment or shame, but to show that he was still in control. As the fabric dropped to the floor, exposing his bare thighs and skin, he raised his head and looked straight into the Captain's eyes - a challenge that clearly stated that she would not get the better of him.

Jade held his gaze, her face unreadable as she stepped closer and closer to him until they were almost touching. Her eyes traveled over his body, lingering on his lower half before finally settling back on his face.

'Why don't you take a picture? It will last longer,' Jackson said through clenched teeth, refusing to show any outward sign of weakness.

Jade stepped away from him with calculated precision and nodded to one of the guards at her side, who flung a white jumpsuit in Jackson's direction. It hit the ground with a muffled thud around his feet, but he drew himself up and glared defiantly back at the Captain, his jaw clenched tight.

'Put it on or go in naked,' Jade said coldly, her icy gaze piercing him. 'It's your choice, Mr. Carter.'

Jackson's gaze shifted from Captain Johnson's face to the jumpsuit lying at his feet, and he slowly bent down to pick it up and slip it on.

Jackson straightened his posture, tried to maintain an emotionless expression, and buried the fear and anticipation deep within.

'Did you enjoy that?' Jackson asked.

Jade stared back at him for what felt like an eternity before giving a sharp nod. Then, with a sharp crack, she snapped her fingers and gestured to the glass structure a few feet away. Instantly, one of the guards opened the cell door. She held Jackson's gaze with a powerful authority until The door slid open with a low hum, and Jade gestured for Jackson to enter the glass box. He stood his ground, his body radiating with a heated rage as Jade stepped forward.

'Get in the cell.'

'Fuck you!' Jackson spat.

The Captain raised her weapon high and drove it deep into his abdomen with a fierce yell. He gasped in pain as his legs buckled beneath him, and the unforgiving ground met his back with an echoing thud.

'Put him in.'

Two guards descended upon him, gripping his arms tightly as they dragged him toward the dreaded glass cell. The door crashed shut, and icy cold air seized him. The sound reverberated with a looming doom as he was trapped inside. Jackson wheeled around to face Jade, whose eyes conveyed a silent warning.

'We will leave you two to get reacquainted,' Jade said.

Without another word, one of the security guards scooped up Jackson's clothing and quickly ushered the others out of the room. Jackson was alone in that glass prison with Rebecca, huddled against the opposite wall, her knees pulled into her chest and tears streaming down her face.

Jackson felt his heart pounding as he stepped closer to

Rebecca. He slowly lowered himself to his knees so they were eye level and cautiously reached an arm towards her.

'Rebecca, it's me, Jackson.'

His voice trembled as he was unsure how she'd react to his presence. She looked up at him in surprise, unable to believe he had come. Their breathing grew labored as they stared at each other in shock, time seemingly frozen in place. Rebecca's breath hitched as Jackson's fingers brushed against hers, and a rush of electricity shot through her body. Gently, he intertwined their fingers, and Rebecca stared deep into his eyes. She could see the same Jackson she had known before but with an intensity that hadn't existed before. His touch felt like fire against her cold skin, and she quivered under its heat.

'Jackson,' Rebecca whispered, her teeth chattering from the chill in the air.

Jackson wrapped his arms around her tightly, desperately sharing his warmth as she rested her head against his chest. Jackson felt his heart racing as he stared into Rebecca's beautiful eyes. He could feel her entire body trembling against his, and he tightly embraced her with his strong arms.

'I can't believe it's you,' Rebecca whispered, breaking the silence between them. Jackson searched her gaze for a sign of familiarity, the tension surrounding them intensifying as he continued to look.

'I heard you were in danger, and I had to come,' Jackson said softly, running one hand slowly over her back.

When she saw Jackson, Rebecca's heart felt like it was being pulled in two different directions. On the one hand, she remembered their happy memories and the love they once shared. On the other hand, the pain and hurt from all that had happened still lingered in her mind.

'Martin helped Scarlett escape. I can only imagine where she is now,' Rebecca whispered.

'Scarlett's in London,' Jackson said.

Her daughter's name had never sounded more chilling, and a million questions filled her mind before she could comprehend what was happening. What would this mean for Ellie? How did Martin factor into all of this? And why would Scarlett resort to such drastic measures?

'Ellie, how is she?'

Jackson shook his head slowly and sighed, his gaze full of pain and anger.

'It's not easy for her, Rebecca,' Jackson said. 'She was adopted into a loving family, but something changed inside her during adolescence. She started abusing alcohol, and it's only gotten worse since then. I've been trying to help her battle her addiction, but it's really tough. And now, with all that is going on and the added pressure, she's just so consumed by rage and fear. I'm genuinely terrified as to what she might do,' Jackson spoke, his voice wavering.

Rebecca looked away, her eyes filled with tears, her heart heavy with regret for what she had done. She reached out to touch Jackson's arm.

'I'm so sorry, Jackson. I know I have let you down. I was terrified and had no idea how to raise our kids. All I ever wanted to do was keep them safe, but I failed,' Rebecca said.

Jackson looked at her with a hollow expression and nodded in agreement.

'I know, we both made mistakes, Becca, and now our children are paying for them,' Jackson said.

'Scarlett is a monster, Jackson! I have tried everything, but I failed her. I can't ignore the terrible things she has done,'

Rebecca said.

Jackson was silent momentarily, his expression torn between sorrow and anger. He wanted to help Scarlett, to save her from herself, but he had no idea how.

'She's our daughter, Becca. I have to believe she has good inside her.'

Jackson held Rebecca tightly, his heart beating rapidly in his chest.

'We have to get out of here. We need to protect Ellie from her. I've already let her down too many times.'

Rebecca slowly unwrapped her arms from Jackson's neck and stood up, her legs heavy and feet icy against the floor. In the corner of the room, a bright red light blinked steadily in the security camera lens.

'They're watching us,' Rebecca said.

Despite their desperate desire to break free of this room, they knew their chances of success barely existed. Rebecca swayed on her feet and steadied herself against the glass wall before sinking back down onto the floor next to Jackson. Rebecca looked into his eyes and noticed the corners of his mouth curl up into a cocky smirk as if he knew something she didn't.

'What?' Rebecca asked.

'You're still as beautiful as ever,' Jackson said.

A deep red blush spread across her pale skin as she tried to escape his intense gaze. Her heart raced in her chest, pounding like a drum in her ears.

'Uh, shut up,' Rebecca mumbled under her breath as She nervously tucked her hair behind her ear and tightly clasped her hands. 'You look good, too.'

Rebecca's hand trembled as she reached out and placed it on Jackson's arm.

'There is something else,' Rebecca whispered.

Jackson's heart constricted like a fist. His mouth dried with anticipation as he waited for her to speak.

'My cancer has returned.'

'When?' Jackson asked.

'A few weeks ago,' Rebecca whispered, her shoulders hunched and shaking with fear.

Jackson held her close, feeling overwhelming terror radiating from her body.

'We'll make it out of here,' Jackson said, trying to sound reassuring but feeling like his words were hollow and unconvincing. 'Ellie will come for us.'

Jackson wanted to believe that Ellie was still alive and could help them, but the odds felt slim. He had no choice but to cling to the faintest glimmer of hope, knowing that their survival depended on it.

25

Ellie stood in the bedroom of the old farmhouse, a single ray of sunshine streaming through the window and glinting off snowflakes as they drifted lazily through the air. Her suitcase lay open on the bed, her clothes scattered around her like a bright patchwork quilt. She methodically folded each piece before zipping it shut. With a heavy heart, she walked to the window and stared dreamily at the snowflakes that gently drifted toward the ground. Ellie's gaze fell on a poster-sized calendar hanging on the wall of the tiny room, and her chest tightened when she saw it was just two days until Christmas. Suddenly, the phone on the side table jolted her out of her meditative state. Its ringing echoed around the room. Ellie gingerly placed the phone to her ear, her fingers trembling as she tucked her hair behind her ear.

'Hello?'

'Ellie, it's mum. You gave us this number to reach you.'

Ellie's face lit up at the sound of her mother's voice on the other end of the line. She felt a wave of relief wash over her as she settled onto the edge of the bed.

'Of course! How are you both doing?' Ellie asked with newfound hope, remembering they were finally out of the hospital.

'Are you still coming home tonight?' Alice asked.

Ellie's hands trembled as she gripped the worn suitcase handle. Her eyes stung as tears pooled, and her throat tightened.

'Yes,' Ellie said. 'I'm just packing my things and I'll be there for dinner. It's just -'

'What is it, honey?' Alice asked, worry laced in her tone.

'Are you sure you want me back?' Ellie asked, her voice cracking.

'Don't be silly. Of course, we do.'

Ellie was silent momentarily and started biting her nails.

'I'm just worried that Ashley doesn't want me around.'

'Ashley loves you; she's just grieving.'

Ellie slowly stepped across the chilly wooden floorboards to gaze out the window. The world outside was transformed into an awe-inspiring winter wonderland. A thick layer of white snow blanketed the hills, and the horizon reached out endlessly in a serene display of softly falling snowflakes. The sky above was a muted ash grey that added to the beauty of the silent landscape.

'So we will see you for dinner? Alice asked.

'Yes, I will see you soon.' Ellie whispered. 'I love you, mum.'

'I love you too,' Alice said before the line disconnected, and Ellie's heart swelled with joy at the thought of being under the same roof as her family again.

She bent down and tucked the last of her belongings into her weathered brown suitcase, the clasp snapping securely shut with a satisfying click. She felt a wave of emotions pour over her as she sat on the edge of the bed. At that moment, the memories of the past days gently embraced her like a whisper. She inhaled deeply and stood tall, her fingers yanking tightly on the laces of her black boots until they fit snugly over her blue jeans. She approached the door, glanced around the small room that had become home for such a fleeting time, and silently said goodbye. With a grunt, she heaved her suitcase down the creaky old staircase. The clomp of her boots filled the silent air as they collided with the wooden steps, reverberating through the house like thunder. Her trembling fingers fumbled around her pocket in search of the keys to Jackson's broken-down truck that he had left her before zipping up her red winter jacket and stepping out into the chilly air. She pulled her coat tightly around her and shivered as the icy wind nipped at her nose. With a heavy sigh, she looked once more at the farmhouse and shut the door behind her with a soft click. The crunch of gravel underfoot accompanied her determined steps to the rusty truck, and she never glanced back.

Ellie's heart raced as she pulled up outside the coffee emporium. The truck's rusty door creaked open and slammed shut as she stepped out and crossed the road. She paused at the window, shielding her eyes from the sun with one hand while peering inside. Her stomach flipped when she gazed upon Jasper standing behind the counter with a green apron tied around his waist. Ellie felt guilt wash over her when she recalled the night at the fair with him. Ellie stepped back onto the pavement, her shoes scraping against the cracked cement. She nervously pulled her hair into a ponytail before gathering her courage and stepping towards the coffee shop. Her heart pounded in her chest as she reached out and pushed open the door, the scent of coffee and baked goods hitting her as she stepped in. The chatter and laughter of customers filled the coffee shop, which bustled with activity. Ellie's gaze landed on Jasper, who had just finished pouring a cup of steaming hot coffee for a woman. Worry filled Ellie as she nervously waited for Jasper to notice her standing there. Would he be pleased to see her, or would he turn away? Jasper had his back to Ellie as she stood in the doorway. He slowly turned around, and his face paled when he saw who it was. His gaze lingered on Ellie for a few moments, taking in her sight before his gaze dropped to the floor.

'Hi Jasper,' Ellie whispered, her voice barely carrying above the low murmur of conversation in the coffee shop.

'Hi,' Jasper said, his voice heavy with emotion.

'Can we talk?' Ellie asked.

Jasper looked around the busy coffee shop and then back at Ellie.

'I thought you couldn't be near me?'

'Please?' Ellie said, her voice a gentle plea.

Jasper inclined his head slightly and gestured for Ellie to follow him. He led her to an unoccupied table, the surface of which was scuffed and scratched from years of service. Ellie stared at him uncertainly as she carefully crossed her legs and placed her bag on the back of the wooden chair. The silence lingered as he watched her with curiosity and apprehension. Ellie's eyes were watery and filled with sadness as she fiddled with a loose string on her sleeve and looked up at Jasper.

'I am so sorry for the other night,' Ellie whispered. 'I have no excuse, and don't blame you if you never want to speak to me again.'

Jasper studied her face momentarily, taking in every detail of her expression before speaking.

'I just don't understand,' Jasper said. His voice was full of pain but still gentle. 'Why did you leave?'

Ellie shifted uncomfortably in her seat and leaned closer to him, desperate to make him understand.

'Look, I want to tell you everything, but please promise you will keep this to yourself. Not for me, but to keep you safe.'

Jasper stared into Ellie's eyes as if willing her to open up and tell him what he needed to know. He seemed desperate for the truth yet scared of how it might change things between them.

'Tell me,' Jasper said. 'Please.'

Ellie's gaze shifted to the window, where a single ray of sunshine peeked through the thick blanket of clouds. A warm glow lit up the shop momentarily, and Ellie felt a rush of emotions she had been repressing. She slowly reached out with her shaking fingers and grasped Jasper's hand.

'you have to believe I was trying to protect you. Leaving you last year was one of the hardest things I have ever had to do. I managed to stick with AA for a year, and apparently, that's a big deal. I just wanted to come home, celebrate Christmas with my family, and start making things right. That night, I was attacked. It wasn't just a robbery. He tried to kidnap me.' Ellie said, her voice trembling and her hands clasped tightly to keep them from shaking.

'I've learned so much in the last few days,' Ellie said, her voice shaking. 'My whole life has been turned upside down. All this time, my birth parents have been out there, and that man at the farm wasn't my uncle--he was my real Father. He had been watching over me since I was adopted. But it turns out I was born in America. What's even crazier is that I have a twin sister, and we were both being experimented on because of our powers. My real Father brought me here to keep me safe and tried to keep me hidden from them. But they found me anyway...'

Ellie closed her eyes and took a deep, shuddering breath as tears streamed down her face. When she opened them again, Jasper's expression had shifted from confusion to concern as he looked at her with sympathy and bewilderment.

'Are you serious?'

'I left you because my sister broke free and came here to kill me. She's been torturing me, and she killed Ashley's girlfriend. I went to the fair with you because I wanted to forget everything but couldn't. You looked so handsome, and that moment we had on the Ferris wheel felt like magic. Knowing that you still loved me made my whole world light up. How you look at me makes me feel that everything will be alright. When we separated in the house of mirrors, I had a vision of my sister killing you, and I panicked. I ran because that's all I have ever done, but I don't want to run anymore.'

Jasper stared at her intently. He opened his mouth to respond but realized words would never be enough.

Ellie held his hands tightly, her fingers shaking as she spoke.

'I know it's a lot to hear, and you may never want to see me again after this. Honestly, I wouldn't blame you. I'm trying hard to face my fears and not run away when things get tough. I want you to know that I love you, always have, and I'm sorry. I hope that one day you can forgive me.'

Ellie's vision blurred, and tears spilled down her cheeks as she tried to stand up, but Jasper's warm hand held her still. He moved closer, his eyes filled with gentle reassurance as he touched her fingers and kissed them softly.

'Ellie, don't go,' Jasper said. 'I may not fully understand

what is going on, and there is no way I can grasp what you are going through. I do know that I love you, and no matter what happens, we will find a way to fix it. You don't have to do everything alone.'

The corners of his mouth twitched upwards in a hesitant expression, and Ellie gave a faint smile that quickly drooped before it could fully form. She took in his features momentarily, amazed at how wise he seemed for his age.

'You are amazing, Jasper,' Ellie said. 'I'm going back to my parent's house tonight; they're home from the hospital.'

Ellie absentmindedly twisted her fingers together, trying to steady her hands.

'I can't believe this is real,' Jasper said, 'Do you think your sister still poses a threat to you?'

'Jackson has gone to Portland to try and resolve the situation, so at least for now, I'm safe.'

'When can I see you again?' Jasper asked.

'I'll call you,' Ellie said as she slung her bag over her shoulder.

Jasper stood and hugged her tight, burying her head into his shoulder.

'Thank you for telling me everything. I know that couldn't have been easy.'

Ellie shuffled closer to Jasper, pressing her petite frame against his. She breathed in his familiar scent and felt secure in his arms, raising her chin to meet his gaze with a smile.

'Thank you for being so wonderful,' Ellie said before leaning in and pressing her lips against his in a tender kiss. Jasper pulled away and glanced at a man hovering near the coffee shop counter.

'You should go back to work,' Ellie said as she smiled and nodded toward the man.

Ellie stepped out into the frigid winter morning, her breath curling around her. She had to fight through the stiffness of cold air that seemed to wrap her up in its embrace. Above her, the sky was overcast and bleak. Looking back at Jasper, she saw him standing in the doorway of a cozy coffee shop, his hands thrust deep into his trouser pockets.

'See you soon,' Ellie said, turning away into the snow-filled sky.

'Be safe, Ellie,' Jasper said. 'See you soon.'

26

Ellie's truck rolled up the long driveway of her parent's house, its rusty engine groaning to a stop. She slowly stepped out, her heart heavy as her eyes fell on the familiar mansion. She grabbed her suitcase from the backseat and dragged it behind her on the gravel drive. Taking a deep breath, she walked up the stairs to the door of her parent's home. Excitement flooded her veins as she anticipated reuniting with her family, but soon, that joy was swallowed up by guilt and regret. As she reached the top, dread overwhelmed her as memories of what happened to them and Shreya filled her with sorrow, making her reluctant to go inside. Ellie's hand shook as she twisted the key to unlock the door, which creaked open with an ominous groan. Sabrina stood in the doorway, her curves accentuated by her skintight black dress and her fiery hair cascading over her shoulders like a blazing cape. Her stunning features were framed perfectly by her deep red lipstick.

'What the fuck are you doing here?' Ellie shouted.

Sabrina stepped forward casually, placing her leg in front of the door to block Ellie's entrance. Her lips pulled into a smirk as her voice dropped to an ominous tone.

'Come on now. Let's be civil,' Sabrina said.

Fists clenched at her sides, Ellie trembled as she glared at Sabrina.

'Where are my parents? I swear if you hurt them, I will...'

Ellie felt the icy sneer of Sabrina upon her skin and heard her cold reply drip with contempt.

'You won't do anything, you pretty little wallflower.'

A chill ran through Ellie's Core as Sabrina sauntered closer, her body language oozing with a false seduction as her gaze roved over Ellie's exposed neck.

'Where is my necklace, my darling?' Sabrina said as her fingers curled, ready to caress Ellie's skin as her lips curled into a sly smile.

'If you dare touch me,' Ellie said in a low hiss of rage, 'I'll tear your fucking arm from its socket.'

Sabrina stepped back, eyes gleaming with amusement.

'Ooh, this kitten finally got her claws,' Sabrina said with a purr, 'I think I like this new you.'

'Where is my family?' Ellie growled through gritted teeth.

'They're in the backyard getting to know your sister,' Sabrina paused, smirking, 'It's a lovely afternoon for it.'

Ellie's face drained of color as the realization of Sabrina's words crashed into her.

'I thought she had gone back to Portland,' Ellie said, her voice quivering.

'Yes, Scarlett wanted your undivided attention, so we required that idiot to disappear,' Sabrina said, her lips contorted into a malicious smirk.

Ellie lunged towards Sabrina with her fists balled up.

'What have you done to Jackson?' Ellie seethed through gritted teeth as Sabrina raised her chin defiantly, her eyes sparking with determination.

'He is no longer your concern,' Sabrina said.

'Get out of my way, or else I'll move you myself.'

Ellie's eyes narrowed as she lunged forward and pushed Sabrina aside. She charged through the hallways, rage inflaming her veins. Her hands shook with each step closer to her parents. When she threw open the doors at the back of the house, there they were: her Mother and Father, tied in ropes that cut into their skin, seated in carved wooden chairs. Mike was wearing a black suit, and Alice was wearing a white dress, their faces pale with terror as they watched their daughter approach them. Ellie's hands shook as she fought to rip the gag away from their mouths.

'Are you okay? Where is she!' Ellie screamed out, desperation and fear lacing every word. For a moment, all was silent until an eerily familiar voice rang out from the shadows.

'Hello, my beloved sister!'

Scarlett's sinister laughter echoed through the darkness.

Ellie spun around to find Scarlett perched atop the old, creaking swing hanging from a grand and soaring tree near an old treehouse. She felt her heart leap into her throat as she watched her sister swing with carefree abandon, her face glowing with delight as her crimson leather trousers and ebony coat clung tightly to her slender body. Ellie's eyes widened with terror as her fingers traced the thick rope that bound her parents' wrists. Scarlett jumped off the swing, her boots thudding against the ground.

'Don't,' Scarlett spat, her voice quivering with rage. 'This is for their protection.'

Ellie stumbled back, her nails digging into the palms of her hands in rage. Her heart pounded fiercely like a war drum as she fought against her boiling emotions, struggling to contain them as Jackson had taught her. Every muscle tensed and shook as the fire inside intensified, threatening to consume her entirely.

'What are you doing here?'

Scarlett glared at Ellie, her lips curled into a sneer as her eyes burned with hatred.

'Time's up,' Scarlett said. 'I'm here to finish what I started!'

Ellie's body shook as fear overwhelmed her, icy dread coursing through every vein.

'Why the hell are you doing this?' Ellie yelled, her voice shaking with fury.

Scarlett let out a piercing laughter, a high-pitched sound that sliced through the atmosphere like lightning.

'You already know the answer to that question,' Scarlett said, her eyes glowing with malice. 'I deserve everything that you have carelessly squandered away. Pathetic as you are, you're still the only other person on this godforsaken planet who possesses power - even if you're too feeble to utilize it. It's my destiny to be the only one worthy of greatness, and just looking at you makes me sick.'

Ellie shook her head, tears streaming down her face.

'No!' Ellie said, her voice raw with emotion as she pleaded. 'There must be some other way.'

Scarlett wavered momentarily, the doubt of her convictions creeping in.

'There is no other way. I have to end this.'

As Ellie stepped forward, her body coiled like a snake, ready to strike. Her eyes blazed with fury, and a righteous rage pulsed through every cell of her body.

'I will not succumb to your evil! I won't let you desecrate my family or anyone else!'

Her fists were balled tightly in anger as she declared her stand against her sister.

'Then fight me, stand for something, and stop being a pussy your whole life. It makes no difference; you will fail, and everybody you love will pay the price.'

'I don't want to fight you!' Ellie said, shaking her head. 'But if you force my hand, I will stop you.'

'Oh really?' Scarlett said. Her emerald eyes glinted with a menacing glimmer. 'This will be over in no time.'

The ground started to tremble violently, rumbling like an earthquake. Without warning, a small tree shot up from the soil as Scarlett raised it above her head with a mysterious supernatural force. It hovered in the air, swaying back and forth ominously. The icy wind bellowed through the garden, lashing the snow into a fury. The two sisters stood tall and resolute, undisturbed by the frigid atmosphere that engulfed them. Snowflakes flew around them in a tornado of white, never touching their skin as if some spectral force had encased them in an impenetrable shield. The garden seemed transformed into an arena of conflict, providing a platform for their test of strength and courage. Scarlett's cruel grin widened as she watched Ellie nervously take her defensive stance in the eerie silence of the night. Ellie's body froze as a vicious wooden projectile flew toward her like a missile. A split second before impact, the branch shuddered to a halt mid-air, stopped by some unseen force that pulsed through Ellie's veins. The suspended shaft of wood hung in time as Ellie stared it down, her eyes blazing with power and her fear turning to courage. It slowly drifted to the ground beneath her, cowed by her strength. Scarlett looked on as five menacing branches erupted from the ground, jagged edges glistening with deadly intent. Swifter than lightning, they flew toward Ellie, their unstoppable momentum ready to take her life instantly. Ellie thought her last moment had come; a deafening silence filled the air before time seemed to pause for a split second. Suddenly, the sharpened branches halted just inches away from her body, crashing into the earth like an executioner's axe. Scarlett felt her power surge as she sent the small tree hurtling toward Ellie. It hit her arm with a sickening thud, and Ellie released an agonizing scream of pain as she stumbled backward. Scarlett's anger surged through her with the force of a hurricane, throwing Ellie like a ragdoll into an ancient well. The strength of the impact rocked her entire body, and she felt her ribs crack like brittle shards of glass. She gasped for air, unable to find it as the blow had forced all breath out of her lungs. The searing pain that raced through her veins was so intense that it felt like molten lava was burning her alive from within. She forced her battered body to sit up, only for the agonizing torment to come crashing down like a tidal wave, leaving her with a raw and desperate wail of anguish. Scarlett sauntered towards Ellie, her emerald eyes glinting with malicious delight. Her outstretched hand seemed to pull Ellie's inanimate body forward without physical contact. Ellie felt her feet lift from the ground as she rose, unable to move. She still managed to look up at Scarlett with an indomitable fury burning in her gaze. Scarlett's eyes gleamed maliciously as her lips curled into an evil smirk. Her voice was like silk, dripping with malice and menace as it filled the air.

'You really are pathetic,' Scarlett spat.

Ellie met Scarlett's gaze, letting the hatred burn through her veins and take hold of her body.

'Fuck you!' Ellie screamed with a voice full of contempt.

The burning rage within her threatened to consume her as she squared off with Scarlett. Her face hardened like granite, and her eyes blazed with a molten fury that refused to be contained. With a deafening roar, she summoned all the strength in her being and the power of the air around her to push Scarlett back with an invisible but unstoppable force.

Scarlett's mouth twisted into a snarl, and she stumbled backward, away from Ellie's wrath. But Ellie was relentless, ignoring the pain throbbing in her bones. She lunged forward with a blistering fury, throwing a punch with inhuman strength. With a sickening crack against her knuckles, Scarlett's chin snapped back from the impact of the blow. The sound echoed like a gunshot as Scarlett crumpled to the ground like a rag doll.

Silence hung in the air as Ellie stood above her fallen sister. Sweat dripped down her face, and her chest heaved with labored breaths.

'You hit me,' Scarlett said in disbelief.

Ellie gritted her teeth, feeling the searing pain in her ribs, as she summoned her power and focused her mind on a nearby rock. Feeling the hard edges dig into her invisible hand, she hurled it at Scarlett with a thunderous roar that echoed in the air. Scarlett reacted instinctively, unleashing a wave of force that smashed the rock through the house window, sending shards of glass flying like deadly shrapnel. Scarlett shivered, feeling a chill descend over her body. Fear rose in her chest in an unfamiliar wave and completely replaced her sense of awareness. Her body trembling, Scarlett sent a surge of energy flying toward Ellie, who responded with one of her own. The immense force between them collided and sent ripples through the air, throwing Scarlett and Ellie back until they crashed to the ground. Scarlett scrambled to her feet, and her face contorted in rage. She ripped her leather jacket off and threw it to the ground in defiance. Scarlett stalked towards Ellie, who had collapsed in pain and was trying to inch towards a nearby tree. Scarlett watched Ellie painfully clamber towards the trunk, finally succumbing to exhaustion and settling in a crumpled heap. Sabrina stepped through the doorway, her eyes alight with a vicious thrill. She had hold of Ashley's arm, fingers digging into flesh, and her other hand around Ashley's throat, restricting the movement of her body entirely. Ellie turned her head and saw Ashley, her eyes wide with fear, pinned to the wall by Sabrina's iron grip around her throat. Her small hands clawed desperately at Sabrina's wrist as she gasped for breath. Ellie frantically tried to make it across the damp grass to help but was hindered by the searing pain radiating through her body. Mike and Alice frantically pulled at their restraints, tears desperately trying to escape their eyes.

'Ash, are you okay!?' Ellie screamed in desperation, her gaze glued to Scarlett standing a few feet away. Blood flowed from a split lip down her face like an unstoppable river, yet her face remained a stoic mask of strength. The air seemed to grow thick with tension as the storm of an impending battle grew closer. Scarlett felt the rage boil up inside her as she stretched her hand to the broken shards of glass. With a savage motion, the shattered fragments rose from the ground in a whirlwind of chaotic energy. They hung suspended mid-air, the sparkling glass pulsing with Scarlett's power, rotating around her like a living entity.

Scarlett glared at Alice, Mike, and Ashley with burning rage, her eyes filled with hatred and contempt.

'This is it,' Scarlett said in a low growl,' Say your final goodbye to Ellie.'

As the glinting shards of glass whirled around Scarlett, a stillness icy enough to bring death itself hung in the air. Sabrina's grip tightened around Ashley's throat until it felt like her windpipe would collapse under the pressure. Ashley's face contorted with rage, and her muscles tensed in defiance. With a sudden, powerful jerk, she twisted her arm free from Sabrina's grip and raised it to strike. She intensely punched Sabrina's stomach, causing her to wince in pain. In one fluid motion, Ashley pivoted and delivered a crushing blow to Sabrina's face. The force of the impact sent Sabrina reeling backward like a limp puppet, crumpling into an awkward heap on the ground. Without missing a beat, Ashley sprinted towards her sister Ellie, who sat helpless against a tree, awaiting certain doom. Scarlett's frosty gaze shot towards Sabrina, lying on the ground, as the cluster of jagged and menacing glass shards flew toward Ellie. In desperate terror, Ellie shut her eyes tight, expecting to feel the coldness of the glass against her skin as Ashley lunged forward, shielding Ellie with her own body. A deafening cry of agony echoed through the air as each shard pierced Ashley's flesh, leaving her back covered in a thick sheet of blood and glass. Ellie's eyes widened in horror as she watched Ashley collapse before her. Her chin trembled, her mouth opened wide, and a frantic yell tore from her throat. Silent tears streamed down her face as she doubled over in anguish. With shaking arms, she wrapped them tightly around Ashley in a desperate attempt to save her. Her heart sank as she felt the warm sensation of Ashley's blood seeping through her clothes.

'Ashley! No! Please don't leave me!' Ellie said, the despair clawing from her throat. Ellie felt Ashley's body go limp in her arms. She pulled away, her hands slick with Ashley's blood. Ellie's eyes blazed with fury as she locked her unwavering gaze on Scarlett. With a scream of rage that thundered through the air, Ellie flung out both arms and unleashed a wave of pure energy that slammed into her sister with enough power to send her flying. Scarlett screamed as the pool house walls crumbled around her, and she tumbled to the ground. The sharp edges of broken bricks bit into her skin, and each impact sent a searing pain through her body until she finally lay still on the ground. Crimson blood poured from deep cuts and lacerations across her body, filling her with anguish.

Ellie clung desperately to Ashley's body as tears streamed uncontrollably down her face.

'Ash, no! Please stay with me,' Ellie said, desperation and sorrow consuming her voice.

Ashley's eyes flickered open, and she gazed at Ellie. Her voice was barely audible now, each word a whisper on the wind.

'I'm sorry. I love you so much, Ellie,' Ashley whispered, her voice fading away as her eyes slowly closed for the final time.

'NO!' Ellie screamed, feeling like an earthquake ripping the world apart. She shook Ashley's limp body as if she could bring her back to life with enough effort. The pain of the impossible became unbearable as Ellie felt herself falling apart inside, her tears flowing uncontrollably and sobs filling the silent void. Despair filled her heart until it crushed her spirit, and her legs gave out in grief, sending her to the ground in anguish. Sabrina stumbled away, quickly fading from view as Ellie crawled over to her parents and tore the bonds from their bruised skin. They embraced Ashley fiercely while Ellie hobbled towards the pool house. Shock and dread flooded Ellie as she stared upon the space where Scarlett had been moments before, only to be met with a horrifying sight: blood-splattered bricks that remained in her place. Ellie's muscles trembled as she hugged her parents, Ashley's motionless body cradled between them. Ellie clung to the embrace, unable to process the events that had just unfolded. Everything around her felt ripped away, replaced with an abyss of nothingness, a void that could never be filled. Tears overflowed down her cheeks as she prayed for it all to be a terrible nightmare.

27

Scarlett sighed as she reclined in the luxurious leather chair of her private jet. Her emerald eyes glimmered, mesmerized by the view out the window. Her heart pounded as scenes from her fight with Ellie replayed in her mind. She had been taken by surprise, overpowered, and outmatched. She wanted answers, but all she could do was watch the fluffy clouds drift across a clear blue sky, reflecting a now uncertain future. Sabrina slowly opened the cabin door and stepped inside, her shoulders hunched as if carrying a heavy burden. She gripped two glasses in her hands, not daring to make eye contact with anyone. Scarlett glanced over at Sabrina and was struck by how much darker and more pronounced the bruise around her eye had become since Ashley had hit her. Sabrina offered the tall sparking water to Scarlett, who turned to face the window again, her expression devoid of emotion. Scarlett's chest was tormented as she gazed upon Sabrina's broken form. Conflicting emotions waged war within her; one part wanted to apologize for being unable to protect her, while the other was angry that Sabrina had distracted her from killing Ellie.

Guilt and shame collided as Scarlett remembered how Sabrina had consistently been the only person to show kindness toward her and make her feel worthy of love and affection. The mixed feelings left her paralyzed.

'I'm so sorry that you got hurt. I don't know what happened,' Sabrina said as she hesitantly reached out and placed her hand on Scarlett's shoulder. She could feel the tension in Scarlett's body as she cautiously avoided eye contact. Sabrina's eyes wandered over Scarlett's body, horrified by the extent of her injuries. Streaks of purple, red, and yellow bruises and cuts decorated her arms. Sabrina immediately tried to soothe her pain and leaned in to kiss her arm. However, when she placed her lips on Scarlett's shoulder, she shrugged it off, causing a deep ache in Sabrina's heart. She peered at Scarlett with a simmering cauldron of emotions. Her heart yearned to be a comfort, to help alleviate Scarlett's suffering. But in the same breath, she knew any effort she put forth would be useless.

'What can I do?' Sabrina asked as uncertainty and guilt washed over her as her lips formed into a macabre smile. 'At least you killed her sister. Did you see how broken Ellie was?'

Scarlett's reflection in the jet window seemed to stare right back at her as she sat, trembling with rage. The muscles in her neck strained, and she could feel the heat radiating off her body. Scarlett turned and stared at Sabrina with a burning intensity, her emerald eyes blazing as she gritted her teeth in rage.

'Are you fucking kidding me?' Scarlett spat.

'That wasn't the plan. I wanted to be done with it, for Ellie to be dead. All you had to do was keep hold of her sister and make her watch.'

Sabrina shrunk back into her chair, unable to look Scarlett

in the eye.

'You distracted me, and now look at me?' Scarlett said.

Sabrina knew she had made a mistake, but words failed her in the face of Scarlett's obvious pain and anger.

'I promise it won't happen again. You need to get home and heal. Then we will get back to Ellie,' Sabrina said. 'She just got lucky this time. She is weak and will pay for what she did to you.'

Scarlett's features softened as she extended her arm to Sabrina, touching her just above the knee. The gesture was an unspoken apology, and Sabrina accepted it with a nod.

'Look, I know you were trying to help me. I'm sorry for pushing you away,' Scarlett said. 'No one has ever cared about me, and I have never cared about anyone else. When I saw her strike you, it shook me to my core. I'm not used to having distractions.'

Scarlett's touch combined strength and tenderness as it embraced Sabrina's. With her eyes closed, Scarlett leaned forward until their lips met in an electric kiss that seemed to last an eternity. She ran her fingers through Sabrina's hair and closed her eyes, savoring the jasmine and lavender aroma. Scarlett exhaled a satisfied sigh, taking Sabrina's head into the crook of her neck. She clung to Sabrina like the lifeline she had been searching for her entire life. Her eyes squeezed shut, desperately savoring every second of their embrace. Scarlett's finger delicately traced Sabrina's skin. Adrenaline coursed through her veins, sending tingles throughout her body. Time had stopped at that moment; the two were one in a way Scarlett had never experienced. She felt their souls intertwine with every caress as if Sabrina spoke directly to her heart.

'I never thought it was possible to feel love like I have for you,' Scarlett said. 'I didn't think I could feel compassion for anything.'

'I love you,' Sabrina said, closing her eyes in contentment.

Scarlett felt a deep wave of emotions swell up inside her, and her throat constricted as she fought back tears. She closed her eyes to center herself and released a long, slow breath as she pressed a tender kiss against Sabrina's forehead. She felt the warmth and softness of Sabrina's skin on her cheek and took a moment to savor it.

'I'm so sorry,' Scarlett whispered, blinking back tears.

'Sorry for what?' Sabrina said as she pulled away and looked at Scarlett.

Sabrina pulled away and looked at Scarlett, seeing her eyes brim with sadness. She felt the sudden tightness in her chest like a vice grip squeezing her lungs and not letting go. The air suddenly felt colder, darker, and more unfamiliar. Her body began to shake as she gasped for air, her wild eyes darting around in a desperate search for escape. Finally, her pleading gaze met Scarlett's.

'Please stop,' Sabrina said, barely managing to choke out the words.

Scarlett grasped Sabrina's shoulders tightly, pulling her close and pressing her forehead against Sabrina's. Scarlett's cheeks were damp with tears, emotion clouding her eyes as she felt the weight of sorrow from Sabrina's trembling body. With every heave of Sabrina's chest, Scarlett ran her hand through her hair to ground her.

'I'm sorry. I do love you, Sabrina,' Scarlett whispered. 'But I have to let you go. Maybe it's because I don't deserve to be loved, but one thing is certain: what happened last night will never happen again.'

Sabrina's face turned red as the weight of Scarlett's words

cut her like a knife. A single sob escaped her lips before she descended into grief-stricken silence. Scarlett felt a hot wave of tears surge down her face as Sabrina's body grew still in her arms. She wept, her eyes streaming and her chest heaving as if it were about to shatter into a million little pieces. Scarlett leaned forward to tenderly kiss Sabrina's forehead, clinging tightly to her body as the roar of the jet's engines subsided as it touched down in Portland.

As the door opened, Scarlett stepped out, momentarily blinded by the dazzling sunlight. Squinting her eyes, she saw Martin standing beside a long, glossy limousine. A flicker of worry encompassed his face as he saw Scarlett's tattered appearance, the bloodstains and mud still visible on her clothing.

'My god, are you okay?' Martin asked.

Scarlett's piercing gaze met Martin's briefly before shifting away. Her face was stoic and unreadable. Her lips pressed together in a tight line.

'I'm fine. Just take me to the facility,' Scarlett said calmly. She turned on her heel and climbed into the car's rear passenger seat, followed closely by Martin, who settled opposite her as the engine roared to life.

'We must get you to the infirmary as soon as we return,' Martin said.

'I'm fine,' Scarlett snapped. 'I want to see my parents.'

'After seeing the doctor, I will take you straight to them,' Martin said. 'I thought Sabrina was joining us.'

Scarlett's expression softened into sadness, but she had already recomposed herself before Martin could register it.

'No, she will not be joining us.'

The car screeched to a halt outside the looming facility, and Scarlett stepped out into the warm air. She looked up at the monolithic structure that had been her prison for many years. Scarlett entered the building, her torn, dirty clothes splattered with dry blood from her encounter with Ellie. The people around her paused to look, and she met their eyes with a smirk, her expression daring them to challenge her. Her strength and determination were evident in every stride as she approached the glass elevator. Knowing that in an instant, she could end all of their lives if need be, she walked confidently through the crowd. Martin stepped into the elevator; his necktie tugged slightly askew. He pressed the button and glanced sideways at Scarlett. He shifted from foot to foot, nervously running a hand through his hair before crossing his arms. The silence was palpable as the doors shut and the elevator ascended.

'I really think you should see a doctor. Your injuries look quite severe,' Martin said.

Scarlett turned her back on him and watched the ground disappear beneath them. Rage surged through her veins like molten lava, threatening to consume her as she felt Martin's patronizing pity. With a scream of fury, she clenched her fists and fought to suppress the urge to hurl him from the elevator in a deathly drop.

'If you don't mind me asking, what happened to Sabrina? The crew discovered her body on the jet,' Martin asked as Scarlett turned to face him. Her face instantly changed as if a wave of emotion had washed over her, and for a moment, she seemed vulnerable.

'What happened between us is none of your concern,' Scarlett said as she blinked her eyes rapidly and cleared her throat, trying to regain her composure.

The elevator doors slowly opened, and Scarlett felt a cold bead of sweat on her forehead, her breathing becoming shallow as she stepped into the long, bright corridor. Fear constricted her chest as dark memories of pain and suffering filled her mind. Scarlett remembered being held within these walls, feeling lost, helpless, and broken. She stepped forward fearlessly down the deserted corridor, encouraged by the thought that her parents were now enduring the same hardships she had gone through. A wave of righteousness surged through her as retribution for her suffering. She approached the entrance of the science division with her head held high and power radiating from her eyes. The two security guards instinctively stepped aside. The air felt tense as they averted their gaze and tried not to draw attention to themselves. The door slid open, startling Doctor Wilson, who was hunched over a microscope. His glasses had been pushed into his unruly hair as he worked diligently on the experiment before him. He jumped up from his chair when he saw Martin and Scarlett standing in the doorway, greeting them with surprise.

'Good morning, Doctor Wilson. How are our guests today?' Martin asked.

'I wasn't expecting you today. We have to let them out, sir. She is not well and needs medical attention.' Doctor Wilson said.

Martin stepped forward, his eyes like two burning coals.

He rested a hand on Doctor Wilson's shoulder and squeezed gently yet firmly.

'Thank you for your hard work, doctor, but they are not going anywhere.'

Scarlett and Martin then turned their attention to the door leading to the cell; it slid open slowly with an eerie creak. A faint light from within illuminated the room's darkness as they stepped inside. Rebecca and Jackson sat in the corner of the glass prison, huddled together like frightened animals to keep from freezing in the cold room. Scarlett slowly approached the glass, her eyes wide and emotionless as Jackson looked up with desperate eyes, catching her gaze with a silent plea for mercy. He stared at Scarlett in horror, his eyes widening at seeing his estranged daughter standing before him. Her clothing was smeared with blood, and deep gashes and sharp bruises lacerated her body, leaving behind a trail of pain and agony.

'Scarlett, what have you done?'

Rebecca stirred beside Jackson, her tired eyes widening as she saw Scarlett, fear pulsing as she scooted closer to Jackson, seeking solace in his embrace.

'I have just returned from London,' Scarlett chuckled.

'Ellie,' Jackson said. 'did you kill her?'

Scarlett's smile widened, revealing her broken and twisted soul.

'No, your treasured daughter is still alive and more powerful than I had anticipated. I mean, look at what she did to me!'

'please let us out of here. Your mother needs medical attention.' Jackson said, desperation in his voice.

Scarlett looked over at Rebecca, her face full of contempt.

'Do you need help, mother? Where were you when I needed help?'

Scarlett smiled as her gaze traveled slowly up and down Rebecca's body. 'You had the appearance of power and leadership, but now that everything has been stripped away, it has revealed you for who you really are. a pitiful coward.'

Rebecca forced herself to stand, her body shaking and barely able to balance. She glanced at Jackson before walking towards the glass to confront her daughter. Scarlett's eyes moved up and down the length of Rebecca's body, pausing momentarily. Her mouth twisted into a smirk, and Rebecca could hear the criticism bouncing around Scarlett's mind. But instead of cowering in response, she took a deep breath and met Scarlett's gaze head-on. Her fingers clenched at her sides, vibrating with rage and terror.

'You look terrible, Mother,' Scarlett spat. 'this is how you've been treating me for as long as I can remember, and look at you, you can't even last a week.'

Rebecca placed a trembling hand on the glass, her eyes welling with tears.

'Scarlett, I am dying,' Rebecca said, her voice choked with emotion. 'My cancer has returned, and I need my medication.'

Rebecca paused, fighting back tears as she looked into Scarlett's eyes.

'I am so sorry for not seeing how much you needed me.'

'I don't need you. I don't need anyone! I will be the most powerful person in the world when Ellie dies!'

Scarlett's hands curled into fists as a fire fueled by hatred and revenge burst across her face.

Jackson stood as his eyes burned into Scarlett's with intensity.

'Power isn't everything. What good will it do you when we are all gone? It won't lessen your pain or stop the suffering. You may have power and influence, but not everyone will kneel before you,' Jackson screamed. 'Are you going to kill us?'

Scarlett glared at Jackson and Rebecca, her eyes burning with fury. She slammed both fists on the glass, startling them so much they stumbled back a few steps.

'No, I will only kill you, Father, but first, I will ask Ellie to join us here. Then I will kill her right before your very eyes.'

Rebecca gasped as Scarlett slowly turned to her, the malice in her gaze almost palpable.

'I would kill you too, but that would be too kind. I'd rather let nature take its course by letting cancer slowly rot away at your body while you suffer.'

Jackson's vision blurred with rage, and he launched toward the thick glass wall of his cell, his fists pounding against it like thunder. Each impact sent shudders through the room, but Scarlett remained unmoved, a stone statue in front of him.

'What the fuck is wrong with you? That is your mother! You may be angry with the world, and she has her share of faults, but in the end, you are responsible for your actions!'

Scarlett pressed her face against the glass partition and stared at Jackson.

'I will blame the world and her, this much, I swear. You know nothing of the atrocities done to me in this place. I will not accept your opinion and will not be broken by anyone again.'

Scarlett spun on her heel and marched to the exit, her cheeks burning with rage.

'Scarlett!'

Scarlett refused to turn as the doors slid shut behind her. Jackson slowly walked over to Rebecca, his heart heavy as he saw her shivering. Jackson's arms tightened around her, but it offered little solace from the chill seeping through her bones. He kept his gaze on hers as a lone tear rolled down his cheek.

'Becca, we must believe we can make it out of here alive. Ellie is strong, and I believe in her.' Jackson whispered.

Rebecca's shoulders sank as she stared up into Jackson's

face. Her eyes were clouded by sorrow, and her voice wavered as she spoke.

'Maybe she's right; this is my punishment. What we did to her was unforgivable. I was so wrapped up in pride and anger that I didn't think about the consequences until it was too late. We made her suffer.'

'No, you can't think like that,' Jackson said. 'Look, are you perfect? No, none of us are. We all make mistakes, and sometimes, there's nothing you can do to fix them. What matters is you learn from them and try to forgive yourself.'

'Did you learn that in AA?' Rebecca asked with a weak smile.

A heavy dread filled the oppressive silence between them as their fearful eyes met in recognition of a shared truth - that they had recklessly meddled in forces beyond their control, pushing forward a type of medicine far too complex to comprehend. The consequence of their actions was clear - bloodshed was unavoidable, and all they could do now was wait and see what fate had in store for them.

28

The snowflakes glided from the sky like a curtain, descending upon the cemetery with ethereal grace. They covered the tall headstones and blanketed the church's rooftop, creating a shimmering landscape of pristine white. Dozens of mourners stood solemnly in an unbroken circle around the fresh grave. They each bowed their heads in reverence as the pallbearers slowly lowered Ashley's coffin into the deep, dark plot of earth. The only sounds in the silence were muffled sobs and a few stifled sniffles punctuated by the occasional whisper while far-off church bells echoed throughout the cemetery. A few brave souls shared fond memories of their beloved Ashley. They spoke through tears, embracing each other for comfort as a blanket of sorrow enveloped them. Alice and Mike stood solemnly at the front, Alice's cheeks streaked with evidence of a morning of tears. Mike's posture was rigid, and his gaze fixed forward, though his face was etched with sadness as he worked to be a pillar of strength for his wife.

Ellie stood at the back of the gathering, her fingers clenched tightly around Jasper's. Her gaze was fixed on her parents, who hadn't spoken to her since Ashley had died. She'd been living at Jackson's farm for a few weeks, and all she wanted was to feel their embrace, but the deep chasm between them seemed too wide to cross. Ellie's heart split in two as she was overwhelmed with the realization that Ashley was truly gone. She could still hear her joyful laughter ringing in her ears and feel her infectious energy that could always light up a room. Ellie's chest constricted with an aching pain that seemed to take away all her breath.

'How are you holding up?' Jasper whispered as he held Ellie close.

'I don't know,' Ellie mumbled, her throat tightening with emotion. 'I just feel numb.'

'You should talk to them; they need you now more than ever.'

'They will hate me for what happened, Jasper.'

'They love you. What happened was a tragedy, but the blame doesn't fall at your feet. You have to remember that.'

Alice slowly approached the podium, her long black dress swaying with each step. She tightly wrapped her thick, soft black coat around her body and crossed her arms to protect herself. She looked at the mourners, finally locking eyes with her daughter, Ellie. She cleared her throat and looked down upon Ashley's coffin, the tears welling in her eyes, threatening to overflow. Alice stood motionless, searching for the words. Her voice wavered when she opened her mouth to speak, and tears fell down her cheeks. Mike stepped up with her, wrapping his arm tightly around her waist and kissing her forehead. He moved to the podium, gathering himself with a deep breath before continuing.

'Ashley was an amazing, strong, beautiful young woman. She brought joy everywhere she went. No parent should have to bury their child. Her spirit will live on in all of us, but her presence is an irreplaceable loss we will all feel until the end of time.'

The air was heavy with grief as Mike finished his solemn words. He spotted Ellie in the sea of people wearing a long black coat and scarf, tears streaming down her face, and grasping Jasper's arm.

'In her last moments,' Mike said, his voice wavering, 'Ashley sacrificed her life so that her sister Ellie could live. She loved you more than you'll ever know, Ellie. We miss you and want you to come home.'

Mike stepped away from the podium and kissed Alice's forehead.

'Thank you all for coming,' Mike said with a nod, 'The wake will be back at the house, and we would love to see you all there.'

Mike tenderly took Alice's hand, and they slowly walked toward Ellie and Jasper, who had almost reached her truck.

'Ellie, wait!' Mike shouted.

Ellie stopped and turned around to face her parents.

'Hi, Mr. and Mrs. Jones. I'm so sorry for your loss.' Jasper said as he solemnly looked down at Ellie. His voice was heavy with sympathy and remorse.

'Thank you, we appreciate you coming and looking after Ellie,' Mike said.

'I will let you guys talk and wait for you in the truck.' Jasper reached out gently and kissed Ellie on the top of her head before saying his goodbye and walking away.

'I'm sorry. I didn't know if you would want me here, but I just had to come.'

'Of course you did,' Mike said. 'Where have you been?'

'I've been back at the farm,' Ellie whispered. 'I hate myself for what happened. I can't imagine how you feel about me. Ashley's dead, and it's my fault.'

'You can't blame yourself for what happened,' Mike said. 'If Ashley hadn't done what she did, you would be dead. You are not to blame for any of this!'

'Maybe it should have been me. Then, all of this would be over. Ashley was so much better than I am. She would have done great things, and I'm just a nobody. It's not fair.' Ellie said, her voice breaking as the tears streamed down her face. Mike stepped in and wrapped his strong arms around her, pulling their bodies close. He nuzzled the top of her head with his chin, making her feel safe and loved.

'Nobody should have died. Ashley wanted to protect you because she loved you so much and always believed in you. 'Mike said as he kissed her forehead and cupped her face with his hands, his thumb grazing her cheekbone.

'Ashley was an amazing woman,' Mike said as he looked down into Ellie's eyes. 'Just like you, Ellie. I know you don't understand why you are different, but I believe everything happens for a reason, and you are destined for greatness.'

Ellie looked up at Mike and wiped away her tears with her sleeve.

'Ashley loved you so much; she would talk about you each night when you were away and all the fun times you shared as kids. If she was here right now, I know what she would say, and she wouldn't change anything. She was always so sure of herself and what she wanted to do in life, and she would protect who she loved with her very life. That's what she did.'

Ellie glanced at her mother, Alice, who was standing rigidly facing away from her, her entire body trembling with tears.

'Mum hates me,' Ellie mumbled as she caught Mike's gaze.

'She doesn't hate you,' Mike whispered. 'She loves you. She's just very broken right now and needs time. We all do.'

Mike stepped back, his left hand still tightly intertwined with Ellie's. He glanced away momentarily before looking at her intensely.

'Why don't you come back to the house, honey?'

Ellie smiled sadly; her lip quivered as she nodded in response. She leaned into him again, embracing him tightly before finally pulling away.

'I will, but not yet. I need to figure some things out first,' Ellie said, looking into his eyes and seeing the understanding there. Mike kissed her forehead and watched as she trudged through the deep snow toward Jasper, who was waiting inside the truck. Mike embraced Alice as they watched Ellie disappear into the vast white landscape.

Ellie stepped into the quiet farmhouse and eased her black leather boots off her feet. She dropped her long black coat to the ground and smoothed down her sleek black dress. Ellie walked over to the worn sofa, collapsed into its cushions, and pressed her body into the armrest.

Jasper hung his coat onto the rack and bent to retrieve Ellie's from the floor.

'I will make tea,' Jasper said, disappearing into the kitchen.

Ellie gazed up at the tall grandfather clock, its long pendulum swinging with steady grace, each clock tick echoing like a hammer in her chest. A tear rolled down her face as she slowly lifted herself off the cushion, feeling utterly lost and exhausted. She ran her fingers through her tangled hair to push the strands away from her face before making her way to the side table, where her phone was vibrating relentlessly. Her heart skipped a beat when she saw the unfamiliar number on the screen. An aching feeling shot through her ribs, and Ellie's heart raced as dread filled her. She raised it to her ear, trembling as she spoke into it and prayed it was news from Jackson.

'Hello, Ellie,' Scarlett's said.

A chill ran down Ellie's spine, and her breath caught in her throat at her sister's voice.

'How have you been?' Scarlett asked in a saccharine tone.

'You are alive!' Ellie shouted into the phone, her voice tight and wavering.

'You thought you killed me? I'm insulted. I will admit that I underestimated you, and you got lucky.' Scarlett said. 'I have given you time to mourn your sister. How was the funeral?'

Scarlett paused, waiting for Ellie's reply, but all she heard was a stony silence.

'Your sister should have never been taken away that night. It was supposed to be just you and me. Mistakes were made,' Scarlett said through the phone as a chill ran down Ellie's spine.

'Look, you've already taken too much from me. I can't take any more,' Ellie said, trembling.

'I told you before. Only one can remain alive, and I won't share power. You are stronger than I imagined, but I promise you will die.'

'If you want me dead, then come and find me! But I promise you, I won't go without a fight.'

Scarlett's voice was cold and calculating as it came through the phone.

'I've had enough of flying for a while, and England was far too cold for my liking. I have a proposition for you. Come to me.'

'Why would I do that?' Ellie asked.

'I thought you might like to see where you came from before you die, to get all the answers you have been craving your whole life,' Scarlett chuckled.

'Go fuck yourself. I don't need your bullshit answers!'

'Oh really? Because if you don't, then Jackson and Rebecca will die, and I will send them in Pieces to you!' Scarlett screamed over the phone, her voice a sharp blade cutting through the air.

Ellie was stunned into silence, paralyzed by fear.

'Our parents have been keeping each other company. Mother isn't doing well and wants to meet you before it's too late,' Scarlett chuckled.

'I swear to God, Scarlett, I'm going to kill you for this!' Ellie said through gritted teeth.

'That's the spirit! I will see you soon,' Scarlett said before hanging up.

Ellie's hands trembled as she flung the phone with such force that it shattered against the wall. Her anguished cry echoed throughout the room and caused Jasper to rush in, his eyes wide with panic. He knelt before her on the sofa and noticed the broken phone on the floor.

'Ellie, what happened? Who were you speaking to?' Jasper asked.

'It was Scarlett,' Ellie whimpered, her voice muffled by Jasper's chest as he wrapped his arms around her. 'This isn't over yet.'

He held her close, wishing for some way to make her feel better but finding no words.

Later that night, the snow had stopped, and the sky was still clear. The full moon's light illuminated the farm, reflecting off the fresh snowfall covering the ground like a layer of diamonds. Everywhere she looked, the landscape was breathtaking white. Ellie walked into the kitchen wearing her favorite cotton-candy-hued shorts and a matching, cropped vest top. Her fluffy dressing gown was a dusty pink and drifted to the tops of her feet as she headed for the fridge. The delicate fabric hid her faded slippers. She grabbed her favorite mug with white daisies painted on its side, filled it with the inviting aroma of hot chocolate, and headed toward the living room. The warmth of the crackling fire in the fireplace was welcoming, and she curled up on the sofa, tucking her legs underneath her and cradling the mug of hot chocolate in her hands.

Ellie's gaze moved from her cup of steaming hot chocolate and fell upon Jasper, who had dozed off on the armchair. A loud knocking on the heavy wooden door made Ellie's heart race as she watched Jasper stir awake.

'Shh, stay here,' Jasper murmured before making his way to the entrance.

Ellie tugged her dressing gown tight around her body as she cautiously watched Jasper approach the door.

'Who is it?' Jasper asked.

'It's Mike and Alice.'

Ellie's face brightened, and her lips curved into a wide smile when Jasper opened the door. Her gaze locked with her parents, who stood on the doorstep.

'What are you guys doing here?' Ellie asked, her voice trembling.

'We just wanted to check on you before we go home to tidy up after the wake,' Mike said. 'Can we come in?'

Ellie gestured for them to enter, leading them into the

living room.

Mike hung Alice's and his coats on the rack by the door before joining them. Ellie sat cross-legged on the sofa next to Jasper, and Mike perched on the armchair beside it while Alice sank onto the empty cushion next to Ellie.

'Mum, I'm so sorry,' Ellie whispered.

"No need to apologize,' Alice said. 'I'm sorry if I've been distant. You are not to blame for any of this.'

Ellie ran her fingers through her hair, still avoiding eye contact.

'I love you both so much. I don't know what to do.'

Mike leaned closer to Ellie, and his lips curved into a warm smile. She nervously tucked a few strands of hair behind her ear as she glanced down at the ground, unable to meet his gaze.

'What do you mean?'

'Scarlett called me today after the funeral.'

'What?'

'She wants me to return to Portland to finish this. If I don't, then she will kill Jackson and Rebecca.'

Alice bit her bottom lip, and Mike wrung his hands nervously as they exchanged glances. A million worries raced through their minds. All focused on their daughter's safety.

'I don't want anything to happen to Jackson and Rebecca, but you can't be serious about going?' Mike asked.

'I am scared to face her again, but I don't have a choice.'

Mike held Alice's trembling hands in his, their fingers entwining together.

'We can't lose you. You don't have to do this, Ellie.'

Ellie took a deep breath and looked away for a moment before bringing her gaze back to meet Mike's.

'I know it's dangerous,' she said quietly. 'But if I don't go, Rebecca and Jackson will die, and the darkness won't stop there. She won't be satisfied until I'm dead—so I'll never truly be safe.'

Mike looked at Alice with a reluctant smile.

'She's right, honey.'

'You can't be serious?' Alice said.

'I don't want her to leave, but we must let her go. She is brave and strong.'

'I'm not brave!'

'You have sold yourself short your whole life. You have been through so much and come out the other side even stronger. Ashley always saw strength in you; she was so proud of you for changing your life,' Mike said. 'You must go to Portland to end this and stop Scarlett.'

'I'm not happy about this, but I understand,' Alice said. 'I'm just worried about you.'

Ellie swallowed hard, fear coursing through her veins.

'I'm scared that I will end up like her, Tied up in darkness and hurting innocent people.' Ellie said.

Mike met her gaze without hesitation.

'That will never happen to you. You are kind, loving, and compassionate. You have way more good in your heart than Scarlett ever will. You don't have to kill her; you only need to stop her, and you have the power to do that. Love is on your side, Ellie; no matter what Scarlett does or says, nothing can defeat you.'

Ellie lifted her head and looked up at her father as memories of Ashley flooded her mind - how she would brave any danger for those she loved.

'I don't have a way to get there,' Ellie said.

Mike cupped her soft hands and gave her a gentle yet

reassuring smile.

'You can take the company jet,' Mike whispered.

Mike and Alice stood up, their arms reaching out to surround Ellie in an embrace. She held them both tightly, feeling the love radiating from them even more strongly as they pulled away.

'I love you,' she whispered in a small voice.

'We love you too,' Alice said as Mike draped a warm coat over her shoulders.

'We have to go. Please be careful and come home to us in one piece,' Mike said gently.

Alice cupped Ellie's face tenderly with her hands and looked into her eyes with determination, making it impossible for her to look away.

'Finish this, Ellie. Make her pay for what she has done,' Alice stated firmly before linking arms with Mike and leading him into the hallway.

'It was good seeing you again, Jasper,' Mike said.

'You too, sir,' Jasper replied with a nod.

Ellie watched them until they were swallowed by the darkness of the night, feeling the pressure of the door against her back when she finally closed it shut. A heaviness seemed to settle deep within her – she knew what she had to do, but did she have enough courage to see it through?

Jasper took Ellie's hand, guiding her back towards the sofa. He gently laid his hand on her knee, and she trembled beneath it.

'I can't believe you are leaving,' Jasper said, desperation lacing his voice.

'I have no choice,' Ellie replied softly, her fear palpable. 'If I don't do this, then who am I?'

'I can't lose you again,' Jasper whispered as he cupped her

face. 'Let me come with you. Please.'

Ellie leaned into him, placing her hand atop his own. She offered a weak smile and shook her head.

'I have to do this alone. I promise I will be careful, and I will return.'

Jasper firmly pulled her body close to his and felt the warmth radiating off of her. He closed his eyes, savoring the moment, and softly kissed her on the forehead as he squeezed her hands in a gentle embrace.

'You better!' Jasper said sternly, a hint of tears shimmering in his eyes.

The two of them sat silently as the fire crackled in the background, both lost in their fears and sorrows.

The first light of dawn slowly illuminated the winter sky as a forlorn figure of Ellie trudged through the graveyard. The snowfall from the night before had blanketed the cemetery, bleaching its shapely mounds and headstones to a pale white. Her red coat stood out in cruel contrast against this sepulchral backdrop, a beacon to her grief. The sun peeked timidly from behind the barren trees, throwing an eerie hue across the cemetery. A fog of breath escaped from her lips with each step, and the biting chill of winter seeped into her skin. She had to force each step forward as if her feet were made of lead. Her vision blurred with unshed tears, and it felt like her heart was breaking all over again. The untouched snow sparkled around her as she looked at the freshly filled grave etched with her beloved sister's name. A solitary tear trickled down her cheek, and a swelling wave of grief constricted her chest. Ellie stood before Ashley's grave, gripping the bouquet of twelve yellow roses. She closed her eyes and let the sweet scent of the blooms fill her senses; she knew that Ashley loved yellow roses above all other kinds.

'Hey, Ash.'

Ellie laid the bouquet of roses at the foot of Ashley's grave, their petals soft to the touch. Friends and family had placed a cascade of colorful flowers there, giving off a sweet scent that lingered in the air.

Ellie slowly sank to her knees in the dewy grass, feeling the chill fall through her black denim trousers. She touched the cold, damp granite headstone, tracing the delicately engraved lettering with her fingertips. Tears stung her eyes as she whispered a broken apology, her voice fragile.

'I don't know how to thank you for everything you did for me. You were the only one who ever saw the best in me. I will never be able to repay you.'

Ellie shivered in the cold air and brought her hands together, cupping them to warm them. Tears spilled down her cheeks as she spoke.

'I hate how much time I've spent away from you the past few years. I thought running away was the only solution, but it was easier than facing myself. You've always encouraged me, but I feel I let you down.'

Ellie stood, rubbing her knee to brush off the flecks of dewy grass, and wiped away her tears.

Ellie slowly and reluctantly placed her hand on the cold tombstone. She tried to find her voice, but the lump in her throat prevented her from speaking.

'I am going to Portland to end this, one way or another. I don't know if I will return, but I promise you that Scarlett will be held accountable for her actions. I hope you can find some peace with Shreya,' Ellie said softly, her voice cracking as tears fell.

'I love you so much.'

Ellie wiped away her tears with a deep breath before turning around and walking away from the grave.

29

Scarlett's breath hitched as she entered the science division chamber, and her chest tightened as the lights flickered on. Her parents were huddled in the corner, their heavy silence speaking volumes. Scarlett slowly walked to the glass cell, her finger running along its smooth surface. It served as a reminder that she was not free despite being released. Jackson opened his eyes and looked at Rebecca, who was pale and drawn. The faint sound of labored breathing filled the cell as they clung to each other with despair.

'Scarlett,' Jackson said, shifting uncomfortably.

'You both look terrible. Don't worry; Ellie is on her way here to free you.'

Rebecca opened her tired red eyes as Scarlett stalked toward their cell with a calculated smile playing on her lips.

'I will bring her to you so you can say goodbye before she dies. It's time for this to end.'

Jackson and Rebecca stared ahead, their faces ashen and stoic, their once lively eyes now empty voids hollowed by despair. Scarlett slowly shuffled across the cold concrete floor towards the large glass wall that separated her from her parents. The chill in the air was intense, and Scarlett could see her parents cuddled together, their arms tightly wrapped around each other, trying their best to stay warm. Memories of her days of isolation in the cell slowly crept into her mind as she clenched her fists and stared daggers at them. Scarlett leaned against the glass with both hands, her foot tapping on the floor.

'Are you cold?' Scarlett asked with a tinge of sarcasm. 'Would you like some heat to warm you up? I wasn't offered such luxuries when I was stuck here in this freezing cell for years, left alone and treated like shit.'

Scarlett gave them a sad smile before turning around, allowing herself to reflect before facing them again.

'But don't worry,' Scarlett whispered. 'This will all be over soon.'

The steel door slid open, and Jade stepped into the room, Her boots thudding against the floor. The imposing figures of two officers flanked her, their armor gleaming in the stark light. With rifles raised and eyes hidden beneath mirrored visors, they stared down at Scarlett, unyielding and silent. Jade looked into the eyes of Jackson and Rebecca before settling her gaze on Scarlett.

'Do you have anything for me?' Scarlett asked, her voice dripping with anticipation.

'Ellie has landed in Portland and is on her way,' Jade said.

'Dispatch the security officers and be ready to contain her on arrival. It's time!' Scarlett said as she turned to walk away.

'Scarlett, please don't do this!' Jackson shouted, but she left the room, leaving Jackson's pleas in silence. Jade's gaze drifted to Rebecca, who hunched in on herself, arms looped around her knees, her body trembling from the cold. A flicker of sympathy crossed The Captain's features, which generally remained stony. She cleared her throat before speaking.

'For what it's worth, Mrs. Ellis, I'm sorry,' Jade said before accompanying the guards out of the room, leaving Rebecca and Jackson alone again.

Ellie trudged towards the foreboding facility, her footfalls echoing in the empty courtyard. She stopped to take in the surroundings; towering evergreens with thick foliage lined the path leading up to the building, casting long shadows in the moonlight. At the end of the path, an immense fountain with an intricate, DNA-shaped sculpture glinted in the moonlight. Around the fountain's perimeter were arranged benches where employees could sit quietly in the shade and enjoy lunch. As she cautiously stepped down the rocky path, she felt the chill of unease as hundreds of armored security officers came into view, each wearing intimidating full-body armor and standing like statues in a line that ran along the perimeter. Before she could react, the barrels of their guns glinted in the light as they swung toward her. She froze, feeling each breath escape her lips like a whisper. She looked up to see more guards in the windows and on the roof, each armed and ready to take action immediately. A wave of raw terror washed over Ellie at the thought of the confrontation ahead, but she knew she had no choice but to press on. Ellie was suddenly aware of a lone figure striding towards her. It was Jade; the scars etched into her skin were a testament to a long history of warfare. The Captain approached Ellie, her face a study of suspicion and disbelief. She searched Ellie's face, eyes passing over every detail of her features with a scrutinizing stare.

'You look exactly like her,' Jade said.

Her eyes narrowed into dark slits as if she was trying to

see through Ellie's identity. Her heart raced, and her mouth went dry as she waited for Jade's next move. Ellie eyed the restraining collar in Captain Johnson's hand warily. Her fists clenched tight as she thought of the implications. When she met the Captain's gaze, her heart sank. The cruel smile on her face told her all she needed to know.

'You must be joking,' Ellie said, her voice quivering with rage. 'You think I will put this on and accept your demands quietly? I swear, if you don't back off and let me through, I'll make sure you regret it!'

Jade's eyes narrowed, and she closed the distance between them.

'I don't think you understand, Ellie. If you don't cooperate, I'll give the signal, and all of these men will open fire.'

Ellie's lip curled into an aggressive snarl as she stepped menacingly toward The Captain.

'Listen,' Ellie whispered. 'I know you have your orders and need to impress your employer, but I've been through too much already, and I'm not backing down. I'm going in there, and I'm going to finish this with Scarlett. You can stand aside and let me pass, or I will move you.' The confidence in her voice was like a shield, and she could almost see fear in Jade's eyes. Suddenly, The Captain raised her arm. A moment later, hundreds of red laser beams pierced the air around Ellie in a chaotic dance of death as the guards drew their weapons and targeted her with deadly precision.

'Don't make me do this,' Jade said.

'Funny,' Ellie whispered, her expression of resignation clear, 'I was about to say the same thing.'

Ellie's eyes flashed with furious power, and a wave of energy surged from her fingertips toward the Captain, picking her body off the ground and suspending her in the

303

air. The Captain squirmed, her body held tightly in an invisible grip, her face twisting in terror as she felt the pressure increasing every second.

'Let me pass, and nobody gets hurt,' Ellie said, trembling as she stepped toward The Captain.

'Fuck you!' Jade sneered as her voice rang with hatred. 'Fire!'

Her command echoed through the air like thunder. The air exploded with the roar of automatic weapons as the heavens above crackled with gunfire. In the blink of an eye, Ellie released Jade's body, letting her fall to the ground with a thud. The Captain's eyes filled with fear and rage as she looked up at Ellie, who held her hands before her. In an instant, the air stilled, and when Ellie opened her eyes, hundreds of bullets were suspended in mid-air as if they were held in place by invisible strings. She then dropped her arms, and the bullets rained down upon Jade, forcing her to curl up into a tight ball as they pelted her body. With eyes wide open, Ellie surveyed the scene unfolding before her. A looming figure clad in heavy armor rushed towards The Captain, who lay motionless on the ground and scooped her up with a single arm before dragging her back towards the entrance of the fortified facility with brute force. Ellie's stomach churned with anticipation as she ground her teeth together. With her eyes clenched shut, she raised her arms in defense, her mind consumed with thoughts of Ashley and the ferocious determination that filled her veins. Suddenly, an ominous creaking and cracking filled the silence of the air, and the trees along the path began to sway and moan, although there was no wind. The hairs on Ellie's skin rose as she felt a power surge through her like she had never felt before. Ellie's eyes opened wide in awe as the trees around her rose from the ground with a mighty groan. The roots tore from the ground, causing chunks of earth to explode around Ellie. With every push, her muscles burned, and she could feel a force coursing through her veins as the trees levitated in the air. Ellie's power was beyond anything even Jackson had anticipated.

'This is your last chance!' Ellie screamed.

No response came, and the air grew heavy with silence. Suddenly, the laser pointers swarmed her body again, a warning of a deadly onslaught of gunfire that was about to come her way. Without a second thought, Ellie lifted her hands towards the trees and sent them hurtling forward with deadly precision, each exploding on impact with the facility in a thunderous roar that shook the earth beneath her feet. Screams echoed across the landscape as Ellie strode forward, eyes blazing with newfound determination. Bullets flew at her from all sides, but none could touch her as her power intensified. Ellie stood in front of the formidable entrance of the facility. Her power pulsed within her like a furnace. A uniformed line of guards stepped menacingly forward, but she didn't hesitate. She unleashed a wave of energy that slammed into them like a force of nature, sending the guards flying through the glass doors in an explosion of shattering debris. They collapsed in a heap like broken puppets on the other side as Ellie strode through the entrance. Amidst the chaos, Jade stood atop a raised platform, her clothing soaked in blood and streaked with dirt from the battle raging around her. Like a dark fog, a wave of fear crept over the room as all eyes fell on Ellie. She stood there with newfound confidence, feeling nothing could stop her. Jade's arm shook with rage as she pointed her weapon at Ellie, her finger trembling on the trigger.

'Stop!' Jade screamed. 'Don't take another step, or I swear I'll fire!'

The Captain's voice was laced with authority, daring Ellie to disobey her as she stared defiantly at her, shielding her vulnerable soul with a mask of courage. Despite the threatening atmosphere, a sly smirk inched across Ellie's lips as she clenched her jaw and narrowed her eyes. A low, menacing hum filled the room as the hundreds of armed guards stood paralyzed with fear, their weapons ripped from their hands, floating in the air and pointing their chilling red lasers directly at their heads. A deathly silence hung in the air as they waited for their fate. The guns were locked and loaded and ready to fire. Even Jade was powerless, forced to stand in Silent fear, arms raised in surrender. Ellie's eyes sprung open, a wave of electric energy coursing through her veins. Her heart pounded in her chest as she took in the scene and realized the immense force she had at her disposal.

'Where is Scarlett?!' Ellie screamed.

Jade's heart raced as her eyes locked on the gun barrel pointed directly at her head, and for a second, her stoic face was broken by fear.

'I don't know,' Jade whispered.

'Take me to Jackson and Rebecca,' Ellie spat.

Jade carefully stepped towards Ellie, feeling the gun follow her every move.

'you won't get out of here alive.'

'take me to them,' Ellie replied.

Jade steered Ellie into the glass elevator, her heart thumping in her chest. Ellie spun around as the door slid shut, her gaze meeting the guards in the foyer. Suddenly, the air snapped, and a loud crash echoed as the guns pointing at the guards disintegrated, their metal shells collapsing and clattering like thunder. Ellie felt a chill run up her spine, her breath held tight in her throat as she went deeper into the facility, not knowing if she would be leaving. With every step, Ellie's heart pounded louder as she followed The Captain down the brightly lit corridor. Her eyes darted side to side as her senses hummed with terror and anticipation. Finally, they reached the room where Jackson and Rebecca were being held, and Ellie felt a chill run through her as the gravity of the situation crashed into her with the sound of the door sliding open. The lights flickered to life as Ellie gasped and stumbled forward, her eyes widening in disbelief as she spotted them.

'Jackson!' Ellie cried out, her voice desperate and distraught. 'Are you okay?'

Jackson squinted and strained his eyes towards her, barely believing his Eyes.

'Is that really you, Ellie?' Jackson asked.

Ellie's gaze shifted to Rebecca, whose face was pallid and frail. She was taken aback when she realized the woman in front of her was her biological mother.

Jackson's gaze shifted from Ellie to Rebecca, and he nodded solemnly.

'Yes, this is your biological mother,' Jackson said, his voice heavy with emotion.

Fury burned in Ellie's eyes as she reached out her arm and unleashed a wave of power, shattering the prison's glass door into a million pieces.

'I need to get you out of here now,' Ellie said with a steeled determination.

Ellie stepped into the glass prison and noticed Rebecca shivering in the corner, her skin white and blue from the cold. Her gaze hardened as she glared at The Captain.

'You're a fucking animal,' Ellie screamed. 'You are no better than Scarlett.'

Ellie gently lifted Rebecca from the floor and placed her in a chair as Jackson wrapped a blanket around her to stop her shivering.

Ellie looked into Rebecca's tired, bloodshot eyes and smiled. She reached up and cupped Rebecca's face in both hands, tears streaming down her cheeks.

'Please stay with us,' Ellie whispered. Rebecca shook her head, marveling that Ellie had appeared out of nowhere when she needed her most. She ran a trembling hand over Ellie's face, tracing her features.

'I can't believe you're here.'

Jackson slowly crept back into the room, his gaze fixed on the vial of pills clenched in one hand and a glass of water in the other. Rebecca took them from him, her hands shaking as she flipped open the lid and carefully tipped two round tablets onto her palm. In one arduous gulp, she swallowed them, chasing them with a sip from the glass of water.

Meanwhile, Jade stood slack-jawed in the corner of the room as Ellie held her in an invisible vice grip, the gun aimed squarely at her forehead.

'Do you think you'll walk away from here alive?' The Captain asked, her voice quivering.

Ellie rose from her knees, all five feet four inches of her looking up to meet Jade's gaze as she strode over.

'Yes, we will get out of here right now.'

'What are you going to do, shoot me?' Jade asked.

Ellie cocked her head to the side and grinned slightly.

'No, I'm not going to shoot you.'

With that, she punched Jade in the chin hard enough to spin her off balance and send her crashing into the chair. Jackson watched in surprised admiration as Ellie shook out her hand and smiled.

'Do I know you?' Jackson asked with a chuckle.

Ellie and Jackson laced their fingers around Rebecca's arms and helped her stand, their shoulders squared and heads held high. They walked down the hall toward the elevator, heat rising in their cheeks with every step. They heard a faint hum that felt like a warning as they descended to the ground floor. The elevator doors opened, revealing an empty foyer. Ellie and Jackson stepped out, Rebecca leaning heavily on their arms. As they advanced, Ellie paused, her sixth sense warning her of danger. She turned in a circle and saw that the armed guards from the foyer had vanished, leaving an eerie silence in their wake.

'Wait here,' Ellie whispered, helping Jackson lower Rebecca. 'Stay with her.'

Ellie's footsteps came to a stop as the faint humming of Scarlett's favorite nursery rhyme filled the grandiose room. The echoes bounced off the walls, growing louder with each passing second. Slowly, she made her way toward the source of the melody, and her eyes soon fell upon Scarlett, perched on the edge of the giant sculpture of Rebecca's father in the center of the foyer. Scarlett's face was glowing with contentment as she swayed her legs from side to side, humming away. Scarlett stopped humming abruptly, and her gaze pierced into Ellie as she stood before her.

'You really brought this place to its knees, didn't you?' Scarlett chuckled.

'It's finished, please let me go with them. Rebecca needs help.'

Scarlett moved menacingly towards Ellie, her eyes blazing with anger.

'They are not going anywhere, and neither are you,'

Scarlett said through gritted teeth.

Ellie stepped forward and stood steadfast in the face of danger.

'Let us end this like we started our life, Scarlett, together!' Ellie shouted as she grabbed Scarlett's arms, and with a sudden burst of energy, they were soaring twenty feet in the air, grappling for control. The air around them crackled with electricity as they hurtled through the sky at lightning speed until an unseen force sent them hurtling in opposite directions. Scarlett's body smashed through a wall while Ellie was thrown to the ground by a water fountain. Ellie frantically scanned the area for any sign of Scarlett as the earth shook with an earsplitting boom. Scarlett stepped out of the billowing dust cloud and advanced towards Ellie, hands raised and eyes blazing with malice. With a piercing screech, the massive statue of Rebecca's father shattered its base and rose into the sky at Scarlett's command. Before Ellie could react, the figure hurtled towards her with unnatural speed and abruptly stopped mere inches from her face. She stared into its lifeless eyes as she summoned her strength to repel it. Ellie unleashed a furious wave of power that hurled the statue like a thunderbolt toward Scarlett. She raised her arms in desperation, deflecting the statue with a crack of energy that caused it to spiral through the air and crash through the wall, shattering the debris into a thousand pieces that spread across the floor like a deadly wave of destruction. Ellie leaped to her feet, her heart pounding in her chest, only to find Scarlett had mysteriously vanished. Suddenly, a barrage of jagged stones and rocks flew toward her. She felt the pain of each impact as the debris pierced her skin, knocking her body to the ground. Scarlett appeared out of nowhere and pinned Ellie to the ground with force, their faces just inches apart.

'Now I will have my fun!' Scarlett said, unleashing a powerful wave of energy as she tried to use her powers to control Ellie's mind. 'You will kill our father!' Scarlett spat, filled with seething hatred.

'you can't get in my head, you fucking bitch!' Ellie shouted.

Scarlett froze in place, her eyes widening with disbelief.

'No! This can't be,' Scarlett gasped. Before she could register what was happening, an invisible force thrust her backward and sent her soaring through the air, smashing into a nearby water fountain. With a sickening crunch, her arm snapped, and she emitted an ear-piercing scream.

Ellie stormed over to Scarlett, standing tall and determined. Scarlett's eyes were wide with terror, brimming with tears as she cradled her broken arm.

'This ends now!' Ellie declared, her outstretched hand demanding submission from Scarlett.

Scarlett's face contorted with rage. Her lips twisted into a snarl as she lunged to her feet, her broken arm held tightly against her body.

'Fuck you! You took everything from me! You fucking bitch!' Scarlett spat, her voice shaking with pent-up fury. 'I hate you- I HATE YOU!'

'I didn't take anything from you,' Ellie screamed, her voice full of scorn. 'Look in the mirror, Scarlett. Have you ever considered that you might have been locked up for a reason? You blame me for what happened to you, but you should take the blame. You are pure evil.'

Scarlett felt a chill run down her spine hearing these words.

'Maybe I'm evil, But what about you? Look at what you've done your whole life!'

Ellie's eyes brimmed with contempt as she shook her head.

'So where's your little pet? Did she finally figure you out and leave?' Ellie sneered.

Scarlett jerked with the ferocity of a wild animal.

'Don't you dare speak of her like that!'

'Don't tell me you actually cared for someone.'

Scarlett roared, her face contorted in fury.

'Fuck you! I loved her!'

Ellie's anger boiled up and consumed her, her face a mask of rage as she bellowed.

'You want to talk about love! You took my sister away from me, you fucking murderer! You hate me? Well, I hate you!' She clenched her fists, felt the power fill her veins, and ran towards Scarlett, lifting her off the ground and throwing her with all her might toward the beautiful crystal chandelier above them. In a shower of glass, Scarlett crashed to the ground, shards of crystal scattered around her.

Jackson's arm tightened around Rebecca as he watched in horror the savage brawl between Ellie and Scarlett. Rebecca pleaded, her voice trembling with desperation.

'Jackson, you have to do something! They'll kill each other!'

Jackson looked into Rebecca's wide eyes and saw pure terror. He clamped his jaw shut and peered around the corner. The scene of destruction that lay before him shattered his soul into a million pieces. He had to act quickly, or it would be too late. Jackson sprinted around the corner and threw his hands up before him defensively.

'Enough!' Jackson shouted desperately. 'We don't need any more bloodshed!'

Ellie gaped at him in disbelief.

'Are you serious? You know what she's done to me and what she will do if we don't stop her!'

'Yes, she must be stopped, but we can help her if we get

her restrained,' Jackson said, his voice ringing urgently.

Scarlett fixed her icy-cold gaze on Jackson, her rage boiling over.

'I would rather be dead than be confined in that box again!' Scarlett screamed as she thrust her hands out toward her sister. An invisible force sent Ellie flying through the air, crashing into the glass elevator with a thunderous boom. Scarlett lifted her hand in a single movement, and the elevator shot up, faster and faster, toward the top floor with a roar and a raging inferno of flames.

'No!' Jackson screamed as he sprinted towards the flaming wreckage.

Scarlett forced herself onto her feet, ignoring the pain in her arm, and limped towards Jackson with wickedness to her steps.

'What did you do!' Jackson screamed, the veins in his neck bulging with rage.

'I told you she had to die. Don't worry, you still have me, Daddy.'

Scarlett glanced over to Rebecca, whose pale face was clenched in terror as she tried to resist an unseen force dragging her across the floor. Her fingers clawed desperately at the ground beneath her as her ankles propelled her toward Scarlett. Jackson cradled Rebecca in his arms, shielding her from Scarlett's wrath. Jackson felt Rebecca's body tremble in his arms as Scarlett's looming figure came closer. Her wild eyes glowed with a sinister pleasure, and her mouth twitched into a cruel smile. She knelt beside them, her presence radiating danger and unfathomable power.

'I will make it swift, I promise.' Scarlett said, her voice laced with malicious satisfaction. 'It's time for me to end your interference and shape the world according to my desires.'

Scarlett looked at Rebecca with evil in her eyes.

'Goodbye, Mother.' Scarlett said.

Jackson felt a gust of air around his feet and heard a low hum. Gradually, Rebecca's limp body began to rise off the ground. Scarlett stood back and watched intently, her lips barely moving as she softly hummed Incy Wincy Spider, the nursery rhyme she would unknowingly be drawn to when her mind filled with dark thoughts.

'Please, Scarlett, let her go. You don't have to do this,' Jackson pleaded.

Scarlett's gaze shifted downward to Jackson, and he felt her power thrust him across the floor like a rag doll until his body crashed against the hard wall, unable to move as she tortured Rebecca. His eyes stayed glued to her, tears stinging his skin as he watched her suffer. Rebecca looked over at Jackson with almost a resigned acceptance in her eyes. Her lips quivered, and she let out a shaky breath.

'I love you, Jackson.'

Tears started streaming down her cheeks, each drop becoming redder until it was no longer tears but blood dripping from her eyes, nose, and ears.

Jackson screamed for her to stop as he thrashed against an invisible force that had him pinned to the wall. Then, with an earth-shattering crack, Rebecca's head dropped to the side, her lifeless body supported by an unseen power as Scarlett's face contorted into a mask of ephemeral regret. Through the haze of smoke and debris, Ellie limped. The calm focus of her gaze turned to pure rage as she saw Rebecca drop to the floor in a crumpled heap before Scarlett.

'What have you done?' Ellie screamed as Jackson ran over to Rebecca and cradled her body.

Scarlett stood in silence as Ellie ran over to Jackson.

'Is she dead?' Ellie asked as Jackson silently nodded.

'You fucking murdered her!' Ellie screamed, echoing in the silence that surrounded them. 'Jackson wanted to help you, Rebecca wanted to help you. But you didn't deserve their help. You are nothing but pure evil, deserving of nothing.'

Scarlett refused to look at her, instead turning away in cowardice.

'I won't be contained again,' Scarlett whispered. ' Please kill me.'

Jackson stepped forward and stood between his daughters.

'No!' Jackson shouted. 'She is trying to make you do something you will regret. Let's get the collar and put an end to this.'

But Scarlett kept pushing, wanting Ellie to succumb to her wishes and give in to the thing she had been fighting against all this time.

'Kill me! We can't both exist. You were always the good one; don't be weak! Get your revenge! I killed our mother; does she not deserve justice? What about Ashley!' Scarlett screamed. 'Remember how I murdered her in front of you? Your poor innocent sister, did she deserve to die like that?' Scarlett spoke with venomous words as she challenged her willpower. Ellie bellowed with unearthly power as she slammed Scarlett against the rocky wall, her hands surging with power.

'Leave Jackson!' Ellie shouted, sending a shockwave of energy through the crumbling ceiling and raining stone down upon them both.

'Ellie, stop!' Jackson yelled, his voice drowned out by the thunderous noise of destruction around them. Ellie unleashed a powerful wave of energy that sent Jackson flying through the air, out of harm's way. The force was so great that it knocked the breath out of him as he soared toward the safety of the outside world.

'This has to end. I'm sorry, Dad', Ellie whispered to herself, her voice trembling with rage and sorrow as she unleashed a torrent of pure anguish into Scarlett's mind, watching in agony as her sister's face contorted in pain and tears cascaded down her cheeks.

'Do it!' Scarlett cried out in desperation as Ellie unleashed all of her power in one last surge that coursed through Scarlett's body like lightning. Blood started streaming from Ellie's ears as the force drained her life away, and everything went dark as she collapsed next to Scarlett's motionless body, surrounded by debris from the building that their wrath had torn apart.

30

Ellie struggled to open her heavy eyelids, and a bright light invaded her vision. Everything was blurry and unrecognizable. As panic began to settle in, she felt a gentle warmth on her hands and slowly turned to see her father, Mike, seated at her bedside. Alice was sitting beside him with a warm smile on her face. Jackson stood at the end of the bed, his face solemn yet caring. Vases of lilies and carnations permeated the hospital room, filling it with their fragrant scent. Ellie's vision blurred until she saw a bright light and strange translucent shapes moving around her. She blinked rapidly, trying to gain her bearings.

'Where am I?' Ellie asked.

Mike gently moved closer and squeezed her hand, the warmth from his palm providing a sense of security.

'Honey,' Mike said soothingly. 'it's Mum and Dad.'

The room filled with an awkward silence until Jackson took a few steps towards the bed and cleared his throat.

'Hey kid, I'm here too,' Jackson said in his familiar tone, trying to mask the worry in his voice.

'What happened?' Ellie quietly asked.

'You saved me, kid.' Jackson said, his voice trembling as he looked down at Ellie in the hospital bed. Her fingers clutched the bedsheets as her eyes darted around the room. Her chest felt tight as she pushed herself up, wincing as her body shifted against the starched white fabric. The fluorescent lights seemed too bright in the sterile room, and she felt overwhelmed by the beeping of the medical equipment.

'How long have I been here?' Ellie asked.

'You have been here about six weeks, Ellie. This is the best hospital in Portland,' Alice said.

'Six weeks!' Ellie gasped as she felt her stomach clench. 'My eyes! I can't focus on anything.'

Mike stood and walked toward the door.

'I'll go and get a Doctor,' Mike said as he disappeared down the hallway.

Ellie watched him disappear around the corner, tears streaming down her face. The memories of her battle with her twin sister flooded back, making fear swell in her chest. She looked around the room with desperation in her eyes.

'What happened to Scarlett?' Ellie asked, voice trembling.

Jackson slowly sat down in the hard, cold chair beside Ellie's bed, his expression somber. He delicately took her hand in his, trying to convey comfort even though, in his heart, he knew it would be useless.

'She died, Ellie,' Jackson whispered.

Ellie's eyes widened, and her mouth opened in shock. Tears welled up in her eyes, and she swallowed hard before she could respond.

'I killed her?'

Jackson saw the shock on Ellie's face and leaned forward, gently cupping her cheeks in his hands. He wiped away the tears flowing with his thumbs and stared into her wide, scared eyes.

'No,' Jackson whispered, 'you had no choice. Please don't punish yourself for Scarlett's decision.'

His voice was deep, like a warm hug, and Ellie felt the tension in her shoulders relax as tears welled up in her eyes. She pulled in a shaky breath and gave a slight nod before the tears spilled over and ran down her face.

'I'm no better than her,' Ellie said, sobbing. 'I tried not to let the anger get to me, but when I saw what she did to Rebecca-.'

The door swung open, and a Doctor walked in with a purposeful stride, followed by Mike, who trailed behind her. Dr. Meyer approached Ellie, her white coat swaying gracefully against her slender frame. Her long brown hair was neatly pulled back in a bun, giving her an air of authority as she adjusted her silver-rimmed glasses and smiled down at Ellie. Her thin fingers expertly worked the straps of the blood pressure cuff around Ellie's arm and nodded in satisfaction as she took the reading.

'Hello, Miss Jones, my name is Doctor Meyer. How are you feeling today?'

Ellie squinted up at her, confusion clouding her bright blue eyes.

'Why can't I see properly?' Ellie asked.

The Doctor's brow furrowed in concern, and she held Ellie's hand reassuringly.

'We need to do some tests,' Doctor Meyer said softly. 'but you suffered an unusual amount of trauma to the brain. We are lucky to have you with us.'

Alice's heart jolted with dread as she stood beside her Daughter, her eyes fixed on the Doctor.

'Will she be alright, Doctor?'

'As I said, we need to do more tests, but it looks like your Daughter is through the worst. She is a tough young woman.'

The Doctor slowly approached the door and gave Ellie a sympathetic look.

'We'll be back to get you soon for more tests,' the Doctor said with a voice full of warmth and compassion.

Mike clutched Alice's hand as they stood close to Ellie, both trying to hide their nerves. Jackson stepped forward confidently and smiled.

'Do you mind if I have a moment with Ellie before I leave?' Jackson asked.

Alice and Mike exchanged a tender look before she pulled her coat from the back of the chair. Mike aided her in slipping it over her shoulders while they both leaned in to kiss Ellie's forehead.

'Thank you, Jackson,' Mike said as they left the room, leaving Jackson and Ellie alone.

'Are you going back to the facility?' Ellie asked, her eyebrows scrunched together.

'Yes, I have to start to rebuild it. For Rebecca,' Jackson said, shifting his gaze to the floor. 'She deserves that. I want to do it right.'

Ellie bit her lip, her eyes welling up with tears as she squeezed them shut. She inhaled sharply and bowed her head, her body shaking with sorrow.

'I'm so sorry about Rebecca,' Ellie whispered, her voice thick with emotion as Jackson's face softened, and he squeezed her shoulder.

'She would have been proud of you, kid,' Jackson said.

'What am I supposed to do now?' Ellie asked as she looked

at Jackson, trying to focus on his face.

'Just live your life and try to find happiness and peace,' Jackson whispered.

Ellie surveyed the room, her vision a kaleidoscope of blurred colors.

'Something feels off,' Ellie murmured, her voice faint and unsteady.

'How do you mean?' Jackson said, squeezing her hand reassuringly.

'I could sense a strength within me before, but now it's like it's been drained from me, and all I'm left with is an overwhelming void.'

Jackson leaned close and closed his eyes.

'What happened between you and Scarlett was so intense. Understandably, it took a toll on you. It may come back to you in time. Don't try and force it.'

Ellie's eyes reflected a world-weariness that comes only to those who have experienced deep pain. She clutched her hands together in a death grip, nails digging into flesh as if trying to keep herself from falling apart. The room was silent except for her ragged breathing, punctuated by small sobs that escaped her lips.

'How do I go back to what's normal? What even is normal anymore?'

Jackson smiled and shrugged his broad shoulders.

'It's like our support group. You make it through the challenging moments and enjoy the good ones while you can. You have a lot of good times to come, Ellie, I know it.'

'I'm sorry I failed you,' Ellie said as she looked up at Jackson, her eyes glistening with tears and her lower lip trembling. 'I said horrible things to you before you left.'

You didn't fail me, Ellie Jones,' Jackson said, full of

admiration and pride as he gently nudged her chin upward, his thumb tracing a soft path over her cheekbone. He stood up, towered over the hospital bed, and stretched out his hand, his smile wide.

'You have done so well, and I couldn't be prouder of all your progress,' Jackson said. 'There is one more thing. I have a gift for you.'

'A gift?' Ellie asked.

Jackson smiled and warmly cupped her palm between his fingers. He gently opened it and placed a small velvet box in her open hand.

'Here,' Jackson whispered.

Ellie felt the velvet box in her palm, not a hint of its contents escaping her probing fingertips. With a gentle touch, Jackson pried open the lid to reveal a silver key. Its ridged edges were unfamiliar to her, and her vision impairment left her unable to make out more than its overall shape.

'What is this?'

Jackson laid the key in the palm of Ellie's hand, his eyes bright and full of emotion. He cleared his throat, his chest rising and falling with a deep breath before he spoke.

'It's the key to my farm. I want you to have it now.'

'Jackson, this is huge,' Ellie whispered, her chest constricting with emotion. She swallowed before continuing, her voice full of determination. 'Of course, I will look after the farm for you.'

Jackson smiled at Ellie, his eyes filled with pride. He pulled out a beautiful silver necklace. Its chain looped around two shiny silver rings.

'What is it?' Ellie asked, her voice trembling. Jackson sighed, and his eyes glistened with emotion.

'These were Rebecca's engagement and wedding rings. She would want you to have them now.'

'Are you sure, Jackson?' Ellie asked as she brushed her long brown hair away from her neck. He nodded, gently detached the chain from its box, and draped it around his Daughter's neck. As he fastened the clasp and stepped back to admire his work, the delicate silver rings of the necklace glimmered in the light, and a proud smile spread across his face. Ellie ran her fingertips over the smooth, silver rings around her neck as a tear escaped from the corner of her eye and followed the curves of her cheekbone.

'Thank you, Dad,' Ellie whispered, her voice thick with emotion as Jackson's eyes widened in surprise.

'what did you call me?'

'Well, technically, you are my father. I guess I have two now,' Ellie said with a smile. 'That is if it's alright with you?'

Jackson stepped closer. His arms outstretched as he pulled Ellie close in an embrace.

'You have made this old man happy, kid.'

Alice and Mike walked into the hospital room and watched as Ellie touched the rings with reverence.

'Would you like us to give you a few more moments?' Mike asked in a gentle voice.

'No, it's fine. I have to get going.'

Jackson stepped back and sighed, shoulders slumped. He tentatively extended his hand, which Mike quickly grasped. Jackson looked up with a heavy heart to meet Mike's gaze as he placed his other hand atop his shoulder, reassuringly squeezing it.

'Take care of yourself,' Jackson said.

'Stay in touch,' Mike said as Alice gave Jackson a warm farewell hug.

Jackson's eyes twinkled as he fondly looked at Alice, Mike, and their Daughter Ellie.

'You all have a wonderful family here. Take care of each other,' Jackson said as he stepped towards the door.

Ellie's face lit up with a hopeful look.

'Are you sure you can't stay a bit longer?' Ellie asked, her voice soft and full of longing.

'I'm afraid I have to be going,' Jackson replied, a hint of regret in his voice as he reached into his pocket and retrieved a pack of cigarettes with a smile.

'These damn hospitals don't allow smoking.'

Jackson winked, waved goodbye, and walked out the door, his gaze lingering on Ellie for one final moment.

Alice and Mike reached around Ellie's shoulders from both sides and drew her close.

'Everything ok, sweetheart?'

Mike peered at the key clutched in Ellie's hands, then glanced up at Alice with a silent understanding that passed between them. He smiled and nodded at his Daughter.

'That's incredible, honey,' Mike said.

The door to the ward opened, and a nurse appeared in the doorway. She wore white shoes that squeaked with each step, a light blue uniform, and her long blond hair pulled back into a neat bun. As she approached Ellie's bedside, the nurse gave her parents a reassuring glance before turning to Ellie.

'We have a few tests we'd like to do if you're feeling up to it,' The nurse said gently.

Ellie hesitated, unsure whether she wanted to leave the ward's safety. She glanced from one parent to the other for reassurance.

'It's fine. We will be right here for when you get back,'

Alice said soothingly. The nurses worked efficiently yet tenderly as they removed the wheel locks on Ellie's hospital bed and wheeled her away. Mike and Alice stood side-by-side, their fingers entwined as they watched Ellie disappear. Worry was etched in the lines on their faces, yet a glimmer of hope remained.

Alice pulled her suitcase behind her, feeling the wheels bump over small stones in the pavement beneath her feet. Mike pushed a wheelchair, carrying Ellie alongside her. The warm breeze whispered through the trees and caused wisps of hair surrounding Ellie's face to flutter around her head. The sun beamed brightly against the silver metal of the company jet ahead of them, causing it to twinkle and shimmer in the light. Despite this brilliant backdrop, Ellie squinted as she tried to take in her surroundings with her imperfect vision, having only slightly improved during the past two weeks. The warm breeze tousled Mike and Alice's hair as they watched two suited men with matching mustaches standing at attention under the open doorway of the jet. Ellie's wheelchair glinted in the sun, its metal frame invitingly adorned with extra cushions. The men rushed over, their polished black shoes hitting the tarmac in unison. They helped Ellie out of her chair and up the metal steps, their faces aglow with pride from their devotion to duty. Ellie settled into a chair by the window and shrugged off her black leather jacket inside the luxurious jet. She gazed out the window, mesmerized by the endless blue sky, and watched as Mike helped Alice with her long black coat. Alice gracefully folded herself into the chair, revealing a stunning emerald green gown with beaded detail along the neckline. Mike sat beside her, looking dapper in his navy blue suit – the fabric contoured to his athletic frame with such precision that it must have been tailored just for him.

'Are you ready to go home?' Mike asked over the roar of the engines.

Ellie nervously fidgeted with her silver necklace as the jet engines roaring grew louder and the aircraft shuddered beneath them.

'More than ready,' Ellie replied

The plane started moving onto the tarmac, and Ellie looked anxiously out the window.

'Do you think Jackson will be alright?' Ellie asked, her worry evident in her voice.

Alice gave her a reassuring smile and gently touched her shoulder.

'He will be fine, honey,' Alice said as the jet lifted into the sky and Portland slowly receded behind them. Ellie pressed her forehead against the cool glass of the porthole window, watching the white clouds streak past as the plane rose steadily in altitude. Ellie twisted the wedding rings that Jackson had given her from Rebecca around her neck. Across from her, Mike surveyed his Daughter's appearance, noting the dark circles beneath her eyes and the wildness of her hair. Despite weeks of grueling tests and pain-filled surgeries, Ellie stood tall with unflinching courage.

'How are you feeling?' Mike asked, though he already knew the answer.

'I'm ok, Dad,' Ellie whispered. 'I was just thinking of Ashley.' Ellie's voice broke, and Mike felt a tear sting his eye. 'I miss her so much.'

'We do, too, honey,' Mike said, squeezing Ellie's hand gently. 'She would be so proud of you for staying so strong through all this.'

Ellie gazed out the tiny airplane window, captivated by

the warm orange sunlight shimmering in the distance. She slowly reclined her chair and sunk into its silky cushion, closing her heavy eyelids.

'I'm going to try and get some rest if that's alright,' Ellie said.

'Of course, honey,' Alice said, her head resting comfortably on Mike's shoulder.

31

Tiny snowflakes swirled in the air and blanketed the rolling hills and farmhouse in a pristine white layer. Ellie had carefully hung strings of Christmas lights around the porch and windows of the farmhouse that added a cheerful glow to the twilight sky. From inside, festive holiday music drifted through the windows, creating a peaceful ambiance as the animals were all tucked away in their warm pens for the evening. Inside the living room, the fireplace glowed brightly with burning logs, casting dancing shadows on the walls. An opulent Christmas tree in the hallway with shining white lights, shiny silver and red ornaments, and a star on the top reached high up to the ceiling. Aromas of roasted turkey, mashed potatoes, and sage stuffing filled the air. Six people sat around the large wooden dining table: Mike, Alice, Ellie, Jasper, Fiona, and Zack, Jasper's little brother. Conversation flowed as they took turns recounting stories from their respective Christmases and savoring the flavor of the home-cooked meal. Alice lifted the glass of sparkling, non-alcoholic red wine to her lips and smiled fondly at Mike. His gaze met hers, and admiration shone in his bright blue eyes. She had twisted her dark brown hair into an elegant bun, secure with shining golden clips. The sleek red silk dress clung to her slim figure, and when she noticed his gaze lingering on her, she gave him a mischievous grin.

'What is it?'

'You look stunning tonight.'

'You don't look too bad yourself,' Alice replied as she playfully rolled her eyes.

Ellie turned to her parents, watching them lovingly smile at one another and fill the room with their adoration. She then shifted her gaze to Jasper, her hands slipping gently atop his on the table. His delicate touch warmed her heart as she ran her fingertips along his skin, feeling their connection. Jasper's mum smiled, bringing a warm glow to her face and lighting up her gold sequined dress. Her eyes sparkled as she enjoyed the conversation and laughter that echoed around the room. Ellie stood with a flourish, her festive red dress with white trim billowing around her like a cape. She smiled as she adjusted her black tights.

'I'm gonna do the dishes,' Ellie said.

Mike glanced toward Ellie, releasing a deep sigh as he reluctantly pushed his chair back and rose to his feet. He knew that if he didn't offer to help with the cleanup, he'd never hear the end of it. Ellie shot him a look that was equal parts stern and playful, her lips pursed in mock anger and eyes narrowed slightly in amusement.

'Don't you dare! You're our guest,' Ellie said in a tone that brooked no argument.

He held his hands in surrender, the corners of his mouth twitching as he returned to his seat, knowing it would be futile to try and win this one. Jasper reached for Ellie's hand

and guided her back to her chair, interlacing his fingers with hers. He wrapped his arm softly around her shoulders and kissed her with a warm smile.

'leave the dishes,' Jasper said in a soft, low tone as she settled back into her chair. Alice's lips curled into a warm, contented smile as her eyes darted around the cozy dinner table.

'I hear you had a big accomplishment this week, Ellie?' Mike inquired curiously from across the table.

Ellie reached down and pulled a shiny metal chip from her bag with trembling hands. She set it on the table between them, her chest puffing out in pride.

'I got my two-year sober chip this week!' Ellie said excitedly.

Mike's face beamed with admiration as he looked at the chip in Ellie's hand.

'Congratulations, Ellie!' Mike exclaimed joyfully. Alice rounded the table, tears of pride welling in her eyes, and pulled Ellie into a tight embrace, planting a gentle kiss on her forehead. Alice closed her eyes and felt safe as Mike's arm draped around her. She slowly intertwined their fingers, a perfect puzzle of knuckles, palms, and fingertips. Ellie cleared her throat, and Jasper took a deep breath, his green tie immaculately knotted, his shirt crisp and pressed. Jasper stood tall and proud next to Ellie, the picture of strength and support as he waited patiently for her words. She turned to face everybody sitting around the table, her gaze catching Jasper's briefly before settling on each of them. Her eyes shone with unshed tears, and she squeezed his hand tightly.

'There's one more thing,' Ellie said.

'What's going on?' Mike asked, eyes darting toward Alice as Fiona smiled and looked away, her lips curling in a knowing smirk.

'Everything is fine, Dad. We just wanted to thank everybody for coming tonight. It's been such a lovely evening,' Ellie said as she surveyed the faces around the room. 'Let's raise our glasses in celebration!'

Ellie lifted her glass of water and held it high in the air.

Her voice quivered, and tears brimmed as she spoke.

'I would like to have a moment of silence for Ashley - the most amazing sister and daughter. We love you, and you are always in our thoughts.'

The room fell silent, and the air was thick as people lowered their heads and remembered Ashley. Everyone in the room held their glasses aloft, creating a moment of stillness.

'To Ashley!' everybody roared in unison, their voices ringing.

Ellie's gaze flickered to Jasper, who smiled reassuringly at her and held her close, her heart pounding with excitement within her chest. She took a deep breath as she addressed their family, their faces glowing with delight.

'We have one more thing to tell you all,' Ellie said, her voice shaking slightly.

Time seemed to slow down as They shifted restlessly, exchanging uncertain glances as they waited for Ellie to break the tense silence and make her announcement.

'We're expecting a baby!' Ellie screamed.

A joyous cheer rang out in reply, echoing off the walls and filling the room. The festive atmosphere at the dinner table buzzed excitedly, and everybody leaped out of their chairs. They circled Ellie and Jasper, clapping and cheering with ecstatic glee. Tears spilled from their eyes as they hugged each other affectionately.

'How long have you known?' Alice asked with wide eyes.

Ellie shifted her weight from foot to foot and adjusted the hem of her dress, finally summoning up the courage to meet Alice's gaze.

'Two months,' Ellie whispered, 'but we wanted to ensure everything was alright before we said anything.'

Fiona gasped, her eyes clouding with tears of joy.

'My baby is going to have a baby!' Alice exclaimed, throwing her arms around Ellie.

Jasper locked eyes with Ellie, a smile spreading across his face.

'Well, actually-'

'What does that mean?' Mike asked anxiously.

'We're having twins!' Ellie cried out, her voice trembling with excitement.

A collective scream of happiness reverberated through the room as the parents embraced joyously while Jasper tenderly kissed Ellie's forehead.

'I love you,' Jasper said, his voice trembling.

'I love you too,' Ellie replied as she looked into his eyes, gently pressing her lips against his.

As their family approached the door, they all began to don their winter coats. Alice pulled Ellie in for an embrace, her affections filling the crisp night air with warmth.

'I'm so happy for you,' Alice said. 'Seeing you happy is my greatest joy.'

'Thank you, Mum,' Ellie said, shifting anxiously on her feet. 'Can I ask you something?'

Alice tenderly cupped her daughter's face with a gloved hand, her eyes shining with unconditional love.

'You can ask me anything,' Alice whispered comfortingly.

'We don't know the sex yet, but I was hoping it would be

alright to name one of the babies Ashley,' Ellie's voice wavered with emotion as she spoke of her unborn child.

As tears filled her eyes, Alice could feel the swell of emotions within her heart.

'That would be lovely,' Alice said as she pulled Ellie in for a hug; both mother and daughter felt the weight of hope for this new life.

Fiona embraced Jasper, feeling his body quiver with anticipation. Their eyes met, and Fiona's heart swelled with paternal love and joy. Her son was about to start a family of his own.

'I'm so proud of you, son. I can't believe I'm going to be a grandmother!'

Jasper's eyes twinkled with joy when he met Zack's gaze.

'You ready to be an Uncle, little man?' Jasper asked as he ruffled the young boy's hair affectionately.

How can I be an uncle? I'm only twelve,' Zack said, shaking his head in confusion as Fiona laughingly helped him into his coat and smiled.

'Happy Christmas, both of you,' Fiona said before stepping out into the snow flurry.

Alice wrapped her arms around Jasper and squeezed him tightly, a broad smile on her face.

'Congratulations,' Alice said.

Mike reached out to Jasper with an air of formality and warmth, shaking hands and then adjusting his arm to drape around Alice's shoulders. Snow blanketed the farm, and the sky was a dismal charcoal grey. Ellie watched as her parents grew smaller in the distance, a chill settling over her until she felt Jasper's lips press against her cheek and his arms wrapped snugly around her waist.

Jasper stood in the doorway of their cozy home, a soft light spilling out into the chilly night. He watched as Ellie shivered in her thin dress that offered little warmth.

'Come on. Let's get you inside where it's warm,' Jasper said, stepping outside and wrapping an arm around her shoulders to guide her back into the house.

'I'm just going to get some fresh air,' Ellie said as Jasper shook his head.

'Don't be long. You'll freeze to death.'

Reaching for her thick wool shawl hanging on the rack, he draped it over her shoulders and kissed her neck before stepping inside.

'I'll make a start on the dishes,' Jasper said with a gentle smile.

Ellie tugged on Jasper's sleeve, her cheeks a rosy pink from the nip in the air.

'Can you come out with me for just a moment?'

Her blue eyes were wide and sparkling, begging him to say yes. He grumbled but couldn't deny her request. He begrudgingly put on his coat and took her hand, leading her onto the icy porch and the wooden swing bench. He could feel the chill from the seat seeping through his clothes as he settled in next to Ellie.

'I think they are so excited to be grandparents!' Jasper said wryly.

Ellie exhaled a ghostly breath and watched it dissipate in the cold night air. A light flurry began, and delicate snowflakes cascaded from the gray sky, gently dancing in the cool breeze. As they touched down, each barren tree was kissed by a blanket of white powder that clung to its frozen limbs like icing on a cake. Ellie hugged herself tightly, trying to keep out the chill. Jasper moved closer and slid an arm around her. Ellie noticed his eyes were intently focused on her face, searching for something he was too afraid to ask.

'What is it?' Ellie asked, curiosity lacing her voice.

'Do you still not feel anything? You know, your powers?' Jasper whispered, almost scared of what she might say.

Ellie's smile faltered, and her bottom lip trembled as she spoke.

'No, nothing,' Ellie whispered. 'It still feels unreal, like it was all just a bad dream.'

Jasper nodded slowly, his face crumpling into a frown as he tried to make sense of the previous year's events that still seemed incomprehensible.

Jasper's teeth chattered as he tried to suppress a shiver. Ellie looked up and smiled knowingly, her eyes sparkling with amusement.

'You get going,' Ellie said, nodding towards the door to the warm kitchen. 'I'll join you in a minute.'

Jasper leaned in and kissed her quickly before shuffling off reluctantly and approaching the kitchen's warmth. He turned to Ellie, who was still sitting on the bench, her eyes focused on the farm in the distance. The relentless wind whipped around them, loudly banging a wooden gate against a post. Jasper shivered as he looked at Ellie with concern.

'Please don't stay out long. It's freezing!' Jasper said before closing the door behind him. Ellie settled onto the rickety bench, her hands automatically reaching to rub warmth into her freezing arms. Her breath formed a fog in front of her as she shivered despite the feeble attempt at generating heat. Before her, the wooden farm gate shuddered and groaned with every gust of wind. She could feel the cold bite of air on her skin as she cautiously stretched her hand towards the gate. As she watched, her fingers seemed to be guiding an unseen force, slowly pushing the gate shut until it clicked into place. Ellie's legs trembled as she rose to her feet, her blue eyes darting around the farm to ensure she was alone. She had no choice but to deceive Jasper. She wanted nothing more than to feel accepted and be happy like everyone else, and the last thing she wanted was for him to see her any differently. She stepped toward the door with a heavy heart, hoping he would never discover the truth. With a gentle push, the door opened slowly, unveiling the kitchen. But Ellie couldn't find Jasper anywhere.

'Jasper?' Ellie called out softly.

'I'm in the living room.' Jasper said.

Ellie took a tentative step toward the living room, her heart pounding in anticipation. As she entered, the warm glow of flickering candles illuminated Jasper's silhouette, standing motionless in the center of the room. Their favorite tune played in the background as if orchestrated for this special moment.

'Jasper!' Ellie gasped, tears of joy rolling down her cheeks.

He looked up at her with eyes that sparkled brighter than the stars.

'Ellie, these past twelve months have been the happiest I've ever experienced,' Jasper said as his voice trembled. 'Seeing you every day - so full of love and life - has inspired me to be the best version of myself, and now with our little ones on the way... I'm only missing one thing to make my world complete.'

Her mouth curved into a nervous smile as she slowly approached him. She could feel her heart pounding against her chest as he dropped to one knee.

'Ellie Jones,' Jasper said, his hands trembling with emotion. 'Will you marry me?'

Without uttering a word, Ellie threw herself around his neck and kissed him passionately till they were both breathless.

'Is that a yes?' Jasper asked after breaking away from their embrace, entirely overwhelmed by emotions.

'Yes! Yes! A thousand times, yes!' Ellie cried out loud.

Jasper rose amid laughter and took her in his arms, swaying along to the music, wishing this night would never end. Ellie nestled into his embrace with a content sigh, safe and secure in this moment of pure bliss.

'I love you,' Ellie murmured against his chest.

'I love you too,' Jasper replied before adding mischievously, 'Do I still have to do the dishes?'

Ellie chuckled against his shirt while she shook her head gently.

'The dishes can wait until morning.'

32

The sprawling grounds of the Portland facility were a stark contrast to the wasteland that remained after Ellie and Scarlett's epic showdown the previous year. Now, life had returned, with vibrant flowers blooming in every color and an elegant fountain casting dancing rainbows across the gardens. Stone walkways snaked through manicured lawns, and towering trees stood tall, providing shelter and beauty. The entire facility hummed with an aura of luxury, leaving employees stunned by its grandeur. A white Rolls Royce pulled up to the curb with a low rumble, its chrome wheels glinting in the morning sun. The driver cut the engine and stepped out of the car, opening the rear door with a flourish. Inside, Jackson sat wearing a navy blue suit, his freshly shaved face practically glowing. He stepped out of the car, grinning. His hair was freshly cut and trimmed to a fashionable style, making his newly slimmed figure appear even more slender. He shook the driver's hand with an air of confidence. Jackson paused to admire the building before walking forward with an inviting smile. He walked toward the entrance, his shoes sinking into the soft, dew-drenched grass. The air carried the fragrance of freshly brewed coffee as people around him smiled and offered friendly greetings. He ran his thumb along the delicate petals of the bright yellow tulips in his right hand as he continued walking until he reached the main doors, where a tall security guard stood.

'Good morning, sir.'

Jackson smiled as he stepped through the security gates, looking around at the newly renovated foyer with its gleaming marble floor, soaring vaulted ceiling, and expansive windows that let sunlight pour in. He slowly approached the spot where Rebecca's late father's statue used to stand. He looked up and saw a larger-than-life, perfect likeness of Rebecca and her father carved out of pristine white marble, standing side by side, hand in hand. He paused for a moment, soaking in the beauty of it all. People bustled around them, but Jackson didn't notice. He read the plaque at the base of the statue with his wife's name, her father's, and their dates of birth and death, forever memorializing their contribution to the company. Kneeling beside the statue of Rebecca, Jackson ran his hand over its smooth surface before carefully arranging a bundle of yellow flowers at its base. Jackson stood back to admire his work and felt a warmth in his chest as he remembered Rebecca's kind eyes. As Jackson made his way toward the new glass elevators installed for the building's staff, he wiped away a tear that had escaped from the corner of his eye. Jackson stepped into the glass elevator, and as it rose through the soaring lobby of the building, he had to tilt his head back to take in the full view. He noticed how the motor's hum blended with the soft classical music from hidden speakers. A sense of serenity swept over him like a warm wave with each passing floor, as if he had escaped all the chaos below. Walking into the reception area of his office, Jackson immediately noticed Rebecca's old secretary, Stacey, sitting behind her desk with her legs crossed and hard at work. She confidently spun her chair to face him, her head held high. A meticulously pinned ponytail hung over her shoulder, its ends delicately brushing the material of her shirt. A bright red lipstick adorned her lips, which widened into a friendly smile at the sight of him.

'Good morning, sir,' Stacey said.

'My name is Jackson, not sir,' Jackson said with a smile. 'Do you have anything for me this morning?'

'Yes,' Stacey said as she shifted uncomfortably in her seat and lowered her gaze to the floor.

'Doctor Wilson asked to see you when you have a moment.'

Jackson's face softened with concern as he observed Stacey's subtle movements.

'Did he say what the problem was?'

'No, sorry sir - Jackson,' Stacey replied.

Jackson entered Rebecca's old office with heavy steps, wincing as the door creaked open. He stumbled across the room, his briefcase dropping to the ground with a thud. Sunlight poured in through the window and cast a soft glow across the desk where she used to sit. His hand shook as he lit a cigarette and inhaled deeply—the smoke filling the room and curling up to the ceiling. He glanced around nervously, knowing that the building strictly prohibited smoking. He paused momentarily, the cigarette precariously balanced between his fingers. He could almost feel the disapproving stares of his family's photographs that lined the edge of his desk. He took one final deep puff, the smoke curling in a gentle wisp around his face like a protective blanket. His gaze settled on a wedding photograph of him and Rebecca standing arm in arm, grinning at each other, a reminder of happier days. On the opposite side was a photo of two chubby-cheeked baby girls, Ellie and Scarlett, snuggled up against his chest.

Stacey rapped her knuckles against the door frame and stepped into Jackson's office. He jumped, hastily stubbing out his smoldering cigarette, and quickly tried to hide the evidence as Stacey made her way across the room. She placed an armload of envelopes on the corner of the desk and flashed him a knowing smile.

'Here's today's mail,' Stacey said politely.

'Thank you,' Jackson mumbled.

Stacey returned to the door, still smiling in amusement as she caught a whiff of nicotine in the air.

'Your secret's safe with me,' Stacey chuckled before exiting the office.

Jackson sighed and leaned back in his faded brown leather office chair, its springs creaking under his weight. He shifted through the envelopes scattered on his desk until one stood out: a thick gold envelope with ivory calligraphy that looped across the front. Jackson gently opened it to find an elegant white card decorated with pink satin ribbons. Murmuring a pleasant surprise, he unfolded the card to reveal a wedding invitation and a personal note.

'Dear Dad,

I hope you are doing well. It's been too long since we last spoke, and I know the facility has kept you busy. I pray you had a beautiful Christmas and that everything is going smoothly in your company. I have some news to share - I am pregnant and expecting twins! You are going to be a grandpa! Also, Jasper proposed to me, and we are planning our wedding. We would love for you to join us on our special day, so please see the enclosed invitation for more details.

With all my love,

Ellie.'

Jackson's face lit up with a broad smile, and he carefully picked up the invitation, admiring its intricate details. He placed it reverently next to the framed photos of his family on the side of his desk, taking a moment to appreciate his past and future.

Jackson squared his shoulders and strode down the hallway with determination. He watched shadows shift beneath closed doors until he reached Andrew's office. With a determined breath, he knocked on the door three times.

'Enter,' Andrew shouted.

Jackson pushed the door open to find a room illuminated with flashing lights from multiple computer monitors. Andrew was sitting in the glow, eyes locked on the screen before him, his fingers dancing across the keyboard. Jackson stepped forward slowly, took a deep breath, and placed a gentle hand on the back of Andrew's chair.

'How's it going, buddy!'

Jackson grinned at Andrew, who was absorbed in his work, taking no notice of the interruption as he continued typing rapidly. His face shone with determination and vigor.

'Any idea what's going on in the Science Division?' Jackson asked.

'No, why?'

'No reason,' Jackson said, shifting his gaze away from Andrew, 'I'm heading there now.'

Andrew spun his chair around to face Jackson and leaned in close, their faces mere inches apart.

'Did you hear what happened to Martin?' Andrew whispered as Jackson shook his head.

'No. What?'

'The trial is over, and they found him guilty. He's looking at 10 to 15 years in prison.'

Jackson's face contorted into a smirk, pleased by the news.

'I still can't believe he orchestrated that whole thing just to embezzle money out of the company,' Jackson said. 'Scarlett was nothing more than an expendable distraction.'

Jackson took a deep breath as he turned towards the door. Adjusting his suit jacket, he tucked his hands into its pockets and slowly shifted his weight from one foot to the other.

'I better see what they want me for,' Jackson said, his voice strong despite the nervous energy he was feeling inside. He smiled gently before continuing, 'It's good to have you back, old friend.'

Jackson stepped out of the room and gently closed the door behind him. He trailed his fingers along the wall as he went to the science division, pausing momentarily at each turn in the corridor to take a deep, calming breath. As he walked by, colleagues cast him knowing glances of recognition. They nodded their heads with respect, their faces beaming with admiration. But despite the acceptance, Jackson could only feel waves of self-doubt rolling over him; he was still trying to shake the feeling that he didn't deserve this. Jackson hesitantly stepped towards the door, feeling the cold glass eye scanner pressing against his skin. A few moments later, a bright green light emanated from within, and with a low hum, the heavy metal doors slowly opened up. Jackson stepped into the laboratory, and his eyes widened at its immaculate white sheen. Scientists, all wearing spotless white coats, scurried around the room. Clipboards and laptops were clutched in their hands as they took notes, studying the various pieces of sophisticated equipment lined up against the walls. Upon seeing Jackson standing at the entrance, Doctor Wilson's eyes widened beneath his thick glasses. He yanked them off his face in a fluster and dropped them onto his desk before hastily rising to greet him.

'Mr. Carter,' Doctor Wilson stammered, a quiver in his voice betraying the nervousness coursing through him. 'How are you today, sir?'

'I was told you wanted to see me?' Jackson said, tilting his head slightly.

Doctor Wilson cleared his throat and ran his hand through his messy hair.

'The subject has returned from the conditioning trials in France.'

The atmosphere tensed as Jackson's eyebrows knit together in anticipation. Doctor Wilson shook his head slowly and sorrowfully, a frown etched upon his features.

'I'm afraid we are still not getting the desired results,' Doctor Wilson said with a hefty sigh. Doctor Robinson strode up to Jackson, her face bearing a distressed expression. Her usually immaculate blond tresses had come undone, cascading down her slender face and framing her delicate features. She tucked the strand behind her ear with a shaking hand as she passed him the clipboard.

'Please sign here, sir,' Doctor Robinson whispered, her voice quivering ever so slightly. Jackson's gaze flickered over the page before he gave a curt nod and scribbled his name along the designated line. He handed back the clipboard to Doctor Robinson without looking at her, an unspoken dread washing over them both. Jackson made his way through the room, a sense of anticipation rising in his chest with every step. He stopped before a large steel door with another security eye scanner before him. He paused momentarily, took a deep breath to steady himself, then leaned forward and placed his eye against the cold glass of the scanner. A low thrumming sound filled the room as the door slowly opened, exposing a vast white chamber with an air of oppressive familiarity. Jackson slowly entered the room and stopped in front of the large glass chamber in the center. Inside was a figure lying on a bed bolted to the ground with white sheets draping over them. Jackson opened his mouth to speak, but a voice bellowed from under the sheets before he could utter a word.

'Go away.'

'I just want to talk,' Jackson said, taking a deep breath.

The figure stirred and slowly sat up, their silhouette still hidden beneath the blankets that cast eerie shadows across their face.

'What would you like to talk about?'

Jackson gasped as the woman in white stepped closer, her sheet slipping from her body to reveal Scarlett's lithe figure. She boldly strode forward, wearing a tight-fitting bodysuit that clung to her curves like a second skin. His breath caught as he took in the vision of her standing there, feet bare and back straight with her head held high, radiating an intensity that seemed to consume him.

'Did it not help at all?' Jackson asked as Scarlett turned away.

'I'm sorry to disappoint you again, Father.'

Scarlett stared at Jackson, her gaze full of resentment and contempt. Rage stirred within Jackson, each word she spoke like a razor blade cutting his heart.

'I have told you repeatedly,' Scarlett said, her voice cold and hollow, 'you should have let me die when you had a chance.'

Jackson's face filled with anger as he stepped closer to Scarlett.

'I don't want you dead, Scarlett!' Jackson yelled, his voice rising in the air. 'Can't you see that I'm trying? I've spent a great sum of money and risked so much to help you!'

Scarlett laughed bitterly and spun away from him.

'You have no idea how much you sound like her! Just look at how that turned out.' Scarlett said disdainfully.

Jackson felt his anger burning through his veins. His voice shook with rage as he tried to keep it from escalating.

'You're just trying to piss me off,' Jackson said through gritted teeth. 'But I won't give up on you, Scarlett!'

'And that's why you will lose. I will get out of here – it's inevitable. When I do, I will act swiftly and without mercy. No games. I will kill you, and then I will find Ellie and ensure she meets the same fate.'

Jackson stiffened in the doorway, his jaw clenched as he watched Scarlett laugh, her head flung back and mouth wide open.

'I still can't believe you made her think she murdered me!' Scarlett screamed. 'That's truly dark. You just can't tell the truth, can you?'

Jackson spun on his heel and faced her. Her lips were pursed tightly together in a thin line, her eyes unyielding.

'Who told you that?' Jackson roared, his voice shaking.

Scarlett's smile evaporated utterly, replaced by a mask of indifference.

'That's not your concern,' Scarlett replied calmly. 'It doesn't matter how much faith you have in the walls here. I have eyes and ears everywhere. You better get going. You have a company to run.'

Jackson nodded and walked out of the room as the large

metal door slid shut behind him, muffling Scarlett's laughter.

Jackson approached Doctor Wilson's desk. His eyes fixed intently on the Doctor hunched over his computer, typing frantically.

'We need to implement protocol ninety-six,' Jackson whispered, his voice stern and unwavering.

Doctor Wilson's fingers paused above the keyboard, and he looked up at Jackson.

'Are you sure, sir?' Doctor Wilson asked as Jackson nodded solemnly. 'protocol ninety-six is very dangerous and has to be a last resort.'

'We have no other choice. It's the only way.'

Jackson strode into the science facility and headed toward Doctor Wilson sitting at his desk.

'It's time,' Jackson declared.

Doctor Wilson studied Jackson cautiously, his eyes pleading for more time.

'Sir, I really don't think we are ready. This could be fatal.'

Jackson paused and met his gaze head-on.

'I have faith in your work, Doctor. Prep the chamber and await us there.'

The door to the room swung open, and two men in identical white lab coats strode through. Each wore a blue face mask and was equipped with thick leather gloves extending up their forearms. Their movements were precise and focused as they wheeled the metal gurney into the room, its four corners adorned with shiny silver clasps. Doctor Wilson's eyes widened as he studied the bed, surrounded by six bulky men wearing black jackets. Their faces were impassive, but their cold eyes promised unpleasant consequences if anyone made a wrong move.

'Please don't make the same mistakes as...'

'Don't finish that sentence, Doctor. You are paid for your mind, and you are a smart young man. I know what is best for my daughter.'

Doctor Wilson hurried toward the door, his head hung low and his fists by his sides.

Jackson stepped to the steel door, wiped the sweat from his forehead, and slowly punched in the access code. A gut-wrenching screech followed a loud click as the door eased open. His eyes widened at the brilliant light emanating from within the chamber. Scarlett stood still, surrounded by six guards with their assault rifles pointed straight at her. Jackson's steps were measured and determined as he approached the glass chamber. Scarlett glared at him from inside, her arms crossed tight against her chest. Despite the palpable tension between them, Jackson stood tall and strong.

'It's time to go.'

'I'm surprised you are here to do it yourself,' Scarlett spat.

'I take no pleasure in where we are, Scarlett,' Jackson said, his expression pained.

The guards entered the glass cell and surrounded her, ensuring she did not move while securing her restraints on her arms and legs to the gurney board. Her body felt heavy and lifeless as the orderlies wheeled her away--her eyes staring ahead, still and unwavering. The squeaky wheels echoed in her ears as they traveled down the hallway and eventually out of sight. Jackson strode ahead, diverting his eyes towards Scarlett every few steps. His forehead was creased; his jaw clenched as if he were battling to repress the sorrow in the atmosphere. Jackson's large, calloused hand lay heavily on Scarlett's shoulder. She didn't move an inch, and her eyes remained wide as she stared fixedly at the ceiling.

'I know it's hard to believe, but I have always loved you, and I am trying to help you,' Jackson murmured, 'I know you have been told many different versions of the truth about me, but I did try to save you both, there was nothing more I could do.'

They stopped at a metal door, and Jackson's grip tightened on her shoulder. He seemed to be searching for something in her expression before letting go.

'I remember the day you were both born like it was yesterday. I looked into your eyes and could see nothing but love. That's why I have to believe there is good in you; that's why we must do this.'

The two orderlies wheeled Scarlett's gurney into the bright, sterile lab. Her eyes widened as the looming white dome-shaped machine came into view and began to hum softly. She watched nervously as the machinery activated with a soft whirring sound that echoed around the room. In its center was an open door, revealing a seat lined with restraints. Scarlett took in the busy scene of the large room, the beeping and whirring of computer consoles, the scientists scurrying back and forth, some on headsets, others tapping away at keyboards. Doctor Wilson sat at his desk stiffly, eyes fixed on the computer screen before him. His face was intense as he studied the data, lips pursed and brows furrowed. He tapped away feverishly at the keys, his fingernails clacking rhythmically against the plastic. Every few moments, he'd pause to scribble an equation on paper or mutter short incantations under his breath.

'Is it ready, Doctor?' Jackson asked, his voice wavering.

Doctor Wilson raised his eyes from his computer, worry

creasing his brow.

'It's as ready as it can be. I would be remiss if I didn't ask for more time, Sir?'

'I have faith in you, Doctor,' Jackson tried to smile, though terror lurked beneath a mask of false confidence.

'There is more than a fifty percent chance this will kill her.'

'I have never been much of a fan of odds,' Jackson replied, his voice barely above a whisper.

His gaze tracked the two guards as they marched Scarlett to the chair in the center of the room. Her eyes were wide with fear and desperation as she was securely bound to the seat. Jackson set his jaw and strode determinedly across the room to check her restraints, his steady hands working quickly.

'Don't worry. I'm not going anywhere,' Scarlett assured him with a sly grin.

'I'll see you when this is over,' Jackson's voice wavered uncertainly.

'I hope this thing kills me,' Scarlett whispered with conviction.

Jackson stood in shock as one of the Doctors advanced towards Scarlett with a menacing mask. Its cold metal surface glinted in the dim light, and a mass of rubber hoses dangled behind it. The Doctor affixed the mask to Scarlett's face, and Jackson could see her trembling. When the latch clicked shut, sealing Scarlett within, Jackson stumbled back, away from the fearful machine.

'I love you,' Jackson muttered softly as a tear rolled down his cheek.

'This is it, everybody!' Doctor Wilson called out, his voice reverberating throughout the room.

Jackson stepped closer to him, his fingers tightly crossed

and his knuckles turning white from gripping the Doctor's shoulder so tightly.

'10...9...8...7...6...5...4...3...2...1.' Jackson said as he gritted his teeth.

A faint hum filled the air as the lights flickered, casting an eerie glow over everyone's faces. Jackson furrowed his brows in deep concentration as he waited for what seemed like an eternity until all that remained was a profound silence.

'Open it!' Jackson demanded.

The heavy door creaked open, revealing a strange and murky silhouette. An unexpected gust of steam rushed out, enveloping the confines of the room. Jackson stood in shock as he watched it slowly dissipate, revealing Scarlett's still figure enshrouded by the chair. His heart stopped when he saw her limp body slumped, head lolled to one side. Jackson sprung into action, desperate to save her, his hands shaking as he hastily removed her mask. He frantically searched for a pulse at her neck, sheer horror overcoming him when he found no signs of life.

'She's not breathing!' Jackson screamed. 'Get help.' Jackson's shouts echoed through the room, his voice cracking with emotion.

Two emergency workers appeared, rushing toward the motionless figure strapped to her seat. They fumbled with the restraints until they finally released her and lowered her onto the frigid tiles. A flurry of activity followed as they scrambled to locate vital signs, unpacked their equipment, and prepared for resuscitation. Scarlett's white bodysuit gave no hint of struggle as they peeled it away from her chest, exposing her pale body. Finally, they applied the paddles to her skin in a last-ditch effort to revive her.

'Clear!' The Paramedic shouted as she placed the paddles

on Scarlett's chest.

Jackson could feel his heart sinking as he watched with dread-filled eyes. The medic seemed to be in a state of panic and desperation, repeating the process while increasing the intensity of the shocks. After several attempts, Jackson saw the look in the paramedic's eyes that told him there was no hope.

'Don't stop.' Jackson stared in horror as the paramedics performed CPR on Scarlett.

Tears brimmed in his eyes, but he steeled himself and punched his fist into the wall. Jackson could hardly bear to look at her pale face and blue lips as they applied electric shock paddles to her chest.

'Come on, keep going!' Jackson cried, desperation and fear driving his voice into a desperate plea.

The paramedics exchanged a solemn glance before they continued their frantic attempts. Jackson dropped to his knees beside them, whispering words of consolation and courage. Scarlett's body suddenly jolted forward, and she gasped for air. Jackson cowered back into the corner of the room while the security guards tightened their grip on their weapons, poised to act at any moment. Scarlett's heart raced as she frantically surveyed the surroundings, her breathing becoming more labored with each passing second. Jackson reached out and encased her trembling hand in his firm grip while his other hand rose and delicately cradled her chin. She found refuge within his eyes, a safe space that seemed to block out all the fear and worry around them.

'Are you alright?' Jackson asked as Scarlett blinked back tears.

'Who are you? Where am I?' Scarlett replied.

Doctor Wilson stood silently watching the exchange with

a satisfied smile.

    'Son of a bitch, it worked.'

33

Alice pushed open the front door of the reception room and stepped out into paradise. She felt the sun's warmth on her skin as she beheld the vast expanse of white sand beach stretching along the island's edge, shimmering in the bright afternoon light. A warm breeze swept across her face and rustled through the colorful bougainvillea that lined the garden aisle leading to the beach. A feeling of peace and excitement washed over Alice as she realized this was her daughter's wedding venue. The sun shone brightly off the rolling waves, which shimmered and glittered as far as the horizon. The sheer beauty of the scene left her in awe, standing for several moments in reverential silence. She glided down the aisle, taking in the beauty of the flowers that lined either side. The smell of burning wax tickled her nose as tiny flames flickered from each candle. As the path ended, a breathtaking archway appeared, adorned with little white lights that sparkled and shone against the deep wood. Carved wooden panels depicted delicate flowers, while long ribbons hung delicately from the sides, fluttering in the gentle breeze. She approached a cozy room where Ellie stood gracefully before a large mirror, wearing a breathtakingly beautiful white wedding dress adorned with diamond embroidery and beading that shimmered like stars in the last rays of sunlight.

'You look beautiful!' Alice said as her face lit up with excitement.

'Thank you.' Ellie slowly turned to her mother and smiled shyly at Alice, wearing a soft yellow silk dress that hugged her curves and a black hat perched atop her head.

She looked like a golden dream. Alice slowly approached Ellie, her heels clicking in rhythm with her beating heart. She reached up and adjusted the delicate lace of Ellie's veil, her fingertips grazing her soft cheek as she smiled reassuringly. Ellie twirled in her flowing white gown, the train trailing behind her like stardust.

'Has there been any sign of Jackson?' Ellie asked as Alice shook her head.

'Not yet, honey. Don't worry, I'm sure he will be here.'

'How are Ashley and Rebecca doing?' Ellie asked.

'They are fast asleep with your father,' Alice replied, beaming with pride at her daughter. 'I'm so proud of you, Elanor. Ashley would have loved this.'

The door creaked open, and Holly peeked around the corner with a huge smile.

'Is it alright to come in?'

'Of course it is,' Ellie replied as Alice approached the door.

'I'll see you out there,' Alice said.

Holly ran up to Ellie and grabbed her hands, jumping for joy.

'Oh my god, you look so amazing, girl!' Holly exclaimed.

'Oh shut up!' Ellie giggled.

'Jasper is a lucky guy,' Holly said. 'I warned him to take

care of you or else.'

'I'm sure he's terrified,' Ellie replied, grinning from ear to ear.

Ellie turned to admire Holly's dress and gasped at seeing her friend's beautiful pink gown.

'Wow, look at you. How dare you look better than me on my wedding day!'

'Nobody could look more beautiful than you,' Holly responded sincerely. 'You are literally a princess.'

Ellie stared at herself in the mirror, inspecting every angle. She felt a moment of anxiety wash over her face, but it quickly disappeared when Holly hugged her from behind, bringing her back to reality.

'What's going on?' Holly asked, sensing the shift in the mood.

Ellie felt comforted by her friend's embrace, and the smile reappeared on her face.

'Nothing, you had better get out there and make sure everybody is ready.'

Holly playfully slapped Ellie across the bottom and walked toward the door, swishing her voluminous dress about her ankles.

'Don't worry, your maid of dishonor has everything under control,' Holly said with a wink as she closed the door behind her.

Ellie walked over to the dressing table and sat down, carefully pulling her phone from her beaded bag and scrolling through the names until Jackson showed up. She held it to her ear, and after a few rings, the voicemail cut in. Ellie's eyes filled with tears as she hung up. She returned the phone to her bag and stood before the mirror again. The white gown fit like a glove on her slender figure, showcasing her delicate curves. She wore an exquisite lace cape with long sleeves that draped down to her wrists, and tiny pearls accentuated the intricate detail of each rose embroidered along the hem. As the last few guests took their seats, Jasper stood at the alter with a nervous but happy look as he stood next to his little brother Zack, who shifted uncomfortably in his smart grey suit and tie.

'How are you doing, little bro?' Jasper asked as he placed his hand on his shoulder.

'I'm fine, just hot,' Zack laughed as he tugged at his collar.

'Don't worry, you will be eating cake soon.' Jasper said reassuringly with a smile.

Mike sat in the crowd's front row with the two-seated pram containing Ellie's beautiful baby girls, Ashley and Rebecca. Alice took her seat next to him and gave him a soft kiss on his cheek.

'Hey, how is she doing?' Mike asked cheerfully.

'She'll be ready for you in a moment,' Alice said warmly. 'How's my granddaughters?'

'Ashley is stirring; I think she's hungry,' Mike replied as Alice lifted the tiny baby girl out of the pram and placed her on her lap.

Ashley gazed at her with Ellie's breathtakingly blue eyes, and Alice paused to savor the moment of joy, delicately kissing Ashley's forehead before offering her the bottle.

'Can you believe we are here?' Alice whispered as she rested her head on Mike's shoulder.

'I know. I can't believe we are grandparents; I feel so old.'

'You had better get going; I got this.'

Mike chuckled as he stood and kissed Alice and Ashley on their foreheads before heading to the dressing room and anxiously knocking on the door.

'Come in!' Ellie shouted in excitement.

Mike walked in and stopped with his mouth wide open at the stunning sight of Ellie in her wedding dress. She was truly radiant!

'Oh my god,' Mike murmured as he approached her slowly.

'What do you think?' Ellie asked as she smiled up at him.

'You are beautiful. Absolutely gorgeous!' Mike responded without hesitation.

Ellie threw herself into Mike's arms, and they embraced tightly for a few blissful moments before parting.

'You ready?' Mike asked with a twinkle in his eye.

'Oh yeah! Let's go!' Ellie beamed as Mike took her hand in his, and they left the room.

The live band started playing beautiful music to accompany them down the aisle, and Mike looked down at his daughter, giving her a gentle nod of encouragement. Suddenly, a car door slammed behind them, followed by frantic footsteps, and Ellie could see a figure running towards them, wrapping a tie around his neck frantically.

'Jackson!' Ellie shouted joyously.

Jackson jogged up to Ellie, his face red from the exertion of running late. She smacked his arm playfully and pulled him into an embrace.

'I thought you weren't coming!' Ellie exclaimed, her voice muffled against his shirt.

Mike coughed, reminding them of the time. Jackson stepped back reluctantly and gave her an admiring look.

'You look stunning; good luck out there,' Jackson whispered.

He looked at Mike and nodded before walking to the front row and sitting beside Alice. His eyes lit up when he saw

Ashley, and without thinking twice, he reached out and carefully cradled the baby in his arms.

'Oh my God!' Jackson gasped, marveling at Ashley's beauty.

A hush fell over the crowd as Ellie and Mike slowly walked up the aisle, Ellie's dress regal against her lightly tanned skin. Jasper's face lit up with wonder at the sight of her bridal beauty; his mouth curved in a blissful smile. Ellie chuckled when her eyes met the sea of smiling faces surrounding them.

'I don't know who half these people are!'

'I guess I might have gone a little overboard - it's not every day your little girl gets married,' Mike said, smiling warmly and squeezing her hand.

As they approached the altar, Mike leaned in and kissed Ellie's forehead before sitting beside Alice. Ellie stood beside Holly with her eyes fixed on Jasper as they stood under the beautiful wooden arch framed by the endless sound of waves crashing against the shore. A gentle breeze blew past them, bringing with it the warm, salty smell of the ocean.

'You look beautiful,' Jasper whispered, barely audible over the sound of water.

'Right back at you,' Ellie smiled softly, unable to take her eyes off him.

Just then, a petite woman with silver-rimmed glasses perched atop her nose stepped up between them and opened an ancient book in her hands. The band ceased playing, and the gentle sound of the sea filled the air.

'Dear friends and family, we are gathered here today to witness and celebrate the union of Elanor Jones and Jasper Johnson in marriage,' The officiant said. 'Throughout their time together, they have realized that their dreams, hopes, and goals are more attainable and meaningful through the combined effort and mutual support provided in love, commitment, and family, so they have decided to live together as husband and wife.'

Mike clasped Alice's hand, his large fingers carefully entwining hers. Ellie's eyes darted to Jackson. In his strong arms, he held Ashley, her tiny body dwarfed by his embrace, a gentle smile playing across his lips. She returned the gesture with a tender smile before turning her attention to Jasper.

'True marriage begins well before the wedding day, and the effort continues beyond the ceremony's end. A brief moment in time and the stroke of the pen are all that is required to create the legal bond of marriage, but it takes a lifetime of love, commitment, and compromise to make marriage durable and everlasting. Today, you declare your commitment to each other before family and friends. Your yesterdays were the path to this moment, and your journey to a future of togetherness becomes a little clearer with each new day.'

Ellie closed her eyes and transported herself to the perfect world she had always imagined. She felt the warmth of Jasper's hands holding onto hers, giving her strength and comfort. Everything around them faded away as they embraced the blissful calmness, celebrating the grandeur of their wedding day. The officiant's gaze swept from Ellie to Jasper and then back again. She cleared his throat before continuing.

'Elanor and Jasper, remember that respect and love will always be the foundation of your relationship. Take responsibility for making each other feel safe. Remain committed to cherishing each other with kindness and tenderness no matter how difficult life may get. Focus on what is right between you, not just what seems wrong. Remember that even if dark clouds enter your relationship, it doesn't mean the sun has disappeared forever. If both of you strive to create a life filled with joy and abundance together, everything will work out wonderfully. Now, if you would like to say your vows.'

Ellie glanced at Holly, who handed her a soft velvet box. With trembling fingers, she opened it and blinked at the beautiful silver ring inside. Holly smiled as Ellie confidently slid the ring onto Jasper's finger.

'I, Elanor, give you, Jasper, this ring as an eternal symbol of my love and commitment to you,' Ellie whispered, her eyes shining joyfully.

Jasper accepted Zack's offering, a beautiful diamond ring gleaming in his fingers. He took Ellie's hand and carefully slid the ring onto her delicate finger.

'I, Jasper, give you, Elanor, this ring as an eternal symbol of my love and commitment to you,' Jasper said.

The officiant's voice swelled with emotion as she spoke while Jasper looked into Ellie's eyes, and they grasped each other's hands tightly. Love beamed from them like rays of light.

'Do you, Jasper, take Elanor to be your lawfully wedded wife, promising to love and cherish, through joy and sorrow, sickness and health, and whatever challenges you may face, for as long as you both shall live?'

'I do,' Jasper said.

'Do you, Elanor, take Jasper to be your lawfully wedded husband, promising to love and cherish, through joy and sorrow, sickness and health, and whatever challenges you may face, for as long as you both shall live?'

'I do,' Ellie said.

'Then, by the power vested in me by the state of Florida, I now pronounce you husband and wife. You may now kiss the bride.'

Jasper leaned forward slowly and placed his lips upon Ellie's. As the world suddenly faded away, time seemed to stand still. They were surrounded only by an overwhelming sense of joy and love. Then, their guests' roaring cheers and applause brought them back to reality. They opened their eyes to find themselves standing before a sea of smiling faces - friends and family gathered to witness their special moment.

As the sun set and the music filled the air, strings of twinkling fairy lights lit up the dance floor and reception area with a warm glow. People chatted and laughed around them, their joyous chatter interweaving with the notes of the merry tunes.

'I'm just going to talk to Dad,' Ellie whispered in Jasper's ear as she approached Jackson, sitting at a table watching the festivities.

'Hi!'

'Hey, kid. Look at you, a married woman,' Jackson said as Ellie sat beside him.

'I was getting worried; I haven't heard from you in a while.'

'I'm sorry, we have had a lot of issues at the facility, and I'm still getting used to being the boss.' Jackson looked into Ellie's eyes and rested his hand on hers. 'I am so proud of you, kid. You look happy.'

'I am happy,' Ellie said as a smile spread across her face.

'Did everything go smoothly with the inhibitors I sent you?' Jackson asked with a sad expression.

'They seem to be working; the girls haven't shown any signs,' Ellie said as she looked down to the ground.

'You still haven't told him, have you?'

'I can't, Jackson; I just want that part of my life to stay in the past. I don't know how he would react if he knew my powers had returned and his babies could be affected.'

'You need to tell him. It will eat away at you if you don't. Believe me, I know,' Jackson whispered.

At that moment, Jasper approached, pushing the twins in a double stroller, and reached out his hand to greet Jackson.

'We are glad you could make it, sir,' Jasper said as Jackson looked at Ellie, who smiled and nodded.

'Sir? Please, call me Jackson.'

His gaze drifted down to Rebecca and Ashley sleeping in the pushchair. He leaned forward slightly to get a better look.

'They're beautiful.'

Just then, the music stopped, and a distinguished-looking man stepped up to the microphone on stage.

'If I could have everyone's attention, please welcome for their first dance as husband and wife, Mr. and Mrs. Johnson!'

Suddenly, the band struck up Ellie's favorite song. Jasper extended his hand towards her, and she smiled shyly at him.

'Will you watch them for me?' Ellie whispered.

'It would be my pleasure,' Jackson replied warmly.

Ellie stood, grasping tightly to Jasper's arm as awkwardness crept up her cheeks; she still loathed being in the limelight. Nonetheless, Jasper guided her gracefully to the center of the dance floor.

'It's just us now; I love you.' Jasper whispered in her ear.

The many guests were left speechless as they watched Ellie and Jasper move together in perfect unison, seemingly gliding on air and lost in their little world of perfection.

When the song finished, Mike approached them and gently touched Ellie's lower back. He extended his arm to Jasper, requesting the honor of his daughter's hand. Ellie glanced at her father with a look of immeasurable contentment. He winked in response, knowing he had given his daughter the day she deserved. Alice approached Jasper and took his hand, swaying in time to the music.

'Thank you, Dad, this has been the perfect day,' Ellie whispered.

'Your happiness is all the thanks we need.'

Alice walked towards Mike with a mischievous glint in her eyes. He bowed his head and held out his arm in invitation; she accepted by clasping her fingertips around his elbow. A swell of music flooded their ears as they moved around the dance floor, their figures twisting and twirling in a graceful harmony. Jasper took Ellie's hand, pulling her tight against his warm chest as the soft notes of the music filled the air. He placed one arm tightly around her waist and started to sway with her, gently humming along to the melody.

'Now, if everybody could join the happy couple on the dance floor.'

The guests began flowing onto the wooden floor, illuminated by the sparkling strings of twinkling lights. Couples intertwined as they laughed and swayed to the beat.

The guests slowly approached the dock and gazed at the impressive yacht. Its gleaming white hull glowed in the moonlight, lighting the harbor like a million twinkling stars. Ellie and Jasper made their way along the path, a sea of white petals scattered with rosemary-scented branches guiding their steps. She had changed into a light yellow dress with delicate spaghetti straps, and the breeze gently swayed the hem of her skirt. Jasper wore tan shorts and a navy blue polo shirt, and they linked fingers as they strolled towards their guests. Both of them were beaming, unable to contain the joy they felt. Their closest family and friends were gathered around the dock, each holding their breath as they watched the newlyweds approach them while Mike, Alice, Fiona, Zach, and Jackson waited by the boat.

'I guess this is it!' Ellie said, tears rimming her eyes.

'Go and have fun. You deserve it,' Alice whispered as she hugged Ellie.

'Are you sure you will be alright with the girls?' Ellie asked.

'It's just one night; we have this,' Mike smiled.

Ellie leaned in and kissed her two daughters on the forehead.

'I love you both so much. Be good girls for Nanny and Grandpa!' Ellie said, struggling to keep her voice steady.

'See you soon, kid,' Jackson said as he leaned in and kissed Ellie's cheek.

'Please don't leave it so long next time,' Ellie said with a smile.

Ellie and Jasper clambered up the ramp of the sleek white vessel as its engines roared into life, vibrating through their bodies. The boat started to turn away from the dock, and a flurry of colorful fireworks illuminated the sky.

'Did you know about this?' Jasper asked, nodding towards the impressive display.

Ellie smiled and shook her head, blushing at the admiration in his eyes.

'Nope, I don't think my parents understand small weddings,' Ellie chuckled softly as the island venue disappeared from view, leaving them surrounded by sea and stars.

'I love you, wife,' Jasper whispered, taking her hand in his.

'I love you, husband,' Ellie replied happily.